Wild Horses

An Eddie Malloy Mystery

Joe McNally

THE EDDIE MALLOY SERIES

This is the eighth book in the ever-growing series. You can find news of all titles on our website at Pitmacbooks.com where you can also opt to join our mailing list.

Mailing list members are first to get news of new Eddie Malloy books, along with the chance to pre-order at a huge discount.

AUTHOR DISCLAIMER

This is a work of fiction. Names, characters, businesses, places, events and incidents are either the products of the author's imagination or used in a fictitious manner. Any resemblance to actual persons, living or dead, or actual events is purely coincidental.

This book is dedicated to all who seek a second chance

1

The only good thing about regaining consciousness in an intensive care unit is that it's better than not regaining consciousness at all. Other than that, I see no upsides. Waking in a hospital bed when your last memory is of riding in a race means you are not going to be riding again anytime soon. While you're down and out, your rivals will steal your rides.

The nurse hadn't noticed I'd come to. I closed my eyes again to slit-level, watching through an eyelash curtain, as she rolled a machine to the foot of the bed, then crouched to organize some tubes coming from it.

What to do?

If I spoke, I might scare her into banging her head on the metal plate overhanging the top of it. I decided a quiet groan should do it.

She stopped. She didn't straighten up, just raised her head slowly, 'Are you awake?'

I opened my eyes. She smiled wide. I did too.

After the doctor had seen me, they let Mave in. She came smiling toward me, along the ward, around the bed to my side, her arms opening to hug me gently, 'You had me worried, Mister Malloy.'

'I'd probably have had me worried if I'd been awake.'

'Well, that doesn't make much sense at all. I'd put it down to the knock on the head if I didn't know you so well.' Her hands rested softly on my shoulders as she eased back to look at me, 'What did the doctor say?' she asked.

'Not much. Said somebody else'll be along to speak to me shortly. What time is it?'

'Nearly eight.'

'In the morning?'

'At night.'

'Jeez! What day is it?'

'Monday.'

'I've been here since Saturday?'

'*We*. We've been here since Saturday.'

I smiled. We hugged.

They didn't let Mave stay long. After she left, the specialist arrived, Mister Crichton. He checked charts, watched machines and shone a zooming light at my pupils. Then he pulled a chair over and sat down. That made me concentrate. 'How are you feeling?' he asked.

'Fine. Good.'

He paused, watching my eyes, then said quietly, 'In jockey-speak that translates to "diabolical" and "wiped out."'

I smiled.

'Jockeys amaze me,' he said, 'had I the chance to do my Ph.D. again, it would be on the pain threshold of professional jockeys.'

'The amateurs are pretty hardy too,' I said.

'What is it that makes you capable of defying acute pain and trauma?'

'Fear.'

'That seems counter-intuitive.'

'We're afraid we'll lose rides on horses we've built up a partnership with. Owners and trainers are superstitious. If I haven't ridden a winner for them in the past ten rides and a sub steps in and rides three in a row, I can probably say goodbye to a source of rides that's taken years to build.'

'And you'd risk damaging your health for that?'

'Crazy, isn't it?'

He watched me for a while then smiled sadly and shook his head. He slid a notebook and pen from his pocket, 'What's your last memory?'

'Watching you take out that notebook.'

He smiled properly this time. I said, 'Sorry...my last memory was seeing my nephew off at the airport...and my sister and a friend...to Australia.'

'When? What day?'

'It was Friday afternoon, the day before the race.'

'I thought you couldn't remember the race?'

'Oh, sorry, I thought you meant my last memory before the race itself. No, I'm pretty sure I can remember everything until the lights went out.'

'Tell me about it.'

'I was riding a horse, a mare, in a handicap steeplechase at Bangor. We were cruising along down the back straight when she took off with me, went absolutely crazy, galloping as though she was trying to burst her heart. Never sat on anything like it...never even seen anything like it. Five furlong sprinters don't go that fast, never mind three-mile 'chasers. Sometimes, when a horse is fresh, on the way to the start or in the early stages of a race, it'll run away with its jockey, but not after more than two miles of racing.'

'Is there a, well, a procedure of any kind for when it happens? Do you plan for it?'

'You can't. If it happens early, you can wrestle with them, haul on just one rein, try to pull them in a circle, but ten men couldn't have stopped this mare, trust me. It was as if someone had shot her with a bullet full of energy.'

'So what did you do?'

'I tried not to look as stupid as I felt, at least at first I did. When I realized she'd completely lost it, I just tried to hold on until she ran out of gas, but she galloped straight into a fence as though she hadn't even seen it and fired me out of the saddle like a human cannonball. Things go into super slow motion when you're halfway though a fall, and I saw the earth coming at me and I remember realizing there was no way I was going to tuck and roll. No way. And that was it. Sometimes, you'll take a kick or two in the head as well when the others pass you…don't know if I did or not.'

'The racecourse doctor doesn't think you did. The damage was done when you landed, and I must say I find it remarkable, utterly remarkable, that you're able to talk so lucidly after being unconscious for so long.'

'One of the advantages of being brainless.'

He smiled and shook his head, then stood up and slid the chair back against the wall, 'You're going to be here for a few days under observation, I'm afraid.'

'It doesn't matter. I won't be riding for a while anyway. Might as well be miserable here as at home.'

'Where is home?'

'Lake District. A farm overlooking Ullswater.'

'Sounds idyllic. And I understand you have someone there to take care of you?'

'I do.'

'You're a lucky man, in more ways than one. I'll see you in the morning.'

'Thanks, Doc.'

'My pleasure.'

'One last thing, Doc, do you know if my horse survived, Montego Moon?'

'I'm afraid I don't.'

2

Next morning, as the cleaners moved among us and some of my ward mates drifted back to sleep, I heard Dil Grant coming, his cowboy heels click-clacking down the ward. Our long friendship had drummed the rhythm of his walk into my memory.

I turned as he came into view, this man from Toronto, this failed movie actor, this crocked stuntman, in whose middle-aged head he was Wyatt Earp.

In Dil's dreams, there was time yet to make something of himself with what remained of his Hollywood looks. All they would have helped with this morning was charming the charge nurse into letting him bust through the visiting restrictions like they were the batwing doors of a saloon.

He stopped. I waited for the fringe-sweep. He did it, that spread-fingered combing of the thick iron-grey hair. It had begun as an affectation, and ended up a habit.

'You look like shit,' he said.

'Gee, thanks.'

'They give you a mirror?'

'Not my own personal mirror, no. I'm one of those people who can rub along without looking at myself every hour.'

'Just as well. You're whiter than that sheet you're lying on.'

'Hollywood tans are hard to come by at Hexham.'

He smiled.

I said, 'I was going to tell you to pull up a chair, but no doubt you've swoonerized the nurses into bringing you a sofa.'

'Was all I could do to talk my way in,' he dragged a chair across.

'Losing your touch, Dil.'

He sat. Our faces were on the same level. I wasn't sure if he was going to smile or cry. 'Did Montego Moon make it?' I asked.

He nodded, 'Bruised and pretty sorry for herself, but she'll live.'

'That's good.'

He stared at me in a strange way, expectant, regretful. I waited.

'What happened?' he asked quietly.

'I was going to ask you the same thing.'

'I've been around horses since I was nine years old, Eddie. Outside of a rodeo show, I've never seen anything like that.'

'Be thankful you weren't sitting on her.'

He resumed the sorrowful staring.

'Spit it out, Dil.'

'I had twenty-five grand on that horse.'

I saw again the actor he'd once been, visualizing himself now in a huge close-up, hurt-looking, eyes glistening. 'Dil, I could say I was sorry to hear that, and poor you and other such bullshit, but all I can offer with any degree of truth is, hell mend you, as my mother used to say.'

'Eddie, I stuck to my part of the bargain.'

'You've lost me now…'

'We had an agreement that I'd never admit before a race that I'd had a bet. I was desperate to tell you when I legged you up. It killed me to hold that in, to not let you know how important that was to me.'

I leaned forward, 'Dil, what are you trying to say here, because it seems to me it's something like if you'd told me about the bet, somehow I'd have stopped that mare doing what she did, and not only that, but I'd have won on her too…is that what you're saying?'

He held my gaze for a few seconds then ducked out with the fringe-sweep, 'I'm not saying that, Eddie, I'm saying…I'm saying what happened nailed me to the wall yesterday,' his voice rose, 'it nailed me to the fu-' I lifted a hand and my anger rose too, 'Dil! Keep it down!' It was a harsh whisper. He saw the threat in my eyes and sat back, and dropped his head, already beaten.

I said, 'Know something? When I heard you coming along the ward, I thought, well, if Saturday did nothing else, it changed old Dil's spots. I believed that for once you were here to see how I was, after being in a coma for more than forty-eight hours. When have you ever visited me in hospital? Ever?'

He stared at his shiny pointed boots, 'That's not the kind of relationship we've got, Eddie, you know that.'

'I'm your stable jockey, have been for, what, three years? And, yes, you're right, that's not the kind of relationship we've got. And that's fine with me. But if you're going to be a dick, at least be a consistent dick. You could have saved this for when I got out. But you're so full of self-pity you come on a round trip of, what, three hundred miles to give me a hard time for almost getting killed on a horse you train? A horse *you* train! And you're asking me where she learned to take off like a Scud missile three quarters of the way through a race? Man, have you got balls doing that!'

He hid behind the fringe this time, ducking, letting it fall, then raising his hands to cover the bottom half of his face, a heavy sigh blowing through his fingers like a whistle. 'I'm sorry,' he said quietly.

'You're sorry for you, Dil, nobody else.' I folded my arms.

He looked up, a spark back in his blue eyes, 'I'm apologizing to you! At least have the grace to accept it!'

I lay back and looked at the ceiling, 'Okay,' I said, 'I'm sorry.'

'You could look at me when you say it!'

I sat up again, 'I'm sorry. Now the two of us are sorry. I'm in hospital, you're in schtuck. Shit happens. We're both still above ground. Think about that on the way home.'

'I've got enough to think about, thanks.'

Silence again, then I asked the hard question, 'Who are you going to replace me with?'

'Haven't thought about it. Probably use the best available.' He swept his fringe and grunted with frustration.

'Why the plunge?' I said, 'You told me a while back you'd quit the five figure bets.'

'Oh, it was supposed to be the start of the great grand plan. I'll tell you about it when you're better.'

I bit back a sarcastic response. Dil went to the end of the bed and gripped the rail and said, 'Even if you're out of here tomorrow, you won't pass the doctor for at least a fortnight. What's your plans?'

'I don't have any. Why?'

'Vita's been pestering me to find a house for her.'

'Hasn't she got enough houses?'

'She wants one near the yard.' His actor's face conveyed a hammed-up hint.

'Near you, you mean?'

He opened his hands in that what-can-I-do pose.

'What's Prim got to say about that?'

'I'm working on her.'

I laughed, 'Prim might not have Vita's money, but I know which one I'd back in a fight. Prim will truss you up. She will boil you in a gypsy cauldron until your balls are the size of rice grains.'

'That's why I'd rather Vita bought the house. Her other suggestion was to move in with me.'

I smiled wide, 'Forget my earlier advice about being thankful you're still above the ground. Was that big bet to pay Prim off, or something? To get rid of her?'

'The opposite. It's a long story,' he said as he let go the bed rail and straightened, 'Know something, Eddie? Good looks have been nothing but a curse to me. When I was young I thought I was so blessed…so blessed.'

'And don't forget the humility God gave you too.'

He looked under his carefully shaped eyebrows at me, 'Eddie, believe me, if I had the choice again, knowing what I know now, I'd settle for being a plain John Doe.'

'No, you wouldn't. Not even your ham-acting face can convince yourself of that, never mind me.'

He shrugged his cheeks, and nodded, 'Well, maybe I'd just have made better choices.'

'Dil, go home and google The Moving Finger by Omar somebody or other. A good tip Mac once gave me.'

'Will it depress me?'

'Probably.'

'I'll pass.'

'I thought you might.'

'Well...want to help Vita with her house-hunting?'

'Er, no. First of all, I'm not an estate agent, second, I like Primarolo Romanic an awful lot more than I like Dame Vita Brodie, and even if I didn't, the last place I'd want to be is on Prim's wrong side.'

'Vita ain't a dame. She pays the bills.'

'Well, she acts like one sometimes...Dil, I've nothing against Vita, but I am going nowhere near this catfight. End of story.'

'Okay.'

'Give my love to Prim,' I smiled.

'Let me know when you're out.'

'I will. And you let me know the schedule for the first wrestling bout between your women.'

'Not funny, Eddie. Not funny at all,' and he set off back along the ward, his boots sending their echo off the hard walls.

A minute later, the blonde nurse was at my bedside, 'I hope you didn't mind seeing your visitor out of hours. He said it was important.'

'Not at all.'

She watched me, 'Seems a nice man...'

'If you're hunting for his name it's Dil Grant. He's a racehorse trainer. Before that he did a lot of things, not many of them sensible.'

'He does seem to have something about him...a kind of presence.'

'He does. Presence of person. No presence of mind, unfortunately.'

'You don't seem to like him much.'

'I like him an awful lot. He's very likeable and that's where he finds most of his trouble. If you're interested, I'll let him know.'

She took a longing look back down the ward and half-nodded.

'How are you at wrestling?' I said.

3

Friday was discharge day. Mave was due to pick me up at nine. I waited in the bright cold, pacing the 18 flagstones between the two columns at the front entrance.

At 9.10 I was still pacing, chilled by the north wind. I reached for my phone, then saw the old silver Volvo turn in through the gates, chugging toward a parking bay. I picked up my bag and started walking as Mave got out.

Halfway to the car, I heard a shout from behind. I thought it was one of the hospital staff.

I turned.

A scrawny man in a short khaki jacket and jeans was limping toward me. Only when he stopped in front of me did my memory bank hazard a guess, 'Ben?'

He nodded and smiled. His teeth were in ruins and his skin was like soft rice paper on the bones of his face. He saw my shock, 'Eddie, I'm sorry. I'm dry now. Been dry for three years.'

I don't know where my tears sprang from. They welled and ran down my cheeks and I swallowed sobs as I opened my arms. Ben moved forward in small steps, like a child, 'Ben! Jesus! Ben!' I said as I held him, afraid to hug in case I broke him. Some of my tears ran down the neck of his thin shirt and he said quietly, 'I'm sorry, Eddie. I didn't think it would be like this or I wouldn't have come. I'm sorry, mate,' and he hugged me, surprising me with the strength in his bony arms.

The emotion had rolled over me so suddenly I felt embarrassed as I took a step back, still holding Ben's shoulders. He was trying to smile while not showing me his wasted teeth. On another day it would have been comical. I became aware of Mave standing at my shoulder. 'I'm sorry…Mave, this is a very old, very dear friend of mine who I thought was dead, Ben Searcey. Ben, Mave's my friend too.'

They smiled at each other and shook hands. Mave's look asked me if I was okay. I nodded, smiling. Ben shivered. 'Come on,' I said, 'get in the car, Mave'll turn the heater on.' I led him and sat him in the front, close to the warm vents.

I moved to the centre of the back seat. Ben half-turned, still trying to smile, to reassure me, 'I'm sorry, Ben, I don't know where that outburst came from. It must have shocked you. I'd heard you were dead. I thought you were dead.'

'Everybody says that, Eddie, don't worry. I'm fine. This is day twelve-twenty-one without a drink. Tomorrow will be twelve-twenty-two. That's how I run things now. I'm doing all right.'

'Are you being treated here?' I asked.

'Never been here before in my life. I came to see you. They showed that race on the news, that race that put you in here, and I thought…well, to be honest, I thought I'd come and see if you'd help me. It's not money or anything.'

I reached to touch his arm, 'Ben, you could have my last penny. Of course I'll help you, what is it?'

'I wondered if you'd be a character witness for me at a children's panel hearing next week. I'm trying to get my girl back, my daughter.'

'Alice?'

He forgot his teeth this time and smiled wide, 'How come you remember her name?'

'I remember her well, Ben, very well. She used to shout "Yeehaa" all the time in the press room when she was about five, didn't she?'

He laughed, 'She did. She heard a gang of punters yelling their horse home and she ran around everywhere for weeks after that shouting Yeehaa and whipping at herself as though she was winning the National.'

'She was a funny kid. How is she?'

His smile dimmed, 'I put her through some tough times, but I couldn't be prouder of her if she was the queen. She's been in a dozen children's homes, kept running away, but I finally talked her into staying put long enough for me to have a chance of getting her back.'

'How old is she now, Ben?'

'She's thirteen. She'd fight dragons for you, for anybody…that's been half the trouble. But we're nearly there now. I've been wracking what's left of my memory to try and come up with two or three people who'd speak for me at the hearing, then I saw you on the telly.'

'Listen,' I said, 'there'd be plenty of your old mates would walk through fire for you. Want me to find you some more for this hearing? How many do you need?'

He waved it away, smiling, and I found myself growing used to the tiny smashed battlements that were his teeth. 'I've got a proper ace up my sleeve, Eddie, queerest thing. I was coming back from visiting Alice the other day, got off the train at Lime Street and I heard somebody shouting my name. At first I couldn't see anybody, with all the crowds moving, but then, as they cleared, there was just me and one man on the platform, and I recognized him right away, which wouldn't be hard given the poor bugger's face. He'd had even more plastic surgery done since-'

'Monty Bearak?'

'Monty Bearak! You got it! Hadn't seen him since I got pissed in his box at Aintree, years back, and didn't half get a shock when he came over. The booze must have blanked me out on just how much damage that accident did. His face is like a big blob of play-doh, just sitting on his collar like it didn't belong there. Tell you what it made me think of, you know the cardboard cutouts at the seaside you stick your head through for a photo? It was like someone had plopped this big pumpkin face on Monty's immaculate suit. Couldn't believe it. You seen him lately?'

I nodded. 'I see him pretty regularly. He's got a box on most courses and goes racing nearly every day. And he's Sir Monty now, by the way, for services to Merseyside charities, so if he's coming to speak for you at the hearing, you're a certainty to get Alice back.'

'They gave him a knighthood? He never said a thing. There you go. Well, that's another piece of good news for me, Eddie, the first one being that you've come out of that fall all right. Never seen anything like that in twenty years on the track.'

'Me neither.'

'What happened?'

'Nobody knows.'

'I was telling Alice about it, I said, that horse must have had a brain haemorrhage, or something like a stroke to have behaved like that. I couldn't believe it. Thank god you were all right.'

'Well there's not much wrong with the horse's brain. She's back in her box as though nothing happened. Something wrong with my brain, though, wanting to get back riding.'

That smile again, 'Some things never change, Eddie.'

'Listen, Mave is driving us home, up to the lakes. Come with us, spend a day or two.'

'I'd love to. Sounds the very thing. But I can't miss my meetings.'

'AA?'

'Saved my life.'

'Where are you living?'

'On a council estate in North Liverpool, not far from Aintree. They call it Deadwood. Rough, but it's where Alice wants to be. She's running a campaign there. I'll let her tell you all about it on Wednesday. I'm working on her so she doesn't start preaching it to the panel,' another wide smile.

'Did you drive here?'

'Got the bus. Can't get insurance, Eddie, too many DUIs. They want about a grand a week to insure me. I do have fun though when they phone me up, you know, those cold callers. Would I be interested in insurance? Sure, I would! Have you got a few minutes now? I got all the time in the world!' He laughed, and I was struck by the purity of his happiness and I supposed he had indeed been dead to all intents and purposes, and maybe he was just glorying in this resurrection, ragged face, ruined teeth and all.

'We'll drive you home,' I said.

'You will not! You're convalescing, my friend, and I've got a free bus pass. I'll see you on Wednesday, eh?'

'At the hearing? Sure. Where is it?'

'Liverpool city centre. I'll email you what you need.'

'Mave, you got a pen and paper?'

Mave flipped the sun visor and unzipped a pocket in the organizer strapped there. I wrote down my contact details for Ben.

'Thanks, Eddie. Drop you a line tonight.'

'Sure you don't want a lift?'

He palmed away the offer, 'Nah! Bus is fine. You meet a few characters, watch the world going by. The good world.'

I got out and opened the door for him and we hugged again. 'You're a dear friend, Eddie.'

'You were always one to me, Ben. Always. I'll never forget what you did.'

He stepped back, still holding my forearms, 'Get away, you'd have done the same for me.'

I saw again that fresh, clean happiness, growing accustomed now to it glowing from such a worn and battered face, 'See you on Wednesday,' I said, 'And Alice. Tell her we'll do a Yeehaa after the hearing.'

Ben backed away, thumb raised, smile open, 'We will, Eddie, we will.' He ducked to look at Mave and raised that thumb again, 'Nice to meet you, Mavis!'

'And you,' she called.

I leant on the open door, watching him limp toward the exit. He shoved his hands in his pockets the way a schoolboy does, and his head came up and he looked around as though trying to take in everything in a new place. Ben Searcey. Reborn.

4

Mave kept her visor down and I lowered mine and pulled the old stained seatbelt across, 'Home, Mavis!' I said, laughing.

'Mavis,' she said quietly, and grinned, 'he's some character.'

'A hell of a man. I'm ashamed to say I'd forgotten about him. He was really well known years ago, big time sports reporter. He'd started in racing, that was his first love. Once he branched out into other sports, he won all sorts of awards. But nothing went to his head. How you just saw him was pretty much the way I'd always found him. Straight to the point. Humble. Even in drink, he was never troublesome or aggressive.'

Mave said, 'Might not have been troublesome for others but he looks a wreck.'

'He was a wreck. Cost him his job, family, home…'

'Shame…' Mave nodded slowly.

'I know. Seems like he has a chance here, though. Will you come with me, to this tribunal thing, this panel?'

'If you like.'

'Good. It should make me seem more, well, human.'

'I'm not sure anything could do that.'

'Very funny. You know what I mean. If I'm to give Ben a character reference, well, it'll look as though I'm more of a family man if you're there.'

'Maybe we should hire a couple of nice kids. Freckled ones.

With fixed smiles.'

'Mave, this is serious. It sounds like Alice has been in and out of care homes and foster homes for a long time.'

'Where's her mother?'

'I don't know.'

'Did you ever meet her?'

'I did. Met her at an awards dinner. Seemed a nice woman. I think she was called Alice, too.'

'I wonder what's happened to her.'

'Well, if Ben doesn't tell us, it'll probably come out on Wednesday at this hearing.'

'Why don't you just ring and ask him? If you're to be a character witness, maybe the panel will ask you about her.'

'I can't just ring him up and say tell me about your wife.'

'Why not?'

'Men don't do emotional conversations, just practical ones.'

She looked across and said, 'Like the practical one back there when he had you in tears?'

'God, that was strange…Can't remember the last time I cried. I think it was just everything that's happened since Saturday, and worry about Kim. Then being back in the fresh air again…It surprised me as much as it surprised Ben.'

'He probably thought *you'd* taken to the booze and gone all maudlin on him.'

'Maybe. Ben will have seen enough tears in his lifetime. I'm glad we've got a chance to help him. Ben was the only reporter who stood by me when I got warned off. Anybody else I called didn't want to know. Ben didn't think twice. He even tried to help me find the guy who framed me.'

'But there would have been a story in it for him, surely?'

'The opposite. His editor had written it off as a lost cause. Ended up costing Ben his job because he wouldn't walk away when they told him to.'

'Proper friend, right enough. Who's the other guy you mentioned, the plastic surgery guy?'

'Monty Bearak, Sir Monty Bearak.'

'A man of means, racing every day. Inherited money?'

I tried to recall what Monty did. He'd been no more than a nodding acquaintance of mine. 'No, I don't think so. I believe he's one of these money market players, a currency trader or some kind of finance guy. He's better known for charitable work on Merseyside, helping kids. I'm pretty sure that's what he got the knighthood for.'

'So what did Ben do for Sir Monty that's made him want to drop everything, well, everything knights do on a Wednesday?'

I smiled. 'I'm not sure. I think they came from the same area, or were at the same school or something. They're both Merseysiders, anyway. Monty's always been into racing. He'll have bumped into Ben hundreds of times. You heard Ben say Monty had invited him to his box at Aintree, though that turned out to be no favour, I suppose.'

'No favour? It sounds positively cruel.'

'Well, I'm not sure how much Monty knew about Ben's boozing habits back then. It's not as if you ask someone to fill in a questionnaire before inviting them in for free champagne.'

Mave nodded and settled to her customary peering over the dashboard driving position, and we travelled in silence until Kim came to my mind once more. I said, 'Any word from our family in Oz?'

'Kim and Marie think it's too hot. Sonny loves it.'

'Did you speak to Kim?'

'Marie. She Skyped last night.'

'I'll ping Kim later. What's the time difference?'

'Eleven hours ahead.'

'I'll try him about ten. Odd to think it'll be tomorrow morning there.'

She said, 'I still haven't told them about the coma, or even the fall. Might be best if you don't mention it.'

'I won't.'

We went a mile in silence, then Mave said, 'You still worried Kim might stay over there?'

'I suppose I am, if I'm honest with myself. At his age, it'll seem like the whole world suddenly opened up.'

'He'll be fine, Eddie. He'll be home by August, they all will.'

'I know that was the plan, but plans don't always work out.'

She reached to put her small hand in mine, 'All will be well.' That was a phrase we used on each other. I nodded and watched the road twist away as it climbed into the hills.

5

The snow came just after dark. Mave and I lived behind the farmhouse in a small cottage. We spent most of our time in The Snug, a room I'd replicated from my previous home in Lambourn. It was big enough for a short sofa and a fireside chair. The Snug was thickly carpeted and we'd added a spark-proof rug by the stove. Three walls were of stone, the other of plate glass, an expensive indulgence, and a bitch to keep clean, but always worth it.

We had views down to Ullswater, the long lake filling the narrow valley between Patterdale and Pooley Bridge. On nights like this, the valley sucked the snow in.

I said, 'I'll turn off these lights, and switch on the ones outside and we can watch the snow.'

'Best tie me down first, in case I'm overcome with excitement,' Maven said.

'Very funny. I think we've had enough excitement for one day.'

She eased back into the sofa, sitting beside me, gazing through the window. The west wind swept the snow past and drove it away into the night. I said, 'It's a bit like going fast in reverse in a snowstorm…In a car, I mean.'

'I suppose.'

After a few moments of silent watching, Mave said, 'You were going to ping Kim.'

I went to the small desk that held Mave's laptop. 'Says here he's offline.'

'Try FaceTime. He'll get it on his phone.'

'Will it cost him?'

'Does it matter? Send him a hundred dollars.'

I clicked on his name, and six rings later Kim's healthy, smiling face loomed at me, 'Uncle Eddie! I thought you'd be in bed!'

'Hey, I'm not that old that I can't keep my eyes open past ten 'o clock. And what's with the uncle all of a sudden?'

He laughed, 'Just winding you up.'

'You look well.' I said, 'Settled in?'

'I don't know about settling, Eddie. You wouldn't believe the size of the place. Look…'

The image zoomed and buffered then steadied on the vastness of a flat green land. 'Where are the sheep?' I asked.

'On the south side. I'll show you!'

In Kim's bumping run I caught flashes of outbuildings and vehicles and glints of sunlight. Kim shouted, 'I'll climb up on this bench!' And, seconds later, I was looking at an ocean of wool. Kim shouted, 'Brian's got a picture on the wall, taken from a plane. They all look like a million maggots!' He laughed.

Kim was my nephew. Brian was his biological father, lately tracked down by my sister Marie to this outback sheep station. Her last sight of Brian had come when she was fifteen, pregnant, and watching him being banished by father in a blitz of yelling.

Kim and I talked for a long time as he moved around what seemed a huge ranch showing me everything that excited his teenage mind.

I said, 'Watch this,' and I carried the laptop to the picture window and turned the webcam.

'Is that snow?'

'Tearing down the valley. Take a good look. You won't see much of it over there.'

'There'll be plenty next winter when I'm home. We'll get the horses back and go out riding every day.'

'We will. Now you go and get yourself a suntan. I'll speak to you again soon. Give our love to your Mum and to Sonny.'

'And Brian,' Mave prompted.

'And to Brian' I said.

'And give our love to the farm,' Kim said, 'and leave a light on there so the mice don't feel lonely.'

'The light's on, Kim, and it'll stay on until you're home.'

'That's good.'

'Off you go. There's a full day ahead for you because it's tomorrow where you are.'

'I know! Strange, isn't it?'

I said, 'If you get to hear tomorrow's racing results in England, let me know, and we'll make a fortune.'

'Ha! I wish tomorrow worked that way.'

'Me too.'

'See ya…Oh, is Mave okay?'

'She's fine. Sitting watching the snow with me. She sends her love.'

'Me too. Us, too, I should say.'

'Off you go.'

'Byyyeee!'

Mave watched me as I walked back toward her, 'Feel better?' she said.

'Much better. He looks great. I'll have a whiskey to celebrate. Want one?'

'Please.'

I brought two glasses from the kitchen.

Mave said, 'Do we get to put the lights back on now?'

I flicked the switch, and took my drink and stood by the stove.

Mave said, 'Let them settle, Eddie. We need to get on with our own lives at this end of the world.'

I nodded, gazing down at the embers.

'Come and sit with me,' she said, 'Relax. Watch the snow.'

I looked through the picture window. 'It's lost its beauty under the lights.'

Mave smiled. 'I know the feeling.'

6

Mave and I met Ben Searcey and his daughter Alice outside the Chambers in Liverpool. Ben's gibbering nervousness proved ill-founded, as the children's panel hearing was a short one, thanks to Sir Monty Bearak. The three women and two men holding the power to release Alice Searcey into the care of her father seemed awed by Monty's title, and stunned by his mangled face. Outside, on the steps between the sandstone pillars, Monty's face in the winter sunlight, fascinated Alice, and Mave, too.

If you didn't know about his car crash history, or the plastic surgery ops, Monty wouldn't tell you. I think he enjoyed the startling gargoyle effect he had on people. The only flaw hidden was his missing right eye. A perfect glass eye had replaced it.

His smile reinforced the starkness, for his teeth were a perfect glittering line in the mashed up flesh around them. But, nobody shied from his hugs on those cold steps, and none refused his invitation to an early lunch.

Face-watchers in the restaurant could switch to Ben if they tired of Monty. Ben's sharp cheekbones and pointed chin beneath that pale papery skin held his face up like a badly pitched tent.

Ben was so ravaged, there was no way of telling if Alice had inherited any of his looks. When I saw Alice, I remembered her mother much more clearly, and could see her in Alice: the fair hair, and springy ears and the flint-grey eyes. The fire in those eyes, and the constant wariness hardened her thin face, stopping her just short of pretty.

Monty was first to leave after lunch, his chauffeur reminding him of a business appointment. He shook hands with all and made Ben and Alice promise to join him at Aintree in April, 'Eddie will come to the box and give us a few winners before racing, I'm sure.'

'Be a first,' I said.

'When do you expect to be back riding?' Monty asked.

'I'm seeing the BHA doc tomorrow for a preliminary.'

'You'll be okay for Cheltenham, won't you?'

I nodded, 'Even if they have to tie me on.'

'I believe you!'

When he'd gone, there was silence. The elephant that was Monty's face had left the room and still no one could talk about it. I watched Ben and Alice, sensing tension. Her jaw was set. Those grey eyes gleamed. Ben put an arm around her shoulder. She didn't move away, nor did she acknowledge anything. She stared through the window, looking at the past, or the future; maybe a fragment of each.

'Can we give you a lift home?' I said.

Ben smiled, 'Nope. Thank you, but no. We're going to walk through the city together. I'll buy two train tickets, and we will sit side by side and count down the stations from Central to Aintree on the Ormskirk line. Then we will gird our loins and conquer Deadwood.'

Alice turned slowly to smile at her father. 'Gird your own loins', she said, 'I'm not even sure women have loins.'

Mave chuckled and turned to me, 'Eddie, do they?'

'How would I know?'

'You're the loin king,' Mave said, and Alice smiled at her and I saw two wits connect. That moment flushed away all my frustration at being absent from racing and I laughed.

Ben laughed, too. He was the oldest there, but when he laughed, he became the youngest.

I said, 'Enjoy your train trip, then. We'll see you at Aintree.'

'I doubt we'll make it, Eddie, but I'll let Monty know in good time. I'd love for us to go, but I swapped my tux a long time ago for a gallon of cider.'

I smiled, 'You'll find the dress code's nowhere near as strict as it used to be.'

Alice said, 'Dad wouldn't pass the dress code for Night of the Living Dead, never mind the Grand National.'

Ben laughed again in that open childlike, infectious way. I said, 'Would you like to go, Alice?'

'I'd love to. We'll find something for him, don't worry.'

I nodded, 'I remember you in your Yeehaa days.'

She cupped her hands on her face, 'Oh, don't!'

Ben pushed her playfully, 'I told you you were famous on the racecourse!'

Mave said, 'Have you been racing since then, Alice?'

She looked from above her fingers, 'No. And if Eddie really does remember that, I'll never be going again!'

'You into horses?' I asked.

'I love watching them, but they're a bit scary. The main thing I remember from going with dad, was that they were like big monsters, all shiny muscles and huge teeth.'

'Yep, they kick at one end and bite at the other, but so long as you know that, you're usually safe. Why don't you come up and see us in the Lakes sometime?'

She said, 'Thanks. Maybe once we've done what we have to do, we will.'

I looked at Ben. He was smiling at her, deferring to her. 'Well,' I said, 'Your dad's got my number.'

Mave said, 'We could time it for when Kim comes home. Kim would love to meet you.'

'How old is she?' Alice asked.

'She's a he,' Mave said, 'and he's fourteen.' She pointed at me, 'If you can picture a much younger version of him, unbattered, finer-featured, someone who smiles much more often, which would not be hard, that's what Kim looks like.'

Alice gazed at me, wrinkling her nose, tilting her head, sizing me up, then, with great comic timing said, 'Nah…I'll pass.'

We didn't need Ben's laugh to set us all off, and everyone in the restaurant stared.

We said goodbye and Mave and I sat smiling as we watched father and daughter walk toward the railway station. Mave said to me, 'A happy day.'

'A rare thing for them.' I said.

'Eddie?' I felt a hand on my shoulder. I turned and saw Calum Crampsey in an immaculate dark suit. Calum had worked for the main racecourse caterers for years and it dawned on me that I hadn't seen him on the track. I stood up and shook his hand, 'Calum! How's it going? Haven't seen you for a long time. Sit down.'

He drew back a chair and eased himself down. His brown hair was greyer and his pleasant face more lined since last I'd seen him. I introduced Mave and he rose again to shake her hand, then settled. He said, 'I saw you from the kitchen. I'm working here now.'

I said, 'You should have come and said hello. You know Ben Searcey, don't you? And Sir Monty?'

Calum said, 'I know Sir Monty, and I remember Ben well.'

Some vague strand of gossip came to mind. I said, 'Did something happen with you and Sir Monty?'

'He got me sacked. Said I'd brought the wrong bottle to his box and caused him great embarrassment, oddly enough with Ben. National day, five years ago.'

I said, 'It's coming back to me now, though I didn't know who was involved.'

'Couldn't get another job in racing after that,' Calum said, 'never a day goes past I don't miss it.' His head went down. I glanced at Mave then said to Calum, 'Want me to have a word with Monty?'

'Would you? If I'm honest, that's why I came over. I was going to ask. I hate to beg, and I'm sure I didn't do anything wrong, but Sir Monty obviously thought I did.'

I didn't know whether to explain what had happened with Ben that day, and how embarrassed he was about it. I said, 'Let me have a word.'

'Thanks, Eddie, though I feel a bit of a hypocrite because I wrote to Sir Monty about a month after it, apologizing. Then I felt bad for doing that because I knew it wasn't my fault, but it was the only way I could think of to try and get my job back.'

'Did he reply?'

Calum shook his head and was quiet for a few moments, then said, 'I'm sorry. I haven't even asked how you are? I still keep up with all the racing news. That was a hell of a fall you took a couple of weeks back.'

I smiled, 'Had a week's holiday in Bangor hospital, now Mave's helping try to piece my brain back together.'

'Mission impossible,' Mave said, and we smiled.

'Never saw anything like that,' Calum said, 'what happened?'

Once more I launched into trying to explain the unexplainable.

At home that evening, I rang Sir Monty and thanked him for his hospitality. 'Not at all,' he said, 'it was a pleasure, and a lovely change from dining with a bunch of stuffed shirts.'

I laughed, 'After you'd gone, I saw Calum Crampsey. He's working as a wine waiter in that restaurant now'

'Calum?'

'He worked on course for years for Selby and Sampson. He was very apologetic about the last time he saw you, that day at Aintree, the National, five years ago...'

The pause was so long I thought he'd gone... 'Eddie, I don't want to be rude, but I'll say this, I rarely get angry, very rarely, but that man caused me huge embarrassment and left me with a heavy conscience over Ben. Ben Searcey was my responsibility that day. I'd had to talk him into accepting my invitation. He was my guest. He was in my care, and I should have looked after his welfare. I failed. And the reason I failed was the incompetence of Crampsey. Ben's had to live with the consequences, and I have had to live with the guilt. There's nothing more I want to say on the subject of Mister Crampsey.'

After we'd said goodbye I looked at Mave, 'He couldn't have

27

made that any clearer,' I said.

'Well, at least we know now why our knight was so eager to help a beat-up alcoholic.'

'You're being awful harsh, Mave.'

She shrugged, 'It's the truth. I like Ben, and I like Alice, but it's the truth. Still, Ben got what he needed and old Monty salved his conscience.'

'And Calum carried the can,' I said.

'It's the rich wot gets the pleasure and the poor wot gets the pain, Edward.'

I reached for my phone, 'I'd best call Calum with the bad news.'

7

I was back in the saddle in time for the Cheltenham Festival, the Olympics of National Hunt racing. It had taken a week's race riding to reach full fitness, and I'd had two winners since my return. Good rides at Cheltenham were awful hard to come by. The four-day event was dominated by three trainers, each with big money owners behind them, and, frustratingly, their own jockeys.

Dil's recently acquired owner, Vita Brodie, could have mustered a few hundred million. Vita had a string of racehorses in America and she had already bought a dozen for Dil to train. One of those was Stevedore in the Supreme Novices Hurdle, a race with a history of huge gambles by the Irish on their 'banker'. Today their big hope was Spalpeen, a stunning black beast who looked so superior in the paddock you got the impression the other horses dared not glance his way.

Spalpeen was odds on. My horse, Stevedore, was twenty-to-one.

We walked round in the holding ring at the start, each small circuit increasing the tension, as though we had banded together to wind up some huge mechanism.

From the packed stands in the distance, the sun flashed glints from raised binoculars held by those with tensions of their own: gamblers, owners, trainers, breeders and bookmakers.

Among us, the chatter levels were unpredictable. It seemed everyone was speaking, or no one. Whatever was being said, nobody was taking it in. Nothing mattered but the race.

We were called, and we filed out, pulling down goggles, jostling for starting positions while trying to keep the horses calm.

'Walk up!' the starter called.

We restrained our mounts as their mouths opened and ears went back and their adrenaline surged and their muscles bunched…'Come on!' the starter called, and the tapes shot up, and we were away, and the customary "Supreme roar" from the stands to mark the first race of the Festival eventually reached us as a whisper below the thunder of hooves as we raced to the first.

Stevedore was unbeaten. But he'd run just once when we had easily won a small race at Doncaster. This was a much hotter contest, but after three jumps, he was moving nicely with the fast pace, easily holding his position and that told me an awful lot about his talent. Had it not been for the cruising Spalpeen travelling so sweetly three in front of me, I'd have been hopeful of my first Festival winner for a long time.

As we galloped toward the top of the hill, three hurdles from home, the brutal pace gutted the weak, the underdogs, the ones who could not respond to desperate urgings from their jockeys as they fell away on this bulletless battlefield, and Stevedore moved easily beneath me, faltering for just a stride or two as we turned downhill and he took the chance to fill his lungs, before resuming his strong, rhythmical gallop.

Whatever the outcome, Vita and Dil had themselves a bloody good horse. On landing over the third last, we'd moved into fourth. I glanced to my left…where was Spalpeen?

Then I spotted him.

He was in sixth. His motionless jockey, Vince McCrory saw me and he smiled the smile of the quiet assassin, killing my hopes in an instant.

But I might finish in the first three.

I concentrated on getting my approach right as we headed downhill to the second last…then Spalpeen passed me so quickly I imagined I could feel the air move in his wake. Seconds later, the

Irish favourite was ten lengths clear and my heart rose, and I smiled, then I forced myself to be more sombre because Vince McCrory was in serious danger. His mount was doing exactly what Montego Moon had done at Bangor and I feared the big horse would smash through the next hurdle and come down, and at that storming, headlong, panicked pace, Vince would be lucky to survive.

I should have been concentrating on the stride pattern of my horse as we got within a hundred yards of the second last, but Spalpeen's wild gallop was all I could watch. Vince stood straight-legged, wrestling with the horse, and I felt like crying out to him that it was useless and that he should stay low and hold tight.

Then Spalpeen veered left and my admiration for Vince McCrory went up ten notches because he stayed in the saddle. At Bangor, Montego Moon had simply lost it and lowered her head and galloped until a fence stopped her. Spalpeen had changed course.

At that crazy speed, one jockey in a hundred would have stayed aboard as the horse veered sharply. Vince did it. And Spalpeen ran past the wing of the hurdle and I felt a mixture of relief for him and elation for us.

By missing out that jump, Spalpeen had disqualified himself.

We flew the next hurdle and Stevedore hit the front, shifting into grafting mode like the professional racehorse he was. I could hear the others, the hoofbeats, snorting nostrils sucking hard, then, as we rounded the bend into the straight, I saw the grey head of the second-favourite, Tomorrowland on my outside, at the flanks of Stevedore, at his ribs, his shoulders, and we went to the last neck and neck. Bomber Harries, a good friend, was riding the grey and I could hear him too, breathing hard as we moved across the track to jump the last.

Bomber got the rail. That would help him. We were close…bumping…Bomber cried, 'Eddie!' I pulled Stevedore away to get a clean jump, hoping Bomber's would stumble, but the horses rose together, a moment's suspension of the sound of galloping as we flew.

Then on the ground again. The noise of fifty thousand people, the screams, the yells and cries were softly there at the edge of my consciousness and they seemed to suck and blow at us as we ran nose to nose, drifting out for a few strides, then back in, heads down, whips flailing, as we fought to raise one more ounce of effort from these brave, battling thoroughbreds whose sweat exploded in micro-drops at each whip strike, whose mouths spumed foam that splatted on our knees and hands, whose courage could not be broken as we passed the winning post inseparable, to a final crescendo before the huge balloon of noise burst, leaving only sighs in the air…

…and then a new sound rose…applause.

And it grew evenly and spread like some audio Mexican wave as the purest of racing fans instinctively congratulated two superb animals who would never know what it meant to surrender.

It didn't take long to pull up, for our mounts were exhausted. Bomber and I brought our horses close and he put an arm around my shoulder, and I put my right arm across his back, and we fought for oxygen, and Bomber in his own mock exhaustion and gratitude laid his head on my shoulder and we found breath enough to laugh.

Only when we stopped to turn and acknowledge the applause from the stands did I see the green screens being erected around the black hulk of Spalpeen. And I remembered Vince, and craned my neck to see if he too was on the ground. Bomber nudged me and signalled with his head and I turned to see Vince lying a hundred yards down the track, his pink colours just visible through the throng of medics.

8

That night, Peter McCarthy rang me. Mac was an old friend, and occasional adversary. He was the security chief for the British racing authorities, the BHA.

'Mac, how I love to see your name light up my phone. It's been so long!'

'Very funny, Eddie.'

'Doubtless you are calling to congratulate me on that fine ride in the Supreme?'

'Well, that would be somewhat disingenuous of me, but, well done anyway. Half a race is better than none.'

'Thank you. I was happy to settle for the dead heat. So was Bomber. Now what can I do for you?'

'I need to talk to you about Montego Moon at Bangor.'

'I'm listening. Oh, what's the latest on Vince McCrory?'

'He's going to be all right. Should be riding tomorrow.'

'That's good news. I heard the horse is okay.'

'Yes. Cracked ribs. Nothing too bad.'

'Dope test results?'

'Clean.'

'Oh dear.'

'Indeed. The horse's adrenaline levels were through the roof. Very high cortisol readings, but nothing synthetic. All the hormonal responses are what you'd expect from the physical behaviour.'

'So how much was Spalpeen laid for on the exchanges?'

'How do you know he was?'

'Because you're calling me. Because it's Festival time and will have a shitload of work you'd rather be doing. Because som e up high has told you to get a result.'

Mac grunted, then said, 'He was laid for a total of one poin million across four accounts, each opened in the past few eeks. Winnings were withdrawn immediately. Police have ap d for permission to examine bank details of the four individuals.'

'Whose names are?'

'Each appears to be an alias.'

'So Spalpeen was got at. No doubt you've checked the b charts for Montego Moon?'

'We have. Nothing unusual. No laying under new accounts or aliases.'

'So your conclusion is that whoever got at Spalpeen was using Montego Moon for a trial run?'

'Correct.'

'But you've not got beyond that?'

'Er,..no.'

'Well, Mac, I'm so happy that after knowing you for more than fifteen years, you've finally stopped trying to bullshit me.'

'I trust your discretion, Eddie, I know I can speak frankly with you. With others, well, sometimes dissemblance is a necessary part of my job.'

'I don't know what dissemblance means, Mac, but I suspect it's a fancy word for bullshit.'

'Harsh people might say so.'

'Count me harsh, Mac, count me harsh.'

He cleared his throat, a prompt I was familiar with. It meant he had nothing more to offer and hoped that I had. I said, 'Any of the vets got an opinion on what set these two horses off?'

'All they agree on is that a sudden high state of panic has been induced, and that it's unlikely it's coming from something that's been administered before the race.'

'So, since I think we can agree that it would not have been administered after the race, your suspicion is that it might have been administered during the race, hence your call to me as the possible administrator with Montego Moon?'

'We need to rule things out one by one, Eddie, don't be offended. If I believed you were up to anything, do you really think I'd just call and ask you?'

'Mac, I'm not so much offended as astonished that the BHA, in its desperation, could come up with a suggestion that a jockey might just have the bright idea of trying to kill himself by giving the half a ton of galloping bone and muscle he's sitting on something to send it into a blind panic. Who was round the table at this particular brainstorming session?'

'It's always easy for you to crab things, isn't it? We're faced with a major incident, which is unexplainable, which might happen again tomorrow, and the next day, and the next. We're under a duty to consider every and any possibility.'

I sighed by way of a grudging apology. 'Okay, Mac. Listen, I said to somebody the other day that it felt as though Montego Moon had been shot with an energy bullet. Has Spalpeen been checked inch by inch for any marks from a tiny dart or pellet or something?'

'How difficult would that have been, assuming you mean someone shot the horse from a distance?'

'Difficult, but probably a less crazy theory than the jockey doing anything. Look at the size of the infield at Cheltenham. Who was out there today? Could somebody have been carrying a rifle, maybe someone in a vehicle? Were there any helicopters up during the race? Or what about the camera blimp? Have you spoken to the operators of that?'

He was silent for a moment, then said, 'No…No I haven't.'

'Well, that's my best guess, Mac. It wasn't dope. It couldn't have been something given to them before the race, unless whoever gave it knew exactly how long it would take to work. For that you'd need to be certain there'd be no delays at the start. A horse loses a shoe, and the race is off five minutes late, bang goes your betting coup.'

'True.'

'It also felt like something immediate. If it had been a drug, there'd surely have been some sort of build up, a gradual agitation. But Montego Moon went from lolloping along to super turbo in a second, maybe less. It would be too late now to check the mare for small skin marks, but maybe there'll be some sign on Spalpeen. And you could check the TV footage to see who was out there during the race, and what was going on overhead.'

'Okay…Okay.'

'Mac, those are your grudging okays, not your decisive I'll get right to it okays.'

'Eddie, I very much appreciate your opinions on this, but if you break it down, assuming it was done from ground level, someone has to get a weapon into the track, a high powered weapon, then find a position where nobody will be around him at exactly the time he needs the privacy, and that same position needs to be the one that best affords a shot at his target, and, hardest of all, the horse he has to hit must be in clear view. If the jockey has him in the pack, or on the far side rail, there is no shot.'

'Fair comment if you're talking ground level. From above, it's a whole different story, especially from the TV blimp. Stationary, clear line of sight, no worries about witnesses, assuming the crew is involved. No issues passing security into the track, and plenty of opportunities to fire.'

'Mmmm'

'Sound more plausible now?'

'I'm coming round, I must admit.'

'Find out who was in that blimp, Mac. Might even be worth grounding it tomorrow.'

'The TV guys and the sponsors would take a very dim view of that.'

'They'd take an even dimmer view of a dead jockey, or a crazed horse bursting through the rails into the enclosures, mowing down racegoers. How would you stop it? If a horse in that state got in among crowds, it would need to be shot just to halt the carnage. If the sponsors think grounding a blimp for a day is bad for their brand, try them with live TV pictures of a slaughtered horse and a dozen dead racegoers lying on the tarmac in front of the grandstand.'

9

On day two of the Cheltenham Festival, I was riding at Sedgefield, which feels like acting in a village play while everyone else is at The Oscars.

Sipping black coffee from a Styrofoam cup in the changing room, I watched Cheltenham on TV. The blimp was flying. Either Mac had binned the theory or he'd been unable to persuade the decision makers.

In the paddock for my first mount, I met Dil. That worried look I'd first seen when he'd visited hospital had etched itself into his face. He legged me up on a narrow chestnut owned by Vita Brodie and said, 'No fame today, win or lose.'

'At least I don't need to worry about being carted.' I told him about my conversation with Mac. Dil said, 'So they think Montego Moon was a guinea pig?'

'Looks like it. And that, my friend, entitles you to at least one smile.'

'If Prim catches me smiling, she'll think it's because I've found a house for Vita.' The horse bucked. Dil eased his grip on the lead rein and began walking us round the paddock.

'I forgot about that,' I said, 'Sounds like you're going to have to make a decision soon.'

'On what?'

'On keeping your owner or your secretary stroke lover. Stroke being the key word.'

'Well, I can't afford to lose Vita.'

'Simple, then. Decision made.'

He turned, glowering at me, 'It's not simple! Prim's a good woman. And she cares for me, which is more than Vita does.'

'Hey! I'm only offering a sympathetic ear! If Vita doesn't care for you, what's her problem?'

'Her problem is sex. That's what she wants. That's what she doesn't want Prim to have, and depriving Prim is becoming more important to her than any relationship she wants with me.'

'Sounds like she wants to deprive you too. Vita's an alpha female, if there is such a thing.'

'She's a rich female. Her horses are already worth two hundred grand a year to me and she's planning to buy a few more.'

'It's your choice, Dil.'

He led me out of the paddock onto the track, unclipped the lead rein and looked up, 'Come home safe.'

I nodded, 'You had a bet?'

He shook his head and walked away.

We finished seventh.

Tracey, the groom, led us back in, patting the sweating chestnut and telling the horse it would win next time.

Dil was in the weighing room when I came out after showering. 'Straight home?' he asked.

'That's the plan.'

'I'll walk out with you,' he said.

'Be my guest.'

We headed for the car park. Dil said, 'I was thinking about Montego Moon...'

'And?'

'Why me? Why pick my yard?'

'Maybe they didn't.'

He looked at me. I said, 'I still think somebody shot Montego Moon and Spalpeen. That panic reaction was generated by sudden pain, had to be. But for the horse to maintain that intense fear, there had to be something to keep the pain level high. Ever had a local anaesthetic injection close to an open wound?'

'Yeah. Stings.'

'It stings for a long time. My guess is something like that. The shot they took at Bangor could have hit any horse, it didn't matter to them. All they needed to check was that whatever they're using worked.'

'They could have checked it in private, on a horse in a field somewhere.'

'Not if they wanted certainty on the reaction. You can't run a race in private. You can't produce the adrenaline levels a horse feels in competition. And if they were going to risk big money, they'd want to be sure.'

'Okay…Okay, maybe they weren't targeting my horse. But they had to be targeting Spalpeen, so how did they make the shot?'

'The blimp was my best bet. It was in the air today and everything went all right at Cheltenham, but that doesn't mean it wasn't used yesterday. I'll call Mac later.'

Dil raised a hand, 'Don't call him on my account. So long as they're leaving my horses alone, I don't care whether they're shooting them, shocking them or doping them. It's not as if we're going to have any odds on favourites in big races.'

'Shocking them…I hadn't thought of that, Dil.'

'Used to carry buzzers in the States, some jocks. The jockey would need to be in on it.'

'Maybe…what if there was something under the girth? Something they could send a remote signal to to keep it pulsing out shocks? That actually sounds more likely. No need for guns, and drugs and having to hit targets.'

'So who puts it under the girth? The trainer would have saddled Spalpeen yesterday. It's hardly going to be him. And once that's done, who else is near the horse before the off, or at least near enough to shove some gadget under the girth without anyone noticing and with enough care to make sure it stays put?'

'The lad? The head lad? The starter's assistant?'

Dil nodded slowly, 'Last one would be favourite, huh? Not the highest paid guys in the world, are they? And they could spend enough time messing around with girths to make sure the thing stays put.'

'Correct.'

'Who checked your girths yesterday?'

'Vogel, Jon Vogel. Been doing it since…hey, Vogel was at Bangor too. He did Montego Moon.'

Dil put an arm across my shoulder. It was the first time I'd seen him smile in weeks.

10

In the car I took my phone from the glovebox, intent on calling Mac. There are heavy racecourse restrictions on mobile phone use by jockeys, and I preferred leaving mine locked up rather than risk misunderstandings. One voicemail waited. It was from Ben Searcey. I called him.

'Eddie, thanks for calling me back so quickly. Listen, I wondered if Monty still had the hotshot security guy on his payroll?'

'Security guy...oh, I remember him, the opposite of the big mean old bouncer. Slim fella, always wore a hankie in his top pocket, dark hair?'

'That's him. Foreign name...short name, just can't bloody remember it!'

'Bruno?'

'Bruno Guta! Bruno Guta! That's him! That's it!'

I smiled at his enthusiasm and said, 'I think I have seen him around, but I can't be sure. He was one of those stay in the background types anyway. I'll check, if you like. I'll give Monty a call.'

'Well tell me first if you think I'm overreacting. And it's kind of a long story. How are you for time?'

'I'm fine. But if it's of any use to you I could come and see you later. I'm doing a Gold Cup preview night at Haydock, one of these racing club things. Want to come? I can pick you up.'

'I need to stay around here until I find out where Alice is going this evening, which is turning into an epic of its own. I could meet you near here if you don't mind coming over after Haydock?'

'Of course not. I'll call you when I'm leaving and we can arrange something.'

Ben was waiting in the pub. It had been his suggestion to meet there. I settled beside him in the corner, as he smiled and held out his hand. When I asked how he was, I had to almost shout, over the level of noise, mostly other voices, but an old fashioned jukebox played too.

I looked around, 'Thought the pub business was dead?' I said.

'Not this place. Always been busy. Used to be one of my favourite haunts. Regulars still have a sense of humour. I got a guard of honour entrance from the smokers, all holding their ciggies up for me to walk under on the way in.'

I laughed, 'And it doesn't bother you watching everybody drinking? The smell of the booze?'

'Not at all. I'm one of the lucky ones. Plenty in AA would never chance going into a pub. But I'm okay. I get a kind of vicarious enjoyment from the memories of the good times. I loved drinking, Eddie. Loved it. That was one of the things. A lot of alcoholics don't even care for the taste of it, they just drink for what they get out of it, escape, whatever. I loved it!' He laughed again in that childlike way.

I got up, 'You want a soft drink or something?'

He rose and grabbed my shoulders, 'I'll get it! You're my guest, sit down!'

I sat and he went to get two diet drinks, returning smiling, 'They never let me pay. Bob always says I provided most of his early capital.'

I smiled, happy that Ben could take all the teasing without suffering any sadness. 'How's Alice?'

He shook his head slowly, 'She's at her mate's house in Crosby right now, so I know she's okay, but things are getting a wee bit out of hand with this campaign she's running in Deadwood.'

Ben explained that the estate they lived in had been riddled with crime and violence for years, and that Alice was trying to stop one of the gangs trafficking young girls out of Deadwood to London, and sometimes abroad.

He said, 'In one of the children's homes she was stuck in, she got to know this kid from Deadwood who told her some horrendous stories about the place. What does Alice do? Runs away, heads for Deadwood and starts looking for the traffickers. The cops would find her, take her back to the home, and first chance she got she was off again, heading for Deadwood. At least the cops always knew where she'd gone. Alice's only condition for moving back into my care was that we got a place in Deadwood, which kind of suited me, because I can't afford to rent privately. And the council would almost pay you to live there.'

'So what does Alice do to try and stop these people?'

'She watches them every night. If she sees a girl near their car, they drive this big silver Beemer, she just runs at them, grabs the girl by the wrist and starts yelling that she's being abducted. For all there's plenty crime in Deadwood, the majority are good, clean living folk. When Alice starts yelling, either the gang drive off or the girl runs away embarrassed.'

'She's a brave kid, but what are the cops doing about these bastards?'

'The gang targets girls whose parents don't give a fuck anyway. Junkies, alkies…I know that sounds rich coming from me, but, well, anyway, the folk living there either hate cops or are too scared to talk to them. You rarely see a uniform in Deadwood. Some say the cops treat it as a no-go area.'

I watched him, wondering how he could be so matter of fact. I said, 'You can't stay there, Ben, not for any length of time. There's room for you at our place and you'd be welcome.'

'I know. Thanks, Eddie. My options are limited just now. Alice is in charge, I'm afraid…that's the deal I made. But I'm trying to kind of ride a sensible race with it. Keep her safe, and work on her steadily.'

'If I can help, you only need to ask.'

He put a hand on my shoulder and smiled, 'Thanks, my friend.

We'll get there, though it might be a longer haul than I'd thought. I saw Alice this morning wandering the streets pushing leaflets through the doors. She'd gone and applied for a community grant to get five thousand printed.' Ben pulled one from his pocket.

In large letters across the top it read DRAT - Deadwood Rejects All Traffickers. There was a picture of a mean-faced boy, I wouldn't have said he was a man, but Alice had made a pretty good Wanted poster out of him. 'Mister Big, I take it?'

'As far as Alice is concerned. DJ he calls himself. Talks like a Detroit rapper, though I doubt he's anything but a gofer. I don't know who's running things, and I don't really want to know, but DJ's warned me a couple of times to keep Alice out of his face, as he puts it. Her latest is trying to get this poster printed in the Liverpool Echo. She took some copies in this afternoon and tried for a meeting with the editor, who I happen to know, Jimmy Baker.'

'But Alice didn't know you knew him?'

'Not until she got back. "Will you talk to him, Dad?" she asks, and I says, of course I will. And I did, I said, Jim, flush those leaflets down the toilet, and don't take any calls from her.'

'Best hope she doesn't find that out,' I said.

'I keep trying to get her to see she can't change the world, but she's not ready to listen yet, so I wondered if Monty might help by sending Bruno over to have a quiet word with DJ. At least that was my plan when I left you that voicemail. I'm wondering now if that will just escalate things with whoever's behind the whole racket.' He sighed heavily and leaned back.

'It's your decision, Ben. I'm happy to have a word with Monty if you want me to.'

'What would you do in my position?'

I'd already thought about that, and had briefly considered telling Ben that I'd deal with DJ, but I didn't want him feeling inadequate or ashamed, 'I'd be doing what you're doing, Ben, trying to find an answer somehow.'

'But would you call Monty?'

'In your situation? No question.'

I was fit and strong, and angry and pig-headed and proud. Ben was wasted, physically weak, always tried to take a balanced view on life and give everyone the benefit of the doubt. Even turds like DJ.

Ben leant forward, elbows on knees, 'Would you mind, then? I know Monty spoke for me last week, and I don't doubt he'd help if I called, but ever since that time I made a complete arse of myself in his box at Aintree, I've felt embarrassed speaking to him.'

'No worries. I'll see him on Friday at Cheltenham.'

'Thanks, Eddie. You're a gem.'

I smiled, 'I don't sparkle much these days. I'll call you tomorrow.'

'And you'll ask him for Bruno?'

'I'll ask for Bruno Guta.'

Ben smiled with relish, 'He's the man!'

11

Maven was in bed when I got home. She lay on the inside where she could see the stars through the window.

She had not spoken.

I slipped into bed hoping not to disturb her. My cold feet sensed the warmth from her legs but knew better than to go there. She lay on her back, her breathing the only sound. When I closed my eyes, the inside of my eyelids replayed my drive home…long, empty, twisting roads…fast in the headlights.

'Bad news,' Mave said quietly.

'I'm listening.'

'Daffodils.'

I turned my head, 'You awake?'

'Yep.'

'Daffodils?'

'Correct.'

'Go on,' I said.

'Outside your picture window. I saw them this afternoon.'

'So?'

'What will you do without the snow to watch?'

'Snow'll be back.'

'Not until winter.'

'Betcha?'

'How much?'

'A pound.'

She drew her hand from below the quilt and spat in her palm and held her hand high, and I did the same and we sealed the bet, and she was silent again for a while.

'Was Ben okay?'

'Pretty much.'

'Hmm. Is Alice okay?'

'She was in Crosby tonight.'

'That's not what I asked,' Mave said.

'I'll tell you about it in the morning. Otherwise your mind will clang into gear and you'll go back to your old ways…just when I'm getting you trained.'

'In my world, night was always for working.'

'I know.'

Silence.

She said, 'I miss the sea.'

'I know you do.'

'How do you know?'

'You're melancholy, mostly.'

'It shows?'

'To me it does.'

'I might go back.'

'You can't,' I said.

'Says who?'

'Them's the rules. Everybody thinks they can go back, or at least everybody who's never tried going back.'

She spoke to the ceiling, 'Ladies and gentlemen, I give you, Philosophy in the Dark!'

I laughed quietly.

'That was a sympathy chuckle.'

'It was.'

'What about Marie,' Mave said, talking of my sister, 'she's going back?'

'She is. It's coming back I'm worried about now.'

'She wouldn't hurt Kim. She'll be home as soon as they've sorted things out.'

'What about Sonny?' I asked. Sonny had been a father-figure to Mave for most of her life, and when she got rich, she employed him and brought him to live with us. She had urged Sonny to go to Australia with Kim and Marie, knowing it would make me feel better if he was watching over them. He'd been getting increasingly restless here, anyway.

'He says he's sent two postcards, but I haven't seen one yet,' she said.

'Do you think he's there for good?'

'Sonny will be there until the NBD, the next big disappointment, and that'll shift his extrovert gearstick into reverse, and he'll look back to the northern hemisphere where the grass will suddenly have become greener again.'

'You've got a fair handle on him, haven't you?'

'Well, I can never remember a time when he wasn't around, so it's pretty much soaked into me. Osmosis, I believe they call it.'

'So, how come you know him so much better than he knows himself? Doesn't osmosis work both ways?'

'Not always. Seldom always.'

'I wonder if Alice knows Ben as well as you know Sonny?'

'Everybody will know Ben. Public alcoholics have no secrets. That's what can make them so endearing, especially the recovering ones.'

'True, I suppose.'

Mave said, 'I think you'll find Alice is looking after Ben, as much as he's looking after her.'

'Well, Ben's now looking for backup.' I told her about Bruno Guta and about what Alice had been up to.

'Jeez! I thought I took chances when I was a kid,' Mave said, 'that's chemistry for you. The teenage brain is hard-wired to risk. Things don't start levelling out until they're pushing eighteen, nineteen. That's a fact.'

'Is it?' I said.

'Scientifically proven.'

'I wish Alice would just have stuck with the normal craziness,

49

then, like playing chicken. Putting up Wanted posters of the local bad guy and canvassing the city press to run the story is teenage risk times a hundred.'

Mave said,' What about the police? I thought there were entire units set up these days to go after these traffickers?'

'Nobody in Deadwood will talk. No witnesses. Ben was saying that some regard it as a no-go zone for cops, full stop.'

'Jeez, what the hell is Ben doing even letting her live in a place like that?'

'It's Alice who wants to be there. Ben doesn't get to choose.'

'Eddie, come on! There's a level where you've got to draw the line!'

'I think Ben takes the view that he lost all privileges with Alice a long time ago. She was running wild for years. At least he has a relationship with her now. And he will protect her. That's why he called me about Bruno Guta.'

'Were you tempted to tell Ben you would have a word with this DJ character?'

'At first, maybe, but it would have been a bad idea for a number of reasons. Best leave it to the pros.'

'What's this Bruno fella like?'

'Very quiet. You'd hardly know he's around. Been with Monty since that car crash. He'll be good at what he does.'

'It sounds like Ben must know what he does, if he remembers him so well through all those hangovers. Why would old Monty want a bodyguard?'

'He doesn't call him a bodyguard. He's a personal assistant. Apparently he was on the same road as Monty when the accident happened, and he pulled him out of the burning car.'

'And got himself a job for life.'

'Looks like it.'

Mave said, 'Monty Bearak. Hardly a Merseyside name. And he talks posh.'

'His father won the pools in the sixties and sent him to a private school, so Ben says.'

'The champagne socialists.'

I sighed, 'Mave, it's late to be getting into political shit.'

She was quiet for a while, then she put a warm hand on my arm. I turned to her. She said, 'Why don't you ask Alice up for the weekend when Kim comes home?'

'I don't think anything is going to sidetrack Alice, not even Kim.'

'Sounds like she'd steamroller him, anyway. He'd be much too gentle for her.'

'Probably.'

Mave turned on her side, away from me. As I drifted off, Mave said quietly, 'Is Alice going to be all right?'

I hesitated, knowing what she was really asking before she could settle to sleep, and knowing too that my whispered answer would be a commitment and a promise, 'Yes.'

12

Mave asked if I wanted to shower first. 'Nah. I'm going out for a run.'

'You've just eaten breakfast.'

'That's why I'm going out for a run.'

'You'll die.'

'Of what?'

'Don't you get cramp or something if you exercise after eating, and fall over and drown?'

'That's swimmers.'

Mave nodded toward the big window, which featured a downpour in all its glory, 'Exactly,' she said.

'I only had toast. And, what would you know about exercise, before or after eating?'

'My brain burns more calories than a whole Grand National full of jockeys, speaking of which, why aren't you going to Cheltenham today?'

'No rides.'

'That's never stopped you. You could miss a good spare.'

'There'll be plenty in the pecking order before me for the Festival spares. No point driving hundreds of miles to mope around green with envy.'

'Well, I'm not babysitting you. I've got work to do.'

'Work away. I might drive back down to see Ben.'

Travelling south on the M6, the rain seemed to ease in five-mile swathes, like layers of curtain, until I reached clear skies. It was bright in Liverpool. Ben and I walked by the canal close to Anchor Bridge, which cut across the Grand National course.

I'd known this canal only through its geographical reference as a Grand National jump, the Canal Turn, where you need to steer your horse at right angles, otherwise you run into a high wire fence bordering the inside of the Leeds Liverpool canal.

'Seems odd walking here, by the actual canal after all these years,' I said.

'Not the place you build in your head when you're watching the big race, is it?'

'I remember it from when I was a kid. I never thought there was a real canal, I just thought that was its name, if you know what I mean, like Becher's Brook.'

'I know what you mean.'

We walked beside the brown water past half-sunken supermarket trollies and old tyres, bottles, bags and a burst football. 'Kind of wish I'd never come, now,' I said.

'Sorry, Eddie, I should've picked a better place.'

I put a hand on Ben's shoulder and laughed, 'Don't worry. My fault for being a romantic.'

'I know the feeling. Met plenty drinkers who were romantics. Was one myself for years, always convinced I'd write a big, big story…win a Pulitzer.'

'There's time enough.'

He laughed. I said, 'Coincidentally, it's one of the reasons I came to see you.'

I told Ben about my conversation with Dil, and about Jon Vogel, the starter's assistant. 'Make a hell of a story for you, if you cracked it,' I said.

'It would.'

He was quiet for a dozen strides, then said, 'What made you think of me?'

'After I spoke to Dil yesterday, I picked up the phone to tell Peter

McCarthy about it, then got your voicemail. That planted the seed.'

He turned to me, 'Aren't you obliged to report this to McCarthy, to tell the authorities?'

'Not really. It's just a theory. It's not as if I have evidence. Vogel might have nothing to do with it. But somebody got at those two horses and there's every chance a few others are lined up. Could be a big story there, no matter who's behind it. Might even be one for the Pulitzer.'

Ben smiled, 'Big as it might turn out, I doubt an American newspaper would be interested, so that's the Pulitzer gone before we start.'

'Shame. We should have one for racing, the Pullupzer prize.'

Ben laughed properly. I was really beginning to like that laugh.

'Maybe Monty would sponsor that,' Ben said, 'you should ask him tomorrow.'

'Let's settle for Monty helping make your lives easier while you're in Deadwood. If you get a big story out of this, maybe it'll land you back in a good job again.'

Smiling, he shook his head, 'The days of high paid reporters are gone forever, Eddie, aside from the elite few. But I'll settle for seeing my name in lights. It'll help land some freelance stuff at higher rates.'

'You working on anything just now?'

'Tractors.'

I looked at him. He said, 'I'm writing a piece for Big Red Tractors.'

'There's a magazine called Big Red Tractors?'

'You'd be amazed what magazines are out there. None of them pays much, but I can rattle out a dozen articles a week.'

'What if this wild horses job starts taking up all your time?'

'We'll get by, Eddie, don't worry.'

I knew better than to offer money, but I'd find a way if he needed it. I said, 'I'll help in the background as best I can. If you do the legwork, you can call me anytime and we'll see what we come up with.'

'Any thoughts on when these people might try again?'

'There's a hot favourite in the Gold Cup tomorrow.'

'You riding?'

'Not in the Gold Cup. Got one in the Triumph.'

'For Dil?'

'For Ben Tylutki.'

'Any chance?'

'You never know.'

'That means nearer last than first. I haven't forgotten the lingo, Eddie!' He put his arm around me, pulling my head onto his shoulder, reminding me of my big winner in The Supreme when Bomber had rested his head on mine. Happy days.

Driving home, I felt a mixture of satisfaction at having Ben involved, and guilt at the thought I'd really just palmed him off with my troubles.

But the troubles weren't mine alone. Dil and Vita would benefit from anything Ben could find out.

When I reached home, I called Ben, 'Listen, why don't you hold off on that Vogel story for now? I think I might be able to find somebody who'll pay you up front to do the legwork.'

'Well, I wouldn't say no to the money, Eddie so long as it's not coming out of your pocket. And it'll give me a day or two to try and get Alice sorted out.'

'That's good. I'll speak to Monty tomorrow, and then I'll try and pin Vita Brodie down. Not literally, of course.'

'Of course!' Ben laughed, 'Is she the paymaster general, then?'

'She's the big boss with the big budget.'

'Tell her I'll settle for NUJ rates.'

'I'll aim for a bonus if you crack it.'

'Ha! Every day's a bonus for me, Eddie, every day.'

I wondered once more at Ben's appetite for life, and wondered too if I would have survived what he'd been through. I'd have counted myself cursed. Ben lived as though he'd been blessed.

13

In Monty Bearak's glass-fronted hospitality box a hundred feet above the Cheltenham crowds, I saw Bruno Guta only because I was looking for him. The box held fifty people. Post-lunch coffee was being served and Monty had just introduced me as the star attraction, who was certain to tip a winner or two.

Guta stood by the balcony exit, framed by the hulk of Cleeve Hill behind him. He gave no sense of being on guard or watchful. The feeling I got was that he was calm, confident and relaxed in this glass eyrie where threats to his boss or the guests would be minimal.

As I stepped up to the microphone and cleared my throat, Guta glanced across and nodded, almost smiling, but not quite. I nodded to him. He was built like a jockey, his navy blue suit sat as impeccably on him as Sir Monty's clothes did on his much larger frame. Guta's boss would have been maybe sixty pounds heavier than him, yet, in that terrible car crash fireball, Guta had hauled him out. Monty chose to see himself as being lucky that day, lucky that Bruno, a man he'd never met until then, had driven past within seconds of Monty coming off the road. Fair play to Monty; very few would call a day like that a lucky one.

I looked again at the smiling Monty. I was strong and fit but could not have dragged him two metres.

I eased into my pitch, nerveless, and enjoying the attention. I talked through each race, highlighting the strengths and weaknesses of the main contenders and offering a selection. I often finished these talks by warning people not to bet more than they could afford, but this glittering crowd might have viewed that as distasteful. I wished them luck. They applauded.

Monty stepped up to the microphone and put a hand on my shoulder, 'What about your mount today, Eddie, Nantafa in the Triumph?'

'He's a brave little horse, but I think he'll find this a bit too hot for him.'

Monty put a sailor's hand to his brow on the lookout across the room, 'I hope his trainer's not here! That's far too honest!'

And his guests laughed as guests do, too hard and too long.

As Monty took his hand from my arm, I grasped his sleeve, 'Have you a couple of minutes?'

'Of course. Shall we go out onto the balcony?'

Bruno Guta smiled and opened the door and Monty and I stepped into the brilliant chilled sunshine of mid March. I told Monty about Alice and how worried Ben was. Monty didn't hesitate in offering Guta's services. I'd been ready to tell the full story, but he gave me a short lesson on being a successful businessman by waving away the details, 'Give Bruno's phone number to Ben, and he can explain everything. Bruno will deal with it.'

As we raced downhill in The Triumph hurdle, Nantafa faltered. I gave him time to fill his lungs, but knew it wasn't a question of fuel, but of engine size. To most people, one racehorse looks like another. To the experienced eye, there are many variations. No matter how skilled the judge, until a horse races, nobody can tell how fast it can go, and for how long.

Galloping toward the second-last, mine was among a string of strugglers being steadily left behind by the top horses. Watching others pull farther and farther away was something I'd grown used to in recent years. My eyes had adjusted…my mind had not. I hated being left behind.

Here on this final day of the Cheltenham Festival, I found myself wishing stupidly that my mount would take off as Montego Moon and Spalpeen had, igniting that whooshing turbo, and that this time I'd be able to control it.

We finished nearer last than first, and the remainder of the day held nothing for me but memories of past glories.

Come Gold Cup time, I walked down to the start to watch Jon Vogel checking girths, especially the girths of the hot favourite, Fenagh Abbey.

Vogel was an ex-jockey. He'd never reached mid-league, but he was a good talker, always happy to help the trainer persuade the owner that the goose he had just ridden was definitely a swan who simply needed softer, firmer, shorter, longer, more time between races, less time between races…whatever excuse had not been used before.

Vogel moved among the runners, checking that girths were tight. A couple of times he shoved buckles up a notch, chatting away to the jockeys.

Fenagh Abbey was a fine big bay, that reddish brown coat with black mane and tail. He walked calmly while a few of his rivals showed some level of nervousness. I watched Vogel's hands as he moved toward the horse, until a chestnut broke my line of sight. I moved, but Vogel's fingers were under the girth, too briefly, I thought, to have planted anything. He made no adjustment, but smacked the horse lightly on the rump and smiled at the jockey, saying something as he backed away.

I looked at the giant TV screen. Fenagh Abbey was evens favourite.

I watched the Gold Cup field approach the tape, unable after all these years to subdue the bitterness that turned the screw in my gut to ratchet up the envy. Still, it no longer made me physically sick. Such is progress, and I was glad to see them away and galloping toward the first.

I looked up. The blimp carrying the TV cameras was there. In the weighing room, I knew Mac would be watching the big bay favourite to the exclusion of all others. The Festival had started with the

Spalpeen shock. The remainder of the meeting had gone smoothly. Fenagh Abbey was the last chance of another big money killing for whoever had nobbled Spalpeen and Montego Moon.

But Fenagh Abbey galloped home at the same pace as he had set out in front. Over the three and a quarter miles it had been enough to wipe out his rivals one by one, as though some invisible rear gunner were strapped to his flanks picking them off with calm regularity over the final half mile. I marvelled at the big bay as he passed me, ears pricked, giant stride carrying him up the hill with remarkable ease and economy.

All eyes were on him as he reached the winning post. I looked around, searching for Vogel. With the favourite's victory, Vogel's status as my chief suspect had just lost some of its credibility.

He'd gone.

The next race was for amateurs. I was beginning to feel like one of them.

14

At Uttoxeter races next day, I could almost smell the charred edges of trouble as I walked into the paddock before the Midlands Grand National.

When I saw Dil's face I knew it was his life someone had set light to. Around his outline I visualized an image of a TV programme my mother used to watch, Bonanza, in which the credits rolled up over an old map, burning from the edges toward the Ponderosa in the centre.

Dil was today's Ponderosa.

At his side, arms linked to his, was Vita Brodie, dressed head-to-toe in black. Her lips were crimson, her smile set harder than her lacquered blonde hair as she tried not to watch what everyone else was watching, the extraordinary figure of Dil's yard secretary Primarolo Romanic, who was leading my mount, Kingdom Come, round the paddock.

She was the most stunning groom I'd ever seen. Normally these lads and lasses find even a basic suit of clothes too uncomfortable, or too expensive. Trousers and a loose jacket are the usual uniform of those looking after the horses.

Prim wore a sky-blue two-piece. The skirt stopped just above knee-level. Below the hem was a six-inch gap of naturally tanned smooth skin disappearing into long high-heeled suede boots. Her big high bust, small waist and swelling hips were almost cartoonishly sexy and as I watched her wiggle her way round, I remembered her telling me at a party that she used an old Marilyn Monroe trick of cutting a half inch from one boot-heel to help emphasize the hip swing.

Most of the frontline crowd against the white-railed oval were men. Not one was looking at the horses.

'Hi Prim!' I said, slipping through the gap between Kingdom Come and the horse in front. Her dark shining hair swung as she turned and her pink lips opened on glistening teeth and for a moment I pictured fangs and glanced across at the raised throat of Vita Brodie, who tended to carry her chin high to even out her neck wrinkles.

Big mistake, Vita.

Big mistake, Dil.

I guessed that war had finally been declared, and Dil had sided with the money woman. 'Vita,' I said as I bent to kiss her cheek, 'you look very elegant.'

Her jaw muscles clenched. Elegant didn't matter. Money didn't matter.

Sexy mattered.

Young mattered.

Prim mattered.

'Dil,' I offered my hand. A permanent look of shock is a difficult thing to pull off, but Dil managed it, and it paled his handsome face and even stilled those habitual finger-sweeps. He was statue-stiff, afraid that any movement would draw attention to his naked pain.

I said, 'I'm surprised to see Prim leading him round? What happened to Melanie?'

'Melanie slipped in the horse's box when she was getting him ready. Twisted her ankle.'

'That's a shame. It was very good of Prim to step in, eh?'

Dil stared at me, knowing I was enjoying this.

Maybe it's because I was rooting for the underdog, but the whole scene gave me immense satisfaction, the warmth of it keeping a smile on my face all the way to the start as jockeys cantered up either side of me with the same question 'Who the hell was that?'

That, my friends, was and is Primarolo Romanic, a woman scorned.

Six fences from home, mid-pack, and tiring in the Staffordshire mud, Kingdom Come finally wiped the smile from my face. Or maybe it was the G-force that did it as the horse took off in terror, ears up, head down, neck straight, tearing toward the next fence.

For the only time in my life, I was glad to be proved a poorer jockey than one of my colleagues. When Spalpeen jinked at Cheltenham, Vince McCrory stayed aboard. When Kingdom Come jinked beneath me, I slipped from the saddle, out of the 'side-door' landing on my shoulder blades, feet pointing back toward the remainder of the field who were moving so slowly, none had trouble avoiding me.

I sat up, watching them pass, splattering me with mud, one dumping a fist-sized clump of it in my lap as I felt the groundwater ooze into my breeches.

I got to my feet and turned and saw Kingdom Come miles ahead of everything else as he swung into the straight. Then he slowed so dramatically that it seemed as though he had met some deep ploughland.

I moved and put a hand to my brow, squinting to see if he had run through the rails into a field.

But he was still on the course. Trotting now. Then walking. He stopped. The others passed him. He remained standing, his nostrils filling the chilly afternoon air with clouds of steam.

I ducked under the rails and made my way across the infield toward him. My smile had returned; one of relief. No hospital this time. No ICU. No two-week layoff. Just the mystery of these wild horses, a riddle now complicated by an absence…the assistant starter today was Bernard Jeffries.

Vogel was out of the dock.

When I reached Kingdom Come he was shaking. He took a step away from me as I moved forward slowly, hand reaching for the reins, and his legs almost buckled. I caught the rein and urged him into a walk, trying to get him moving, making it less likely he'd collapse.

I saw the vet's car coming and the sight triggered my common sense. I stopped walking and undid the horse's girth, letting it swing free, hoping, despite Vogel's absence at the start, that something would fall to the ground.

But nothing fell. I ducked to examine the girth strap as it hung loose; it was marked only by sweat stains. No buzzer-shaped indentation. Perhaps it had been lost in the crazed gallop…I sighed. Perhaps I was deluding myself. No drugs. No buzzers. No remote controls. What the hell was going on?

15

Dil came to the weighing room after the vet had examined Kingdom Come. He asked me to drive back to the yard and meet him there.

'Why?' I said.

'We need to get to the bottom of this.'

'We, as in?'

'You and me, and Vita.'

'What, the three of us around the table?'

'You got a problem with that?'

I stared at him. The tension of Dil's day was seeking an outlet. I straightened and said quietly, 'Don't talk to me like that.'

'Like what?' he reddened.

'Like I'm some kind of lackey. I'm your stable jockey. You pay me. Vita pays you. If you want to let her talk to you that way, that's fine. But don't talk to me as though I'm some kind of lowly employee that has to come to your office and explain myself.'

'That's not what I said!'

'It ain't what you say, it's the way that you say it.'

His shoulders slumped, 'Well, it wasn't what I meant. I'm sorry. It's been a shit day.'

'It has, and it's not going to get any better with us sitting down to try and come up with some kind of answer just because Vita's pissed off.'

'So we just wait for the next time?'

'No, we don't just wait for the next time, Dil. We go home and we sleep on it, and I call Mac and find out what the dope test showed. Then I ask him if he's made any headway with his enquiries. And I get access to whatever betting info he has from the bookies today, and then we have something to sit down and talk about. In the morning. When Vita is not bursting her corsets because Prim blew her out of the water today. When you've thought about how much you're going to let your relationships fuck up your business. And when it's finally sunk home with you that I don't exist just to make sure you get what you want.'

I didn't wait for an answer.

In the car, I dialled Mac's number and put him on speaker, then I cancelled the call with a frustrated jab, knowing he wouldn't yet have any information on Kingdom Come. I banged the steering wheel with my fist, still angry at the way Dil had spoken to me, at the helplessness when these horses took off.

I turned the key, and revved the engine hard, then the tiny shred of sense that remained got me to shut the engine off, step out of the car and go for a walk until I was calm enough to drive.

In The Snug, in the dark, looking over the rim of my whiskey glass at the burning logs in the stove, I had a vague awareness of Mave's keyboard clicks from the next room. I wandered through to see her, working in the gloom with just the faintest flickers of flames from the stove reflecting on the paintwork of the open door.

'Can I come in?' I asked.

Her fingers clicked on as she looked at me, 'What ails thee?'

'Crazy horses. Crazy trainer.'

'What's the latest theory?'

'I don't have one. I'm waiting for Mac returning my call, but I'm pretty sure he won't have one either.'

'What about Ben and Alice?'

'I gave Ben Bruno's number last night and told him to call me if he needed anything else.'

'And he hasn't, so maybe Bruno is doing the sorting out that his boss seemed so confident about.'

'I hope so. One less thing to worry about. I ought to ask Bruno to come to Dil's with me in the morning and join me at the table with him and Vita.'

'Or send him Prim's way as a flirting target. Let her swinging hips lock onto his heat map and draw him in so she can make sure Dil suffers plenty collateral damage.'

I ducked sideways to look at her screen, 'You playing a war game, or something?'

'Nope.'

'Designing one?'

'Nope. Don't over-interpret my military metaphors.'

My phone rang.

'Mac. Any news?'

'The dope test is clear. None of the four accounts that bet on Spalpeen were used today at all. At this stage there's no evidence of any unusual betting or laying on Kingdom Come, or indeed on that race. I should have a full report in the morning.'

I sighed, 'I take it my blimp theory didn't pan out?'

'All hot air, I'm afraid.'

I smiled wearily, 'You were dying for me to ask you that.'

He chuckled in that deep Richter-scale way he had.

I said, 'Nice to hear you relaxed enough to find some humour, anyway.'

'If I didn't laugh, I'd cry, Eddie. This is very unusual.'

'You ought to be sitting on one when it happens.'

'The motive, I mean. Whoever's behind it neglects two opportunities out of three to make money. Okay, if we allow for the first one of yours to be a trial of some sort, it's still a fifty percent opt out rate. Why? Whatever they are doing to control these horses cannot be easy. It must take meticulous planning. Why not cash in, especially once it's proven?'

I said, 'And why were two of them from the same relatively small yard? If somebody had something against Dil, or me, or the owners, why not nobble Stevedore and deprive us of a Supreme winner?'

'Because they didn't expect him to win anyway? And because money could be made from laying Spalpeen? But it is interesting that Grant's yard has been affected in all three cases...I hadn't considered that. How is security there?'

'Well he's hardly protecting the crown jewels. It'll be no better or worse than at most yards outside of the big boys.'

Mac sighed, 'I'd better come and speak to Grant, anyway.'

'I'm seeing him in the morning. Want me to tell him?'

'No. Hold off. Let me get the full report.'

'Okay.'

Despite finding nothing under Kingdom Come's girth, I considered mentioning the assistant starters, simply because I had nothing else to work on. 'Mac, will you get me the patrol film for those three races? I want them from five minutes before the off, so I can see the full starting procedure.'

I sensed the hesitation, but he knew me well enough now not to question it. 'Okay. I'll get the online versions and send you a log in.'

'Thanks.'

'Goodbye.'

Still working her keyboard, Mave said, 'You told me you found nothing under that girth. I thought you'd dropped Vogel?'

'There was nothing under the girth, but maybe I got fixated on that. I should have checked under the saddle too. And it might be Vogel and crew. There's more than one assistant starter. And none of them earn a fortune. Not from working, anyway.'

'Illicit fingers on the buzzer, you reckon?'

'Maybe. Can you dig around and find out how those buzzers work? Dil mentioned they've been used in America.'

Mave reached to the shelf in front of her and passed me a black, beaten-up laptop. 'Digging is for manual labourers. Here's your shovel.'

Smiling, I took it. 'It's got more dents and scratches than a shovel,' I said, 'what've you been doing with it?'

'Chewing it. It is the coder's equivalent of chewing a pencil.'

'Mave, you never chewed anything that wasn't fried.' I opened the laptop, she nodded toward it. 'That qualifies,' she said.

I gave her my quizzical look. She stopped typing and turned to me, 'Chips.'

16

I reached Dil's as dawn broke. He had three horses for me to school before our breakfast meeting. I parked by the big paddock and walked round past Arnie's cottage. Arnie was the head lad, so he qualified for a place of his own. The other grooms shared a hostel, which had recently been upgraded at Vita's insistence. She was certainly putting Dil through the financial wringer. Maybe that's why he'd returned to betting big.

As I passed Arnie's cottage, I heard the front door open, and I turned to bid him good morning.

It was Prim.

She closed the door. 'Morning, Eddie.'

'Morning...Prim.' It was an auto response. My brain was working through the possibilities. Arnie was sixty-seven. Prim was the boss's mistress. Or had been. Even for revenge, she would not be sleeping with the head lad. My face must have shown her every turn of the tumblers as my mind tried to unlock the puzzle. She said, 'I'm living here now.'

'Since when?' It was more surprise than curiosity that prompted me.

'Since Vita Brodie decided that, contrary to the age-old protests of Mister Lennon and Mister McCartney, money can indeed buy you love.'

'Dil slung you out?'

Her nose wrinkled and her lovely mouth half-frowned then half-smiled, 'That's not quite the way he put it. When we got back from Uttoxeter, Dil managed to persuade me it was actually a very good idea.'

Her dark hair was drawn up tightly in a bun. Prim had the most elegant neck. She had been born in Spain and, looking at her, I was often reminded of that framed print you used to see everywhere of the Flamenco dancer in the red dress. The whites of her eyes shone. I said, 'You serious?'

'Dil says that once the business is secure, he'll move her on.'

'Vita, and all her horses?'

She nodded, and blinked once, then held my gaze with a professional smile. I said nothing, but Prim read me again and said, 'I'll be forty next week, Eddie. You'd be amazed at what women my age can believe.'

'And you'd be amazed at what women your age deserve. And it isn't Dil Grant. And I'll happily tell him to his face he's a fool.'

She raised a finger, 'Ah, you'd be in trouble there…Dil assures me often he is nobody's fool.'

'But you don't believe him.'

'He isn't nobody's fool. He's my fool.'

I leant forward and kissed her softly on each cheek, then I nodded toward the main house, 'Is he in the kitchen?'

'I believe so.'

'And Vita's there?'

She nodded slowly, those sparkling eyes still looking assured and patient. I said, 'Keep torturing her with the thigh boots and the tight two-piece.'

'I'm afraid I've promised trousers and loose jumpers until she's gone.'

I shook my head, smiling, 'Pick a line you won't cross, Prim, or he'll have you in a Nun's habit.'

'He has,' she said softly, as I turned away, 'several times.'

We sat at the table below Dil's ceiling light, the long shade hanging by chains, like those you see in pool halls. The harshness the glow

70

cast on Vita drew my eyes to the tiny wrinkles that the collagen treatment had failed to fill. Her brow and cheeks had the smoothness of a well-prepared corpse.

She spooned marmalade onto brown toast, raising her eyes to look at me as she did so, 'What do you think, Eddie? Why have they picked on us?' Vita had been born in Stirling, Scotland, the only child of a man with a global biscuit business. "Shortbread!" Vita would have corrected me as I'd heard her do to an elderly trainer in the winner's enclosure one day.

The Stirling Shortbread brand, castle, kilted piper and all, had been sold by her before the grass had regrown on her father's grave. She'd lived most of her life in London, but spent a lot of time in New York. She was a pedigree woman with a mongrel, mid-Atlantic accent.

I said, 'I wish I knew why they picked on us, Vita.'

Dil said, 'We shouldn't rule out coincidence. Not yet. I know we're two from three, but let's see who's next.'

Vita said, 'I'd rather catch whoever is doing it before there is a next.'

I said. 'It's how as much as who, I think. If we can find out how, we can check each horse before the start. Then the who doesn't matter so much.'

Dil said, 'It might not matter for the future, but this guy's deprived us of prize money...well, of the chance of prize money, not to mention a couple more winners on the stats table.'

I said, 'And, not to mention either, the services of your stable jockey for two weeks. Or indeed, from a purely personal viewpoint but I hope you don't mind me raising it, of almost killing me.'

Vita smiled and bit into her toast. I let her chew long enough to be able to speak then said, 'You have horses at Pimlico, don't you?'

'I do. A dozen.'

'You come across any incidents over there of jockeys using buzzers?'

Vita said, 'I heard that at Ruidoso Downs at one time so many were using them it sounded like a full blown orchestra. But we know this is not buzzers, right? Buzzers are used by jockeys.'

I said, 'But what if someone fitted one under the girth or the saddle just before the race and it was set off remotely?'

She broke toast with both hands, and raised her eyebrows.

Dil said, 'I thought that was off the list? Vogel wasn't on duty yesterday.'

I said, 'It doesn't have to be just one of the starting team.'

'Who is Vogel?' Vita said.

I told her.

'Sounds like small fry,' she said.

'They could be working for somebody big,' I said.

Dil said. 'You seem pretty fixed on this, Eddie?'

'It's all I've got. Other than jolting the horse with a major shock, I can't think how else they're doing it.'

Vita said, 'Could someone be shooting them?'

'That was my first thought,' I said.

'And?'

'And I got talked out of it by Mac who reckoned it was impossible unless they knew the exact position of the horse at the time they wanted to make the shot. If their target is buried in the pack, the betting coup's buried with it.'

She propped her chin on her hand, elbow on table, 'But what if the jockey was in on it? Present company excepted, of course. They're trialling things with us, then, when the cash is down, they're bribing the jockey?'

I said, 'I don't know Vince McCrory well, but I can't see him risking his life for a few quid.'

Dil broke in, 'But how much risk was involved if he knew it was coming? Didn't you say you were amazed how he stayed on when the horse jinked? Maybe he steered it round the hurdle to make sure of disqualification.'

I reran the incident in my mind...'That wasn't steering, Dil, he jinked, I'm sure of it.'

They both looked at me the same way, a way that said, are you really sure? I said. 'I've asked Mac to get me the patrol films for each race. I'll watch Vince again a few times. I'll watch them all.'

'When will you have them?' Vita asked.

'Pretty soon. They're online. He's sending me a link.'

She said, 'Why don't you call him and get it now and we can all watch it?'

I glanced at Dil. Vita said, 'Six eyes are better than two.'

I picked up my phone and walked outside to get a signal. Prim crossed the yard. She turned and smiled at me, seeming confident again of her place in Dil's world. But in the room I'd just left there was no doubting who'd been in charge.

Mac answered, 'Eddie, good morning. What can I do for you?'

17

Dil put his laptop on the kitchen table, adjusting the lid until Vita was happy with the angle. She said to me, 'Can you see that okay?'

'Fine.'

'Right, Dil, let's play the first one.'

It was the official patrol film from Bangor. Every race is filmed from different angles for what Mac calls 'integrity purposes'. In the old days, there were stories of jockeys at fogbound country courses pulling up on the far side and rejoining the race when the runners came around again.

I watched myself on board Montego Moon as we circled at the start, and was surprised to find a nervous lump in my throat. This was my first viewing of the race that could have killed me.

'Watch Vogel,' I said, as the assistant starter moved toward me. Smiling, he looked up at me as he felt the girth, twanged it then slapped Montego Moon's rump and turned away.

'Rewind that,' Vita said.

We watched it six times. Vogel took no more time with my girth check than with the others, except for two where he notched the girths up.

The film moved to where we lined up to start. Vita said, 'Spot the difference?'

We looked at her. She smiled, still watching the screen, 'Just pause it, Dil, will you?' she said, and turned to us, 'What was different about Montego Moon?'

'With Vogel?' Dil asked.

She nodded. He shrugged. I'd noticed nothing and felt it best not to ask for another replay. I said, 'Go on.'

Vita said, 'Ours was the only horse he slapped on the rump.'

We ran it once more. She was right. Vita looked at me, no sense of superiority about her, just a keenness to move on, and we watched the rest of the race.

Seeing myself flying from the saddle as the mare ran straight into that fence stopped my breath. I held it involuntarily until I saw my head hit the ground…the air trickled from me as I realized how lucky I'd been to survive.

She reached to pause it. 'You okay?' she asked.

I nodded.

We watched the Cheltenham footage. Vogel spent no more time on Spalpeen than on any other that did not need a girth adjustment. Spalpeen was one of four who got a slap on the rump from him.

The film showed Spalpeen being switched to the inside going down the hill, offering a rifle shot to anyone on the infield who was skilled enough. But the manoeuvre McCrory had made was far from unusual. The inside was the shortest route.

McCarthy had included the aerial footage from the blimp, and while the side-on film had been inconclusive, the overhead shots left no doubt in my mind that Spalpeen jinked before the hurdle. 'No way did Vince steer him,' I said.

The Uttoxeter clip showed nothing out of the ordinary in the girth check, unless you count the fact that Bernard Jeffries gave every horse a soft rump slap before walking away. We watched the manner in which Kingdom Come veered to avoid facing any more jumps, and it seemed more controlled than Spalpeen's move, less of a sudden jink. I said, 'That looked more like I steered than that McCrory steered.'

'But you didn't, obviously?' Vita said.

'Nope. He went sideways. I fell off.'

We watched it twice more. Dil said, 'Well, exact same behaviour each time. Went from moving easy and relaxed to off the wall, like the hounds of hell were after them.'

Vita nodded slowly.

I said, 'They weren't exactly the same.'

They looked at me. I said, 'Montego Moon didn't veer of
ran straight into that fence. Blind.'

Vita tilted her head to look at the ceiling while she con
'You're right. When you say blind, do you think the mare wa;
blinded somehow and that's what panicked her?'

'No, not literally, though you're making me wonder, now.'

Dil said, 'Maybe she really was in what they call a blind pai.
She's in a race, her eyesight goes, her blood's up, she can hea
everything around her galloping. Would she stop or would she panic
because she couldn't see?'

'How would they blind her in the middle of a race?' I asked.

Dil shrugged. Vita uncrossed her arms and said, 'Let me see t
Cheltenham start again.'

After several attempts to freeze frame Vogel as he raised   left
hand to slap Spalpeen, Vita got what she wanted, 'There!'   yelled,
leaning forward and pointing at the screen. Dil hit the pa   button
'That glint. Is that a ring?'

'On his finger?' Dil asked then seemed suitably embarrass   when he
saw how Vita looked at him. She turned to me, 'Can you ask   friend
McCarthy if his guys can get a good quality blow up of that fra

'I can ask. You think there's something on the ring?'

'I'm thinking it could have a tiny spike on the inside whi   night;
have been dipped in something. Let's have a look at the ot   two
starts again.'

No ring glint was obvious at Bangor or Uttoxeter, both   and
overcast days. I went outside again and tried Mac's nu   er;
voicemail.

Vita asked when he'd be likely to return my call. 'No kn   g,' I
said. She was excited.

I couldn't go with this blind theory, but she was getting   d on
it and I'd learnt enough about her in the past hour to know   ing
was pointless.

I took my leave and set off for Stratford where I had two mounts booked. On the drive, images of Vita shuffled in my mind like a playing card set full of queens with different facial expressions.

The gathering energy from her as we'd watched those films had flushed Dil out onto the margins. Her interest in me had been like a prosecutor's concentration on a witness.

Her money had brought her all the worldly things, and it had given her a servant in Dil, and the satisfaction of depriving Prim Romanic of a man she cared about. Vita's joy with each 'purchase' hadn't lasted and now, bizarrely, the attacks on her horses were giving her pleasure in her attempt to solve the mystery.

18

After a luckless day at Stratford, I drove north to see Ben Searcey in Liverpool. He was waiting in the pub we'd met in last time. I settled in an old chair as Ben got soft drinks from the bar.

When he'd sat back down, Ben said, 'You're getting good at escaping from these runaway horses. I watched that Uttoxeter race again before I came out...slick dismount.'

I smiled, 'If they start awarding points for it, maybe I'll win something this season.'

'What's the news?'

I told him what had happened. He said, 'So Vogel's still in the picture?'

'Long shot, a very long shot, but Vita Brodie's getting quite attached to it, so I think you might be back on Vogel's case soon.'

'But you think it's a waste of time?'

I sighed, suddenly feeling the weight of a long day, 'I think Vita's wicked stepmother fantasies are taking over. A silver ring dipped in some kind of potion that blinds a horse at a certain point then unblinds it.'

'Unblinds? Good word, Eddie,' he chuckled.

'I wish I could unblind Vita, but she's just getting started. And I haven't a bloody clue myself, so it's not as though I can come up with an alternative.'

'Well, maybe the best we can do is rule Vogel out?'

'Might not be easy. Whatever you come up with in Vogel's favour, I suspect Vita will find a way of objecting.'

'We can only try,' he said, smiling as he raised his glass toward me. I toasted his optimism, 'How is Alice doing?' I said.

'At a wee bit of a loss, if I'm honest.'

'What's up?'

'Nothing, that's the problem. Young DJ has not been around since I called Bruno Guta.'

'Quick worker.'

'And effective.'

'What's the gossip in Deadwood?'

'If anybody knows, nobody's saying. Word is that DJ just disappeared. His "troops" as he calls them, are claiming he's away on some kind of special mission.'

'To a toilet somewhere, shitting himself, I'd think after meeting a proper pro.'

Ben smiled, 'I'd like to have been there, to see his face.'

'Alice must be pleased. Did you tell her about Bruno?'

'Not yet, but I'm thinking maybe I'd better. She's kind of lost her focus without DJ around.'

I thought again of Vita Brodie. 'Is it humans that are strange, or just women?' I said.

'Men are too simple. We're all still cavemen at heart,' Ben sipped his orange drink and settled back, 'Looking at it Darwin's way, I'd say men clumped their way straight up an evolutionary set of rock stairs, lifting their big feet only when they had to whereas your woman, well, she's kind of glided up a smooth, silky ramp, all twists and turns, seeing the signs well in advance and changing course as necessary.'

Half-smiling, I looked at him, 'You've thought about this a lot, haven't you?'

He sat forward and put down his glass, 'Since I got sober, I probably have. I very probably have. Alice, my wife that is, was a clever woman, and she tried all she knew to get me to stop drinking. Alice, my daughter, was even cleverer than her mother, she realized from very young that I was a lost cause entirely and didn't waste her time on me.'

'You mentioned she jumped ship when her mother went to America, what actually happened? How did she get out of going?'

'She jumped ship. Literally. She read her mother as skilfully as she read me and made sure she didn't give her the faintest idea that she wanted to stay here. Colin, Alice's man, had this romantic vision of a new life, starting with a long voyage. They all got on at Southampton and, not long before the ship sailed, Alice quietly got back off again.'

'How old was she?'

'Ten.'

'Where did she go?'

'She came to me.'

Ben's eyes dulled and his head went down. I reached to clutch his arm, 'I'm sorry, mate, that was really thoughtless of me. I'm sorry.'

He nodded slowly and rubbed his face with both hands. He looked up, 'Want to get some fresh air?'

'Sure.'

We headed down Melling Road and Ben told me he'd been along here yesterday with Alice, 'Had to go and see the social worker. Took us fifteen minutes to walk this road and I was nervous. It was the first check on us since I got Alice back and you'd have thought I was the kid and she was the adult the way she was keeping my spirits up…we stopped here.'

We were at the big gates where the Grand National course crossed this highway. On raceday, the road was closed and a special surface laid for the forty runners to gallop over as they headed for the first fence. I'd crossed here on horseback many times. Ben pointed at the outline of the grandstands against the dark sky, 'I told Alice that's where we'll be come National day, the Queen Mother Stand, special guests of Sir Monty Bearak. For once in our lives we'll be somebody, I said, and Alice went mad.'

He was smiling again as he turned to me, 'She was poking me in the chest with her finger shouting "you are somebody, Dad! We're all somebody! Nobody's any better than anybody else. Just because your friend's got a Sir before his name, doesn't make him better than you! Wise up!" Got a proper bloody lecture, so I did.'

'Deserved, by the sound of it. I'm with Alice. We're all equal.'

'In the eyes of God, maybe.'

His sadness was returning, and I took his elbow, 'Let's go down to Anchor Bridge. You're giving me another education here, like walking the canal last time. I've galloped across this road lots of times and never thought of it as a road, if you know what I mean, a normal road.'

On cue, truck headlights showed around the bend, then a motorcycle passed us. Ben's words were drowned out as the truck thundered by. I leant closer, 'What did you say?'

'The long and winding road, I said. Talking to myself. Ignore me.'

We walked on in silence. Ben shoved his hands in his pockets, 'The long and winding road,' he repeated quietly, and I could think of nothing to comfort him.

19

It was almost midnight when I reached home. I steered the car into the long driveway, and smiled as I saw the old oil lamp burning on the windowsill of The Snug. When darkness fell and I was not home, this had become Mave's habit. I looked forward to the night I could do the same for her, but she seldom ventured far from the farm.

I found her where I knew she would be, in the tiny workspace on the high-backed chair, right calf tucked under her left thigh. Aside from the oil lamp on the sill, only her PC screen gave light. It was her habit not to look at me when I came home, as though I had never left. The screen kept most of her attention. She said, 'Home is the sailor, home from the sea, and the hunter home from the hill.'

'Guided by the light.'

'And at very cheap rates.'

I put down my bag and stretched and yawned, then went and stood by Mave's chair, 'You're just always going to be a nighthawk, aren't you?'

'It's beginning to look like it. I did try.'

'You did. That's true. Want a drink?'

'No, thanks.'

I poured a whiskey and reached for my laptop and sat by the embers of the last firelogs. Mac had sent me a blown up picture of the frame Vita had asked for. Vogel was wearing a ring. I called out to Mave, 'What does a silver ring on the wedding finger mean...on a man?'

'That his wife is tight with money.'

I smiled, 'Seriously, is there any significance you know of?'

She came to sit beside me, 'It could be white gold. Why?'

I told her of Vita's theory. She turned to me, 'She believes that someone who's working with his hands all the time among half ton beasts who are very unpredictable would risk pricking himself with whatever it is that's driving these horses crazy?'

'Those were my thoughts.'

She lowered her brow, looking accusingly at me under her eyelashes. I cleared my throat and said, 'Well, they are now.'

She smiled, 'Sounds like Vita's getting her teeth into this good and proper.'

'I think she has a short attention span coupled with a desire for...er, frequent stimulation.'

'Frequent stimulation? Isn't that Dil's job, and some would say he is appropriately named for such work.'

'Dil looked more like a waiter hanging around the breakfast table, anxious not to offend the woman with the shiny credit card. If Prim had been there, maybe it would have helped bring her to her senses.' I went over my conversation with Prim.

'That just makes me sad, Eddie. Jeez, look at her, she could do a whole lot better than Dil. I'd bed her myself, were I that way inclined.'

I smiled, 'Would you, now?'

'Wouldn't you?'

She held my gaze. I held my breath, then said quietly, 'Were I that way inclined...'

'Smart answer, Mister Malloy, smart answer,' she got up, 'I'm going back to work. Tell Vita from me she needs to take more water with it, as my dad used to say. Sounds like she's the last kind of detective you need for this caper.'

'I'm hoping she'll pay Ben to do some legwork.'

'How was he?'

'Okay. Managed to put my foot in it about Alice, but he held up.'

'How is Alice?'

'At a loose end. The devil she's been chasing has hurried off to hell by the look of it, after Mister Bruno Guta offered him some mature advice.'

'This DJ character?'

'That's him.'

'Gone?'

'Disappeared. No stand-in so far. Ben's hoping Alice will ease off and find another project.'

'You should invite them for the weekend. You riding on Sunday?'

'Not at the moment.'

'Why don't you take the day off, ask the pair of them up?'

'Good idea. I'll give Vita the news about this ring in the morning, and see if she wants Ben to do some digging, then I'll call him.'

'Be nice to see Alice. Weather forecast is good, too.'

I got up and went to her, and squeezed her shoulders. She reached back to put a hand on mine.

'I'm going to bed,' I said, 'the comforting clicking of your keyboard will be the soundtrack to my slumbers.'

'Slumbers is a good word. One I don't hear much these days, and all the better when I do.'

'Has a kind of reassuring weight to it, hasn't it?'

'A heft. A harmonious heft.'

'Good night,' I went to the window to blow out the lamp.

'Just leave it burning, Eddie.'

I looked at her and she stopped typing and turned to me, and said, 'For the lost souls.'

20

Next morning, I called Dil to ask if he'd be at Warwick in the afternoon. I had three rides there, two of them for Dil, but trainers don't always attend the track when they have runners.

'I'll be there.' Dil said.

'You sound like you're still under pressure.'

'When am I anything else?'

'Vita coming with you today?'

'Yes.'

His tone had tightened a notch. 'Is Vita there now?' I asked.

'Yes.'

'Well, I'd best let you go. If you keep barking out one-word answers she's going to know we're talking about her. See you later.'

'Okay.'

I heard Vita say something. Dil said, 'Eddie! Eddie, you still there?'

'I'm still here.'

'Did you manage to get hold of those blown up photos?'

'Mac sent them last night, but they're what he would call inconclusive, and what I would call useless.'

'Could you bring them to Warwick?'

I sighed, 'Dil, I only have them on email.'

'You can print them off, can't you?'

I pictured him looking at Vita as he spoke and imagined her nodding approvingly.

'I can print them, but they'll probably look even worse.'

'We'll see. It'll do no harm.'

At Warwick, Vita was waiting for me at the door of the weighing room. Normally, she'd go to her private box and leave the running around to Dil. She wore a camel coat and a bright, multi-coloured scarf, the first time I'd seen her on track dressed in anything but black. She offered a cheek and I kissed her, 'No black?'

'Thought I'd try and change our luck.'

'Well, no better place. Racing put the super in superstition. Where's Dil?'

'Gone looking for your friend, McCarthy.'

'Mac's here?'

'I don't know. But he should be, don't you think? His concentration ought to be on finding out who's interfering with our horses.'

I bit back my instinctive response, 'Mac will have something in mind, I'm sure.'

'I hope so. Did you bring those pictures?'

I set my bag on the wooden rail and drew the big envelope from the side pocket, expecting her to rip it open and pull out a magnifying glass. But she slid the envelope under her arm and said, 'I'll take a close look at them in the box.'

'Fine. I'd best go and get changed for the first.'

'Did you see who the assistant starter is?'

'Jon Vogel.'

She nodded down toward the envelope, 'Is he wearing a ring in these pictures?'

'He seems to be.'

She smiled, 'Do you think you could somehow try and get a closer look today, especially at the inside?'

'Of the ring?'

She nodded, gazing at me, warming again, the way she had yesterday as her mind strung things together in the order that excited her most.

I said, 'Let me think about it.'

'You're creative and persuasive, Eddie. You'll find a way.'

I said, 'I'll see you in the parade ring,' and I followed Bomber Harries through the door. As it swung closed, Vita called out, 'Maybe a left handed high five!'

Bomber looked at me quizzically. 'Don't ask,' I said.

I cantered to the start more quickly than usual, keen to be there to see all the girth checks. Vogel moved among us in his usual efficient manner. Girth checks were always done with his right hand. I watched to see if he ever put it in his pocket. He didn't.

He came toward me, smiling. It was the first time I'd taken a proper look at him. He reminded me of the actor Philip Seymour Hoffman. He smiled, 'Eddie.'

'Jon.'

'Try and stay on this one, will you?' he laughed, as he twanged the girth, then slapped the grey's rump with his left hand.

'Glued myself to the saddle this time,' I said, 'That's why I got to the start first, give it plenty of time to dry.' He wore his watch with the face by the heel of his hand. I said, 'Can't be long till the off now, can it? What's the time?'

He turned his wrist. I tried to see the inside of the silver ring, but his fingers curled over it. He said, 'Two minutes to go.'

'Thanks.'

'Good luck,' he strode toward the next horse. There were three left to check. He rump-slapped the last of them, the favourite. I made a mental note to check the order he'd gone round in at Bangor and Cheltenham.

I had seven rivals and an idea. As we walked toward the starting gate, line abreast I said to the others, 'I'm going to lead until he runs out of gas, just in case he takes off. No point putting anyone else in danger.'

A couple grunted their thanks. One said 'Good man!' The starter let us go and I set off a couple of lengths clear of my nearest pursuer.

With a circuit left to run, they remained content to sit behind me and I steadily increased my lead to three lengths, then I cried out 'Ahhh!' and kicked the gelding on, crouching low to drive him for a dozen strides. He took fright and set off, and I stood theatrically as though fighting with him, then bent low again for a few seconds before standing once more, and with three to jump I glanced round to find myself fifteen lengths clear.

I was in full control and the horse wasn't going too fast for this stage of the race, but the others had done what I'd hoped and sat back to stay out of trouble, expecting him to veer off and run out. As we went toward the last, I looked round again to see a lot of very busy jockeys and I laughed out loud as we galloped home to a ten length victory.

They called me a few names as we walked back toward the enclosures, but it was all good natured. They knew they'd been conned, and respected someone who'd outwitted them.

Unusually, Vita came to meet us. She rarely led her horses back in, preferring to let Dil do that. Laughing, she wagged a finger at me then clasped the rein, 'Very clever, Eddie, though Dil almost had a heart attack.'

Dil's jaw muscles were working like a strong pulse. I knew what was really wrong. He wouldn't have been able to admit it to Vita, but he walked with me toward the weighing room as Vita stayed behind chatting to the few who were congratulating her.

Dil gripped my arm, 'Why the fuck didn't you tell me you were going to do that?'

'Because I didn't know.'

'He was sixteen to one! I could have got all my losses back!'

I stopped and flexed my forearm muscle against his grip. He eased his fingers loose. I turned and stared at him, 'Dil, I only got the idea after Vogel had spoken to me. And I didn't know if it would work.'

'You stole the race!'

'I did. And if I'd said to you before I went out that I was going to try that, would you have rushed off to have three or four grand on?'

The fire left his eyes. His posture slumped and he looked much smaller. I said. 'Would you even have had three hundred quid on?'

He looked at the ground, 'Probably not.'

I waited. He kept staring at his shoes. I said, 'Dil, look at me.'

He raised his head. I said, 'You've trapped yourself. You're behaving like a cornered animal, snapping at everything and everyone. You got yourself into the trap. You chose Vita. You chose money. You chose to give up control. Deal with it, or get back to your old self.'

'Easy for you to say.'

'Easy for you to fix, Dil.'

'It's not easy! It might be obvious, but it's not easy!'

He was heating up again. Pointless wasting any more breath trying to cool him off. I said, 'For you? No, I suppose it isn't,' I walked away. He called after me, 'Vita wants a meeting after the last!'

'Fine. She knows where to find me.'

21

The meeting was in Vita's private box. The glass front was bigger than my picture window, but all it showed as I walked in was the deepening dusk over an empty track. If you squinted hard you could see the trail of hoofprints in the turf beside the winning post.

Dil sat opposite Vita. She turned and dismissed the last member of catering staff and watched the door swing slowly closed behind him.

She looked at me, 'I got hold of Peter McCarthy on the phone.'

I nodded, 'Good.'

'He was in London. I wanted to leave him in no doubt that we simply won't allow this to slip below the BHA's radar. They need to do something.'

It had taken me years to learn that it's always best to humour people who believe they're right about something. Whichever way you steer them, whatever evidence you produce, it never matters. But I wouldn't be able to stand months of this. 'What did Mac say?' I asked.

'That they were very much aware of the importance of finding out what has happened in these three cases.'

She seemed pleased. I said, 'Mac's one of the good guys. I've known him for years, and he'll do his best, but nobody's best will be good enough. Nobody at the BHA at any rate. They struggle to keep tabs on the day to day stuff. When something like this comes up, they just try to look calm and they pray.'

'For what?' Vita asked.

'For somebody to call and offer to trade information. For an angry man who might want revenge, or to take out a rival. For something to come up.'

'I thought they employed investigators?'

'They do. Just not enough of them for something like this. And those they've got are plodders. They wouldn't know where to start.'

She looked at Dil as though all this were his fault. She turned back to me, 'What about you?'

'What about me?'

'These people, these criminals have put your life in danger.'

'Collateral damage. Nothing personal.'

'How do you know?'

'Because they bet Spalpeen. It's money they're after. And I also think they might be trying to perfect whatever they're doing in order to protect the jockey and the horse. Or maybe the horse and the jockey, depending on their priorities.'

'Why do you think that?'

'Because when Montego Moon took off, she ran straight until a fence got in her way. The other two were steered somehow around the jumps and along the flat part of the track.'

'You're making it sound as though they've been fitted with some sort of remote control.'

'Maybe they have. When you last crossed the Atlantic, you were sitting in a comfortable chair, thirty thousand feet up watching a movie or using the internet. I wouldn't put it beyond somebody to have come up with a high tech way to make a dumb animal do what they want.'

She straightened in her chair, seeming to narrow as her shoulders tightened and her neck stretched, and her blonde hair topped her off like some kind of pointed beacon of superiority. 'Don't patronize me, Eddie.'

I sighed loud and long then bent forward to bang my forehead lightly on the table three times. I got up, and slid the chair in, 'I'm going home. No doubt you'll talk about me when I've gone. Include in that conversation whether you still want me to ride for you or not, and text me or email me or something. If you decide you still want me as your stable jockey, then I'll ride your horses. You sort out all the other shit. If you'd prefer me to sort out the other shit, let me know.'

I opened the door. Dil stood up, 'Eddie!'

I went out. Dil followed me into the thickly-carpeted corridor, 'Eddie!'

I went through the double doors and skipped downstairs, my reflection in the huge windows reminding me of old black and white movies where the leading man danced down the central staircase. I was as light of heart as he'd have been, even if the footwork didn't match.

Unburdened.

Unemployed too, perhaps, but it didn't matter. It would free me from crazy horses and crazier people.

As I got in the car, Dil rang me. I didn't answer.

Driving the last mile up to the farm from the floor of the valley, the sky got steadily bigger. The clouds had gone, letting all the heat out of the earth and exposing the starry blackness. I parked by the farmhouse so I could walk toward the light burning in the window.

Mave was at her dark alcove desk and she called as I closed the door. 'You survived another day, then?'

I dropped my bag in the hall and answered, 'Survived the riding, not so sure I survived my meeting with Bonnie and Clyde.' I told her what had happened. She came and sat with me in The Snug and we stayed silent by the stove until the ice in my whiskey cracked. Mave said, 'You're getting grumpy.'

'Life's too short.'

'Think she'll sack you?'

'I don't know.'

'And you don't care.'

I shrugged, 'Not much. Up until now I could handle Dil and I could handle Vita, but not both at the same time.'

'Last night you seemed quite amused at her playing detective.'

'I don't mind when it's the pie in the sky stuff, but she's coming over all officious now, like she was the sheriff of sin city. She made a clumsy attempt at prodding me into at least saving my own skin by helping find these people. That annoyed me. As if I don't care about anyone else.'

'Sounds like she wants you to eschew those ornery old brown horses and mount your white charger.'

I smiled and sipped whiskey and turned to her, 'Eschew. I like that. You and Mac are the only ones I know who use it. Mac told me once he was eschewing lunch, which tickled me.'

She drew her right leg up and tucked her foot under her left thigh. I said, 'What do you think I should do?'

'If you walk away, you're out of danger, assuming it is Dil's horses they're targeting. But then you're back freelancing and hoping to get lucky. You said Vita's looking to buy some more good horses.'

'You want me to prostitute myself for the sake of winning a couple of grade ones?'

'Yep.'

I laughed. Mave got up and stood with her back to the stove, feet apart, her legs forming a spindly arch. She watched me, 'You know you're free to do whatever you want? You needn't worry about money.'

I nodded. Mave had won millions from betting, using software she'd spent years developing. 'I know,' I said.

'Sounds to me like Vita's already trying to shuffle this problem off onto either the BHA or you. Why don't you go back to your earlier idea and see if she'll pay Ben to do his investigative journalist stuff?'

I sighed and laid my head back. Mave's long thin shadow loomed over me, 'Look how tall you are in your shadow life,' I said.

She glanced up, 'First eschew, now shadows. You keep trying to change the subject Mister Malloy.'

'I know.'

'You already said Ben would be up for it.'

'I'm not ringing Vita or Dil to beg for favours.'

She opened her arms, casting shadows like rails either side of me. She said, 'Who's asking you to beg? You said Dil's called you three times since you left. He'll be on the phone first thing in the morning. If Ben wants the job, tell Dil you're making it a condition of coming back.'

I pulled out my phone and found Ben's number, and just before I pressed dial, I had an odd sense of resistance. Foreboding would be too strong a word, it was a sort of sniff of suspicion rather than a lungful. I hesitated then put my reaction down to tiredness and frustration, and whiskey, so I made the call.

22

At six-thirty next morning I phoned Dil Grant.

'You're sharp,' he said.

'Thought I'd best find out early if I'm in for a good day or a bad one.'

'Well, you still have a job if you want it. I told Vita she just has to accept your quirks. Nobody's perfect.'

'Ain't that the truth. And what did Vita say?'

'She's happy to go with my judgement'

I smiled. Dil seemed to believe I hadn't noticed how cowed he was around her. 'And what about this investigation she's so hot on?'

'Well, she's not lying down on that, and I don't think you'd want her to.'

'I never said I wanted her to. She just needs to decide who's doing what because it's not a show she's capable of running. And the BHA aren't up to it. I'll do what I can, but I'm taking no orders from her or anyone else. If she wants to play a part she can put the money up for Ben Searcey to do some legwork.'

'Who's Ben Searcey?'

'An old friend. Investigative journalist. Before your time. He's good.'

'She'd want to meet him.'

'That's fine, so long as she realizes it's not some cattle call. She won't be giving Ben any orders.'

'What about the old "he who pays the piper" you used to quote at me, Eddie?'

'Dil, I'm not debating this with you, or with Vita. I'm seeing Ben tomorrow, and I think he will be interested in doing this. Best I can do is bring him to your place on Sunday if Vita will be there.'

'I'll speak to her and we can talk at Carlisle this afternoon.'

We left it at that, and I called Ben.

'Sunday would be fine for me, Eddie, but I don't want to leave Alice behind.'

'Of course, I hadn't meant for you to leave her. I should have made that clearer. Everyone at Dil's place will be happy to see her.'

When I hung up, I cursed myself for forgetting about Alice. I'd need to make sure she got a warm welcome at Dil's place.

On Sunday morning I picked Ben and Alice up outside 'our' pub. They were in the doorway, sheltering from cold rain. Ben got in the front. I turned to greet Alice as she slid into the back seat, 'Blame your dad for you getting wet. I offered to come to your house, but he won't let me over the borders of Deadwood.'

She smiled, 'You're not missing anything.'

Ben said, 'It's for our good as well as yours, Eddie. The curtain twitchers are on twenty-four-seven duty. The less they have to talk about, the better it suits us,' he glanced over his shoulder, 'Doesn't it, Alice?'

'I don't care what they say about me.'

Ben smiled and raised his eyes, and shrugged, 'Well, we'll be looking for somewhere else soon, now that DJ's gone.'

Alice said, 'As soon as we leave, he'll show up again.'

'Then I'll have another quiet word with Bruno,' Ben said.

Alice shifted forward quickly in her seat, just as I drove off, toppling her back, 'Oops,' I said, 'sorry.'

She leaned forward once more to speak to her father, 'Who is this Bruno fella anyway?'

'One of the good guys,' Ben said, 'I'll introduce you to him next weekend at the National.'

'Do you think he'd answer my questions?'

'Depends what they are.'

'Like, what did you do with DJ?'

'I think he'll blank you on that one,' Ben said, 'ask him if he can make sure DJ stays away once we leave.'

We drove past Aintree racecourse, and I was getting more of a sense of what Ben had been facing in letting Alice have her head while trying to protect her. I butted in, hoping to take some of the heat out of things, 'You got your eye on some place else, Ben?'

'Not yet, but we don't want to stay there forever.'

Alice said, 'Wherever DJ is, Dad, he'll likely be doing what he was doing in Deadwood.'

'And that's why I keep telling you that you can't solve the world's problems. You can't follow even one bad guy, never mind all of them. You do what you can, and beyond that, you've just got to leave it to the next person.'

'What if there is no next person?'

He turned and spoke softly, reaching for her with his right hand, 'I'm the last one that needs to tell you that shit happens...you've probably seen more of it than I have.'

'And I've seen more people explain it all away by saying shit happens'

Ben said nothing, just turned and settled into the seat, put his head back and folded his arms. I heard Alice slide slowly backwards, too and recognized the family ritual of a silent truce, one without rancour, where a social conscience had grown used to subduing a guilty conscience.

We left the northern suburbs of Liverpool behind as I steered onto the M58 motorway into a heavier swathe of rain, and that seemed to kind of close the curtain on the debate.

Alice said, 'Is it okay if I listen to music on my headphones?'

'Of course,' I said, 'feel free.'

Ben turned, 'Not too loud, eh?'

I glanced at him and saw from his smile that she had made a face.

When the tinny sound of pop reached a negotiated level between

Ben and his daughter, he said to me, 'If I get this gig, do you think your pal, McCarthy will help?'

'Yes. Definitely. It'll suit him.'

'Could he get all the data on those four betting accounts?'

'Such as it is, I'm sure he could. But they were bogus. Whoever opened them closed them again the same day they collected on Spalpeen.'

'What do you know about Vince McCrory?'

'Very little, other than he's better at staying on a crazy runaway than I am.'

'What about Spalpeen's trainer?'

'Sean Quinlynn. Champion Irish trainer…after your time. He has no need to be pulling stunts for money.'

'He won't be enemy-free if he's that successful, Eddie. Who knows what about him, and how quiet might he want something kept?'

'Sounds like you've started this job already. Save it until Vita starts paying.'

'What's she like?'

'Smart. And cruel.' I told him about Prim and her relationship with Dil and about what she'd done to embarrass Vita at Uttoxeter.

'Prim by name. but not by nature,' he said.

'Primarolo Romanic. Hell of a name, isn't it?'

'Certainly rolls off the tongue, though it takes a fair time to reach the tip of it. Where does she hail from?'

'Born in Spain. Says her mother was a gypsy queen, and her father was a bullfighter. Prim ends up with Dil. A bullfighter at one end of her life and a bullshitter at the other.'

Ben laughed, 'What about Dil? Who'd be his enemy number one?'

'Easy. The bookies.'

'They're hardly going to be spiking his horses, though. He sounds like somebody you'd love or hate.'

I went through Dil's long history.

Ben said, 'From would-be James Dean to widow-hunting on cruise liners. Sounds like old Dil could write a book.'

'No doubt.'

'You sure he restricted himself to widows on the ships?'

'I wouldn't be sure about anything with Dil Grant.'

'Could he have pissed off some poor husband enough to end up a target?'

'Every chance. But if his horses are being got at, why wouldn't this husband make some money from it?'

'It would be a purer form of revenge, don't you think? He crocks Dil's horses just for the satisfaction of screwing him. Maybe he's sold the recipe to the people who pulled the Spalpeen coup.'

'Maybe. Aintree starts on Thursday. Spalpeen's due to run again there.'

'Dil got anything between now and then that you'd expect to win? Or anything at Aintree?'

'He's got the Supreme winner, Stevedore turning out against Spalpeen.'

'The one Vita Brodie owns?'

'Well, she owns a few, but Stevedore is her best horse.'

'That could be interesting. Spalpeen would be favourite again, eh?'

'He will be.'

'I'll do some digging between now and then.'

I put a hand on his shoulder, 'Best wait and hear your terms of employment.'

'I'd do it for expenses, Eddie. Better than writing about tractors.'

'Don't tell Vita. She can afford to pay you,' I smiled across at him, 'she might even run to the price of some high class dental work.'

He smiled extra wide, showing the battlefield ridges in his mouth, 'Nah. The price I paid for these was close to the highest you can get. It's good that I only need to look in a mirror to be reminded of that.'

I reached to put a hand on his shoulder, 'Ben, I'm sorry, that was in poor taste, my comment.'

The music grew louder as Alice leaned forward, 'You're getting implants when we get the money, Dad. You've got enough old memories to hang your guilt on.'

He turned, smiling, 'I thought you were lost in music?'

'The bad news for you is my ears can multi-task. The worse news is I've got two of them.'

Ben laughed, 'You'll be keen to meet this fella, Dil Grant, then?'

'I'm keen to meet the vamp with the long name.'

'Primarolo Romanic,' I said, 'you'll get on well together.'

Alice said, 'I bet she gets a big kick out of being called Prim.'

I said, 'Your Dad said Dil Grant could write a book. The one I'd really want to read is Prim's. And you're in luck, because Dil told me he's arranged for Prim to show you around.'

I glanced in the rearview mirror. Alice's grey eyes had that faraway look you see only in the young, when life is still long and most of the questions are yet to be answered.

23

On the approach to Dil's, Alice leaned forward from her seat in the back and pointed to the wooden building dominating the skyline, 'What's that, a church?'

I said, 'That's Dil's American horse barn.'

'He brought it from America?' Alice asked.

I smiled, 'No, that's what they call that style of barn. A lot of the British stable yards have individual boxes in stone buildings. The American barns are kind of open plan, one building with lots of stalls in it.'

'So all the horses can watch each other?'

'Pretty much. Well, at least their closest neighbours. You'll soon see, anyway.'

Prim greeted us as we walked into the yard. She wasn't quite in her Sunday best, but she was geared up well beyond the limitations of jeans and loose sweaters. She wore tight jodhpurs and a black silky top under a shaped waistcoat of blue quilted stitching. Her black leather boots shone.

'Alice!' she said, reaching for Alice's hand, 'I've heard a lot about you.'

Alice put on a deliberate knowing smile, glanced at her father and me and said, 'And I've heard quite a lot about you, too,' and Prim looked at us and laughed.

Dil came out of the back door of the main house and strode

toward us, smiling, holding out his hand to Ben before he'd reached him, 'Ben! Good to meet you!' He turned then to Alice, held her lightly by the shoulders and kissed her cheek, 'You'll be Alice!'

'I am,' and I could see her biting back a remark as her natural guardedness took over. He said, 'Prim has been so looking forward to showing you around. After that, we can have lunch, if you're all hungry that is?'

Alice gave a single nod, keeping her eyes on him, unblinking.

'Enjoy yourselves!' Dil said, giving Prim a light push, touching her just above her hip with an open hand, a habitual action for him, but one which gave away their relationship as effectively as Ben and Alice finding them in bed.

Dil turned toward the house only to see Vita watching from the window, her dark eyes nailing him with the message that she'd seen that intimate touch with Prim.

Vita was cool with Dil, and overly warm with Ben, holding onto his hand too long then walking with him toward the big oak table in the dining room.

We clustered at the window end of the table, and Dil tipped coffee from an elegant white pot.

Vita offered milk to Ben and poured it for him. 'Eddie tells me you're a hardened investigative reporter, Ben.'

'Natural curiosity, Miss Brodie, I could never keep my nose out of anything.'

'Call me Vita.'

Ben smiled and nodded. Vita said, 'Eddie will have filled you in on the situation here, with the horses?'

'He did.'

'And is it something you feel you could help with?'

'I'm always happy to give it a try, though I'm not big on miracles.'

'As in?' Vita said.

'As in quick results…any results, really. It tends to be a slow trudge with stuff like this. So long as you're okay with that, I'm happy to have a go.'

Vita said, 'Eddie was keen that I emphasize to you that no

chances should be taken with your own safety.'

Ben looked at me and his eyes twinkled. He turned back to Vita and said, 'Eddie thinks there's not much holding my body together these days.'

Vita said, 'Sometimes it can be an advantage to look not quite what you are.'

Ben gazed at her as though awaiting a revolving target coming back round, then nailed her, 'I can understand that,' he said, and Vita smiled in acknowledgement that Ben was much smarter than she had assumed.

Twenty minutes later the deal had been done, and Dil handed Ben an envelope of cash for expenses. We went looking for Alice and Prim. Dil stayed behind with Vita.

In the brightly lit barn, Alice was scratching the neck of a beautiful chestnut mare. Prim was on the other side, stroking the mare and telling Alice about the importance of breeding.

'That would be your specialist subject, Prim, would it not? Good breeding? You being of royal descent,' I said, and Prim laughed, 'You mean my mother, the gypsy queen?'

'I'd like to have met her,' I said.

'There's still time, Eddie.'

'Good.'

Alice played with the mare's mane and said to Prim, 'Your mother really was a gypsy queen?'

'In Granada,' Prim said.

Alice smiled, 'That makes you a princess.'

Prim laughed, 'I told them all that when I came here, but they laughed!'

Alice said, 'You should make them curtsy...like this,' and Alice stepped back and bent gracefully, strands of her fair hair almost touching the deep straw. Prim laughed and looked at Ben, 'You have a princess of your own, Ben. You're a lucky man!'

Ben had his forearms flat on the door of the stall and he gazed lovingly at his daughter and said, 'I am.'

Prim glanced up at the big railway clock that hung in the triangle above the barn entrance, 'Time for lunch,' she said, 'Let's get you back to the house.'

They walked ahead of me and Ben, along the concrete aisle down the middle of the barn and out into the sunshine and across the yard, Prim with her arm linked in Alice's all the way. We stopped ten paces short of the back door and Prim turned to us, 'Enjoy your lunch. Dil's as good a cook as he is a trainer,' and she smiled and winked and eased her arm free from Alice's.

Alice looked concerned, 'Aren't you coming?'

Prim didn't answer right away, but she held Alice's gaze then said, 'Maybe next time.'

Alice turned to us. Ben shrugged. I looked at Prim who reached to touch Alice's shoulder, 'We will have a girls' lunch, you and I, very soon. We won't wait for a next time.'

Alice said, 'I'd like that,' and she leant and kissed Prim's cheek and Prim looked straight ahead, avoiding our eyes in the hope of hiding her wounds.

24

On Wednesday afternoon, the day before the start of the three-day Grand National meeting, I was driving home from Kelso when Mac phoned me.

'Mac, how are you?'

'Harassed, as ever. How are you?'

'Sanguine.'

'Ha! You've been saving that up, haven't you? Learning a word a day to throw at me?'

I laughed, 'A word a month, more like. So, what's harassing you that I can help with?'

'I just wanted your thoughts on an idea I had.'

'Go on.'

'The big novice hurdle tomorrow, I was thinking of getting all the runners thoroughly vetted before the race.'

'As in what, blood tests, heart and lungs, scopes?'

'We'd take veterinary advice on what should be covered.'

'Short notice, Mac, isn't it? Would you tell the press?'

'Not beforehand.'

'Well there wouldn't be much point in telling them afterwards. If Spalpeen or something else goes wild, all you'd be admitting is that the tests picked up nothing. If the race goes to plan there's no point telling the press then, is there?'

'Hmmm, no, I suppose not.'

'Seems to me you'd be on a loser whichever way it pans out.'

Mac cleared his throat, 'But if something does go wrong, at least we could say that we took what precautions we could.'

'In that case, you'd need to do it for every race…or, at least, every race with a short priced favourite. If Spalpeen wins easy, and the favourite in the next gets crocked you're going to look a right bunch.'

'You've persuaded me.'

'Good.'

'Had you any more thoughts on it yourself?'

'Maybe we can talk tomorrow, Mac? Vita Brodie has taken someone on to do a bit of digging. If you could arrange some help for this guy, I think it would work in your favour.'

'Who is it?'

'Ben Searcey.'

'The journalist?'

'That's him.'

'I thought he was dead!'

'So did I. He only looks dead.'

'What's his connection to Vita Brodie?'

'It's a long story. I'll tell you tomorrow.'

'I'm travelling up tonight. What time will you be there tomorrow?'

'Come and stay with us, Mac, we're only an hour away from Aintree.'

'Well, it would be nice to see everyone again.'

'Kim and Marie and Sonny are away at the moment. I'll tell you all about it tonight. But Mave will be happy to see you.'

'How is she?'

'As brainy as ever. She's doing fine, Mac.'

'Good…good.'

'We'll get your room ready.'

'See you about eight?'

'See you then.'

After dinner, Maven excused herself to work on her laptop in the bedroom. Mac and I moved to the Snug where logs burned in the stove and a brandy glass sat on the old coffee table. I poured cognac for him and whiskey for myself.

Mac settled back on the low sofa, his weight making the cushion wheeze. He said, 'Looks like you have everything the way you want it now.'

When we'd first moved here, Mac had visited with his friend, Broc Lisle. That had been shortly after the death of Mac's wife, and we had invited him to join our little commune. 'No regrets about declining our offer of a place here?' I said.

'That's a hard one to answer. It's difficult to have regrets about something you've never experienced, if you know what I mean?'

'I suppose so. But you're doing all right on your own?'

'Well...' he sipped from the glass, 'I've made some tiny adjustments, day by day, week by week, and things are not quite so bad as they were after Jean died,' he smiled at me then gazed at the embers in the stove.

'I'm glad to hear that, Mac. What about Broc, has he stayed in touch?'

'He calls from time to time.'

'What's he doing?'

'Working for a London charity, I believe, supporting victims of crime. Apparently he did a big job in the middle east which means, financially at least, he'll never need to work again.'

'Good for him. He's a real character.'

'I suspect we don't know the half of it. Anyway, tell me more about Ben Searcey and this job with Vita Brodie.'

I went though the details. Mac said, 'I can't see this assistant starter theory going anywhere. Perhaps it had some merit after the first two, but when Vogel was elsewhere for the third one, that knocks rather a big hole in it, don't you think?'

'I don't believe it will come to anything. It was Vita who latched onto it with this fixation on the ring Vogel was wearing. What do you know about him?'

'Well, he was never cautioned as a jockey. Started a retraining course before he quit the saddle, so he was a better planner than many of your colleagues. And he applied regularly for jobs at the BHA until he landed this one.'

'What about his private life?'

Mac shook his head, 'Not our line, beyond basic background checks, Eddie. Couldn't justify probing that until evidence supported it. He lives on his own in Swindon. That's as much as I know.'

'Fair enough.' I got up to put more logs in the stove.

Mac said, 'So it sounds like Ben's employment might be cut short if Miss Brodie wants him to concentrate on Vogel.'

'He's going to do some digging on Vince McCrory too,' I told Mac about the discussion on whether McCrory had steered the horse off the course at Cheltenham, and about buzzers.

Mac smiled and drained his glass, 'A horseman of exquisite skill if that turns out to be the case.'

'Agreed,' I reached for the cognac and tipped a short, slow stream over the rim of the brandy balloon. Mac nodded and raised a finger to stop me. I said, 'What's happening your side with this?'

He sighed and settled his bulk back, 'We've adopted our specialized HIDHA approach...' I knew Mac well enough to wait silently for the punchline. He said, 'Hoping it doesn't happen again.'

I smiled. He said, 'You know as well as I do we're buggered on this. Unless somebody decides to tell tales, or the perpetrators make a mistake, we just need to hope for the best. One of the benefits of twenty-four-seven news, and this virulent social media is that nothing stays in the headlines for long.'

'Spalpeen will be the shortest price of the meeting. You can probably breathe easy if you get past that race.'

'You don't think yours will beat him?'

'He won't. One of my memories of Cheltenham for as long as I live will be how sweetly that horse was travelling when I looked across at him. And we know he finds plenty when asked. He'll win barring accidents.'

'Dil Grant and Miss Brodie will surely be more hopeful than you about the chances of Stevedore?'

'Up front, they will. And maybe Vita believes it. But Dil's not daft.

Well, he's stupid but he's not daft, if you know what I mean.'

'I hear he's punting big.'

'Is that so?'

We smiled the same smile. Over the years, almost all the barriers between us had dropped, but, much as Dil aggravated me at times, some things were sacred. Trainers were not barred from betting, but Mac would be uneasy about the stakes Dil was playing in. It was none of my business.

Mac leaned forward and put his glass on the table, and the shallow pool of cognac glowed in the light as the new logs caught fire. I reached for the bottle, but Mac raised his palm, 'No, thank you, Eddie. You've been a gracious host, but it was a long drive and if you don't mind, I'll head for bed.'

I got up, 'Sure. We've a nice big room for you in the farmhouse. This place is a bit too small. I hope that's okay?'

He shuffled forward and pushed himself up from the low sofa, 'Of course, of course. Anywhere at all. Wherever I lay my hat, as the old song goes. I can haunt the corridors while the clan is in Australia. When did you say they'd be back?'

'August. That's the plan. Kim's supposed to be starting at boarding school in Edinburgh in September.'

'Ah, good. Which one?'

'Can't recall, Mac. One of the fancy ones. They're not my line, as you probably know. Not Kim's either, poor bugger. His mother's idea.'

'It will do him more good than harm, if I can paraphrase an old saying.'

We went outside and walked toward the patch of light cast on the drive by the side window of the farmhouse kitchen. Mac said, 'I know it's just three lines of latitude above Lambourn, Eddie, but I always find it noticeably chillier up this way.'

'You're getting old, Mac. Though it is colder here in the hills.'

'An unusually still night, too, I'd guess?'

'It's been an unusually still week. More like June than April.'

'Calm before the storm, eh?'

'Likely, knowing our luck.'

We covered the remaining fifty yards in companionable silence, and I felt oddly reassured by Mac's dark bulk beside me that the big house would soon be alive again when Kim and the others came home.

Back in our small cottage, the clickety-clack of Mave's keyboard as I approached the bedroom sounded like a busy typing pool sound-effect from an old black and white movie. And when I opened the door, the weak light from a small lamp in the corner reinforced the monochrome feel.

Mave sat on the bed, a slim silhouette. Even if the lampglow had reached her, it wouldn't have found much.

She spoke without breaking her finger-rhythm, 'Early night for the boys?'

I sat on the edge of the bed, 'Mac's tired.'

'He's getting old.'

'I think losing Jean sucked about ten years out of the poor sod.'

'He'll adjust, Eddie. They don't spend their whole childhood moulding those stiff upper lips for nothing.'

I sighed, and laid back, easing off my shoes, 'That's funny, that's what Mac said, he's adjusting...day by day, a tiny bit at a time.'

The clicking stopped as she reached to touch my arm, 'Stop worrying about him. You've enough to worry about.'

'Thanks for reminding me.'

'You're welcome.'

I tried to get my trousers off, still lying down. Mave laughed and pushed me, 'Get up, you lazy bugger!'

I grabbed at her, trying to keep my balance, and my phone rang.

By the time I'd scrambled it from my pocket I'd missed the call.

'Who was it?' Mave asked.

'Ben.'

'This late?'

I called back.

25

Ben answered on the first ring, 'Eddie, sorry to call so late. Did I wake you?'

'No, not at all. Everything okay?'

'Well, yes, but I wanted to let you know before tomorrow, assuming you'll be seeing Vita tomorrow?'

'Yes, she'll be at Aintree.'

'It's just that, well, this probably sounds stupid, but I'd rather be safe than sorry, tell her to be careful from a personal viewpoint.'

'What's happening?'

'It might be nothing, but I think Vogel is some kind of woman hater, and he is so anti-American, they'll lock him up if he ever lands there.'

'How'd you find this out?'

'A friend of mine is an accomplished…well, let's call him a high tech eavesdropper. He's very discreet.'

'A hacker?'

Ben cleared his throat, 'That would be a crude term. This guy's the best.'

I glanced at Mave, keen to speak up, but this wasn't the time. 'So what's he found?' I said.

'Vogel's posting on message boards under an alias. Big time conspiracy theorist, especially where America is concerned, you know, the moon landing never happened, nine-eleven was down to the government, Obama's a terrorist etcetera.'

'What's he saying about women?'

'American women, specifically. They're conspiring to take over from men, look at the jobs they have already, see how competitive they are, how insolent, that's his word, they all are, how they're bringing up their little girls to compete with men, that they need putting back in their place, blah, blah, blah.'

'Nice man, but just so we're clear, Vita's not American. I know she's got one of these mangled accents, and she lives in New York most of the time, but she was born in Scotland.'

'Ah, right. Maybe that changes things a bit...though Vogel might be thinking she's a Yank.'

'Look, we'll tell her, to be on the safe side.'

'You ought to see some of the stuff on these boards. A few of them call Vogel the voice of reason, trying to promote him as some sort of viable public spokesman come the day.'

'Come what day?'

'The day democracy is finally exposed for the sham it is. The day politicians pay the price.'

I looked at Mave, 'Ben, I'll get some more details about this. Mave's a superstar too at all things technical, maybe she can help track Vogel and the places he's hanging out online.'

'That would be good, Eddie, take some pressure off me for now. Alice has kicked off on another link with DJ and I'm trying to help her too.'

'Is he back?'

'DJ? No, but Alice has found the guy who's doing what she thinks is a lot of his work. She started following him, but a few of his regular stops are betting shops where she can't get in, so, since I have no trouble these days convincing staff I'm over eighteen, I've landed the job of hanging around in the bookies.'

'You'll find a few conspiracy theorists in there, too.'

He laughed, 'You said it.'

'So, what's this guy doing, passing money to DJ or something?'

'I think he might be laundering it through slot machines. My trouble is keeping up with the guy once he leaves the betting shop. He travels on foot until he comes out, then there's usually someone waiting to pick him up in whatever fancy car's available.'

'Want me to have a word with Monty tomorrow and get Bruno back on it?'

'Nah, not worth it. I think once Alice knows what he's actually doing, she'll calm down a bit. I'm learning that if I humour her, she doesn't kick and scream so much, figuratively speaking, of course.'

'Of course.'

'Sorry,' Ben said, 'just getting paranoid after reading so much of Vogel's bile. Anyway, send me Mave's details and I'll forward some stuff. I'll see you on Saturday.'

'Alice excited about the National?'

'She is. She's asking if Prim will be there.'

'I don't know, Ben, and it's not one I'm inclined to get involved with as far as Dil is concerned.'

'Don't worry. Just leave it. I think maybe she's missing her mother more than she thought she would. Prim's about the same age as Alice, Alice senior that is, and, well, you know how it is.'

'I do. Let's wait and see. I know Prim wouldn't want to miss the National, so maybe she'll stick two fingers up to Vita and Dil. If she does, I'm sure I can get Monty to invite her up to the box.'

'That would be cool…as Alice would say.'

'It would. Listen, I'll speak to Dil and to Vita about Vogel, I'll call them first thing.'

'It's probably nothing, but she's paying me to find things out, and, well, I found something out.'

'I'll let you know how it goes, Ben. See you Saturday. Give our love to Alice.'

'I will. Good night.'

26

We lay side by side in the April darkness. Mave said, 'Shall we open a window?'

'You mean will I open a window, since it's on my side?'

'Oh, so it is!'

I got up and reached through the curtains and slipped the latch.

'Thanks,' Mave said, 'we'll sleep better with fresh air.'

'If I'd suggested opening the window, you'd have said it was a subliminal reaction after hearing that foul stuff about Vogel.'

'You could well be right, Mister Malloy.'

'You going to be okay delving into that sort of crap?'

'I'll be fine. I try to leave my emotions this side of the keyboard.'

'Let's see what turns up and we can go from there, eh?'

'I'll be okay. I'm just wondering how Ben found out so much so quickly.'

'Well, I don't want to set you up for a challenge, but Ben says his techie guy is Bull Goose Hacker. None better, according to Ben.'

'I didn't hear you defending my honour?'

'Thought it best not to get you into a pissing contest...figuratively speaking.'

She turned, 'Think I couldn't win a pissing contest?'

I laughed. She said, 'I'd bet my urethra against any man's.'

'You haven't got a urethra!'

'Since when?'

'I thought they were men only things?'

'Well, they're not. And allied to my pelvic floor, I'd take any man on.'

I smiled at her, 'You'd need to get into a funny position.'

'Handstand. Floor flex. Squirt. Job done.'

I laughed again, 'You're a hell of a woman!'

'And don't you forget it!' she wagged a finger at me.

We lay flat and quiet for a few moments. I said, 'So, you don't mind putting aside your work to help Ben out with Vogel?'

She sighed, 'The work I'm doing's meaningless, Eddie. Same old, same old. Can't wean myself off it.'

'You're still developing the betting software? I thought you were building a new game?'

She said, 'It was a large chunk of my life. It was supposed to be my holy grail.'

'But you did it. It worked. You made millions. I know that's not particularly what you wanted, the money, but you proved yourself.'

'I know. But things change a tiny bit everyday. Every race result brings a grain that could hold new information.'

'But it's of no more use to you now than information on how to live on Mars. You're done with it. You were certain of that when we moved here.'

'I know. Funny the things you become certain about when you're in danger.'

I thought of the mountaineering stories I'd read, and the epic journeys. Mave was right. When things are at their absolute worst, a man will swear that all he really wants is home and family, and if he can be delivered from whatever danger he is in, he'll stay safe forever. Then, after six months of home life, the thirst returns.

I said, 'Second thoughts, then?'

'Maybe. Not so much about the decision, but about how I took it. I can't go back to using the information the system's spitting out, I know that. It's just that I shouldn't have gone cold turkey.'

'I think you miss that little clifftop eyrie of yours more than anything else.'

'I lie here sometimes when you're asleep, remembering the sounds of the waves and the wind.'

I turned, my head still on the pillow. She turned to face me. I said, 'If you were back there, now, you wouldn't be humouring me by lying in bed trying to reset your body clock, would you?'

'I'd be at my desk, listening to the weather and the keyboard clicking.'

The darkness hid the longing in her eyes, but her voice betrayed her. I said, 'We can go back there.'

'You said the other day a man can never go back.'

'I know. Maybe a woman can.'

She made a sound that was half laugh, half sob, 'You said "we". You're a man.'

'Ahh, but I wouldn't be going back, would I? We never lived there together.'

'What about Kim, and Marie and Sonny?'

'We can visit. It's barely a hundred miles…by crow.'

She smiled, 'We'll see.'

We lay quiet again.

'If you want to get up and go to your desk, I don't mind,' I said.

'The clicking will keep you awake.'

'It's a lullaby to me now, Mave.'

'Man, you can be positively poetic at times.'

'That's alliteration, isn't it?'

'It is.'

'Between you and Mac, you're educating the hell out of me.'

'We'd never do that intentionally. I'm sure I speak for Mac, there, too.'

I pushed her gently with my foot, 'Away to your work, woman.'

She rolled gracefully out and got to her feet, 'Aye, aye sir.'

'Log in to my email, will you, and see if Ben has sent those links on Vogel? Or would you rather leave that until daylight?'

'If it's there, I'll make a start. See you in the morning.'

'You will, Miss Judge, you will.'

116

27

I rose early to make breakfast for Mac. Mave was still at her PC and I learned that she had not been the only nighthawk. Vogel had been flitting from site to site, unaware Mave was following him. She looked happy.

I sipped black coffee and said, 'If anyone saw us and wanted a bet on which one had had a full night's sleep, you'd be odds-on favourite.'

'My natural zest will always top that groggy Malloy morning mope.'

'You've got a massive advantage, though, you don't have to shave…well, not yet, anyway.'

She smiled and rubbed her jaw like Desperate Dan.

'Tell me about Vogel,' I said.

'Not much to tell. He drifts around these forums like a bit of a lost soul looking for some kind of recognition, some fulfilment. He's just an aimless wanderer who'd like people to think he's an action man. My bet is that the guy is harmless.'

'Was the stuff Ben's bloke found as bad as he said?'

She shrugged, 'More sad than bad, I'd say.'

'But worth mentioning to Vita Brodie?'

'It'll do no harm.'

When Mac left for Aintree, I called Ben, and told him what Mave had found. He said, 'Always good to have a backup source. Mave's found him on sites I couldn't get to. You going to call her ladyship?'

'I think you should do that, Ben. You did the digging.'

'How do you think she'll take it?'

'I don't know. She seems pretty tough. I suppose we should check with Dil first.'

'Want me to call him?' Ben said.

'I need to speak to him anyway about Aintree. I'll mention it and see what he advises.'

Dil advised that Vita Brodie ought to be told face to face, and we arranged a meeting in her box at Aintree at eleven. I asked Dil to make sure an entry badge was left for Ben to collect at the Owners and Trainers entrance. Dil said, 'What about his Press badge?'

'They took it off him years ago. This job should help him get it back.'

The four of us sat in the quiet, glass-fronted box at the top of t grandstand. The morning sun lacked strength, and mist lay low (Aintree's 270 flat acres making the Melling Road the outer limi⁺ what we could see.

Vita's brief nod and cold smile dismissed the catering staff, v had the knack of opening the heavy door just enough to ghost aw. through the gap. They'd left behind hot coffee in silverware, and Γ filled our cups.

Ben's new suit of navy blue, his white shirt and pink tie chang him utterly. It would have been all for the good had it not contraˢ so starkly with his crumpled face and ruined teeth. His head see like an ancient gravestone uprooted and laid on a neat lawr discomfort was obvious, and I felt sorry for him.

Dil finished pouring. Vita glanced at him expectantly aι turned to Ben, 'Ben, do you want to make a start?'

Ben told them what he'd told me, and he added what Ν discovered, though not mentioning her. I'd told him to take a credit as he could on this.

Vita surprised me by staying silent until he'd finished. Maybe t was something to do with the way Ben delivered it in news-lik fashion, the story already written in his head.

She said, 'No mention of my name, though?'

'No,' Ben said.

'Then he's just a run-of-the-mill woman hater. There are plenty out there, believe me,' she said.

'Maybe,' I said, 'but none of them have access to your horses.'

She turned, 'So long as he doesn't have access to me.'

I hesitated briefly, but decided it was better said, 'He does, though, doesn't he?'

Dil clenched his jaw and looked at the ceiling. Vita said, 'In what way?'

I said, 'Well, he's on the racecourse, never far away, physically, at least.'

She said, 'So, where do they go between races, these starter's assistants?'

'Good question,' I said, 'I've never thought about it.'

'Who do they report to?' she asked.

'The starter, I suppose.'

'And who does he report to?'

I shrugged, 'I'll ask Mac.'

Dil said, 'While you're at it, why don't you let him know he's employing a ticking bomb right there?'

'Well, if you want me to. But I'd rather Vogel didn't know we were tracking him. Not until we find out if he's involved with these horses.'

Vita looked at Ben, 'He never mentioned horses, did he? Mine or anyone else's?'

'Not a word,' Ben said, 'it's almost as though this online stuff is his life, and the day job's just, well, a day job.'

Dil said, 'Did he mention any woman by name?'

Ben shook his head, 'Nearest he got was "my ex". Never named her. Never even said "ex-wife", just "ex".'

Vita straightened in her chair and stuck a spoon dead centre into her coffee, and stirred slowly, 'Ben, you've done a great job to come up with all this so quickly, but I hope you don't mind me saying that

I think it's pure coincidence, and nothing more, that this Vogel character is such a disgusting slug.'

'I hope you're right, Ms. Brodie, Ben said, 'and you might well be. But that's not for me to decide. You wanted me to find out as much as possible about this case, and I couldn't ignore that.'

'Indeed you couldn't,' Vita said, 'but I'd tick it off now, and move on, if I were you.'

'Fine,' said Ben, and he pulled at his tie knot, then reached for his cup.

Dil said, 'Ben, what put you onto this angle with Vogel? How did you find out he was that way inclined?'

Ben wiped his mouth, and tried to refold the heavy napkin, 'An old contact. I made half a dozen calls. Had to spend the first few minutes of each explaining where I'd been for years. The rumour about me being dead must have taken root like that Japanese knotweed stuff.'

'Oh,' Vita said, 'my friend had about an acre of that in her garden. Nightmare to shift, by all accounts.'

'So I hear,' Ben said.

I sat back, and looked over their heads and through the glass doors at the pale sun, heavily dulled by the mist. I'd come here expecting Vita to be horrified, to demand bodyguards, and here she was sipping coffee and discussing the horrors of unwanted garden plants.

Another lesson for me not to make assumptions about Vita Brodie.

28

The first big contest of the day was sun versus mist, and the sun won and we cantered to the start though the mild air of a fine afternoon. This was the top race of the meeting for novice hurdlers. Dil had led me out on Stevedore before hurrying back to join Vita in her box. He assured me he hadn't bet anything, and I congratulated him on good judgement. I, like most others, believed the Irish horse, Spalpeen, would do what he'd been stopped from doing at Cheltenham.

He was 4/7 with the bookmakers to do so. Stevedore was 4/1. I expected to finish second, but had assured Vita we'd make the favourite battle all the way. Fighting talk. I had scant ammunition to back it up with, but owners always prefer optimism.

We arrived at the start where Spalpeen stood head up, ears pricked, coat gleaming black in the sunshine. Nine of us settled to a circular walk as Jon Vogel began his work with his usual cheery public persona. I watched with fascination as I pictured him crouched each night at a screen, typing vitriol and hatred in those echo chambers of the internet.

He looked up, smiling as he approached me, and I had to glance away in case he read in my eyes that I knew so much about him. 'All right, Eddie? You'll struggle to beat that fella today if he stays on the track.'

'We all will,' I said, watching him reach under the girth. 'Hmm, could do with going up one, I'd say. All right?'

'Sure,' this was the first time he'd adjusted my girths. His hands moved smoothly, and quickly in a job he'd done a thousand times, and I saw nothing untoward. Then I remembered the silver ring, and I watched as he raised his left hand to slap Stevedore's flank. 'Good luck!' he said, and moved on to check the chestnut behind me.

Two minutes later, the tapes flew skyward and we were away, galloping on perfect ground on Aintree's flat, tight oval track on the stands side of Melling Road.

Tactically, there's not much you can do to beat a horse that's better than yours. McCrory, on the favourite, knew that his eight rivals could only try to slow the race down in the hope of beating him in a sprint. Spalpeen's key strength was his staying power, his ability to maintain a high speed longer than his rivals could. Dawdling wouldn't suit him.

Most jockeys generally prefer to sit in the pack and come with a run at the time they judge best. It seldom works that way, because you need to react to what's happening around you, especially to who is in front and how fast he's going.

Vince McCrory would have been content in the pack, but by the time we jumped the first, he knew he'd have to make his own pace and he got straight down to it, stretching five lengths clear, then eight until he drew us along with him, our choices reduced to a single one: trying to keep up.

Four hurdles from home, a sensation that was becoming queasily familiar hit me once more as Stevedore exploded into that head-down, neck-stretched panic which took us tearing past Spalpeen on the outside.

I heard Vince curse as I went by, more from fright and surprise than any feeling he might lose the race. The only certain loser now would be me. It was just a matter of how much I could limit the damage.

The ground, though perfect for racing, wasn't soft as it had been last time. Bailing out at almost forty miles an hour would be like jumping from a car roof. It was small consolation that grass awaited me rather than pavement. A fracture would be close to certain, a broken neck not unlikely, depending on how I landed.

Standing up and wrestling with him would be pointless. Staying aboard until he exhausted himself was the best option, and I crouched and gripped with knees and ankles, and grabbed his neckstrap as he bore down on the next hurdle. If it went to pattern here, he'd jink soon, to avoid jumping this, and that helped because the only way he could jink was to his right. And that was exactly what he did fifty yards from take-off, and I was ready for it, and read it spot on and felt a surge of pride as my balance was undisturbed.

I settled now, adrenaline pipe slowly closing as I realized I could just sit and let him run himself out.

Then he slowed so suddenly I slid right up his neck, and almost off over his head. He had gone from full pelt to half speed, ribs heaving, nostrils snorting, and now, as the others passed us on the inside, he made a brave attempt to quicken again, to stay with them, to get back to the safety of the herd. But he had no more to give, and I pulled him up, and felt a quiver go through him. I slid quickly off, and tried to get him walking round, but he went down as his legs gave way and he thumped onto the turf, groaning out the wind from his lungs as his ribs compressed in the fall.

A minute later, the green screens were around him, and two vets were at his head.

29

We gathered again in Vita's box at the top of the grandstand. [ ]
was down and, through the glass, the streetlights on the reopen[ ]
Melling Road glowed orange. Below us, litter pickers in hi-vis vests
cleared up in preparation for the second day of the Grand National
meeting.

We sat in the chairs we had occupied this morning. The only good
news was that Stevedore had eventually got to his feet and walked
shakily into the horse ambulance, then onward to Liverpool
Veterinary School for further checks on his fibrillating heart.

Vita turned to Dil, 'Is there any way the fibrillating heart could
have caused him to bolt like that?'

Dil chewed his thumb and shook his handsome head, 'More likely
that bolting brought on the fibrillation.'

Vita looked at me for confirmation. I nodded, 'I've ridden horses
before with the same condition. That shakiness, sudden weakness-'

Ben said, 'Could that have been what stopped him so quickly?'

'I doubt it,' I said, 'he was running because he was scared, very
scared. He'd still have shown that fear when he stopped if the source
of it was still there, but he didn't.'

Dil banged the table with both fists, 'This is fucking stupid!' he
shouted. Vita glanced sideways at him and I thought I saw a
triumphant glint in her eye.

He massaged his face and groaned, and tried to collect himself.

He looked at me, pointed at me, and said, 'Don't tell me now that they're not having a go at my horses!'

'I wasn't going to.'

'What have I done, what have we done for this to happen?'

Vita turned fully and looked at him, 'We being?' she said.

Dil said, 'Me, you, Eddie, the yard!'

She watched for a few moments, then lowered her voice to almost soothing level, 'Calm down. We'll get nowhere if everyone panics.'

But, like Stevedore, Dil had gone already, 'It's okay for you to say don't panic! I've got a yardful of horses I can't run anywhere because of this fucker!'

Vita seemed to luxuriate in her own calmness, 'A quarter of that yardful belongs to me.'

Dil glared at her, 'Meaning?'

'Meaning, Dylan, that I'm paying the price as much as you are. I'm taking the hits too. If it's you they're after, I'm paying for the collateral damage.'

Dil stood up, gripping the table edges, 'Then take them away! Move them! At least I'll be able to sleep at night…on my own!'

She'd stayed calm until his final three words made her wince. Ben looked away, out into the deepening dark.

I watched them both, betting mentally that Dil would start back-tracking very soon.

I called it wrong. He left, although his theatrical exit did not go to plan. He tried slamming the door behind him, not realizing it was set on a heavy spring to help catering staff. He stormed out and the softly closing door mocked him for ten seconds before quietly clasping to its lock.

Vita turned slowly to look at me, her eyebrows rising. I held her gaze then raised my eyebrows too, and she laughed.

She said, 'I'm guessing it's not the first time you've seen Dil's tantrums?'

I said, 'And I'm guessing it's the first time you've seen one in public?'

'He's fraught, poor dear.'

I had plenty of reasons to complain about Dil, but I wouldn't give Vita the satisfaction of teaming up with her against him. Especially now I knew that this was a game for her. Stevedore, didn't matter much. Winning races meant little. Manipulating people was what drove Vita Brodie.

She turned to Ben, 'What do you think, Ben?'

'About what, Ms. Brodie?'

'Oh stop calling me Ms. Brodie, will you? Ms. Brodie! Mizzy Brodie! You're a step away from a southern black on a plantation.'

'I think my Scouse accent will save me from any miscasting there. At least on this side of the Atlantic.'

Her jaw clenched.

'What do you like to be called?' Ben asked.

'Vita. I told you that before...Vita!'

Ben slowly pulled a notebook from inside his jacket, carefully opened it and searched for an empty page, which he smoothed out, then clicked his pen and wrote "Vita". He closed it and unhurriedly put it away. 'Got it,' he said.

It was rude of me, but I smiled. Vita got up, 'Excuse me,' she said, and left, remembering not to slam the door.

Ben and I smiled at each other. Affecting the accent, he said, 'Mizzy Brodie, she gone. She gone to Cry me a River, an Ol' Man River!'

I laughed and slapped his shoulder. It was dark now, and we could see our reflections in the glass. Ben said, 'What are we laughing at? It looks like I'm unemployed and it looks like somebody's trying to kill you.'

'Well, Ben, you might be in trouble, but the odd thing, the very odd thing is that someone is actually trying to keep me alive.'

30

I parked by the end of the farmhouse and walked toward the lamp burning in the window. It didn't register until she raised a pale hand in welcome that Mave was there too.

I closed the door on the outer dark and dropped my kit bag in the short hallway. I smiled at Mave, 'Waiting for someone?'

'Cowboy Joe,' she said, 'that looked like a rodeo act when he stopped so suddenly. Not your most dignified moment.'

'I'll take survival over dignity any day.'

'Do you think this is anything to do with us stalking Vogel so closely online in the past twenty-four hours?'

I leaned back against the windowsill and crossed my arms, 'Well, is there any way that he could have found out you and Ben have been stalking him, as you put it?'

'If he's smart enough.'

'But if he was smart enough, surely you wouldn't have been able to track him in the first place?'

'Unless he wanted us to.'

'Why would he want us to?'

Mave crossed her arms too, and tilted her head sideways, mimicking me, 'Damned if I know, Edward, but it all seems a bit too coincidental, and I saw him adjusting your girth today. Is that a first?'

'Since this caper started, yes, it is.'

'And, if it had been for money, the favourite would have been the sensible target, so why you, again?'

'Well, whoever it is, they don't want to hurt me.'

She laughed, 'You'll convince yourself of anything.'

'No. Tell me, what was different about today?'

My phone rang. It was Mac. 'Mac, can I call you in five minutes?'

'Please do.'

I switched off my phone, and watched Mave. She said, 'The horse stopped and you were still on it?'

'Exactly. He stopped because whoever set him going, stopped him as soon as he'd disqualified himself by running out.'

Mave moved to stand beside me. She put a hand on my shoulder and said, 'I'm listening.'

I said, 'The first time was some kind of experiment. Montego Moon galloped until she ran into a fence. The second time Spalpeen was steered around the jump. At Uttoxeter, Kingdom Come pulled himself up on the bend after unseating me. Today Stevedore was stopped as soon as the money was landed.' I pointed at my phone, 'That was Mac. I'll bet you now that he was calling to tell me Stevedore was laid on the exchanges.'

Mave said, 'Ring him back.'

I did. 'Mac, sorry about that. What can I do for you?'

'The boss would like to see you at Aintree at nine tomorrow morning. The chief constable of Merseyside will be with him.'

'What boss? What's it about?'

'Nigel Steel, and what do you think it's about?'

'Okay, I can understand Steel, but whose idea was it to rope in the chief constable?'

'It seems it was the chief constable's idea to rope himself in'

'Why?'

'Well, we will find out tomorrow.'

'Mac, to use an old cliché, I don't like the smell of this. Okay, it's criminal, whatever's going on, but routine criminal, surely, not chief constable criminal.'

'I can't disagree, Eddie. Fascinating, isn't it?'

'For you, maybe. I could do without it.'

'Well, you're in the clear, we both know that, so don't worry about it.'

'Will you be there?'

'Yes. I'll meet you in the car park and take you up to the chairman's box.'

'What time?'

'Quarter to, for nine?'

'Okay. Listen, was Stevedore laid today on the exchanges?'

'Yes, but don't mention it to anyone.'

'How much did they get?'

'Seventy-eight grand.'

'They could have doubled that, maybe tripled it by stopping the favourite.'

'Indeed.'

'Mac, that was a loaded "indeed". It was one of your "don't I know it indeeds". Are you sure I won't need a lawyer tomorrow?'

'All you'll need is a pleasant smile and a well restrained temper.'

'Should I wear a cap, too, so I can doff it, then stare at my shoes?'

'Now don't start winding yourself up! I'm ending this call now. I think I make you worse at times like these.'

'Mac!'

'Good night, Eddie.'

31

I only had one ride booked at Aintree on this Friday, and nine o'clock was way too early to be arriving for it. But it was a fine morning, mistless, and promising warmth, and the drive through the valleys of the Lake District then south on a quiet M6 had been pleasant.

My dealings with the police had seldom been peaceful. Most cops I met had already judged me, based on the time I'd spent in prison many years ago for beating up the man who'd cost me my riding licence and a career at the top.

In the early days, I'd been angrily anxious to explain to the police that my assault on Kruger was justified. But, when the tenth pair of eyes glazed over, I gave it up.

Mac met me in the car park. I knew how anxious he was when I saw that he was already out of his car and on his big flat feet when I drove in. Mac preferred sitting. I'd never known him to wait standing up.

I took my kitbag from the back seat as he walked toward me. He called, 'Just leave that, Eddie. You'll have plenty time to come back for it.'

I left it, and locked up, and we walked toward the grandstands. Mac said, 'I've been thinking about this, it's probably just box-ticking. Grand National meeting, plenty of press attention, an unusual betting fraud takes place on Chief Constable Bradley's patch, and he wants to be seen to be taking it seriously. So long as he can make the claim that he's spoken personally to the jockey who's been most affected by these incidents, then he'll be happy with that.'

'What about the trainer most affected?'

'Well, I suppose they'll take a view on that after they've spoken to you.'

I stopped. Mac took two more strides before he turned, 'What is it?'

'I'm not having it, Mac.'

He looked at his watch. 'Not having what, Eddie? For God's sake it's ten to bloody nine!'

'Dil Grant's horses were involved in these 'incidents', as you call them. I just happened to be riding them. The horses were got at, not me. The horses are trained by Dil, not by me.'

'Eddie, it's just a bloody PR exercise! Come on!'

'It's a PR exercise until a reporter asks if Dil has been interviewed. Then it becomes a witch hunt. And the silhouette on the broomstick against the moon bears a striking resemblance to me.'

Mac's eyes were bugging. He looked at his watch then inclined his wrist toward my face, 'Look at the time!'

'It's upside down.'

He grabbed my arm and dragged me, 'Eddie, you owe me so many favours you won't live long enough to repay them. Now, please, for God's sake, just let me deliver you on time!'

I stumbled forward, 'Deliver me? Well, that says it all, Mac, that says it all.'

But, he was right. I owed him plenty. And he was my friend.

Nigel Steel was a recent appointment by the BHA. I hadn't met him before, but had heard he was a decent but careful man who tried to get on with everyone. He rose as we entered, and came forward, smiling, hand out, 'Mister McCarthy, nice to see you. And so good to meet you at last, Mister Malloy. I've watched you ride a number of times, and just never have found the time so far to come and say hello,' he clasped my hand 'so kind of you to leave home early to accommodate us.'

I was charmed. 'My pleasure, Mister Steel.' He walked with us to the table which lay in a wedge of sunlight from the east-facing window. The chief constable, in full uniform, stood to be introduced.

Steel said, 'This is Chief Constable Bradley of the Merseyside police.' Bradley didn't beam quite so much as Steel had, but seemed pleasant enough.

Steel poured coffee for everyone, then settled down to business.

'May I call you Eddie?' he said.

'Feel free.'

'I know this is most unusual. Mister McCarthy's department would almost always deal with these matters exclusively, but Mister McCarthy himself wisely suggested that a meeting with you might well help us in presenting the most effective possible case to the public.'

I glanced at Mac, who shifted in his seat and smiled nervously. I said, 'Mister McCarthy's advice has always proved interesting.'

The chief constable said, 'You two know each other well?'

I looked at Mac, who said, 'Mister Malloy is a veteran of the weighing room, sir.'

I smiled. Steel asked me to tell the story of each of the three races 'in my own words'. Mac was watching my face and his eyes flared a warning not to reply 'who else's words would I use?' So I told the tale of the three races.

Chief Constable Bradley scribbled the occasional note in a leather-bound book.

Steel, looking serious, hands joined, leant forward and said to me, 'What's your take on it, Eddie?'

Five years back I would have lunged at the lure of such flattery, but I thought it would do more harm than good to offer my opinions on blimps and bullets and theories that no harm was meant to me or to the horses. I said, 'I'm as baffled as everyone else, Mister Steel.'

He nodded. The chief constable sat back in his chair and said, 'I understand you have something of a reputation when it comes to situations like these?'

I watched him. He stared at me. I'd heard too many of these slanted comments by senior police officers. We both knew he was baiting me without accusing directly.

'Situations?' I said. 'You'll have to explain what you mean, chief constable, just so I don't get the wrong end of the stick.'

He crossed his arms and eased himself lower in the chair, 'You've been in difficulties more than once and, from what I hear, you seem quite accomplished at resolving matters on your own.'

'Resolving matters? Are you accusing me of something here?'

From the corner of my eye. I saw Mac bend his neck to look to the heavens.

Bradley said, 'Not at all. Should I be?'

I glanced at Steel. He smiled, like a head teacher silently urging a student on. I said to Bradley, 'Look, racing starts at two o'clock. How long do you want to go round in circles?'

He said, 'Do you know a man by the name of Sydney Ember?'

'Never heard of him. Ember as in burning ember?'

'E-M-B-E-R.'

'Don't know him.'

'He's a very successful gambler according to all the records he shows the police when we ask how he can afford a Cheshire mansion and half a dozen cars.'

'Well, there you go, what would I be doing knowing a big time gambler? Even if I did know him, I'd give him a wide berth.'

'Why?' He was easing into interrogation mode now.

I said, 'Because any jockey that ever got into trouble with the BHA did so through knowing gamblers.'

'A bit like you and your old friend Mister Kruger?'

He was trying to bait me into a temper. I said, 'That was more than fifteen years ago. And Kruger was a doper. And I didn't know him at first. I was a silly kid who got taken in too easily by Kruger's so-called friends. Also, as Mister McCarthy can tell you, Kruger later admitted I'd had nothing to do with either doping or gambling.'

Bradley watched me, trying to outstare me. I held his gaze calmly until he spoke, 'Do you think you might know Sydney Ember without knowing his name?' He opened his notebook and took out a brown envelope. He handed me a six-by-four portrait shot of a man who looked to be in his late fifties. He was smiling, showing teeth which had been bought at some expense and his smile was exaggerated as though he wanted to show off every bright tooth right down to the gum. I said, 'Looks like he's in a gurning contest,' and handed back the picture.

Bradley said, 'Ever seen him on the racecourse?'

'Not that I can remember.'

'Are there people you see often enough on the course to know them without knowing their names?'

'Plenty,' I said.

'So, wouldn't you expect to know a man who says he's made his living from betting for many years?'

I sighed and leant forward, 'Why would I not tell you if I did happen to know this guy, Ember? Why would I lie?'

'I'm just trying to work through logical progression, Mister Malloy. You're on the racetrack most days of the week and have been for a long time. So is Sydney Ember.'

'Well, maybe it's Sydney Ember who is lying and not me.'

'We've seen the accounts from the on-course bookmakers he uses.'

'Look, I don't know the man. What's the problem here? Has Ember been betting in these races where the horses have bolted?'

'We haven't asked him that yet.'

'Perhaps you should, then.'

'And give him early warning?' Bradley said.

I said, 'Listen, I'm always happy to help the police and the BHA, but I can't find you a link to something just to suit your theories, no matter how long you want to sit here. I don't mean to be rude, chief constable, but at what point are you going to stop asking if I know this guy?'

'What I'm asking now is that you make yourself aware of him.'

'I'm aware. More than aware. What do you want me to do, call you if I see him?'

'Well, as we touched on a few minutes ago, I believe you often find your own ways of resolving problems like this. If you happen to run into Mister Ember during your own…inquiries into these horses, maybe you could bear in mind that we'd very much like to finally get some evidence to convict Ember.'

'Of what?'

'Organized crime. He is a very smart operator who not only has avoided getting his hands dirty, there's not even a speck under one of his fingernails.'

I said, 'As clean as his teeth, then? Listen, if I come across the guy, I'll remember what you said.'

'I'm glad to hear that. Ember's a dangerous man and a very clever man, who's made millions over the past thirty years, all of it, he says, from betting. He's based in the north, but travels around the country to racetracks and betting shops. He maintains immaculate records that all stand up to investigation, but I know he's a criminal, and he knows I know he's a criminal.'

He was becoming agitated. I said, 'Now that I've seen his picture, I'll look out for him.'

'I believe there's a strong likelihood he will approach you to see if he can get in on this racing scam, probably through a third party.'

I watched him. He held my gaze. I said, 'And that's the real reason you wanted to see me, isn't it?' I looked at Steel, but his bland smile didn't change. I said, 'What was this supposed to be, some kind of early plea bargaining? A deal in advance on the assumption I do know something about this scam?'

Bradley said, 'It was planned as a courtesy meeting, to alert you to the danger.'

'Courtesy my arse.'

From the corner of my eye, I saw Mac's head go down. Bradley said, 'Believe what you want. My main concern is that if Ember is involved, or becomes involved in this, that you do not try to deal with him yourself. That would be dangerous for you, and damaging to…to the police.'

'To you,' I said, 'you were about to say that and you stopped yourself.' He remained silent. I said, 'Well, at least you didn't deny it.'

Steel said, 'Well, I think we've all made our positions clear, gentlemen. It's always been BHA policy to cooperate, indeed to give every assistance possible to the police. We know that everyone we licence, especially jockeys and trainers will be keen to support that policy to the utmost in this fight for integrity in the sport.'

I said, 'Well, talking of trainers, I'd have said it was as much Mister Grant's fight as mine, if you want to put it like that.'

Bradley looked at Steel, who said, 'Dil Grant trains the horses Mister Malloy told us about.'

'So why do you say it's Mister Grant's fight too?' Bradley asked.

'He trains them. I just ride them. If they get beat, I'm never happy, but it doesn't affect my livelihood, or, at least, not much.'

'Whereas?' he asked.

'Whereas, Mister Grant looks after those horses round the clock. He knows them inside out. His job, his whole business depends on people trusting his skills as a trainer, and the security at his yard...not that I'm casting any doubt on that. Dil's a friend of mine. But I'd say that as far as this goes, he's the organ grinder, and you're currently talking to the monkey.'

Bradley looked at Steel and Steel turned to look at Mac, who didn't seem to know where to look. I said, 'This is like watching some kind of mental pass the parcel, only it's actually pass the buck.'

Steel got up, smiling once more, and holding out his hand, 'Mister Malloy, I really can't thank you enough for taking the time out from your busy schedule.'

I rose and shook his hand, 'Not at all.' I moved sideways as the policeman got up and I reached for his hand, 'Nice meeting you, chief constable.'

'Indeed,' he said.

I raised a hand toward Mac. He nodded, stern but seemingly relieved I hadn't blown completely.

I left the door to its soft, slow closing and moved silently across thick carpet toward the staircase, frustrated that I hadn't avoided digging myself deeper into this shit.

I was convinced nobody meant me harm, and I'd gone in there intending to stay out of other people's battles. That's why I'd pitched

Dil into it. But Bradley seemed to want me in there fighting on his behalf, a refreshing change, I suppose. Most cops usually warned me off carrying out my own "inquiries" as Bradley had put it.

Downstairs, on the next level, I caught sight of the bookies' 'ring', the bear pit they all worked from, and it set me wondering why I'd never noticed this Sydney Ember. I knew a few professional punters. In fact, I was confident I knew all of them who'd been at it more than four or five years, because most didn't last that long.

It sounded like Mister Ember had found a very effective method of laundering money. If he was the sharp criminal Bradley had painted, he'd have no problem setting up a handful of bank accounts to use on the betting exchanges. Was it him who'd collected the big money on Spalpeen at Cheltenham?

Maybe it was time to start asking a few questions of my own about Sydney Ember.

32

My one ride, in the third race, was for Ben Tylutki. The horse was unbeaten in two runs at small racecourses, and he was stepping up in grade, big time. That's when you find out what a horse is made of. Competing against the best exposes all hopes and dreams and lays your investment bare on the green track. Come the end of the race, owner and trainer either have a potential champ to take home, or a headful of shattered plans.

This horse was a lovely compact bay named Indamelia. He managed to stay with the others at a fierce pace, and was just beginning to weaken when the even money favourite scorched past in that flat-out run of terror. My mind went back to this morning's meeting, and I took mental refuge in the fact that here was one I wasn't riding. Then it dawned, that, riding them or not, these runaways were happening only in races I rode in.

Like Stevedore had done, this favourite ran out two hurdles from home, and, thus disqualified, he slowed and was pulled up. I glanced across as we passed him. Tim Jacobs, his jockey, looked at me and shook his head.

Was he disgusted at me or the horse?

The jockeys' changing room, especially the one at Aintree, had seen pretty much everything, but when I walked in with my kit, all eyes seemed to be on me. Gary Conlon said, 'This is getting crazy. What the fuck is going on?'

Riled, I stopped in front of him, 'You asking me?'

'No. I'm just saying, right? This is fucking madness!'

'It is madness. But it's everybody's madness. It's not mine!'

Bomber walked over and put a hand on my shoulder, 'Take it easy, Eddie, nobody's blaming you.'

I sighed and threw my saddle onto the bench, and reached to touch Gary's arm, 'I'm sorry,' I said.

'Don't worry about it. It must be driving you twice as mad as the rest of us. Don't you know anything? You're not exactly the man who ducks out of shit like this.'

'Gary, your guess is as good as mine. I just realized back there that it's only happened in races I've been riding in, and it's not just happening to me. If there's a connection, I'm fucked if I know what it is.'

Bomber said, 'What's McCarthy saying about it?'

'Oh, they know less than we do, as usual.'

I wondered briefly if the news had leaked that I'd been interviewed earlier by the high ups. If it had, no-one would raise it now, not after I'd blown a gasket with Gary.

'What about Grant?' Colin Parker asked, 'most of the horses have been his.'

'Two haven't,' I said, 'counting today, three of the five have been Dil's, and he's no wiser than the rest of us.'

Heads were shaken, words were mumbled, feet were shuffled and the changing room morphed softly back into its routine.

Normally I'd have stayed around in the hope of picking up a spare in one of the remaining races, but I was sick of everything. This morning I'd congratulated myself on avoiding any possibility of being drawn into this. Even beforehand, I'd shied away by persuading Vita to employ Ben, and by nudging Ben into taking it on.

All we'd learned was that Jon Vogel didn't like women or democracy. And the only place my ducking and diving had led me was down an ever-narrowing alleyway. And I hadn't the faintest idea of how to find my way back to daylight.

I took my phone from the car's glovebox. A text from Mac told me not to leave the track without speaking to him. I called him…'Eddie? Where are you?'

'In the car. I'm going home.'

'Can you put up with a lodger for the night?'

'Sure…of course. Has something happened? They haven't sacked you, have they?'

'Not yet. And only because it would have taken too much explaining to the mob in the media tent.'

'Shit…that's bad news, Mac. Where are you now?'

'Up at the stables. I can't leave until racing is finished, so you go on home, and I'll see you tonight.'

'I'll have a glass filled and waiting for you.'

'Thanks. And if you get any calls from the press, don't answer, not until we've spoken.'

'Why?'

'Eddie, just leave it until later, will you? It's best kept off the airwaves.'

'Okay.' I hung up and sighed and headed for home.

33

In the Snug, standing by the fire, Mac drank the cognac in two swallows, then wriggled out of his coat.

'That bad?' I said.

He ran his fingers through his thick, greying hair and sat heavily in the big chair, and looked at me. I said, 'They wanted to stand me down, didn't they?'

'Worse than that.'

I waited. Mac liked to try and build suspense. He just kept watching me. I said, 'Mac, it doesn't get worse than that as far as I'm concerned.'

'Oh, it does...Bradley wanted to put a phone tap on your mobile, after getting your past records.'

I sat forward, 'He's got my phone records?'

'No, he wanted to get hold of your past records, then put a phone tap on you.'

'Why?'

'Because he doesn't believe what you said. He's convinced you must know this Sydney Ember.'

I sat back and stared at the ceiling. Mac said, 'I persuaded them that it would be a very very bad idea.'

'Who took most persuading?'

'Bradley.'

'How do these guys get to the top positions, tell me? How much plainer could it be that I was innocent back when I was warned off. Did you tell him it was you who actually found Kruger's confession?'

'As a matter of fact I did.'

'But it obviously wasn't enough.'

'I had to tell them that if they tapped your phone you would cause the biggest shitstorm they've ever seen. Steel said, "But how would he find out?" and I said, "Because I would tell him."'

Mac paused for effect, as he was well entitled to do. I said, 'Mac, I don't quite know what to say to you. That could cost you your job.'

'It doesn't matter, Eddie. You and me go back a lot further than any of them, now.'

I got up and walked the three steps to where he sat and slowly offered my hand. He took it. Neither of us spoke.

I went to the kitchen to get some alcohol.

Mac nodded a yes to the cognac and I poured, then sat back and sipped whiskey. I said, 'Before I got your message in the car, I'd decided it was time to get more involved in this. I'll see Ben at Aintree tomorrow, he's been invited by Monty Bearak. I'd been thinking of sitting down with him and trying to figure something out...split the workload somehow.'

'Eddie, if you do that now, Steel will believe there was some merit in Bradley's suggestion.'

'He obviously thought there was, anyway, or he wouldn't have let him put it to you. Did they try to get you to promise not to tell me about it?'

'They tried.'

'And you said no?'

He nodded, then sipped his drink.

'And Steel didn't threaten you?'

'No. He hadn't thought it through. The last thing they expected was for me to go against them. They had no plan B.'

'Well, they might be developing one now, so you'd better watch your back.'

'Eddie, I don't care anymore. I'm tired of the years and years of politics and bullshit. When Jean died, I began wondering what it was all about. I used to come home and moan to her about work, about office politics and she tried to be sympathetic, but I always felt there was some unspoken disappointment about the compromises I was making.' His eye twitched and he looked away through the window then raised his glass again.

I said, 'No point torturing yourself, Mac. We all do what we think is best at the time. None of us ever gets it dead right.'

He nodded, still looking into the distance. I said, 'You thinking of quitting?'

He smiled and half laughed, 'I'm thinking of taking a leaf from your book and causing havoc.'

'You've made a good start.'

He laughed. I said, 'Don't bugger up your pension, old fella.'

'Hmm, I suppose it is late in the day.'

'I need you as an inside man, anyway.'

He watched me for a while then said, 'You used to frustrate the hell out of me, but I always admired you...always.'

'Now, Mac, I could have said that exact line. Listen, you're tired, take it easy and don't go all soft on me. It makes me uneasy when you're not, what's the word you use, curmudgeonly?'

His smile widened, 'I don't think I've ever heard you string so many syllables together.'

'You won't have. Not without a swear word fitted in somewhere.'

He raised his glass, 'Here's to curmudgeons.'

I toasted that. Mac finished his drink and said, 'Do you think there is a way for you to get involved, to muck in with Ben Searcey on this? I could help, too.'

'Let me talk to Ben tomorrow, and see where he is with it. In fact...' I reached for my phone and found Ben's number.

Ben answered on the first ring, 'Eddie! I was going to call you, but I guessed you'd have enough to do after today.'

'You guessed right, Ben. Could you use an apprentice?'

'I could certainly use an extra pair of everything, ears, arms, legs. What are you thinking?'

'I'm thinking I shouldn't have fobbed you off with this. I'm thinking I ought to carry my share of the weight.'

'And I'm thinking you might be timing things just right.'

'Go on?'

'Well…I'd rather hold until tomorrow. I just need to do a bit more cross-checking.'

'You onto something?'

I saw Mac perk up, and I smiled.

'I could be. Just might be. But I don't want to build up any hopes, so don't mention anything to Vita for now, or to Dil, will you?'

'I can't mention anything, Ben, you haven't told me!'

'I know, I know. Just want a double-check on my sources. It's my old training kicking in.'

'You have sources?'

'Well, resources, if I'm honest. An educated hunch beginning to gather some credibility through research, nothing more. We won't be solving anything tomorrow, but we might just have a break.'

'In the shape of?'

'In the shape of a hunch, Eddie. You know what a hunch looks like, don't you?'

I laughed, and Ben echoed it back at me. 'Okay', I said, 'see you tomorrow. Alice all set?'

'She is. Handbags and gladrags.'

'Binoculars?'

'Pretty useless for the National. All you see is horses' arses for most of it.'

'True, and not just the animal kind. I'll come up to Monty's box as soon as I get there.'

'Oh, you're the resident tipster, aren't you? I forgot.'

'You'll want to forget after I've tipped them, that's for sure.'

He laughed, 'See you tomorrow. By the way, Alice is still asking if Prim will be there?'

'I'll be speaking to Dil shortly. I'll find out. But I wouldn't hold my breath if I was Alice. How's she been?'

'Tigerish, as ever. Has me following DJ's old mates in and out of the bookies, still trying to get her evidence.'

'As if you didn't have enough to do.'

'I've a feeling things are finally turning our way, Eddie. watch this space!'

'See you tomorrow, Ben.'

'You will. I'll be whistling Dixie for ol' Mizzy Vita.'

'Ha! Goodnight.'

'Goodnight.'

'Good news?' Mac asked, as I put the phone on the table.

'Put it this way, it's the most positive I've heard Ben since the old days.'

'No clue as to what he's picked up?'

'I don't think it's groundbreaking, Mac, but it sounds like a lead, something to latch onto properly.'

'By God, I hope so,' he picked up his glass, frowned when he saw it was empty, but raised it anyway, 'To leads!'

I returned the salute. Ben's confidence had been a real boost, and I reached for my phone again and found Dil's number.

34

Mave's sharp elbow jabbed me out of a dream so vivid I was unsure if I was truly awake. 'Mave?'

'Your phone is ringing.'

'My phone?'

'Your phone.'

'Oh…where?'

'Sounds like it's in the kitchen.'

I rolled out of bed, 'What time is it?'

'It's after one.'

'Jeez…who…' My phone was on the kitchen table, silent. I picked it up and did not recognize the number on the missed call message. Then it rang again.

'Eddie?'

'Who's this?'

'Eddie, it's Prim. At Dil's place.'

'Prim, hello. What's wrong?'

'Alice just called me, Alice Searcey, she thinks something's happened to her dad.'

'To Ben? I spoke to him earlier. He was fine.'

'He hasn't come home. His phone is ringing out. He left no message. He's never done this before.'

I finally woke up properly. 'Did Alice leave a number?'

She gave me the number and asked me to call back after I'd

spoken to Alice.

Alice answered on the first ring, 'Alice, it's Eddie, Eddie Malloy.'

'Something's happened to my dad!'

'What? What's happened?'

'I don't know! I just know something's wrong. I know it. He hasn't come home. He's hurt somewhere. I know it!'

'Look, Alice, listen, when did you last see him?'

'He was here, at home when I went out this afternoon. He'd never stay out without calling me.'

'I spoke to him. This evening. About seven, I'd say. He was in good form. He sounded great.'

'Eddie, Listen! Listen! Listen! Something's happened to him! Please believe me!'

'Okay. All right. Are you on your own?'

'Yes!'

'At home?'

'Yes, at home!'

'Do you think you're in any danger?'

'I don't give a shit about being in danger, I just need to find my dad!'

'Have you called the police?'

'No! You know they won't do anything! I called Prim, that was the only number I had of anybody I trusted. I didn't have your number.'

'That's okay. Listen, I'll get ready and drive to your place. I just need fifteen minutes to get dressed and get my gear.'

'Can you call that fella, the one that helped us with DJ, the bodyguard guy?'

'I haven't got his number, Alice.'

'Can you get it?'

'I'll see. Maybe. Look, let me get ready and drive down there. Don't open the door to anyone, okay? Lock it. Now. I'll call when I'm outside your house. What's your address?'

She gave me it. I memorized the postcode for the satnav, and turned to go back to the bedroom. Mave was behind me. 'Shit! You scared me then!'

'Sorry. What's wrong with Ben?'

'He didn't come home. Alice thinks he's in trouble.'

'What kind of trouble?'

'Harm kind of trouble.'

Mave followed me to the bathroom, 'What do you think?'

'I don't know. She's frantic.' I brushed my teeth.

'Booze?'

I shook my head.

Mave raised a doubting eyebrow. I spat into the cold stream from the tap, wiped my mouth and said, 'Ben would sooner kill himself than drink again.'

'What are you going to do?'

'I'm going to make sure Alice is okay. If half of Ben's stories about Deadwood are true, it's not somewhere to leave a kid at night.'

'I'll come with you.'

'I wish you could, but I don't want to leave Mac to wake up with nobody here.'

'Why don't you wake him now?'

'He's not long gone to bed. Anyway, he'll just try to nag me into calling the cops. Why don't you travel to Aintree with Mac and I'll see you there?'

'Of course. Sure. Should I pack an overnight bag for us?'

'It'll do no harm.'

We went to the bedroom, and I dressed and began checking my kitbag. Mave said, 'Leave that, Eddie. I'll do it and bring it with me later.'

'Thanks,' I kissed her and felt in my pocket for my car keys. Then I remembered Prim and scrolled back for her number and told her what I was doing.

'Call me as soon as there's any news,' she said.

'Can you come to Aintree, Prim? Alice thinks a lot of you.'

'I...I don't think Dil wants me to.'

'Fuck Dil. Tell him you're the guest of Monty Bearak, and that you'll be in his box looking after Alice Searcey, and that I said so.'

'Okay.'

'Do it, Prim!'

'I'll do it! I'll do it! I promise!'

'Good. I'll tell Alice.'

'Call me when you get there, just to let me know she's all right.'

'I'll try to remember,' I said, going out the door, waving to Maven.

'I'll call you, then.' Prim said.

'Fine. Do that.'

I got in the car and drove hard and fast into the deep darkness.

35

My invisible companion, confidently guiding me from the satnav speakers, would have changed her bright tone had she seen where her "now, turn left" command had taken me. This was Deadwood, marked at its border with a row of broken street-lamps and graffiti-covered gable ends.

I slowed, watching for the next turn. From a house on the right, music blared. I glanced through the dimly lit, uncurtained window and saw dancers moving, and cigarette ends glowing. It was almost 3.a.m.

Outside the Searcey house, I stopped and switched off the lights, reaching for my phone as I looked around.

In the long terraces, a few windows showed light. Toward the bend in the crescent, a hundred yards away, two youths walked, their brash swagger marking their age and their vulnerability.

She answered on the first ring. 'Alice. I'm outside.'

'Hold on.'

I watched the three windows on the house front and saw her peek from the curtain edge of the wider upstairs one.

Thirty seconds later she was unlatching the security chain. I went in. She'd been crying. Her fair hair was untidy and damp and pressed against her temple.

I felt like hugging her, but I was still too much of a stranger to risk her being comfortable with that. She led me into a small, warm living room where a lamp glowed in one corner, and a TV screen, wide and black, dominated the opposite corner. Two rugs sat neatly on a laminate floor. A gas fire burned low, only the central column glowing, an armchair and two-seater dark sofa angled toward it.

'No word?' I said.

She shook her head, staring at me, wide-eyed. I took three steps toward her and put my hands on her shoulders, 'I'll fix this, for you, Alice. I promise.'

'How?'

'I don't know, yet, but I'll fix it. This is what I do. Outside of riding horses, this is what I do. I'm good at it. Okay?'

Her shoulders were high, making her neck look just half its normal length. The tension in her seemed to be keeping her upright. She just watched me. 'Okay?' I repeated.

She nodded, then said, 'Did you get that fella's number?'

Bruno.

I'd forgotten, and I realized what I'd just said had washed right over her. She didn't want a jockey promising he'd fix things, and find her father. She wanted a proper hard man.

I said, 'I'll speak to Sir Monty tomorrow, and if I think Bruno can help, I'll get him on our side. But you need to believe what I'm telling you, for your own sake. I do stuff like this. I find people. I deal with problems. I've been offered jobs in the past, jobs just doing this, finding people, fixing problems that the police can't, that other people, even people like Bruno can't. Understand?'

She nodded, more slowly this time, looking at me with deeper concentration. I said, 'If you want me to, I'll tell you the details of all the jobs I've done that are like this.'

Fear was coming back into her face. She said, 'Like what? Do you know what's happened to my Dad? How do you know it's going to be like the other things you've done?'

I moved my hands down onto her upper arms and squeezed, 'I don't know anything about what's happened, Alice, that's not what I meant. I just wanted to reassure you that if something has gone wrong, I'll fix it. I'll find him. Listen, he could walk back through that door anytime, and I believe that's probably what he'll do. But if I need to go looking, then I'll find him. Okay?'

'Okay. Should we go out now and start looking?'

'No. We should sit down and you should tell me everything about what he's been doing lately, especially with DJ's people.'

'Then what?'

'Then, I'm going to ask Mave to help us track his phone activity. Mave's good too. She's helped with some of that other stuff I mentioned.'

'She could start now, then, couldn't she? What does she do, work for a mobile company, or something?'

'Better than that. She's a genius. A walking talking genius.' I took out my phone. Alice was right. Mave could have been working on this. So much for all my boasting. I brought up Mave's number, and asked Alice to write Ben's down. I told Mave I'd arrived safe and asked her to let Prim know. 'Will do. How's Alice?'

'Alice is fine. I've promised her we're going to find her Dad, so Alice is fine.'

'Good.'

'Can you get into the system of his phone supplier and track his activity?'

'Er, yes, but I don't know how long it'll take. I haven't done anything like this for a while. They'll have upgraded their security.'

'Can you start now?'

'Of course. Give me the number.'

When I ended the call, I told Alice that Mave was as confident as I was about finding her father, and steadily, I could see Alice begin to unwind.

'Now let's sit down and try and work out where he might be,' I said. Alice told me of the trailing work Ben had mentioned, from betting shop to betting shop, watching these guys put large amounts of cash into Fixed Odds Betting Terminals then taking most of it back out, suitably "laundered", ten minutes later.

The more she talked, the more confident she grew that this was the line to take.

I wasn't so sure that it was the DJ stuff behind Ben's disappearance. He'd been tracking these bookie boys for weeks, but had disappeared soon after telling me he had a lead on the wild horses side.

Alice was still talking, working her way through the different players in DJ's girl-running scheme, describing each in detail and giving me their backstory, when Mave rang, 'Eddie, I've found Ben's phone. Well, its location. It's still live and pinging the closest masts.'

'Where?'

Alice stared unblinking at me. Mave said, 'Weirdly, it's west of mast BLU831, the BLU standing for Blundellsands.'

'Why weirdly?'

'According to the system map, that mast is on a building right against the sea wall at Crosby.'

'So, all that's west of it...' I tailed off as I realized Alice was obviously hanging on everything we talked about. Mave said, 'Yep, all that's west of that mast is the sea, and maybe fifty metres of beach at low tide, which it is just now.'

'If we drive there, could you pinpoint my phone in relation to Ben's?'

'Yes.'

'Okay. I'll call you when we're parked.'

Alice said nothing. She just reached involuntarily and clasped my forearm. I said, 'Crosby isn't far, is it?'

'Has she found him?'

'She's found his phone.'

Alice got up, 'Crosby's only about twenty minutes! Come on. Dad liked Crosby. Used to take me there when I was a kid.'

When I was a kid

I couldn't picture a time when she had been any more childlike than she was now; eyes beaming, gripping and pulling at the sleeves of her denim jacket, elated at the promise of something special.

She ran down the path to the car.

36

We drove through the suburbs of Crosby until we reached the long sea wall. Mave had been tracking my phone as I spoke to her. She guided us to a parking spot closest to the straight line west she had pinpointed.

We got out. The wind off the sea blew Alice's hair above head height, but she didn't reach to smooth it or hold it down, 'Which way?' she said.

We had driven past a flight of stairs leading to the beach. I pointed back toward it. Alice, hands in pockets, jogged and I quickened my step, still talking to Mave, 'It's black-dark out there, but I can't hear any waves.'

'Tide's out, remember' she said, 'I checked the tables. You'll be safe to walk. Wet and splodgy maybe, but safe.'

Alice looked up at me as I took the last few stairs and stepped onto dry sand. 'How far do you reckon?' I asked Mave.

'Hard to say. Start walking, and keep moving. This'll play catch up. It's not quite a GPS, but it should make sure you're on the line to cross where Ben's phone is.'

'Hold on,' I said and I called for Alice to come back and stay beside me, 'we're going the right way. A few minutes, but I don't want you getting out of my sight in the dark.'

She nodded, but wouldn't come right alongside, staying a step ahead, putting her hand to her forehead as though it were bright sunlight she faced. I knew what she was trying to do, the streetlamps on the prom were leaking enough yellow light to stop our eyes from adjusting fully to the darkness.

'Keep going,' Mave said.

And we walked toward the sea, though I could neither hear nor see it.

Then I saw a man.

Big. Upright, ahead of me.

I put a hand out, pulling Alice back. She turned. I pointed. She shook her head, 'Those are statues. It's art. There are quite a few of them scattered along the beach. Been here for years.'

My memory dredged up an old news article about a sculptor, Antony somebody. I told Mave.

'Antony Gormley,' she said, 'sorry, I should have told you to expect those.'

'No worries.'

We walked on, over wet ridges and through troughs of tidewater. The farther we got from the sea wall, the better my eyes coped.

'You should be close, now,' Mave said.

I told Alice. She called out, 'Dad! Dad!'

Something in me wanted to silence her, but that was senseless.

'Is she okay?' Mave asked.

'On the edge...I think she's hoping he's drunk, and he's passed out here somewhere.'

'I didn't think I'd be saying this, but that would probably be a blessing.'

'I know what you mean.'

'Go right a bit, Eddie.'

Alice was almost gone from sight, still calling for her father. 'How much is a bit, Mave? It's pitch dark.'

'If you see it as walking now toward twelve on a clock face, go off toward ten past.'

'Okay.'

A few silent moments, then she said, 'That's it, that's the line. You're very, very close.'

'There's another statue about ten yards ahead.'

'Keep going.'

I reached the statue, 'Fuck,' I said.

'What is it?' Mave asked.

'Ben's jacket is on the statue. Looks like his trousers are tied to it.'

'Jeez! Where's Alice?'

'She's out of sight, off to my left.'

'Check the jacket pockets.'

'I am…his shoes are on the ground on top of what looks like his underwear.'

'Oh, no,' Mave said quietly.

'The phone's here, Mave. In his inside pocket.'

'Anything else?'

I moved to the northern side. 'I can smell whiskey…there's something in the big jacket pocket…a bottle…a half bottle…empty.'

'I'm sorry, Eddie.'

'I'm not buying this, Mave, no way. It's not even Ben's style. If he was going to kill himself, he'd do it quietly. The only thing that stinks higher than the whiskey is this set up.'

'I hope you're right.'

'Go to be…got to be.'

'Who do you think?'

'I don't know. Whoever Ben had picked up on with the horses, I'd think.'

'What about this DJ guy?'

'Ben got him warned off, didn't he? He's gone.'

'Maybe he's back.'

'No way. From what I've heard, this wouldn't be the kid's style. He's got a single cell brain. And he'd be too scared of Bruno Guta.'

'What are you going to tell Alice?'

I sighed, long and heavy and reached stupidly to lean on the cold metal arm of the statue, covered with Ben's jacket, 'I don't know, Mave.'

'I'd best let you find her. Call me when you've decided what we're doing. Do you want me to tell Mac what's happened?'

'Yes. But tell him to speak to no one until he's spoken to me. Try and get to Aintree for eight. We've got a lot of sorting out to do before racing.'

'I will. Good luck.'

'Thanks, Mave.'

I stood with my phone in one hand, and Ben's in the other, and I heard Alice call again for her Dad, her voice carrying on the southwest wind.

'Alice! Over here!' I shouted, and swallowed the lump in my throat.

37

Two hours later, Alice and I were still waiting for the police. We took turns in the car, out of the wind. Her shock had long ago turned to anger, then, through half a dozen calls to Merseyside police, into rage.

I had twice talked her out of removing her father's clothing from the statue. I didn't think Ben had committed suicide, but there was a chance he'd been murdered, and I knew enough by now about the importance of Scene of Crime Officers, and not disturbing anything. Trouble was, I couldn't tell Alice the reason I was holding out. I'd spent most of the first hour trying to convince her that he wasn't dead.

I walked the beach, trying to stay warm. Each time I moved downwind of the statue, the smell of whiskey was strong, and I knew it must have soaked into the fabric of the jacket.

It was still dark, but I could hear the tide coming in. If the cops didn't turn up soon, the crime scene would be under the Irish Sea.

I saw Alice marching toward me out of the gloom, powering forward, head down.

'What is it?' I asked, as she stopped in front of me.

'I just spoke to a knobhead sergeant who said they had more to do with their time than run around after alcoholics who got lost after a beach party!'

'Did you get his name?'

'I hung up on him. I said "fuck this" and hung up on him!'

158

I almost smiled. Alice came past me and unbuttoned her Dad's jacket, 'Come on,' she said, 'we'll find him ourselves'.

Driving back to Deadwood, I asked Alice what she wanted to do about the invitation to Monty Bearak's box for the Grand National.

'I want to go. I want to ask that Bruno fella to help. I know you'll help me, but I think he'll want to as well, once he knows.'

That solved one problem and created another. I had to be at Aintree for two rides, but I wasn't leaving Alice on her own. Monty would want a day of fun and relaxation for his guests. If Alice was going around the box the way she'd stormed the beach, people were going to have a day to remember.

'Okay,' I said, 'I'll make arrangements for Bruno to help. You won't need to ask. He'll be happy to, and Sir Monty will want to do all he can. But I think you should still come. Prim will be there.'

She folded her arms and nodded firmly. I said, 'I'll stay in the car while you get ready, and I'll make a few calls.'

When we got to the track, Mave and Prim were waiting by the weighing room, as arranged. Monty had told me he'd meet us in his box.

Prim and Mave hugged Alice, and she half-heartedly hugged back. Monty was the best tonic. He spent the first five minutes reassuring her that he was certain everything would work out, and that all his powers were at Alice's disposal.

She told him what the sergeant had said.

Monty said, 'I know the chief constable very well. That man will be dealt with.'

Alice seemed more pleased about this than anything else, that is until Monty called Bruno Guta over and said to him, 'Bruno, you know the situation with Alice's Dad, Ben, and I want you to make Alice your priority today. You're to be her shadow. Unless, of course, she expressly requires a female shadow in the shape of Prim or Mave!'

Bruno smiled. Alice blushed. I went to meet Mac in the stewards' room, where he'd persuaded the caterers to bring him hot toast and jam with a pot of tea. 'Would you like a cup?' he asked, as I sat down.

'No, thanks, Mac. I'm fine.'

'An eventful night, I hear?'

I told him what had happened. He said, 'I'll have to tell Steel.'

'Well, it'll give him something to think about, other than me.'

He nodded, and chewed, looking thoughtful, 'So close last night,' he said, 'when you spoke to Ben, I had high hopes he was onto something solid.'

'It looks very much like he was. Trouble is we'll now have to do all the things he did and try to find out what he found out.'

'You sound as though you're not confident about ever finding it out from Ben.'

'Not in the near future.'

'You fear the worst, then?'

'Not really, but it can only be one of two things. They've killed him or they've got him. If they were going to kill him, they'd just have done it. No need for pantomimes with beach statues.'

'So you think he's alive?'

'I think he's alive, and I think we're dealing with amateurs. They didn't want to hurt jockeys or horses, and they'd rather do some daft comical set up...they even poured whiskey on his jacket, for God's sake! It's straight out of an old Ealing Studios movie.'

Mac nodded and picked up another piece of toast, 'Catching them should be easy, then, eh?'

'Well, put it this way, it didn't take Ben long to discover a big enough clue to scare them into grabbing him. How long can it take us?'

'Very true. Very true. You're bolstering my confidence for my meeting with Mister Steel.'

'Good.' I got up. 'It's Saturday morning. It's spring. It's Grand National day. Anything can happen, Mac. Anything.'

38

By dusk, as we prepared to leave Aintree, a 100/1 chance had won the National, I had fallen at the last when still in contention in the Aintree Hurdle, and the BHA boss, Nigel Steel, seemed satisfied that the disappearance of Ben Searcey had given him some respite from the pressure: not a single horse had gone wild.

All in all, the planning, the early phone calls, the stewardship of Prim and Mave, had worked exactly as we'd hoped. Stage two was not going to be so easy.

We sat at the table in the corner of Monty's box, me, Mave, Prim and Alice. I said, 'We've got a room fixed up for you at the farm, until we find your Dad.'

Alice said, 'Thanks, but I'm staying in Deadwood. Dad might come home, and there's other stuff I need to be there for.'

I said, 'We can leave a message for your Dad. It's not safe for you to be there on your own.'

Her grey eyes hardened, a look I'd seen a few times now. She said, 'I'm not leaving Deadwood without Dad. And there are young girls there who still need my help.'

'The last thing your Dad would want is you living there on your own. And you can give the girls you're worried about your number. They can always call you. And DJ's gone, anyway, hasn't he?'

'He could come back anytime.'

'And if he does, you're alone in that house,' I said, conscious that

Mave and Prim had decided to stay quiet.

Alice said, 'He doesn't scare me.'

'I know, but that won't matter to him.'

'It will. If Bruno's looking after me, it'll matter to him all right.'

I watched her as she turned to glance at Monty, laughing with his guests at the table by the door. I said, 'Did Sir Monty say Bruno would stay with you all the time?'

'I'm going to ask him.'

'Is that fair?'

She stiffened, 'What do you mean?'

'You'll be asking Monty to release one of his best men for an unlimited period of time, just because you want to do what you want to do.'

'Then I won't bother.' Alice got up and lifted her small handbag from the table. I said, 'I'm not trying to upset you, Alice. I know that what you do is for other people. What I'm trying to say is that it's time to start thinking of yourself for a change. And of your Dad.'

'That's blackmail!'

I stood, 'It's reality. You don't owe your protection to every kid you meet. You owe it to your Dad to stay safe until we find him.'

'What about the girls in Deadwood who've never had a father, Eddie?' her voice was shaky, rage building again. I didn't know what to do and admitted as much by looking to Prim and to Mave.

Prim got up and reached to put an arm around Alice's shoulder, 'Come on, darling, let's go and get some fresh air.'

Alice drew away from her, sharply avoiding Prim's reach and frowning at her, 'I'm going home,' she said, and walked out.

We spent what seemed a long time debating what to do about Alice until Mave said, 'She's probably a better survivalist than us lot put together. How many children's homes has she been in? How many times did she run away to get back to Deadwood and do her duty?'

'Some duty,' I said.

Prim said, 'Sir Monty said he knew the chief constable. Wouldn't he help Alice?'

Mave said, 'He's the guy who thought Eddie was in on this scam. Anyway, he'd have to enforce the law, which means Alice would be back in a children's home. She can't live alone at her age.'

I looked at Prim, 'Maybe that's the answer,' I said.

Mave said, 'Eddie, you can't put the police onto her, she'd never forgive you.'

'I don't want her forgiveness. I just want her to be safe. That's what Ben would want, and if I hadn't left him to do everything, we probably wouldn't be in this position.'

Mave stifled her reply, and her look told me that this wasn't for debating in open company. I sighed heavily, and massaged my face, and we sat in silent gloom. Then, Prim stood up, 'Well, if the mountain won't come to Mohammed…'

We looked at her. Prim shrugged and said, 'I'll go and stay with Alice in this Deadwood place until, well, until we find out what's happened to her dad.'

I said, 'Prim, you need to see this place.'

She said, 'Eddie, you ought to see some of the places I've been.'

I got up, 'Staying here with her is just letting Alice have her way.'

Prim put her pink-nailed hands on the table, leaned across and said, 'You got a better idea?'

'Jeez!' I said, 'What about your work at the yard? What will Dil say?'

'Eddie, I don't care anymore what Dil says. Dil will say what Vita tells him to, like he always does.'

'And this will be a proper result for her, won't it, with you out of the way?' I said.

Prim said, 'Well, maybe that's just what Vita needs. She'll get to see Dil Grant for what he is, and there'll be no more games to play. She…' Prim raised a finger to her own lips, hushing herself, smiling.

'Believe me, Prim, this is not a good idea. If I-'

'Eddie…' It was Mave, with another one of her looks, the look that meant "Enough. Drop it."

'Okay,' I said, looking at Prim, 'What about your stuff? You're going to need to go home and pack a suitcase or something.'

Mave got up, 'I'll drive you and bring you back here,' she said to Prim.

I said, 'I'll drive to Deadwood and have one more go at talking Alice out of this.'

Prim said, 'Eddie, why don't you leave Alice to me, to us?' she glanced at Mave, 'Maybe you could concentrate on Ben. We'll take care of Alice.'

She seemed confident, reassuring. I looked around at the happy throng, the box still half full, Monty holding court at three tables pulled together…laughter rose, champagne flutes clinked, and bright lights shone on the rich and the lucky. Less than a mile to the west, Alice would be picking her way home through dark, narrow streets where the clink of glass came from dirty, broken bottles in the gutter.

39

I waited up, standing by the lamp in the window. Mave saw me as she closed the car door, and she raised a hand in a weary wave.

She came in, and dropped her bag by the sofa where she flopped then settled in her corner of it. I turned, resting my hip against the windowsill. We looked at each other. Mave slowly shook her head, 'I thought I'd been a maverick kid. Alice is a one-off. If a bunch of mavericks banded together, Alice would be the one who'd break away first, and run farthest.'

'I'm glad. I was beginning to think it was just me she had it in for.'

'Prim will get her eyes opened. She was full of plans on the drive to Deadwood. Then Alice laid down the law when we got there.'

'Which was?'

'Pretty much, "don't try to stop me doing what I'm going to do".'

'Did Prim stay?'

'She stayed. I don't know how long she'll last. She'd been confident she could persuade Alice to move in with her at Dil's place.'

'Did she see Dil?'

'She left him a note. Picked up her stuff and left a note on the desk.'

'I can almost hear Dil crying from here, Vita playing games at one end, now Prim playing him at the other.'

'I don't think she's doing that, Eddie. She really is concerned about Alice.'

I pushed away from the window and stood straight, 'Mave, sh obsessed with Dil. Look how she's let him treat her. She knows humiliation. She as good as admitted that to me.'

'Well, all she talked about was Alice and her dad.'

'It's a game. Believe me. I'm not saying she doesn't care Alice or Ben, but if Dil crooks his finger, Prim will come runn

Mave sighed, 'Oh, we'll see…we'll see,' she hung her elbows on her bony knees. I touched her hair, pulled it so from her eyes, 'Want a drink?' I said.

'Nah. No, thanks. I need to shut my brain down for a v Sleep.'

It was pointless asking if she wanted something to eat. Mave ha never uttered the word hungry in my hearing. 'Bed?'

She nodded, her hair falling again over her bowed face.

Lying flat, in the dark, she spoke, 'I've got a bad feeling abou this, Eddie.'

'Me too.'

'Do you think Ben is still alive?'

'The way I've stacked things up, yes, I do.'

'Do you think you've stacked things up right?'

I hesitated, 'I don't know.'

'What are you going to do?'

'I'm going to try and find out what Ben found out terday. That's what I think has got him into trouble.'

'You got any idea what it is?'

'None. Not a clue.'

She sighed. I reached for her hand below the covers and w nked fingers. I said, 'It'll work out.'

She squeezed my hand. I said, 'Once you've cranked t giant brain into gear, you'll slot every piece into place, and I'll just he out and collect the jigsaw.'

'You'd better take a big box. That's what bothers me. I time, with Bayley Watt, and Jimmy, and the others, it was kind o y…or easier. We knew they were dead. We knew it was one sour There weren't pieces scattered everywhere, like this. There was not to worry about. I know that sounds crazy, but you were never in any real danger.'

'I'm not in any danger here.'

'Yet.'

'All will be well.'

'That's your get out quote, which means "I've run out of logical things to say". Jeeez!' She sighed long and loud, 'life used to be simple. I lived by the sea and wrote computer code. I swam at midnight and slept all day.'

'Then you had the bright idea of going to Bangor races and climbing onto the roof of my car.'

She turned her head toward me, 'You know, that seems like a lifetime ago somehow.'

'Well, I suppose we've squeezed a lot in since then.'

'I was sure I'd thought of everything. I hadn't planned on you turning me into an everyday member of the human race. I was fine until that happened.'

'You were superwoman.'

'You were Kryptonite.'

'Is that your way of saying I'm your rock?'

I sensed her smiling. She said, 'Don't you ever get tired of all this?'

'All what?'

'All these scrapes. All this righting of wrongs.'

'Shit happens.'

'Yes, and most people walk away from it. You walk toward it.'

'Only when I think it needs cleaning up.'

She turned to me again, 'You know you're just another Alice? An older, male version? At least she's got the excuse of being a teenager. What's your excuse?'

'Pig headedness is about the best I can offer.'

'It's more than that, Eddie.'

'It is.'

She lay still and we were quiet for a while. She knew what drove me. She'd just been running through a routine because she was tired and maybe a bit regretful again at the loss of her solitude and her independence. She knew well what had lit that fuse in me as a boy, and she knew too that it would burn until the day I died.

'I'm sorry,' she said softly.

I squeezed her hand, 'Good night,' I said.

'We'll make a start in the morning,' she said.

'We will.'

40

Dawn was just breaking as we had breakfast, Mave nibbling at a thin slice of brown toast, when Monty Bearak rang.

'Monty, good morning.'

'Eddie, any news?'

'Nothing so far.'

'How is Alice?'

'She'll be okay. Prim is staying with her.'

'She went back home?'

'Wild horses, pretty apt in this case, would not have kept her away. She says she's staying because her friends are still in danger, and because Ben might come home.'

'She has balls, you've got to give her that.'

'Fearless. So far,' I said.

'Indeed. Listen, I was thinking of asking Bruno to speak to some of his contacts on the street, nose around a bit.'

'That would be helpful, Monty.'

'Good. I'll organize it. If you hear anything, give me a call right away, will you?'

'Of course. And I'll let Alice know. She thinks a lot of Bruno.'

'He's a good man.'

'Well, I think Alice is still on her crusade chasing the Deadwood hoods. If she gets herself in too deep, do you think Bruno would bail her out?'

'He'll take care of it.'

'Good. At least I'll sleep easier.'

'Right, I'll let you get on. Let me know if there's anything else I can do.'

'Thanks, Monty.'

I put the phone on the table. Mave picked up the piece of toast she'd been eating and held it in front of her chin. She'd chewed it into the shape of a smile. I laughed.

Mave said, 'All guns blazing?'

'Perfect start to the day,' I stood up, 'I'd better get ready.'

Mave dipped the toast crust into her tea, 'That's disgusting,' I said, 'look at all the grease floating on top.'

Mave shrugged, 'Best I can offer is a promise not to do it at the Lord Mayor's banquet.'

'I'm going to shower.'

'Eddie, what have you got booked this week?'

'Two tomorrow at Market Rasen. Why?'

'What about the weekend, Dil got any big plans?'

'Not that I know of.'

'Why don't you take a break until we find Ben?'

'No way.'

'Why not?'

'A million reasons. The BHA believe these horses are bolting only in the races I ride in, so they'd be glad to see me grounded. I don't want them thinking I've got anything to hide. And people would say my nerve has gone if I stop now.'

'Nobody who knows you would say that.'

'Maybe, but somebody will start whispering. Anyway, Dil is hardly going to sign me off on holiday, is he?'

'I'd have thought it would be a bonus for him and Vita. He wouldn't saddle anything with any confidence now, would he? Why don't you talk to him about it?'

I leant on the chairback, 'Mave, I need to keep riding. There's more chance of me picking up something on track about Ben, than if I'm just drifting around.'

She shrugged, 'Fair enough.'

'I need to speak to Dil anyway. I'll call him after I've showered, and maybe drive down there.'

She nodded, and picked up her tea cup, 'I'll see what I can find in Ben's phone records.'

'What about tracing his movements on Friday via the phone masts?'

'I did that on Friday night, while you and Alice were waiting for the police. He hadn't been anywhere, or at least his phone hadn't, outside his normal stamping grounds.'

'What about the route he took to the beach?'

'From his house, he went along Melling Road, a regular walk for him, down and across the canal, then back toward home, and-'

'Could you map it out?'

'Sure. Give me two minutes.'

Towelling myself, I sidled up to Mave and her laptop. She flipped the lid so I could see the map and I leaned forward, water from my hair splashing and dotting the screen. Mave stood and snatched the towel from me, wrapping it roughly round my head, 'Malloy! Did nobody teach you to dry your hair first?'

'Sorry,' I smiled.

She smiled, too, 'Boy, do you look cute.'

'I'll bet. Show me the map.'

A purple line ran from Ben's place up toward the pub we usually met in, then down Melling Road, and south east along the canal, before heading northwest toward Southport, then dipping back south west to the beach at Crosby.

Mave said, 'He was in a vehicle when he left that spot at Melling Road,' she pointed with her pen. 'Pings are happening far too fast for someone on foot.'

'What's around there?'

'A pub called the Blue Anchor. Otherwise, just houses.'

I straightened. Ben knew that area well. The canal runs behind The Blue Anchor. We had walked past it that day we were out. I said,

'You know the pings Ben's phone was sending to the masts, is there any way of tracking the phones of whoever was with him?'

'There'd be thousands of phones pinging those masts at the same time…It would be possible though.'

'How?' I worked on my hair with the towel. Mave chewed the end of her pen, then said, 'I could write a short programme to suck in all the numbers at each mast and filter through until we find one or more that's shadowing Ben's.'

'How short is short, timewise?'

'Maybe an hour?'

'Go to it, Maven Judge!'

41

Mave's programme turned up nothing. No mobile numbers travelled that route other than Ben's. Mave cupped her chin in her hands and mumbled, 'Frustrating.'

'It is.'

She turned to me, 'You said he didn't drive, so he couldn't have been on his own.'

'But whoever's trying to make it look like suicide wants us to believe he was on his own. Am I right in saying that if they had their phones switched off, they'd be invisible to the masts?'

'Yep. They can't ping, if they're not on.'

'Would that be generally known, do you think?'

Mave made one of her faces, where her cheeks went up and her nose wrinkled, 'Well, first you'd need to know that your phone is always looking for these masts anyway, and I doubt that ever crosses anyone's mind, unless they're battery saving or criminal.'

I dragged a chair over and sat close to her, 'So, would you say that any criminal turning off his phone was pretty tech savvy?'

'Not necessarily. They'd just pick up the advice from someone they trusted. They wouldn't necessarily be interested in the technical facts. Why?'

'Because, if they're nobbling horses, maybe they're using hi-tech to do it rather than drugs or guns.'

Mave picked up her pen again and tapped it on her chin, 'Were you thinking of something in particular?'

'Remember the ID chips, the ones Watt and Kilberg were using before we caught them? I just wondered if that could be adapted and some kind of signal sent to it?'

'A signal could be sent, but what would it activate? It would need to be something linked to a neural pathway. Anyway, how would they get access to the horses? We're talking surgery here if I remember correctly. Minor surgery, maybe, but they'd still need to get at the chip, or plant another one.'

I leant forward, elbows on knees, 'Vets.'

Mave looked quizzical. I said, 'I was fixated on Vogel, on the starter's assistants. I never thought about vets.'

'You know Dil's vet well, though, whatshisname?'

'His name is Winslow Mimnaugh, Winnie.'

'And would you trust him?'

'Almost with my life. But the horses weren't all Dil's, were they?'

'Who else does this Winnie guy work for?'

'I'll find out,' I stood up, 'I'd bet my life he's straight, but I'll find out if he has anything to do with the other yards. I'll call Dil…Where's my phone?'

'Probably in the pocket of your trousers on the bedroom floor where you kicked them off to shower.'

I went to the bedroom and came back waving the phone, 'Mave, while I'm speaking to Dil, will you make a start on checking which vets were on duty at each of the tracks?'

'Aye, aye, sir!'

I smiled and scrolled for Dil's number.

Dil and I rode out in the early afternoon, shoulders brushing the white blossom on the hedgerows. I was surprised by the depth of its scent, which obliterated the smell of horse and leather.

It had been Dil's idea to saddle up and get away from the yard. As the path widened, I moved alongside him, 'Not like you to seek fresh air,' I said.

'I had to get away from Vita. She's suffocating me. She was

supposed to be flying home today and changed her mind, again.'

'You know what they say, be careful what you wish for.'

Dil turned toward me, and held up his right hand, finger and thumb an inch apart, 'I'm this close to kicking her out.'

I smiled. Dil said, 'Seriously, I've had enough.'

I suspected that Prim's departure had pushed him to this edge, but I said nothing. Dil just needed to vent, and he did that for the next half mile, until we reached open fields.

When Dil had got all his frustration out, and had been quiet for a minute, I went over the conversation I'd had with Mave about vets, 'I've known Winnie longer than you have, and I trust him, but I wanted to know how you felt?'

Dil's shoulders rocked gently as we kept the horses at a steady walk. He said, 'I wouldn't say Winnie has been himself since all this shit started. He's turned Stevedore inside out trying to find some physical cause for the bolting. He even had a friend of his at Newmarket do dozens of different cross comparisons on bloods from Stevedore and Montego Moon and Kingdom Come.'

'Why didn't you tell me this?' I tried not to sound confrontational, but was annoyed that so much had been going on without Dil telling me. He said, 'Tell you what? That Winnie had nothing to report? Would you expect a newsman, say, Ben Searcey to ring you up and say, "Guess what, Eddie, no news!"'

'That's not what I meant, Dil. I just didn't know you'd gone to those lengths.'

'It wasn't me, it was Winnie. He's not even charging for the bloods work. He's as pissed off as everyone else.'

'I'll go and see him.'

'Do that.'

'I will. Now, what are you going to do about Vita, and Prim?'

He turned and reached to do his fringe-sweep, but forgot he had the helmet on, and he ended up just tucking a few hairs inside the rim, 'I don't know, yet...What would you do?'

'You want the truth?'

He nodded. I said, 'I don't know because I wouldn't have got into the position in the first place.'

I expected an outburst, but he turned again to look straight ahead at the path worn into the grass along the field edge, and he spoke quietly, 'And I shouldn't have got myself into it.'

'Well, maybe it's time to give Vita her marching orders.'

'I can't do that, Eddie. I told you, I was this close to it, but it would make me look a quitter. She'd think I was baling out because of Stevedore and the others. I could live if I lost her business, but I'm not having her saying I'm a quitter.'

I looked at him. He'd quit Prim quickly enough when it suited him. He'd quit more jobs than I'd had winners, but he didn't want a woman who cared little for him to think he was a quitter. I shook my head, but managed to keep quiet.

42

Winnie Mimnaugh had blue eyes that were slightly popped, as though he'd fitted his stethoscope and blown a short blast into his ears. His fair hair popped too, in a crew-cut carpet a centimetre high. It would have been a dense growth for a man half his age, and each time I saw him I felt a weird temptation to stroke it. It looked as tough as a welcome mat.

Dil and I were in the office at Winnie's practice. He shook my hand, 'Eddie, I should have called you. To tell you the truth, I was embarrassed by the shambles I've made of these horses.'

I smiled, 'What shambles? Don't be daft, it's not your fault.'

'But there has to be a physiological reason for the way they're behaving, and I should be able to find it!'

'Can I offer you a theory?' I said.

'Please do.'

I told him about the microchips and signals and all that Mave and I had discussed, but the more I talked, the more those poppy blue eyes clouded over. The polite smile stayed on his mouth, but those old windows on the soul had misted up. When I'd explained everything, I added, 'You think I'm crazy, don't you?'

'Well, I'm hoping you're crazy, because if someone's developed a technique that advanced, I can't see how it could be combatted.'

Dil said, 'But, in your opinion, Winnie, could something like that be possible? Links to neural pathways, all that kind of stuff?'

'Dil, I think we're in the realms of Frankenstein here, if you want an honest opinion. The unravelling of equine neural pathways into something as predictable, and as utterly consistent as what's been happening just isn't possible. I'm not saying it won't be in thirty or forty years, but I'm not buying it today.'

I sighed long and loud and Dil and Winnie looked at me. I raised my hands, 'Maybe it's hypnosis for horses.'

Winnie smiled, but he looked resigned, and tired. I said, 'If we were just talking about setting a horse off here, then we're looking at a rifle, or a laser beam or something, but they're not just setting them off. The horses are being started, then steered, then stopped, and each of those has been added since Montego Moon. Whatever they're doing, they're refining it.'

Winnie said, 'Maybe we should stop looking for the what and start looking for the "they".'

'We are,' I said, 'and I think we probably found them, or, at least Ben did.' I turned to Dil, 'Have you told Winnie about Ben?'

'Yes,' he looked at Winnie, 'Ben was brilliant at finding these guys, not so brilliant at avoiding them once they knew.'

I said, 'Dil, we don't know that yet. Don't blame Ben.' Dil shrugged and did his fringe-sweep. He was building resentment over Ben. Prim leaving to look after Alice had stoked his ill-feeling.

I turned back to Winnie, 'Look, whatever's happening to these horses, somebody's got access to them, somebody who shouldn't have. If it is a microchip, or a drug of some kind, there has to be physical contact with the horse at some point. You've done nothing to them, so who has? What about the vets at the track?'

Winnie said, 'If there's a bent vet, he'd be working alone. That would be my bet.'

I said, 'By working alone you mean it would all be his idea?'

'No, I mean I'd be amazed if you can find one crooked vet on track. The chances of finding more than one, are remote, to my mind, at least.'

'If you had to name one who might be worth checking out, who would it be?'

His eyes popped even more and he raised a hand, 'I know half a dozen who work this area, Eddie, and I'd pretty much stand by any of them. I can't speak for the ones down south.'

'Okay,' I said, 'No offence meant. I'm not having a go at your profession, Winnie, I'm just working through a process of elimination. Somebody with a lot of knowledge is getting at these horses. It's not you, and it's not me, and it's not Dil. It's got to be happening at the track.'

Dil reached to nudge my arm with a soft fist, 'About time your buddy McCarthy did some work then, don't you think?'

'He's on it, Dil.'

'Well he's not on it heavy enough. Have they come up with a single lead? A single idea?'

'Fair enough,' I said, 'I'll call Mac later.'

Dil drove us back to the yard. He was quiet for the first minute of the trip, then he started in on what I knew had been building all day, 'Has Prim told you what her plans are? I mean, has she said when when she's coming back?'

'Not to me, she hasn't. Why don't you call her?'

'That's not how I work.'

I gazed at him, 'So, how do you "work", as you put it?'

He set his jaw then relaxed it, and made to turn and look at me, but changed his mind. He said, 'Once you start chasing a woman, you might as well forget it.'

'Ah, right. So what were you doing on those cruise ships when you were widow gathering?'

'That's not chasing. There's a subtlety to it…an art. It was something I had to learn, then perfect over the years.'

I smiled, watching him, and said, 'You make it sound like some great achievement that will leave lasting benefits for mankind.'

He glanced across, 'Listen, you've never tried it. There's a skill to it, a finesse that can border on genius.'

I knew him well enough to realize he was serious, and I said, 'Dil! You're a fucking hustler! You might not be a two-bit hustler as they say in your old homeland, but, well, in fact, I take that back, you are a two-bit hustler at heart, it's just that you work the upper end of the money scale.'

'Don't knock it till you've tried it.'

'Dil, I'd sooner try riding a fence of red hot spikes than prowl the bars and casinos on a floating prison.'

'Well, you're hardly Mister Right yourself going on your record with women.'

'Maybe. But it doesn't make me treat them like I learned how to do it in a correspondence course for dickheads.'

He laughed, 'You're jealous.'

'Of what? All the moaning you were doing this morning about Vita? You're only beginning to realize what a good woman Prim is, and you're going to burn through her pretty soon. Can't even pick up the phone to her because the manual says no.'

He tried to keep smiling, but it was hard work, and it faded and he said, 'Seriously, has she mentioned me?'

'Seriously? I haven't spoken to her since yesterday, but as it happens, I'm calling her tonight to see how Alice is.'

'Don't tell her I've been asking about her!'

'Don't worry, I've got better things to do.'

'How long is she planning on staying?'

'Not long, I hope, for her sake. I'd like to get Alice out of there, and Prim.'

'Well, I would too. It's not as though I don't care for her.'

'No, it's just that you're an idiot.'

He smiled again, but only with his mouth.

43

Mac promised he'd round up the information on racecourse vets. When I finished that call, I rang Prim, 'How's it going in Deadwood?'

'Eddie! How are you?'

'I'm okay, Prim. How are you and how is Alice?'

'Oh, Alice is a six stone fuse that never seems to burn out. I came here thinking how much she reminded me of my young self. Now I know I could never have held a candle to her. She's a remarkable kid. Have you any news of her father?'

'Afraid not, Prim. Mave's doing what she can online with mobile phone data and stuff, but nothing to report so far.'

'Alice has been non stop here trying to find out where he is. We ended up doing house to house calls last night.'

'Seriously?'

'Seriously. I went with her from door to door. She just knocks and won't leave until somebody answers, then you either get dog's abuse or they listen to her. And when they listen to her, most of them agree to do what they can, and that's saying something around here.'

'But you're okay?'

'I'm fine.'

'Is Alice there?'

'She's in the bath.'

'Do you think there's any way of persuading her to come and live with us until Ben turns up?'

'Not a chance, Eddie. Not a hope. She's here until he's found, dead or alive.'

'That's about what I expected. Do you want me to try and make arrangements to relieve you, if you'll pardon the question?'

'Eddie, I feel more alive here, than I have for years. Alice isn't leaving her Dad, and I'm not leaving Alice.'

'Well, I'm pretty sure it's tied up with this wild horses scam, so if we find the scammers, we find Ben. Hopefully it won't be long.'

'Have you got anything to go on?'

'Not yet. But Ben found something pretty quick, so it shouldn't take us too long to figure out the same as he did.'

'What about this Vogel guy?'

'He's out of it. Ben had some stuff on him, but it didn't fit with the horses. It was when Ben moved on from Vogel that he found whatever got him carted away.'

'It was the Blue Anchor pub he was last seen, is that right?'

'It was at that location. Whether it was in the pub or not I don't know. Why?'

'Well, that's where we're heading this evening. Alice got some posters printed with her Dad's picture on. We're both going to the pub, and it's my job to go in and hand them out. With a smile, and a phone number.'

'Whose phone number?'

'Alice's. And, I know, don't tell me. I've been through it all with her. Save your breath.'

'But do you even know what the pub is like? It could be worse than Deadwood for all you know.'

'Well, we'll soon find out.'

'Prim, look, why don't you hold off and I'll drive down there and come with you?'

'I'd love to, Eddie, but I reckon you've got about ten minutes. As soon as Alice has dried her hair, she's heading for the Blue Anchor, and she won't be waiting for you or me or anybody else.'

'Let me talk to her.'

'Eddie, listen…we know each other well enough you and me?'

'Of course, but-'

'Eddie…I now know Alice better than I know you, better than I know Dil, better than I know anyone. She doesn't take much knowing, because what you see is most definitely what you get, and if I tell you that Alice will listen politely to you, then put the phone down and head out, then trust me, that's exactly what she'll do.'

I sighed, 'Okay, Prim. I'd better go and try making alternative arrangements…where the hell did she get posters printed on a Sunday?'

'There's a community centre, open seven days a week. They seemed to know Alice well.'

'There's a surprise.'

Prim said, 'You mentioned alternative arrangements, of what kind, if you don't mind me asking?'

'Of the Bruno Guta kind.' I said.

'Ahh, now much as Alice admires Mister Guta, and she has mentioned him more than once, I think she'd throw a hairy fit if he pitched up at the Blue Anchor and scared all her potential informants.'

'No doubt. But Bruno, or should I say Monty, will have other people, much less recognizable, but just as capable of making sure you're both safe.'

'Well, you'd best make double sure Alice won't recognize whoever it is, because if Alice comes looking for you, Edward, I would not want to be in your Chelsea boots.'

I laughed, 'Will you call me this evening and let me know how it went?'

'I will.'

'Take care, Prim.'

'I'll try.'

I ended the call, and stared out of the window from my seat on the arm of the sofa.

'Trouble?'

The voice startled me so badly I grunted, and it came out almost like a yelp as I jumped to my feet and spun. It was Mave. 'Jeez, you scared the shit out of me!'

'Not literally, I hope.'

'I thought you were out!'

'I came back.'

I released the breath I hadn't realized I was holding in, and smiled and went to hug her, 'Sorry, Mave. I was a bit tensed up thinking what could happen to Alice and Prim.'

'What's wrong?'

I looked at my watch, 'Nothing. Yet. I'll tell you in a minute. Let me call Monty.'

Ten minutes later, Mave and I sat by the stove drinking whiskey. Monty had handled the request in his usual smooth manner and promised he'd have 'a guardian angel' at the Blue Anchor within half an hour.

Mave raised her glass, 'Fair play to old Monty, he's delivered time and again for Ben. I hereby apologize for ever doubting him.'

I joined her in the toast, and as I lowered my glass I stared through the crystal at the fire flames. Something was trying to push its way to the front of my mind, and I scrabbled in the mental dust trying to uncover what it was.

Mave watched me, 'You're thinking again, aren't you?'

I nodded, still staring at the blend of firelight, whiskey and cut crystal.

'It's bad for you,' Mave said, 'especially this close to bedtime.'

I nodded again. Mave said, 'That means "be quiet".'

I didn't answer. We sat in silence a minute more, and then it came to me. I found it. Mave had dropped it and I had found it. I turned to her, 'You almost made me jump in the air earlier.'

'I know. Funny, wasn't it?'

'Why did I react that way?'

'Because you got a fright.'

'How? What caused the fright?'

'Surprise?'

'You spoke. You made a noise.'

44

Mave watched me pace the short room. She said, 'That's hardly worth the walk. Nine steps.'

'I know. I need to think for a minute. I was just about to dial Winnie's number to ask if he'd checked Stevedore's ears. But maybe we shouldn't tell anyone.'

Mave settled back and crossed her legs, 'I'm listening.'

'If I call Winnie, he might blab, or feel guilty and go running to Dil and Vita. If I tell Dil myself, he'll tell Vita and she's the potential problem here, because she's in charge and there's no way of guessing what she'll do.'

'What about Mac?'

I nodded, still pacing, 'He'd probably be okay…probably…but he'd feel some pressure to tell Steel and try to ease his situation there.'

Mave smiled, 'It's killing you, in a way, isn't it? It's like being the kid in class who solves the tough problem and is dying to jump up and down.'

I smiled, 'It wasn't so long ago that I'd have made five calls by now to let everyone see how smart I am. I'm getting old and cynical.'

'Old and wise, Eddie. It's human nature to want to tell the world, especially when it's caused so much trouble.'

'I know. The only thing I should be concentrating on is Ben. What's best for Ben. That's all that matters.'

'You're right. Ben and Alice.'

'Yep.' I stopped and rested my hands on the mantelpiece above the stove, looking into the mirror.

'Reflecting on things?' Mave said.

I smiled and caught her eye in the mirror, the shape of the glass making her look even smaller, almost distant, 'The old ones are the best, Mave.' She raised a thumb.

I said, 'What if we get the list of vets from Mac and work through that, see who's been at the track on the days in question and find out where they're going to be in future? Then, when the next one happens, we catch them in the act, literally. Wait until they're dipping into the horse's ear after the race and nail them.'

'What if it's not a vet? If you're right and it's a relatively simple radio transmitter hidden in an earplug, then a lad could have shoved it in there, or the stable manager on track.'

I turned from the mirror, 'It's not so much the putting it in, it's getting it safely back out again before there's any detailed examination.'

'True.'

'The vet would be first on the scene once the horse stops.'

'Fine,' said Mave, 'but there's more than one vet on the course, is there not? In which case, you not only need to find out who was there on the relevant days, but which one attended each incident. Can you remember any of them from yours?'

I sighed, 'No. I should have paid more attention.'

'Well, don't be too hard on yourself. You were thirty-six hours waking up the first time.'

I sat beside Mave, 'I'm going to have to bring Mac in, to find out who went out on the track for each of these.'

'Just tell him in advance that it's off the record. He knows you well enough by now.'

I nodded, and reached for my phone. Then I put it down, 'I'll give it an hour, see if I can come up with anything else. The big problem's going to be asking Mac to keep it informal, but getting him to set up the sting for the next time it happens. I can't do that without his help.'

Mave put a hand on my shoulder, 'Even with a successful sting, is your man going to tell you where Ben is?'

'He might not even know. Whoever's doing it will be working for someone else.'

'Why do you say that?'

'Because it's more than a one-man job, isn't it? They've got to get the money on, they've had to kidnap Ben and hold him somewhere...got to be three or four of them. There were four accounts laying Spalpeen at Cheltenham...though I suppose that means nothing, does it?'

'Could easily have been one man doing that.'

I turned to her, 'You don't just go from being a trusted vet working the tracks to a villain, though, do you?'

'Probably not. And a vet makes sense. We know it's someone who's trying hard to avoid injury to horses and jockeys.'

'Exactly.'

Mave sat forward, 'Look, why don't you press Mac on the list first? Maybe something will jump out from there and you can then line everything up before asking him to work on the security side?'

I nodded. Mave said, 'Once you get the list, do you think Sir Monty would help?'

I looked at my watch, 'I forgot. Prim and Alice will be at the Blue Anchor now. I hope Monty's guy made it on time.'

'Prim said she'd call, didn't she?'

'She did. She will. And you're right, I should ask Monty. He's just as keen as we are to help Ben.'

Mave reached to get my phone from the small table, 'Here, ring Mac.'

Slowly. I took the phone, then I looked again at my watch, 'I don't want to risk missing a call from Prim. I'll wait until I've spoken to her.'

Mave's eyebrows went up, telling me she knew I was putting this off. But she said nothing. I sat back, staring at the ceiling, seeking another way, wracking my brain. Mave said, 'I'm going back to work. I'll listen out for Prim calling.'

I put a hand on her back, pushing her up from the cushion, 'Mave, you know those phone masts you checked to find Ben's mobile?'

'Uhuh?'

'Do you need a number? I mean, could you check the masts closest to, say, Bangor on the day Montego Moon bolted and find out what numbers were pinging that mast, and when?'

'I could. There'd be plenty. You've got to account for passing traffic, not just those at the track.'

'But the ones at the track would be static for hours, wouldn't they? They'd be sending multiple pings from the same location?'

'You're right, they would.'

I looked up at her, 'So that programme you wrote to track Ben from the Blue Anchor to Crosby, you could use that to check which phone numbers were at Bangor, Cheltenham, Uttoxeter, and Aintree?'

'Yes. But you've got a horde of jockeys for a start. Most of them will be repeats.'

'But they'll be easy to filter out, because there won't be more than a few pings. The rules mean that most of them do the same as I do now and just leave their phones in the car, or leave them switched off. You should end up with a manageable list.'

She watched me, and she smiled, 'So all you'd need to ask Mac for just now is a list of phone numbers for the vets?'

'Correct. And if we can single just one out, you could also discover which numbers he was phoning, right?'

She gazed at me for a while, then reached and pinched my cheek gently, 'You're not just a pretty face, Mister Malloy, are you?'

I smiled, 'Remember that, Miss Judge.'

45

I rang Mac, 'Anyone with you?' I said.

'At half-past nine on a Sunday night?'

'Well, you're always warning me not to make assumptions, Mac. Could be you're hosting the Lambourn Pole Dancers' Convention or something...how would I know?'

'That's a grotesque suggestion.'

'Each to his own, Mac, each to his own.'

'Indeed. So, now that we've established that I face no distractions, what can I do for you?'

I told him about my speaker theory.

'Interesting. How would they transmit the sound?'

'Radio waves, I suppose, or some sort of Wi-Fi receiver.'

He was silent for a few moments then said, 'Makes a lot of sense...'

'You know that list of vets I asked you to get, made any headway there?'

'I've asked the question. Should have the answers tomorrow. You think these speakers are being put in by a vet?'

'Put in and, more importantly, taken out again very quickly when the vet arrives on the scene.'

We talked that through and Mac could find no holes in the theory. He said, 'I'll get the list of vets first thing, and take it from there.'

'We'll take it from there, Mac. Me and you. Don't tell Steel about it, or anyone else. And a list of phone numbers for those vets would help a hell of a lot.'

'Fine. I'll ask no questions on that front.'

'Good. Just on the off chance, have you got a list of all vets working on track, along with their mobile numbers?'

'I've got it on a spreadsheet somewhere.'

'How long would it take to find it?'

'Ten minutes. I'll email it.'

'Thanks, Mac. Goodnight.'

'Goodnight.'

At 10.17, Prim called. 'Are you home?' I asked.

'Yes.'

'Alice okay?'

'Her old enemy's back.'

'DJ?'

'He's just trailed us through the streets, all the way to the gate, him and his friends in a big BMW. Sat right on our heels crawling along.'

'What did he say?'

'Nothing. He was in the passenger seat. Every fifty yards or so they'd move alongside and he would just smile. He is a creepy guy.'

'What did Alice do?'

'Stopped three times and yelled at him. He just laughed and did some obscene stuff with his tongue.'

'Where's the car, now?'

'It's gone. They sat outside the house for a minute, then left.'

'But they could come back anytime?'

'I suppose so.'

'Listen, Prim, we've got to get you two out of there. It doesn't matter what Alice wants or what she says.'

'She won't go, Eddie. No way. That's made it worse, the fact that this guy is back.'

I cursed silently, 'She's going to have to move, Prim. We'll need to come up with something. Give me five minutes, will you? I'll call you back.'

'Okay.'

'Oh, did Sir Monty's man turn up at the pub?'

'I don't know. There were at least three guys who could have been him, if you know what I mean. It was hard to say. I went in expecting a wild west saloon, but it's an upmarket place, selling nice meals. All lamps and soft music and thick carpets. Almost everybody took a leaflet, and no one was rude to me.'

'Sounds like DJ made up for that.'

'He's a horrible bastard. Alice came in ranting about Bruno Guta and what he'd do.'

'She didn't say that to DJ, did she?'

'No, to her credit she didn't. Just went off on one when we locked the door behind us.'

'Where is she now?'

'Upstairs.'

I sighed long and hard then realized how harsh and shrill it must have sounded down the phone to Prim, 'Sorry, Prim…it's been a long day.'

'Don't worry. Have you seen Dil?'

'Rode out with him this morning. Didn't stop talking about you, but his head's up his arse.'

Now Prim sighed. I said, 'He's not worth it, Prim, he really is not worth it.'

'I know…I know.'

'I'm sorry. It's not my place to be saying that.'

'It's okay.'

But it didn't sound like it was okay, and I regretted speaking up. I said, 'Prim, I'll call you back as soon as I've worked out what to do about this DJ character.'

'Are you going to tell Bruno Guta that he's back?'

'That'll be what Alice wants.'

'Yes. It is.'

'I'll think about it. No point in just putting a patch on this. We need to fix it. DJ's not the problem here, I'm afraid, Alice is. And I need to try and handle this the way Ben would want me to.'

'I know. I know you do.'

'I'll call you soon.'

'Okay, Eddie. Thanks.'

'But, you call me if anything happens, especially if DJ starts causing trouble.'

'I will.'

I ended the call and cursed three times, hard and harsh, and heard Mave giggling in her study. When I turned, she was in the doorway. She said, 'Sorry, I shouldn't laugh. But you do make me laugh…in a good way.'

'Can you laugh in a bad way, then?'

'In several bad ways. What's up?'

I told Mave what had happened. She nodded and said, 'I'm guessing you are not going to ask for Bruno Guta's help?'

'No, I'm not. I've asked Monty for enough for now. And Alice needs to learn that her crusade isn't everybody's crusade. She's coming out of Deadwood, like it or not.'

Mave raised her eyebrows. 'Good luck with that project.'

'What about your project, how's it going?'

'On the vet's phone numbers? Pretty good. Should be ready to run the query by the time you've made me a coffee.'

'I'm afraid you'll have to make your own coffee. Then you can maybe make up a bed for Miss Alice Searcey.'

'For tonight?'

'Yep.'

'Best buy a cage, too, when you're out. Or a set of manacles.'

'I'll do just that, if I have too.'

Mave leant against the doorway, all the humour gone from her face, 'Seriously, Eddie, she was escaping from children's homes to get herself back to Deadwood. She's not going to stay here, even if you manage to get her to come.'

'We'll see.' I picked up my jacket from the back of the chair.

'You going to Deadwood now?'

'I am.'

She watched as I buttoned my jacket and pocketed my phone,

then she said, 'Good luck, Eddie.'

I smiled, 'Will you call me if that query throws anything up?'

She nodded, still looking serious, 'Listen, you don't need to prove to Alice that you're tougher than Bruno Guta.'

I took my car keys from the windowsill, 'I'm afraid that's exactly what I'm going to have to do.'

I kissed her, and went out, and when I turned the car, my reversing lights flared and showed Mave at the window, beside the burning lamp, eyes closed, brow furrowed, alone and afraid.

On another night, I'd have felt guilty at leaving her, but not tonight. There was work to be done.

46

I sped down the valley through the hamlet of Glenridding and along the shores of Ullswater. This was my route to the motorway and I knew every kink and rise on this twisting road and I tore along it with confidence and concentration, all thoughts of Alice gone, replaced by ultrafast frames in my headlights of thick tree trunks, low branches, flashes of dark water and pinpoints of moon, and on the rare straight stretches a tunnel of mainbeam light through the darkness.

It ended at a large roundabout, which seemed like the winning post after a hectic race. Here were streetlights above dual carriageway and, a minute to the east, the M6 motorway. I'd be in Deadwood in an hour.

I arrived just before eleven and parked on the main street at the border of Deadwood. When the time came to bring Alice and Prim out, I didn't want to find my car full of broken glass, or sitting on knifed tyres. I reckoned we could reach the main street in under five minutes walking, or, once I'd talked Alice into it, I could jog back for the car and wait at the gate for them.

I locked the car and hurried across to the road that led into Deadwood. After three hundred yards, I had taken the two turns I remembered from my first visit. Without headlights, I was much more aware of the number of broken streetlamps. About one in every six cast light. Below the others lay smashed orange shards from the plastic casings.

Approaching the house in which I'd seen the dancers last time, I could hear the music once more, and as I passed the window, the dancers were still dancing, the cigarettes still glowing, and I wondered if everyone inside was doomed to some eternal party in this grim place.

I turned into the street where Alice lived, a long crescent, where most of the buildings were four storey flats showing a patchwork of window lights.

Ahead, to my left, a window was open on the third floor and a man and woman were arguing. He was shouting, she was screaming. I was alone on the street and I stopped beneath the window, the viciousness and volume of the fight making me wonder if it was physical too…maybe the woman needed help… but I could hear no blows.

I could pick out only the odd word. The impatience of each to get their argument across, and the strong Liverpool accent, plus the screaming and bawling made almost everything incomprehensible.

Such was the venom in each voice, I guessed it had to be about some sexual betrayal, but the longer I listened the more attuned I became to the accent and the overall rhythms and I finally learned they were fighting over the remote control for the TV.

Now that's what you call passion. Smiling, I walked on.

Alice's house was in a terraced section, between two higher blocks of flats. There were four front doors. Alice's was the end one on the left as I looked across at the building. All the lights in the house were on, all the curtains closed.

I crossed the road and went through the gate. On the doorstep, I phoned Prim and told her I was outside.

Prim welcomed me hurriedly, then closed and locked the door.

Alice was in the kitchen with her coat on. She didn't seem surprised to see me.

'Going out or just come in?' I asked.

'Just came in,' Alice said, not looking at me, tapping her fingers on the worktop.

Prim looked almost haggard, and that told me as much as I

needed to know about how she felt. She said, 'Alice has just been to see one of DJ's friends.'

'Girls,' Alice said, 'they're not friends, they're just stupid girls who think he's some kind of man instead of a piece of shit.'

Prim looked at me and said, 'Well, it seems DJ knows nothing about Ben or where he is.'

'He'd say that anyway, wouldn't he?' I asked.

'No, he wouldn't,' Alice said, 'he'd try to torture me with it if he knew anything.'

'Hasn't he just come back, though?' I said, 'there's time enough for him to be taunting you, and it seems to me he'd do that anyway, even if he didn't know anything.'

Alice looked hard at me, 'He doesn't know anything,' she said.

I raised my hands in surrender, 'Fair enough. Let's see what he's got for us in the next few days.'

Alice's look hardened. 'Us?'

'Me and you and Prim,' I said.

'You're staying?' Alice asked.

'That's right.'

She got up, 'Why?'

'Because your enemy number one is back, and I need to make sure you're safe.'

'I thought you were looking for my Dad?'

'I was. Been working on it pretty much nonstop. I've left Mave writing a programme which will track and filter phone numbers, and maybe bring some leads. But I can't follow any leads while DJ is here threatening you.'

'He's not threatening me!'

'He followed you home from the Blue Anchor.'

'That's just his creepy style.'

'Alice, do you trust your Dad?' I said.

'What does that mean?'

'Do you trust your Dad's judgement?'

'Well, yes, I trust his judgement, when he's here and I can see him and figure things out around what he's saying.'

'But he's not here. I trust his judgement. I always have. I've known him for a long time, long before you were born. He's a smart man. It looks like he figured out in forty-eight hours what a team of us couldn't do in weeks. He's a very clever man.'

'I know he is! I know!'

'Well, he says DJ is very bad news. He told me DJ has been easy on you because you're young, and that DJ had warned him more than once that he wasn't going to cut you much more slack.'

She watched me now. Her mouth had opened, but she'd stopped the words in her throat. I said, 'So, I'm here for the duration, because you are more important to your father than anything else, even his own safety.'

'But there's nothing you can do! Can't you get Bruno to come and speak to him?'

I gazed at her. Prim cleared her throat and shifted her weight to lean against the edge of the worktop. I said, 'No more Bruno. No more Monty Bearak. I'm taking over, and I'm staying here until DJ goes away again.'

'But if you find my Dad, he'll be here to look after me!'

'My first responsibility is you, Alice. No point me finding your Dad if you're gone.' I slid my jacket off, 'So, I'll sleep on the couch if you don't mind. Mave is bringing some stuff for me tomorrow.'

'Don't you have to go to the races?' she said, looking increasingly worried.

'Well, I work for Dil, mostly, and your Dad was working for him too on trying to find out about these horses. Anyway, Dil's happy for me to take all the time off I need to make sure you're safe. Now, can I use your bathroom?'

Prim said, 'I'll show you where it is,' and she led me upstairs. Outside the bathroom door, Prim smiled and said, 'I hope this works. You'll only get to call her bluff once.'

'Well, it's over to you for the next five minutes. See what you can do.'

Prim went back down. I went into the bathroom and closed the door against any verbal fireworks.

When I entered the kitchen, they were talking quietly. Prim looked up, smiling, and said, 'If it's okay with you, Alice is going to come back with me, to Dil's.'

I stayed silent until Alice looked up at me, 'I said, that's a big help, but I'd feel better if she came with me to the farm.'

Alice got up from the table, 'But if I come with you, you won't have the time to go looking for Dad!'

I nodded and put a hand to my chin, 'True. Would you stay with Prim until I find your Dad?'

'Yes.'

I resisted asking her to promise, 'Okay. It's a deal,' I reached to shake her hand and she offered hers slowly, still unsure, and maybe wondering if she had been conned into this.

I said, 'I've parked the car five minutes away. I'll go and get it, if you want to pack your things?'

Prim smiled wide. Alice nodded slowly. I let a silent sigh of relief trickle through my nostrils, 'I'll go and get the car,' I said.

47

Prim opened the door to let me out. I was halfway to the gate when she said, 'Eddie!'

I stopped and turned. Prim nodded toward the road sloping down toward us. I looked behind me. A big silver BMW was parked, lights on, fifty yards from the gate. Prim said, 'I think that's DJ's car.'

'Go inside. Lock up. I'll be back soon.'

I hadn't reached the first broken lamp post when I became aware of the car trailing me, engine at a whisper, headlights casting twin beams ahead of me.

I glanced back without stopping, and ducked to look inside: four heads, faces in darkness.

I kept going at the same steady pace. They moved closer, almost on my heels now. I looked to the junction at the head of the crescent, about three hundred yards away. A left turn there and a quick jog across a patch of wasteland would get me off this road, into the warren of high-rise blocks. The car drew alongside.

I walked on.

It stayed with me.

The front passenger window came down. 'Hey, man!' I stopped and turned. The Mister Muscles in the front passenger seat had to be DJ. He smiled up at me and drew on a long reefer. Big strong-looking guy, but with a covering of fat. Maybe nineteen or twenty. 'Hey, yourself,' I said.

'What were you doing with Alice?'

'None of your business.'

'Everything that happens in Deadwood is my business.'

'Well, this'll make a refreshing change for you, give you a little mystery in your life.'

His smile widened and he drew on the reefer, 'You're not a copper.'

'How do you know?'

'Cops only come in here in teams.'

'That's the locals for you.'

He kept smiling and turned to look at his friends, then back to me, 'So, where are you stationed?'

'That's none of your business either. There you go, two mysteries for the price of one. In the same night too.'

'You're not a cop, man. What do you want with Alice?'

'I'm in the ensurance business.'

'You mean insurance.'

'I mean ensurance. I'm a friend of her father's ensuring she's going to be okay, and nobody's going to give her any trouble.'

'Well, you're robbing jobs from hard working people like me, doing that.'

'So, be happy. I'm giving you some time off.'

'You're taking money out of my pocket, man. If there's protection needed, I'm the guy, and I'm the guy they pay.'

'Well, I work for free, so, no contest.'

He drew again on the reefer and blew the smoke up at my face. He said, 'So, you pay me. You never hear of the Deadwood tax?'

'I never did. Send me an invoice.' I glanced sideways and saw Alice and Prim coming toward us. I began walking to draw the trouble away from them. The car moved alongside.

'Hey, man!' I heard a click as I turned to look down, and a flashlight came on, the beam dazzling me. I covered my eyes, but walked on.

'Hey! I'm talking to you! You want little Alice looked after, you pay the tax.' I stopped. Alice and Prim were a hundred yards away and still coming. I said, 'Okay, okay, How much?'

'Two hundred. For now.' I reached into my back pocket for my wallet, and counted out some notes. DJ smiled. I switched the cash to my left hand and offered it to him, keeping it just far enough away so he had to put the big metal Maglite on the seat between his legs and reach with his left hand, resting his arm, palm open, on the sill.

I swung hard and fast, bringing my fist down in a chopping motion, and hit DJ's wrist and heard his forearm crack. He squealed. His friends were caught between surprise and uncertainty and if I didn't go through with this now, and make their minds up for them, I might die in this dark street. I grabbed DJ's head and pulled it toward me and down until his left ear was hard against the sill of the car. He was squealing still from the fracture, and I reached and grabbed the foot-long black metal Maglite, its beam flashing the open-mouthed face of the driver as I raised it then smashed it down on DJ's right ear, then on his jaw, his temple, his nose, bang, bang, bang, swinging from the side, the front, spraying blood, drawing howls, then, grabbing his hair, raising his head, I spun the two pounds of black metal and smashed the butt up into the point of his jaw.

Instant result.

His neck relaxed, his head flopped over the sill, and the howling stopped. I held my breath, wanting to drive home the effect of the sudden silence, to keep the others hypnotized by the unexpected. Then I bent and aimed the beam at them, holding it for five seconds on each wide-eyed face. 'I'll remember you,' I said quietly, 'now remember me.' And I put the bright broad lens below my chin to shine on my face, like a kid at Halloween.

I said, 'And remember this…your only job until I see you again is to make sure nothing bad happens to any girl in Deadwood.' They stared at me, as I crouched over their bleeding, unconscious friend, and I could feel some splattered blood spots wet on my face now, highlighted by the ghostly beam from below. No wonder they looked scared. 'Understand?' I said. They nodded. I smiled, and straightened, and flipped the Maglite in the air. It twirled and I caught it by the head and offered the handle to the driver, who hesitated. 'Take it. It's a quality piece of merchandise. Maybe you guys could have filmed that and sold the footage to Maglite.'

Still they stared, unmoving. I pushed the flashlight closer to the driver, 'Take it. I won't bite. Not this time, anyway.' I smiled again as the driver reached slowly. I said, 'Now you'd better get your fat friend to hospital and see if they can save his eye.' I glanced down, 'And then to the car wash before all this blood dries on your nice motor.'

All three looked at me. I grabbed DJ's hair and shoved his head inside, then pointed along the road, 'Move!'

They moved.

I watched them take a right at the junction, then I turned. Alice was within touching distance, staring at me, just staring.

Prim was ten yards back, her hands at her mouth. She too looked at me as though she had never seen me before.

I said, 'Go back and get your things. I'll pick you up in five minutes.'

By the time I reached the car, I was empty of adrenaline and rising instead was a mild disgust with myself. Never before had I deliberately broken a man's bone, nor beaten anyone so savagely. But I had known within a minute what was needed back there. I had learned long ago from men in prison that it wasn't the strongest who won a fight, nor the smartest, nor even the one with the bigger army. It was the man willing to resort most quickly to brutality.

I sat for ten seconds, reliving it, then reached in the back for a bottle of water. My mouth was so dry my tongue was stuck as my mind carped keenly at me about what might have been. How it could have ended with death in a dark gutter surrounded by houses where people fought like animals over a TV remote. I started the engine, and headed back into Deadwood for what I hoped would be the final time.

48

We got safely out of Deadwood and on the road to Dil's yard. Alice hadn't spoken. Prim stayed silent until we reached the motorway. She said to me, 'Are you all right?'

'I'm fine, thanks.'

'That was a big chance you took.'

I kept my eyes on the road, 'There isn't an option with people like that. You can't show weakness.'

'What happened?'

I told her. Alice leant forward, 'He said he was being paid to protect me?'

I glanced back at her, 'It was just an excuse to have a go.'

'Did he mention my Dad?'

'No. Not a word. It wasn't about your Dad or you, it was about DJ showing his mates he was the big chief.'

Prim said, 'He picked the wrong man.'

'This time he did. Unfortunately, he'll go for a nice soft target next time to try and get his mates back onside. Anyway, it's time to stop worrying about him. And, Alice, I warned the others in the car that if anything happened to any of the girls in Deadwood I'd be back.'

'Do you think that will work?' Alice said.

'For a while. Depends how long it takes DJ to get back on his feet.'

'Did you hurt him bad?' Alice asked.

'His arm's broken. So is his nose. There'll be at least one fracture in his jaw, probably more. The rest will depend on the blow that put him out. With a bit of luck, it'll have knocked some sense into him.'

'I doubt it,' Alice said, 'But he'll remember you now. I don't know what Bruno Guta said to him, but he'll remember you. He might even think you work for Bruno.'

'Well,' I said, 'that would be no bad thing if he did.'

'Boys against men,' Prim said.

'Literally, I'm afraid. Nobody in that car looked more than nineteen. There'll be others. Those kids are just cannon fodder.'

Alice's phone rang and she scrambled to find it, 'Hello?'

I could hear a male voice but couldn't make out what he was saying.

'When?' Alice said. Prim was watching for her and reached to reassure her.

'Did you see them?' Alice said, 'Do you know them? What's your name? Can you give me your name?' She was getting panicky.

'Fuck!' she said.

I slowed the car. Alice said 'That was somebody we gave a leaflet to in the pub. He said he saw Dad leaving there with two gypsies on Friday night.'

'Did his phone number come up?'

'Withheld.'

'Did he know the men your Dad was with?' I asked.

'No, he just knew they were gypsies. "Pikey bastards" he called them.'

Prim flinched. I glanced at her and there was a look of distaste there, then I remembered she'd always claimed to be a gypsy princess. I said, 'Did he say if it looked like they were forcing your Dad to go with them?'

'He didn't say. I should have asked.'

'Don't worry.' I turned to Prim, 'Did you notice if there was CCTV outside the Blue Anchor?'

'I didn't.'

I was about to ask her if she had access to any connections in the gypsy world that might be able to help, but she still looked upset at the Pikey jibe. I passed Prim my phone, 'Get Mave for me, would you, then hit hands free.'

'All well?' Mave answered, her usual greeting.

I told her what had happened and she called out a cheery hello to Prim and Alice. I said, 'Can you find out what CCTV cameras are in place between the Blue Anchor pub and Crosby beach?'

'Will do.'

'And Alice will give you her mobile number. Is there any way you could get the number of the guy who just called?'

'I'll try.'

'Thanks, Mave.'

'Want me to call you back?'

'It'll hold until we reach Dil's. I'll ring you from there.'

'Okay.'

Prim called out, 'Mave, would you be able to find out if there are any travellers camped in that area?'

'Just around Aintree?'

I butted in, 'Go for Merseyside, Mave, will you?'

'Will do.'

I turned to Prim, 'Anything else you want to ask Mave?'

She shook her head, then, realizing Mave couldn't see that said, 'No. No, thanks.'

'Alice?' I called.

'No…well, just anything else you can think of, Mave. Please.'

'I'll get right on it,' Mave said, 'speak to you all soon.'

We choired a goodbye, which brought the first smile of the evening. Alice leant forward until her head was past the back of our seats. She said to Prim, 'Is that how gypsies really live, travelling around all the time?'

I sensed Prim preparing herself to answer. She said, 'My family were Roma. Are Roma, I should say. They used to travel, mostly in Romania, then in Europe, but my grandfather settled on a farm in the mountains in Spain. There was no more travelling then for us.'

Alice said, 'So are the gypsies here not Roma, then?'

'I think most of them are Irish travellers. They were Ireland's version of Roma, if you like. But not many travel any more. Things are too hard for them.'

Alice said, 'So, would they mix, the Roma and the Irish ones?'

'Not really, I don't think they would. I don't know all that much about them, but if you're asking if I know anyone who might be able to help find your Dad, then I'm sorry, but I wouldn't be hopeful about that.'

I watched Alice in the rearview mirror, her face in deep shadow, but her eyes bright. She seemed to be thinking up the next question. I said, 'Let's wait and see what Mave comes up with'

49

It was almost 2 a.m. when we got to Dil's. I switched off the headlights and we stepped out under a clear sky into the silent, sparkling blackness.

Dil had waited up and he hurried toward us across the cobbled yard, his heel-clicks reminding me of that hospital visit, which seemed so long ago.

Dil's thick hair shone under the gallery of security lights, each firing up as we tripped the sensors, and when he reached us, he smelt of fresh pinewood, and the lamp glare shone on a newly shaven jaw as he fixed his gaze on Prim. So, before he spoke, I knew that Vita had gone.

Dil spoke, 'Are you all okay?'

Alice nodded, and Prim and I said we were fine, Dil stretched a welcoming arm, 'Come in! Come in out of the cold!'

I began walking, as did Alice. Prim stayed where she was.

Dil looked at her for a few seconds, 'Aren't you coming in?'

Prim said, 'Vita's gone then?'

'She left yesterday. She has business in New York.'

Prim watched him, 'And when she comes back, will you be so keen to ask me into your house again?'

The harsh chemical light spared no shades of red as he blushed and said nothing. Prim said, 'Then I'm not coming in now.'

Dil said, 'Well, we can't stand here all night.'

'Go and get the keys to the cottage,' Prim said. I suspected it was the first command she'd ever given him, but he didn't hesitate and two minutes later, we were inside Arnie's cottage, where Prim had been living until she'd left.

Dil hurried around, turning radiator dials and switching on lights and Prim filled the kettle, then took Alice upstairs to her bedroom.

Dil stood with his back to the sink, leaning against it, looking at me. I said, 'Well, you couldn't have made that more obvious if you'd come charging out with a silk dressing gown on and a band of violinists behind you.'

He smiled and did the hair sweep, 'She'll come round.'

'I wouldn't bet on it.'

'We'll see. Tell me what happened, you were a bit vague on the phone.'

I told him. He said, 'Did Mave come up with anything?'

'The guy who phoned Alice was using a throwaway phone. No CCTV close enough to catch anyone on foot.'

Dil stood up straight and swept his fringe again, 'You're n having much luck on this, Eddie.'

'We, Dil. We're not having much luck. You, me and Vita, w decided to get out of the country just when the man she hired to some dirty work goes missing.'

He spread his hands, 'Listen, it was sudden. She told me she'd h here for the duration. She'll be back in a week. Vita's not one running away, you should know that.'

'Good, because she's probably going to have to put some mor on the table. If we can get a handle on this gypsy story she can a reward.'

'I'm sure she will.' He looked to the ceiling at the sou footsteps on creaking floorboards. Prim led Alice downstairs, a if she was hungry.

'I'm fine,' Alice said, then, to me, 'what's next? Can M keep trying to track those phones?'

I said, 'I'm heading home now. Mave will work through the I think she's done all she can for now on phones and CCTV, we'll stay on the gypsy angle and see what we can find out. And in the morning I'll call Monty and ask if his man at the Blue Anchor picked anything up.'

She had watched unblinking as I spoke, but the doubt about me had gone from her eyes. Alice detested violence, and it annoyed me that she appeared to find no irony in the fact that she had needed to see me beat DJ up before she felt I was worth her full respect. Then I chided myself silently for expecting too much. She was tough and independent, but she was still little more than a child.

I said, 'You look knackered. Try and get some sleep. I'll call you in the morning and let you know what's planned.'

Alice said, 'Call me through the night if Mave finds anything. I'll leave my phone on.'

'Okay,' I turned toward Prim. Alice grabbed my arm and turned me back. She said, 'Promise?'

'I promise! Lord help the man you marry!'

'Amen to that,' said Prim and we all laughed…even Alice.

50

Next morning, Mave had to remind me what day it was, and that I was riding at Newcastle. She'd been up all night, with nothing to show for it. 'Try and get some sleep,' I said.

'I will.'

'Do me a favour and call Alice first or she'll be on the phone to me. Try to persuade her that no news is good news.'

'Yes, boss.' I smiled and kissed her.

I'd just started the car when Mac rang, 'Eddie, can you talk?'

'Sure. What's up?'

'Ever heard of Kelman Hines? Used to be a vet.'

'Name rings a bell from somewhere, but I don't know the guy.'

'He used to work on-course in the midlands and the north, then set up a big practice in Ripon, and began providing vets that were registered with him to work the tracks throughout the UK. Gave that up three years ago to open a lab in Newmarket. He specializes in equine nutrition now, though his company has various spin-offs.'

'Is this the Hines of Byerley Hines, the big company?'

'Same one. Listen, Hines contacted Bangor out of the blue the week before Montego Moon ran to say he was considering getting back into the business of supplying vets to tracks, and would they like to help him out.'

'Well, well, well…and Bangor booked him?'

'They did. Well they booked his company. And he pulled the

same stunt with Cheltenham, and Aintree and Uttoxeter.'

'His guys were on duty at every track?'

'One guy, Mike Boffo. He covered every raceday where a horse bolted.'

I slapped the steering wheel in celebration. 'This is looking good, Mac! What's Boffo's background?'

'I don't know yet. I'm more interested in pulling all the CCTV footage from the stables when he was in there.'

'How long will that take?'

'A couple of hours.'

'And you're keeping this quiet as agreed?'

'As agreed,' he said.

'What about Hines? Any sign of him being less than pure?'

'Not so far, but it's early days. He's certainly ambitious. Byerley Hines is a private company, so there's not much information in the public domain. Aside from nutrition they do portable blood testing machines, GPS-based exercise monitoring, non-invasive scoping, blah, blah, blah.'

'So going backwards to hiring out their guys piecemeal to tracks for a couple of hundred quid doesn't quite sit right?'

'Exactly.'

'And he has a lab, a lab full of high-tech kit including GPS stuff, so getting hold of some tiny speakers and some bandwidth is hardly a major challenge, eh?'

'That's what I was thinking,' Mac said, 'and sending the same guy each time.'

I said, 'Was this guy, Boffo, on that list you emailed last night?'

'No. Just the regular vets on the long term roster.'

'Okay. And the powers that be at Bangor and Uttoxeter etcetera who usually work off the roster, ask no questions when this top businessman rings them up out of the blue to say he'd love to be back in the business of collecting horse piss in plastic fucking buckets?'

'Well, they do more than dope testing, Eddie, but I take your point. I suspect he called the chairman in each case. They'd be old friends of his, or, at least, they'd be aware he was a big shot now. Human nature at work.'

'Well, one thing you could find out, is when Boffo's due back on track. That would give us a chance of nailing him with the radio kit.'

'I'll check on the rosters.'

'You sure you can ask these questions without anyone at your end sussing this?'

He sighed long and loud and I said, 'Okay! Okay, Mac, I'm sorry. I'll leave it with you. Let me know if there's anything on the CCTV footage, will you?'

'Where are you today?'

'Newcastle. Do me a favour and check if Boffo's going to be there. Oh, and double check that whoever is on duty doesn't work for Hines.'

'Boffo is not on duty anywhere today. The vets at each track are locals. Been on the books for donkeys' years.'

'In that case, see if you can get a price off a bookie that there'll be no wild horses taking off today. Then we can all retire on the winnings.'

'Good luck at Newcastle.'

'Thanks, Mac.'

Newcastle was east of home, almost a straight drive to the opposite coast. I arrived at the start on my first ride of the day to see Jon Vogel's fixed smile as he raised a hand to greet me.

I hadn't bothered checking who was on duty at the start. That was an old theory, filed under "failed". But still, I watched Vogel as he went cheerily about his job.

As we circled, and the sun broke through, Vogel moved toward a brown mare for his final check. He twanged the girth and smiled and slapped the mare's rump, and she reacted by lashing out with her near-hind and connecting with Vogel's left leg bang on the side of his knee joint. The cracking sound was so loud some of the horses spooked and every jockey turned as Vogel howled and went down.

Five minutes later, as the ambulance pulled slowly away, with a sedated Vogel strapped onto the bed, Bomber Harries said, 'Strange to see the ambulance heading back when all of us are still in the saddle.'

A few nodded, but nobody spoke and as the ambulance trundled toward the stand, another one lined up behind us ready to follow for this three-mile steeplechase.

Most jockeys are superstitious and many believe bad things come in threes. Vogel was the first casualty of the day. Looking around at some worried faces, I wished I could at least offer them the reassurance that there would be no horses in this race going wild.

51

Dusk was just giving way to darkness as I turned at the end the barn, and I saw in the cottage window the spark of a match, en Mave's face in the flare before she leant to light the homecoming lamp. I smiled.

Inside, I said, 'The shortest burning.'

'Indeed,' she said, holding the spent match between her raised fingers, 'I could have saved a match.'

'And a pennyworth of wax.' We smiled, and hugged and she said, 'Another winnerless day, I see?'

'There's always tomorrow,' I said, as I dropped my kitbag, 'At least I left the course under my own steam which is more than can be said of our old friend, Jon Vogel.'

'What happened?'

'He slapped one female rump too many. A mare kicked him. Apparently, when the doctor looked at his x-ray he described Vogel's knee as "mush". Probably not the precise medical term, but it gives you a good picture.'

'A mare. Ironic, in a way, for the anthropomorphic among us, at least.'

'Indeed. I believe she was American bred too, rubbing salt into the mush.'

'Karma.'

We settled over Mave's laptop, the steam from our coffee mugs drifting beyond the small desk lamp into the darkness. She turned to me, 'This could take half an hour.'

I shrugged, 'I'm not doing anything else.' I had asked Mave to try and get into the IT system at Byerley Hines and take a look at Kelman Hines's email.

'Go away,' she said, 'You'll fidget and you'll mumble and you'll sniff and I'll slap you.'

'I don't sniff!'

'You always sniff when you're waiting for me to find something. You just don't realize you're doing it. It's like sniffing something on the cooker to see if it's ready.'

'I promise not to sniff.'

'Go away! Light the stove. In fact, Call Kim. You haven't spoken to him for ages.'

'Because I feel like I'm intruding on the big family reunion. If he's missing home, he'll call,' I stood up, 'but I take the hint, I'm going. I'll check tomorrow's runners.'

Half an hour later, Mave brought her laptop to the kitchen table. I shifted my chair closer to hers and she paged through what she'd found, 'This is a list of the people Hines has spoken to in the last three months, by mobile phone. Here are the companies he's called. The yellow highlights link person to company.'

She clicked the next tab and rolled the cursor down through lines of text, 'These are the emails with his company address on, originating or terminating at the company server.'

'Good. What about his home email address?'

'You won't need those.'

I knew that look of Mave's and I felt a nervous jolt of anticipation, 'What did you find?'

'Hines travels a lot, mostly to North and South America. He uses software that pulls together his itinerary, you know, taxi pickup at seven, flight check-in at eight, land Chicago at eleven, and so on. It collates everything and sends him one email.'

'Uhuh?'

'On the first Thursday in February, he made a one-day trip to

Spain. A chauffeur met him at Malaga Airport and drove him up into the Sierra Nevada. The final leg of his journey was by donkey.'

She waited for my reaction. I just nodded. She said, 'The donkey carried him up a long and steep cliff path to here...' she clicked on another tab, which opened showing an aerial picture of what looked like a ranch set on a vast plateau. The buildings looked dangerously close to the cliff edge which dropped into a ravine so deep and dark, the bottom couldn't be seen. In what looked like a paddock of about five acres, was a herd of white horses, maybe a hundred in all.

I said, 'I'm guessing Hines wasn't there on a vet call.'

'You'd have to ask the owner of said horses.'

'Who is?'

'Senor Valentino Romanic.'

52

My instinct was to jump up and grab the car keys, but I forced myself to stay seated, still staring at the clifftop residence of Prim's father.

Mave was watching my face. She said, 'We're not done yet.' She brought up a YouTube page and clicked play on a video with the title: The Gypsy King Horse Whisperer. A white horse was being led around a large circular enclosure by a smiling young girl. A crowd lined the wooden rails of the enclosure. Ten seconds in, the horse went crazy and took off and began racing around the ring as the girl tumbled in the dirt and rolled theatrically before coming to rest on her front, apparently unconscious, as the horse ran and bucked and the crowd took fright.

Then a long-haired man in a jewelled waistcoat and flapping white trousers jumped from the top rail into the enclosure and held his right hand high as he moved to stand by the girl. The man watched the racing animal, turning on his heel, his arm still high, his lips moving…then he walked slowly toward the perimeter of the ring until he was right in the path of the galloping horse. As it rounded the bend, ten strides from him, he lowered his right arm, put both hands on his hips and spread his feet.

The horse stopped so quickly that dust rose in a cloud, drifting around the man as he walked slowly toward the shaking animal and touched it gently between the eyes.

The horse lowered its head and was still. The man turned to look at the girl and she stirred and slowly sat up. The crowd cheered and the girl got to her feet and went to the man, who hugged her to his side and stroked her head.

The horse moved forward gently to join the man and the girl, who reached to touch the horse's nose as she smiled. Mave hit pause and zoomed the screen to an enlargement of the girl's face. Much pixelated as it was, there was no mistaking the beauty of a teenage Primarolo Romanic.

I turned slowly from the screen to look at Mave, 'Prim?'

'Looks very like her.'

'How old? How long ago would that be?'

'She looks younger than Alice there…maybe twelve, thirteen.'

I turned again to the freeze frame…'Jeez, look at her, the whole world waiting for her. You can see it in her eyes, can't you? Everything still possible. She could have done anything…'

'If her father, I'm assuming that is Senor Romanic, hadn't been using her as a shill.'

'Is there anything more? I don't suppose you see him switching anything or touching the horse's ears?'

'He'll have somebody in the crowd throwing the switches.'

I looked at Mave as I counted back, 'Prim is forty, so that's almost thirty years ago. How would they be sending remote signals to speakers back then?'

Mave watched me, as though waiting for a punchline. I opened my hands and said 'What?'

'Ever heard of a transistor radio?'

'Bit big for stuffing into a horse's lug.'

She shook her head, 'Very funny. The speaker out of a basic nineteen-sixties transistor would easily fit.'

I turned back to Prim's face, 'So that's where she got the idea.'

'Well, playing dead every day at that age with a wild horse galloping circles round you would kind of tend to stick in the memory, don't you think?'

I nodded, still staring at Prim, feeling pity for her and anger at what had become of her life, of her potential. I said, 'Mave, I just need a sexist check, here. I need you to confirm that Prim really was as stupid as I think she was?'

'Was or is?'

'Tell me she wouldn't have set all this up just to keep a man like Dil Grant?'

'That wouldn't have been her only reason. I suspect she did it to kill off Vita Brodie, metaphorically, of course.'

'And to win enough money to put her up there with Vita?'

'I don't think so. I believe that would have been daddy's part of the deal.'

'Why?'

Mave shrugged, 'I don't know. Prim just doesn't seem the type who's ever lived for money.'

'The old crime of passion, then? Except that it extended to kidnapping Ben Searcey.'

'Well, at least you know he's safe...and she did look after his daughter.'

I closed the laptop lid, 'Well, one little piece of the puzzle falls into place, Prim going to Deadwood. It never sat right with me that she would just up and leave Dil and Vita cozily together. That was like awarding Vita a big fat You Win badge.'

'Proves she has a conscience, or half a conscience, I suppose,' Mave said.

'I doubt Alice will see it that way.'

Mave leant forward and rested her chin on her hands, and her eyebrows rose together, asking what I was going to do. I sighed and massaged my face. I checked my watch, 'Is there any way that Senor Romanic could know that we're onto him?'

'Nothing's impossible, but I doubt it would be through anything I've done.'

I reached for her hand, 'I'm not criticizing you.'

'I know. Just saying.'

I sat back again and made a noise that was half sigh, half moan. Mave smiled, 'You're inventing a whole new acoustic for this little kitchen.'

'There's more to come, Maven…What do we do now? Call Dil? Mac? Alice?'

'I think you should stop being all logical just for my sake, and just do what you want to do.'

'What I want to do, in a way, is go and see Prim and have her tell us we've got it all wrong, and give us rock solid one hundred percent proof.'

'Well, that's what we'll do.'

'Now?'

'As soon as you like,' she said.

I stood up, 'Final question, do we do it all in front of Alice?'

Mave hesitated, then got to her feet, 'Let's talk about that in the car.'

We headed southeast for Dil's place, working through contingency plans. What if Prim wasn't in the cottage? What if she was in Dil's bed? It would be close to midnight by the time we got there.

What if she was in her own bed, asleep? Were we to call her on the phone? Ring the doorbell? Ask her to wake Alice? Did I need to ring Dil and tell him to expect to see me rolling into the yard but not to come out and speak to me?

Finally, Mave said, 'This would be best left until the morning, wouldn't it?'

'Can't now, though, can we? We'd be awake all night wondering if Prim had somehow found out and taken off…with Alice.'

'How likely is that?'

I shook my head, 'We can't wait, Mave.' I glanced at the dashboard clock, 'It's not ten yet. I'll call Dil and tell him we need to see Alice because of something that's happened back in Deadwood and that he's not to go near her in case she spooks and runs.'

'Best tell him not to speak to Prim, then, wherever she is, which might just be lying right beside him when you make the call.'

She was right. We were just going to have to keep driving, and handle things as they spun out.

53

We parked on the narrow road, 300 yards away from Dil's and set out between the hedgerows under a half moon. Mave said, 'One light on upstairs. Is that Dil's bedroom, do you know?'

'Haven't a clue.'

'How will he take this?'

'He'll go fucking mad. I can guarantee. Whatever he feels for Prim will be sunk by the thought of the twenty-five grand he lost on Montego Moon.'

'She couldn't have known he'd had that bet, could she?'

'No way. No one would know except Dil.'

'She's entitled to have that loss offset against him winning The Supreme…well half The Supreme. If they hadn't nobbled Spalpeen, Stevedore would just have been placed.'

'Dil won't be sitting there rationalizing, believe me. He'll go apeshit. And it sounds like Prim gets your sympathy in this.'

'She got the good looks and the bad men. You'd be amazed how many do,' she turned to me, the light wind lifting her hair, and she parted it to look at me, 'you're not exactly short on sympathy yourself, or we would be knocking on Dil's door first.'

I shrugged. We were a hundred and fifty yards from the gate when a cloud hid the moon, and Mave stopped. I turned to her, 'You okay?'

'Just had a sudden memory of that really dark night we were prowling around Nina Raine's place.'

I laughed and took her arm, 'You were just a wee bit scared that time.'

'I was officially shitting myself. Really. I remember the cramps in my bowel.'

'Good old mother nature. Fight or flight. And if it looks like flight, you need to be carrying no excess weight so you can flee fast. That's why you'll often see a bird shitting as it takes off, if you surprise it.'

'Well, you almost saw this bird shitting that night as she took off.'

I laughed.

'Sshhh! You'll wake the dogs.'

She was right. Best be quiet until the dogs caught my scent. They'd be fine then.

As we turned the corner behind the barn, the cottage was fifty yards away. No lights were on inside, but after five more paces the security light on the gable end clicked and fired up a sodium circle of light. Our right hands came up to shield our eyes.

We stopped at the front door. I looked back at the main house. No lights had come on inside.

Mave took out her phone and called Prim.

I watched Mave's face in the harsh light. I could hear the ringtone.

'Hello?'

'Prim, it's Mave. I'm outside. Can you let me in?' All this in an anxious stage whisper, and it did its job, for Prim asked no questions. Twenty seconds later she opened the door. Her red housecoat brought that old flamenco dancer image once more to my mind.

Prim looked at Mave, and Mave looked back, saying nothing. Prim swallowed, then turned slightly to look at me...she held my gaze for just long enough to be sure that what she had seen in Mave's eyes was in mine too, then as the shame rose in her, she lowered her head to stare at the ground. She did not look up as she stepped back, silently inviting us in.

Just before Prim switched on the light in the small living room, I saw in the hearth the pale red of the last embers. The ceiling light made everything in the grate look grey, but Prim must have sat up quite late. She looked alert, so we hadn't wakened her. She sat at the end of the longer of the two old leather couches, the worn rug running between them to the tiled hearth.

Alice's denim jacket lay over the back of the short couch on which Mave and I sat to face Prim.

I thought for a moment that she was going to try some bluffing small talk, but the longer the silence had stretched, the tighter the noose had become, as though all three of us could see it.

I said quietly, 'Is Alice safe?'

'She's asleep.'

I said, 'I thought it was best to talk to you first about your father and Kelman Hines. I wasn't sure what to do for the best, but we've known each other a long time and I thought I owed you this.'

Her shoulders went back, and her big breasts, still in a bra, came up and showed their cleavage in the deep neck of her scarlet dressing gown, and she reached and closed that gap and kept one hand holding the gown shut. But she didn't cower. From somewhere, she was finding a brave face without seeming proud. She said, 'You know why I did it?'

'I think so, but tell me.'

'I wanted her out and gone. For good.'

'Even at the cost of Dil going under?'

'Once she'd taken her horses away, we would have got new owners.'

'New widows. You know Dil's routine by now.'

'No more widows. Things would have changed.' She stared at the wall as though that wished-for movie of her perfect future were playing out there.

I said, 'Where's Ben being held?'

She turned quickly, looking afraid, 'We haven't got Ben! I'd never have allowed it. I promise!'

'You might never have allowed it, Prim, but I think you lost control after Montego Moon.'

'I did not! It was me who said they had to find a way of not hurting the jockeys, the horses. I almost died when you were injured on Montego Moon.'

223

'That makes two of us.'

'It wasn't what I wanted. My idea was to put something in the feed. Or take something out, just the feed that was delivered here.'

I recalled that Dil had met Prim when she'd been working as a rep for her father's company, which supplied horsenuts for thoroughbreds.

I said, 'So who's idea was it?'

She opened her mouth, then stopped, reluctant to blame the only one it could be. I said 'Your father?'

She just kept looking at me. I said, 'He suggested that old trick you used to do when you were a kid, where he'd set the horse off in the ring and then stop it.'

'How did you know about that?'

'I,' I glanced at Mave, 'we, I should say, and more than seven thousand others have seen it on YouTube.'

Prim's pride finally gave way and she slumped and put her head in her hands.

I said, 'How old were you then, Prim?'

She massaged her face and sighed long and low then looked up at me, 'Depends. I was nine when we started doing that. But it went on for years.'

'Did you mention it to your father when you went to see him about Vita?'

'No. We didn't talk about it. He had a deal with Kelman Hines to let him use his special ingredients in the horsenuts. Kelman had bought his business. My idea was to substitute our supplies with something low energy or maybe get Kelman to introduce a virus.'

'Why would Hines do that?'

She hesitated, then said, 'Father was confident he could persuade him.'

'But then your father came up with a better idea, one he could use on any horse.'

She became much more animated, especially with her hands, 'Eddie! I warned them at the start. They promised me the horse would just keep running until it got tired. They said there was no way it would try to jump a fence in such a panic.'

I nodded slowly, caught between sympathy and anger. I said, 'What sound were they playing through the speakers?'

'A wolf pack. A hunting wolf pack.'

'Radio-controlled?'

'Yes.'

'And after Montego Moon they turned off one speaker to steer the horse around the jumps?'

'That's right…that helped. They promised me it would.'

I nodded, 'And after that they turned the sound off as soon as the horse had disqualified itself? That's why Kingdom Come stopped at Uttoxeter the day you led him up?'

'Yes, yes, yes! That's all correct. Everything! And I'm glad it's out now. But we don't know where Ben is, I promise you that! I swear on it!'

'Maybe you don't know, Prim, but your father will know, won't he? Wasn't it him who arranged for the two gypsies to grab Ben at the Blue Anchor?'

She got up quickly, 'It was nothing to do with us!' She glanced up at the ceiling, obviously wary of her rising voice waking Alice. She came over and stopped to look down at me, 'Stand up,' she said.

I stood. She reached for my hands and raised them and gripped them firmly, 'Eddie, I promise you, I will swear on anything you ask me to, I would never allow Alice to suffer like this. We do not have Ben. My father is as upset as I am that he has gone missing. He has been trying everything he can to find him.'

I looked straight into her dark eyes. If she was lying, her acting was far better than Dil Grant's had ever been. She said, 'My father is worried too, because whoever has Ben must know what we've been doing. He has been expecting a blackmail call.'

I eased my hands free, and Prim slowly clasped hers at her waist, then reached to close her gown collar once again. I said, 'What about Hines? Apart from his guy handling the speakers on track, where does he come in?'

'Nowhere. That's all he's done.'

'So who scooped the betting winnings off Spalpeen at Cheltenham?'

'My father.'

No hesitation.

'On his own?'

'He paid for some false documents to open bank accounts with, that's all.'

'So what does Kelman Hines get out of this?'

More hesitation…her gaze dropping again, unable to look me in the eye. She said, 'When my father was launching the horsefeed business, he paid Mister Hines for endorsements.'

'Was this when Hines was running the equine nutrition lab?'

'Yes. My father was paying him a percentage of each sale.'

'Undeclared, obviously?'

She nodded, then kept her head down. I said, 'And this was back when you were the travelling sales rep for your father's brand?'

'Yes,' quieter now. I watched her. She would not look at me. I said, 'So, since then, Hines has built a…well, an empire, I don't think that's too strong a word for it. And you're telling me he'd risk that because of an old debt to your father?'

Prim looked up, fighting to raise that pride again, but looking sadder, 'Mister Hines also had an affair. His wife had just had their first child.' She managed to hold my gaze, but the sadness in her eyes had been replaced by shame.

Mave shifted in her seat.

I said to Prim, 'So, your father, who you say is anxiously awaiting a blackmail call, was blackmailing Kelman Hines?'

Still she held my gaze, unwilling to duck out of her responsibility, 'We both did.'

'But your father made the approach?'

'Yes.'

I sat down beside Mave. Prim walked slowly back to her seat by the cold hearth. She settled there and looked at me, and then at Mave, 'We don't have Alice's Dad. We don't know where he is. I'll take you to see my father tomorrow. You can search his place. I won't call him. We can sit up all night.'

I believed her. I turned to Mave. She pursed her lips and raised her eyebrows. I said to Prim, 'The night before Ben disappeared he told me he'd found a lead that was very promising, and that there was just one thing more he had to check before confirming it.'

She listened without blinking, her concentration fixed on me. I said, 'The most logical find Ben could have made was that Kelman Hines's company had supplied the vet in charge at each of those tracks. It was information that would have been reasonably easy to find as a layman. All Ben would need to have done was put two and two together.'

Prim said, 'Ben made no contact with Kelman. Not that night, not ever.'

'So says Kelman'

'Eddie, this has been Kelman's worst nightmare come true. All he's ever wanted is for it to be over.'

'Exactly. So what would he do if he gets a call from a guy who used to be one of the best investigative journalists that ever picked up a telephone?'

Her head went up, her jaw muscles clenched, and her hands went out, 'Eddie, listen-'

I broke in, 'If Hines was afraid of your father blabbing, how scared is he going to be of a top reporter?'

Prim said, 'Have you ever met Kelman Hines?'

'No.'

'Well, one minute in his company would prove to you that he'd shit himself if a child phoned him about that…if Alice phoned him.'

'All the more reason for him to call up a hit man.'

Prim clenched her fists and leant forward, 'But he didn't, did he? You said that yourself right from the start that Ben wasn't dead, that somebody had him. Why a call a hitman to go through all that palaver on Crosby beach?'

I watched her. She had a point, but I wouldn't concede it, though I sensed she was telling the truth. She watched me, then she shook her head quickly, as though trying to dislodge something, and she sighed heavily then looked at me again, 'Eddie, I'm done. There isn't any other way I know to try to persuade you. So you'd better tell Dil now, or call the police, or do whatever it was you planned to do next.'

I sighed and slumped back against the fat old leather cushion, 'What I'd planned to do was to drive out to wherever Ben was and bring him home.'

'I'm sorry,' Prim said, 'sorry for everything.'

I turned to Mave, 'What do you think?'

Mave said, 'I think we should tell Alice.'

I delayed my answer long enough to be courteous to Mave's suggestion, then said, 'That might not be the best thing for her just now.'

Mave looked at me for a moment or two, then said, 'So, are we to deceive her, too?'

I hesitated.

Prim finally covered her face, and wept.

54

Mave showed no indecision in crossing the room to console Prim, who was trying to suppress her sobbing. Not waking Alice would be in Prim's mind, but the more she tried to stifle the sound, the more guttural and broken the sobbing became.

Mave put an arm around Prim, pulling her head down on to her shoulder, and that broke the dam and Prim moaned and howled eliminating any chance of planning how we were going to tell Alice.

A minute later, she appeared in the doorway, pushing tousled hair back behind those springy ears, and I saw again that children's home expression: assessing the situation, trying to figure out where the threat lay and how best to tackle it.

I said, 'Come in, Alice. Prim's just had some bad news...family news.'

Alice came in and closed the door. She wore pale blue pyjamas and white fluffy socks that sparkled, even in the dim light. She went to the other side of Prim, and she too put an arm around her, and Prim's howling hit that note of desolation which said that she might as well be in the desert, a thousand miles from the closest comfort.

I went to the window and watched the inevitable play out as the first of the yard's dogs barked, setting off the others in a firecracker string of noise. My glance moved to the window of Dil's bedroom, and I found myself counting silently...at 12 the light came on and at 14, Dil's wild-haired head and shoulders loomed into the yellow-lit window frame.

The circus was well and truly rolling.

Twenty minutes later we were in Dil's kitchen. The story had been told in the cottage, its details steadily chiselling at the closeness that had formed around Prim.

Dil had suggested we move. His face told me he was reformulating his Prim-plan and that it was now very much advantage, Mister Grant.

Alice had said little. Reading her face was way harder than reading Dil's. In the cottage, when I'd been telling Dil and Alice what had happened, Prim had pleaded with Alice to accept that Ben's disappearance had nothing to do with her. But Alice had remained silent.

Now, seated around this long pine table, Prim turned her haggard face once more to Alice, 'Please tell me you believe me! I would never hurt your father! I have no idea where he is!'

Alice, emotionless, said, 'I believe you,' and Prim's head went down and she tried to find more tears, but they'd dried up, and she covered her face with her hands and moaned long and low.

Dil said, 'Why don't you go upstairs and lie down?'

It was more a directive than a question and Prim's timid response of rising silently and walking toward the hallway laid bare their relationship as it had really been and always would be, in spite of her small rebellions. I looked around the others to see their responses: Mave sat straight-faced and unblinking. Alice seemed cool...her mind working. Dil looked triumphant. Yes, Prim had betrayed him, but for reasons that would boost his ego. He knew his worries about the next runaway horse were over. And there'd be no further desertions by Prim: she owed him now, forever.

He looked at us, careful not to let the smile in his eyes spread.

'What now?' Alice said, looking at each of us in turn, and seeming effortlessly more mature than Dil, seated alongside her.

I said, 'If we're accepting that your Dad's disappearance has nothing to do with Prim and her scheme, then we're back to square one.'

Alice said, 'Do you believe her?'

'Yes. I think she's telling the truth of what she knows. I'm not convinced about her father, or about Kelman Hines. Her father collected almost two million from laying Spalpeen at Cheltenham. How easily would you give up that source?' That brought a sudden thought of how stupid I'd been. I turned to Dil, 'Will you go and see if Prim has her phone?'

Mave said, 'I've got her phone,' and she took it from the pocket of her jacket, showing no emotion. I smiled at her. She did that cheeks-shrug that I saw from time to time, the one that meant "What else could I do?" And although we'd had no chance to speak privately, it told me that Mave's suspicions echoed mine.

I said to Dil, 'Is there a phone in your room she could use?'

'I think mine is still up there,' he rose, 'I'll go and check.'

Alice said, 'How can we find out what her father knows?'

Mave said, 'If Prim will cooperate, I could get into his PC very quickly.'

'Do you think she will?' Alice asked.

Mave said, 'I think she probably will. She seems like she'd bet her life that he's not guilty...not with your dad, at least.'

I said, 'If she won't cooperate, that would be an admission that she's got doubts about it, so we might as well find out.'

Dil came back, waving his phone and smiling. He put it on the table and said, 'I'm going to pour a large brandy for Prim, see if it will get her off to sleep. Anyone want a drink?'

I got up, 'Not for me, but I'll walk through with you. Mave?'

'No, thanks.' she said.

I looked at Alice, 'Coke?'

'No, thanks.'

I followed Dil across the hall and into the room where his 'bar' sat, an old piece of maplewood, recovered, he had claimed from a Yukon saloon. A silk replica of the Canadian flag was pinned to the bar front.

Dil poured whiskey for himself and gestured at me with the neck of the bottle, 'No, thanks,' I said.

He filled the glass with soda and drank the lot, big Adam's apple bobbing, strong and regular as a heartbeat.

He put the empty glass down, 'Aaahhh! Sounds stupid, but it feels almost like a celebration drink.' He gripped the brandy bottle and tipped it, then stopped. He picked up the heavy crystal tumbler and took a cloth and polished it in a manner so careful it seemed seductive. I said, 'Dil, can you forget about your plans for the remainder of the night, just for now? We've got a lot to work out.'

'What plans?' But he reddened as he protested and it took nothing more than a raised eyebrow from me for him to nod once and put the glass down.

'Pour me a whiskey,' I said.

He did, and another for himself. He pushed the glass toward me, 'Ice is in the kitchen.' He wanted away, back to the safety of numbers. I said, 'It's fine. Come and sit down.'

We sat by the leaded window overlooking the dark cobbled yard, quiet again now the dogs were asleep.

Dil settled across from me and looked out, and drank a mouthful and swallowed with relish and said, 'Jesus…I can plan again…at last.'

'You think so? What are you going to tell Vita?'

'I'll think of something.'

'And do you think this something will allow for keeping Prim out of prison?'

He waved that prospect away with his free hand, 'Vita's satisfaction will come from saying "I told you so".'

'Dil, Vita will gut her. She will stand her up in a courtroom and she'll pay to fill the press gallery and she will break your woman apart piece by piece. All those eyes that were on Prim's swinging hips at Uttoxeter that day, Vita will want to see focused on the tearing down and the public shaming. It will be all she can do not to lick her lips as she watches.'

He smiled, swept his fringe and said, 'At first, maybe. I'll talk her round.'

'How?'

'I'll figure it out, okay? It's not your concern. why are you so worried about Prim, she almost got you killed?'

'Because she did something stupid for what she thought was a good reason. Not for money, not to hurt me or anyone else, well, physically, at least, but to try and keep you…and, even as I say it, I find it hard to believe.'

He smiled and raised his glass, 'Well, cheers, my friend. I love you too!'

'Dil! Postpone the fucking party, will you? Ten days ago I had the chief constable of Merseyside and the head honcho in the BHA asking what I knew about these wild horses. What do you suggest we tell them? The guys who got conned out of a whack of money over Spalpeen are going to want a posse of Spanish fucking donkeys to ride up that cliff face and pin Prim's old man to the wall. And, apart from all that, where is Ben Searcey?'

'Well, if Prim's right, he's not tied up with this, so that's a relief, at least.'

'A relief for you. What about Ben? What about Alice?'

Dil held his glass low and leant forward, 'Eddie, don't take this the wrong way, but, as you just said, there's plenty other stuff for me to work out before I get around to Ben Searcey.'

'Ben is working for Vita and you. You employed him.'

'But the job's done, now, ain't it?' he swallowed the rest of his drink.

I watched him, believing he was winding me up. But there was no telltale smile, just a shrug to dislodge from his shoulders all responsibility for the safety of Ben Searcey.

'You serious?' I said.

The shrug again, 'First things first,' he said.

I got to my feet, 'I'm done with you, Dil.'

He looked up, did the fringe-sweep and said, 'You're overreacting, as ever.'

'Go and bring Prim down. Mave needs her to help us check out her father's involvement.'

'Eddie, she's not well enough.'

'She's well enough for you to be planning to shag her all night. Go and get her.'

He glared at me, leaving the fringe alone this time, 'Don't talk to me like that in my own house.'

I bent forward until my face was a foot from his, 'Go and fucking get her or I'll go!'

55

Alice came with us when we left Dil's place. Also with us was the knowledge that there was nothing on Valentino Romanic's PC to suggest he or Kelman Hines had any involvement in the disappearance of Alice's Dad.

In the car we considered our next move. I said, 'Prim's father might simply have been smart enough to keep all the sensitive stuff offline.'

'What about the panicky emails with Hines?' Mave said.

I shrugged, 'Double bluff?'

'Didn't read like that to me,' Mave said.

I said 'I don't think I'd be happy writing Senor Romanic out of this until I see him face to face and ask him the questions?'

'What questions?' Alice said, leaning forward through the gap in the front seats. Mave said, 'Alice, put your seatbelt on, will you? When we find your Dad, we want you in good condition.'

Alice slid back and clipped in, asking again 'Eddie, what questions do you think need to be asked?'

'I don't know, Alice, I just meant that I want to see his face, watch for his reactions.'

Alice said, 'But we'd lose a couple of days if you had to go to Spain.'

'We could all go…the three of us,' I said.

Mave said, 'I think Alice is right, Eddie. Put together Prim's denials and what was on his PC, well, I don't think they've got Ben.'

'I don't think they have, either, but it doesn't sit right with me just leaving it at this. Not with a guy who's had it away with all that money.'

Mave said, 'Call Mac. Let him deal with it. Or the chief constable who was so keen to implicate you in all this. You're going to have to tell them anyway.'

'But what about Prim?' I said.

Mave said, 'It's not just Prim, though. If she'd done all this alone, maybe you could have swung something for her. All she wanted was the horses stopped. She didn't want a penny from it. It's her father who's the criminal, the old Gypsy King. Let Prim take her chances with the police. She'll be okay.'

I glanced in the mirror to catch Alice's eye, 'Alice?'

'Prim will be all right. I wouldn't worry about her. But this gypsy thing seems strange now, to me, anyway. Do you think that man who called could have been trying to push us onto Prim's Dad somehow?'

I glanced at Mave. She held my gaze for a moment then raised an eyebrow. I said, 'That would mean two things. First, the Spanish connection, if you want to call Prim's side that, is telling the truth. They don't have your Dad. Second, whoever is holding your Dad knows about the Spanish connection. It could be that your Dad had sussed out the Spanish connection on the night he disappeared, but that means we'd have to swallow a hell of a coincidence.' I turned to Mave, 'What do you think?'

'It's not impossible, I suppose. Maybe Ben had put everything together and maybe he tried to trade the information with whoever took him. If he told them what was happening, they could bet on any future races, or maybe they could blackmail the Spanish connection, as you call it.'

Alice said, 'But the main thing they'd want to do is throw us off their trail and onto Prim's. So what reason would they have for kidnapping Dad?'

I said, 'I wonder if it's a combination and your Dad just got very unlucky.' I glanced again in the rearview mirror at her, 'Remember your Dad was going into betting shops, following DJ's guys?'

'He did that quite a lot,' Alice said.

'Did he ever say anything about them putting money on horses?'

'He said it was the machines, the FOBTs, they call them. You can put a hundred in, or five hundred or whatever, and then play just ten pounds' worth and cash out, and it prints a slip with the amount, which is obviously an official piece of paper. Dad reckoned they were just doing that to clean the money.'

'Do you keep a diary?' I asked.

'Yes.'

'Would you have put in it that your Dad had tracked someone to a bookie's that day?'

'Not every time, but probably some of the time. I've got it with me.'

'The diary?'

'It's in my bag.'

'When we get home, will you check it and give me those dates?'

'Sure. What are you thinking, that they might have been betting on those wild horses on the day they ran?'

'They wouldn't have been betting them if they were in on this, but they might well have been betting something else in the race. And their bets would be anonymous. No need for usernames or passwords or bank accounts.'

'But they were DJ's yobs,' Alice said, 'how would he get to know about the horses?'

'Alice, DJ will be working for somebody else. There'll be some Mister Big somewhere, probably with no criminal record because he employs kids like DJ to make sure they are the ones who end up in court.'

'He's only interested in girls, young girls, I can tell you that for a fact.'

'Do you know any of these girls who have actually, well, gone with him? Someone who might be able to tell us something more about what he's doing?'

'I know a few of them, but I'm not exactly their best friend. They usually spit at me.'

'When DJ followed you home from the Blue Anchor did he say anything?'

'Nothing. He was just trying to scare us.'

I said, 'There's got to be some connection there, though. Your Dad disappears and DJ is suddenly back on the scene.'

Alice said, 'Can't you find out what Bruno said to DJ to warn him off? Why would he think that the warning didn't apply anymore when Dad went missing?'

'Good question. I'll call Monty in the morning.'

Over the final few miles, climbing up the valley toward the farm, I grew more and more optimistic that the Deadwood connection was now the likeliest solution.

But when we reached home, Alice's diary closed the book on the betting side. Of the eleven entries with dates of betting shop visits, none was within three days of a bolting horse.

Mave settled Alice in the one guest room we had in the cottage. Most visitors slept in the much bigger farmhouse, but we wanted her close by.

Alice's bedroom was next to ours, so there'd be no discussions in the dark for fear of being overheard. I waited in The Snug where the walls would soundproof our conversation. Mave came in.

'How is she?' I asked.

'Settled, calm...I can see her eyes working through options. She's a remarkable kid.'

'Did she say anything about Prim?'

'Not a word, why'

'I know how close she'd got to her. I just didn't expect her to shrug off the deception.'

'Alice has had more disappointments than you and me put together. She'll be a pro by now at handling them.'

'Looks like it.'

I yawned, and groaned and said, 'I feel as though I've been awake for a week.'

'Well, we'd better get to bed. It's nearly six.'

I looked at my watch, 'I ought to just stay up for another hour and call Mac and Monty.'

'What difference will it make? Ring them at ten. Are you just going to leave Mac to deal with Prim and her father, and Hines?'

I sighed, massaging my face, 'I don't know…I think, well…we could probably still keep Prim out of it. Just tell Mac it was her father who was behind it.'

'Which is fine until old Valentino then starts saying it was a labour of love for his only daughter, his princess.'

I hung my head, 'Jeez…'

Mave ruffled my hair, 'Come on. Your brain's useless when you're this tired.' She offered her hand and I took it and followed her to bed.

56

A hot shower ending with a forced minute below a very cold shower blasted me awake as it always does. Mave was already up and at her desk.

'Morning,' she said.

'Is it? I don't know what end of the day I'm at.'

'You seldom do.'

'Is Alice okay?'

'Still asleep, or, at least, her eyes were closed. You making coffee?'

'I am.'

'Black for me, please.'

I filled the kettle then headed for the door, 'I am going outside, Maven. I may be some time.'

She smiled, but didn't look up.

The air was chilly, but the sun warmed my face, and I walked to the rear of the cottage to stand looking down the valley to the snaking Ullswater, its surface dark blue in the shadow of the surrounding fells. I called Dil, 'How's Prim this morning?'

'Sad. That's all she'll say, that she's sad and sorry. How is Alice?'

'Cool. Determined. Remarkable.'

'She is an unusual kid. Most of Prim's tears have been over Alice.'

'Tell her I don't think Alice will hold it against her. But tell her too that I'm going to call Mac and give him the whole story, names as well.'

'Eddie! Not until I've spoken to Vita!'

'Well, you'd better get on the phone.'

'She's in New York! It's five in the fucking morning there!'

'Okay, okay, calm down. I'll hold until this afternoon.'

'What about Prim?'

'She'll need to take what's coming, Dil, plain and simple. I've tried every way of looking at it and I can't find one that'll suit her.'

'Eddie, come on! How long have you known her?'

'Don't pull this shit on me, Dil. She's right at the heart of it. She thought it up, she-'

'She didn't think it up! It was her father who came up with that. Her idea was for him to get some bad feed for the yard to make all the horses sick. She told you that!'

'So she wanted to poison them instead? Ahh, that'll be fine then, eh?'

'Eddie!'

'Listen, Dil, whatever the original plan was, what actually happened was that the old man resurrected his con from thirty years back. Very dramatic, very entertaining, but very law-breaking.'

'Look, there must be some other way out. I promised Prim I would fix this for her.'

'You'll never slide yourself out of that Hollywood hero skin, will you? How the hell are you going to fix it for her?'

'What if I can get Vita onside?'

I smiled, shaking my head, 'Jeez, that must have been some night you just spent with Primarolo Romanic. You've always been deluded, Dil, but do you seriously believe you are going to tell Vita what Prim did to her horses, and Vita is then going to come out on her side?'

'Give me a chance, at least.'

'You can have a chance. Take it. No problem. If by three this afternoon you can get Vita to phone me and say she wants Prim protected in this, then I won't call Mac.'

'Good. That's enough. I can do that.'

'Dil, listen to you...you're trying to persuade yourself.'

'Just give me until three.'

241

'Fine. But remember, I want to speak to Vita. I want to hear from her, not you.'

'No problem.'

I walked to the front of the cottage and met Alice coming out the door, leaving it half open. She smiled with her mouth, 'Hi,' she said.

'Good morning. Where are you headed?'

'I just wanted to get my bearings. See where we are in the daylight.'

'I can give you a guided tour.'

She hesitated briefly, then said, 'Okay.'

'Want to get a jacket? It's breezy away from the shelter of the buildings.'

'I'm fine, thanks.' She wore her jeans and a tight pink t-shirt with a big glittery flower on the front. I said, 'Your nice white trainers will probably get dirty. Mave's got some wellies that'll probably fit you.'

'I'm okay, thanks. I can chuck the trainers in the washing machine…if you have a washing machine?'

'You put shoes in a washing machine?'

'Why not?'

'They're too heavy. They'll bust the drum. The soles will melt.'

She inclined her head in the same mock-thoughtful way she'd done at lunch that day in Liverpool, after the hearing, 'None of the above,' she said.

I laughed, 'Come on!'

We walked down the drive to the front door of the farmhouse, 'Oops,' I said, 'I forgot the keys. I won't be a minute.'

'It's okay. I don't need to see inside. Not now. Just want to kind of see where I am in relation to things.'

'What kind of things?'

She looked out across the fields, through the ranks of budding trees and hedgerows toward the horizon, 'Civilization?' she said, and I laughed again.

'We'll walk the perimeter and I'll tell you when we turn from north to south etcetera.' We walked. She said, 'Where's Liverpool from here?'

I pointed south, 'Thataway, about a hundred miles going straight.'

'Where's the nearest main road?'

'Over that way, maybe five miles straight, twelve driving.'

'Shops?'

'Glenridding for basics, ten minutes. Penrith for everything else, half an hour.'

She nodded and we walked on along the front of the farm by the dry stone wall. Alice said, 'I've only ever seen this much green from a train window, or on the telly.'

'What do you think of it live then?'

'Big. The sky's massive.'

I smiled, 'I know what you mean. I like big skies.'

We went ten paces with just the sound of footfalls then Alice said, 'Did you speak to Bruno Guta yet about what he said to DJ?'

'Not yet. I just spoke to Dil, and he's asked me to hold off telling anyone until he's spoken to Vita Brodie. He is...well, he's hoping to find a way out of this for Prim.'

I didn't know how Alice would react, but she stayed cool and just nodded slowly. The breeze blew strands of her hair across her face. She pulled them away and looked out across the fields. I said, 'Dil reckons he can get Vita to let Prim off the hook. Completely. How would you feel about that?'

'Whatever. It doesn't matter to me. She wasn't involved in Dad disappearing so I don't really care.'

'Fair enough.'

'But if it means you can't speak to Bruno, then I think we should go back to Deadwood and see what DJ knows about Dad.'

'Funny, that's exactly what I was thinking.'

She smiled, 'Really?'

'Really. The only other people your dad was pissing off were in Deadwood. If it's not to do with the horses, it's got to be connected with whatever DJ's doing. I shouldn't have jumped to the conclusion that night that your dad had been picked up for something he'd found out about the horses.'

Alice said, 'You're going to have a problem getting anywhere near

DJ now. He'll do a runner as soon as he sees you.'

'No, he won't. He might be scared, but he'll be even more scared of losing face again. He could shoot me or knock me down in his fancy car, but he won't run.'

'Are you ever scared?'

'Often.'

'Of people like DJ?'

'They're the ones you should be scared of, the ones who've been embarrassed in front of their friends, the ones who've been, what do you say, dissed?'

She smiled and was quiet for a few strides, then said, 'You know you said that DJ was probably just a kind of runner working for whoever's doing the trafficking?'

'Uhuh?'

'I was thinking last night that if Bruno could get DJ to back off without even touching him, there might be a chance that he knows whoever DJ's working for.'

'And that maybe he spoke to Mister Big rather than DJ?'

Alice nodded without looking at me, almost as though she'd moved on in her head to the next step. I said, 'That's a good shout, Alice. I'll give Sir Monty a call when we get back.'

'I was going to mention him too. He's never failed once to help Dad. Not once.'

'That's true.'

'He knows the chief constable, doesn't he? Do you think he could maybe press him harder?'

'Every chance, yes, every chance. I'll ask him.'

'Good. Should we go back now? I've left my phone in the bedroom.'

'Sure.'

Mave was at the kitchen table, flipping through the newspaper. 'On strike?' I said.

'Fingers overheating.'

'That why you couldn't pour your own coffee after the kettle boiled?' I hit the switch again to reheat the water.

'I didn't want to dine without you, darling.'

'You mean you didn't want to do anything that approximates manual work in any form whatsoever. You would literally starve to death or dehydrate if I wasn't around.' I rinsed the yellow mugs, 'What the hell did you do before you met me?'

'Enjoyed a quiet life without nagging.'

'No, but, who fed you, meals on wheels or something?'

'Eating's overrated.'

I spooned instant coffee, then tilted the kettle, 'Seriously, did you ever actually cook? Have you ever in your whole life cooked a meal?'

'I put hot milk on my cornflakes one epic winter...well, one morning one epic winter.'

I laughed, and shoved the mug toward her, 'I'm laughing, but you're not joking, are you?'

'I'm not. It taught me a big lesson.'

'Obviously not one about nutrition.'

'No, one about how hard it is to get dried burnt milk off the hotplate when the pan bubbles over.'

'Well, leaving it for a year before picking up a scourer probably didn't help.'

She sipped like a bird, watching me, then said, 'You are an old woman.'

I smiled and raised my mug to toast her. She said, 'You're an old woman in a young man's body...well, a youngish man. In twenty years, you'll be sitting at your bloody picture window with a tattered black shawl around you pedalling an ancient Singer sewing machine and mumbling complaints about the price of fish.'

'And you'll be at your desk, with your leg tucked under you, still ignoring me.'

'Probably.'

'Good!'

'How was Alice?'

'Ruthlessly effective, as ever. When we set off for a guided tour, I thought I was leading her around, by the time she'd got everything she wanted I began to realize she had been leading me.'

Mave smiled and sipped again and said, 'You're just never going to figure women out, are you?'

57

Dil didn't wait until the 3pm deadline, he called just after one o'clock, 'Eddie, good news. It seems like we've found a way out of this for Prim.'

'I'm listening.'

'We'll need a bit more time, but it looks as if her father will take the hit for everything.'

'How can he do that, Dil? Hines is obviously the man as far as the BHA is concerned. They already know about him. And Hines will name Prim, won't he?'

'We're working on that. That's why we need until tomorrow.'

'Working on it how?'

'Prim's father is trying to square things with Hines.'

'Square things? Working on it? A bit vague, Dil...have you spoken to Vita?'

His sigh was deliberate, to make sure I felt the force of his exasperation, 'Eddie, if this works out, I won't need to speak to Vita, Prim will be in the clear.'

'Prim kicked the whole thing off! How can she be in the clear?'

'You know what I mean! I thought we were all trying to keep her out of prison?'

It was my turn to sound exasperated. Much as I liked Prim, and felt sorry for her, it didn't sit right with me that she was going to walk on this. But Dil had me; we'd spent much of last night trying to come

246

up with a way to protect Prim. I couldn't complain now. I said, 'So, by tomorrow, you expect Señor Romanic to have agreed some sort of deal with Kelman Hines?'

'We might get it done tonight. But give me till tomorrow, will you?'

'All right.' It was grudgingly conceded.

'Will you tell Alice and Mave? We don't want anything slipping through the cracks.'

'I'll tell them. Call me as soon as you know what's happening, but remember, it's going to have to be digestible enough for Mac to swallow. And Vita.'

'Leave it to me, Eddie. I've got a good feeling about this now. Call you later.'

Good feeling. Huh. I stuffed my phone in my pocket, annoyed that I'd painted myself into a corner, allowing Prim to paint herself out of one.

I went to the farmhouse. Mave and Alice were in the kitchen drinking coffee. That brought a smile to my face as I said to Mave, 'You actually made coffee?'

She glanced up at me, then across at Alice, who smiled. I said to Alice, 'She got you to make the coffee?'

Alice said, 'I wracked my brain on those old home economics lessons and came up with the one on how to boil water.'

'I give up,' I said, pulling out a chair.

I told them what Dil had said, trying not to sound judgmental. Alice shrugged. Mave read me, 'No point agonizing over it, we're concentrating on finding Alice's Dad now. Let them do what they want. You've got enough on your plate.'

'It's me that'll have to sell it to Mac.'

Mave raised her mug in both hands, 'What's to sell? Tell him what Dil tells you, then give him Dil's number. Then you walk away and we can get on with finding Ben.'

Alice said, 'Did you speak to Sir Monty?'

'I left a message for him.'

Alice said, 'Do you think we should go home tonight? To

Deadwood, I mean? See if we can find DJ?'

'I'd sooner speak to Monty first and try to find out who DJ's boss is.'

Alice said, 'Do you think Sir Monty would know that?'

'I think his pal the chief constable will know. The tricky bit will be getting him to tell.'

Mave said, 'I take it this is the same chief constable that gave you a hard time at Aintree?'

'Bradley? Must be,' I said.

'So, if Monty knows him that well, why didn't he speak up for you back then?'

'He probably didn't even know Bradley was meeting me. What reason would Bradley have to mention it to Monty?'

Mave hesitated, 'I don't know...maybe Chief Constable Bradley just latches on to everyone with a close association with racing in the hope of catching this Nemesis of his, what's his name?'

'Ember,' I said, 'Sydney Ember.'

'Any chance he's involved in this?' Mave asked.

'Not his line of country according to Bradley, if I remember correctly. Organized crime. Big time stuff.'

'Like trafficking teenagers,' Mave said.

'I got the impression it was more, well, I don't know, drugs, money laundering...put it this way, Bradley hasn't been able to lay a finger on him for thirty years, so he wouldn't have time bombs like DJ working for him.'

'Mention him to Monty, will you?' Mave said.

'I will.'

'And Bradley, too.'

'Okay.'

I was getting changed to go running in the last of the afternoon light when Monty's secretary called and asked me to hold for him...'Eddie! How are you? Sorry I couldn't get back to you sooner.'

'No worries, Monty. I'm well, thanks, how are you?'

'Sailing along. Things are going worryingly smoothly, actually. Any word on Ben?'

'Nothing, I'm afraid. That's why I was ringing. I had a, well, a short chat with the fella that Bruno spoke to a while back, the guy he warned off in Deadwood, DJ?'

'Oh, yes?'

'Well, I kind of got the idea that whatever he's involved with, he's just a runner. I'd like to find out who his boss is. I wondered if your friend the chief constable might know?'

'I can certainly ask. Do you think these people might have information about Ben?'

'I'm hoping so. If they don't, well, I'm not sure where to turn next.'

He paused a few moments then said, 'Is there anything else that Bruno might be able to assist with here? Perhaps he could speak to this young gun you mentioned and persuade him to say who he works for.'

'Whatever fits best, Monty. I'm not bothered who the information comes from.'

'Well, look, don't feel limited to these one-off issues. If you need Bruno to get a bit more deeply involved, just say so. I mean, I know you are extremely capable in these matters, Eddie, extremely, but Bruno has considerable experience in the field of quietly resolving things in a fuss-free manner.'

'Monty, I'll take any help that's going, especially Bruno's.'

'Then why don't I get him to give you a call?'

'That would be great.'

'Good. Done. But do keep me up to date on Ben, will you?'

'Of course.'

'And how is Alice, do you know?'

'She's in good shape. She's staying with us now, until Ben turns up.'

'Ahh, I'm glad to hear that. She's a determined young woman, so it's reassuring to know she's in good hands. Please give her my regards. And Mave, too. And your other charming friend with the wonderful name.'

'Primarolo Romanic. I will.'

'An exotic and most personable woman.'

'She has many talents.'

He chuckled, 'Oh, that sounded a rather knowing assessment, Edward!'

I laughed, 'Listen, Monty, I'm very grateful for your time, and your generous help, yet again.'

'Not at all, not at all. I'll have Bruno call you shortly.'

'Before you go, ever heard of a guy called Ember, Sydney Ember?'

He hesitated, 'You haven't, by chance, been speaking to Chief Constable Bradley lately?'

'A few weeks back, actually, yes. He was with the CEO of the BHA when we talked about these wild horses, but all Bradley wanted to talk about was-'

'Sydney Ember.'

'Correct.'

'He's obsessed with the man. He spoke to me about him years ago, then angled for invites to my box at big meetings, where he'd go around asking the other guests about Ember. I had to stop inviting him. Ember is his long time bête noire.'

'Ah well, at least I know Bradley wasn't just picking on me. You ever come across this Ember bloke?'

'Never. Not once. There are some who think he's a figment of Chief Constable Bradley's imagination.'

'Well, I hope I'm not putting you on the spot asking you to speak to him?'

'Let's try Bruno first and see what he knows. I'll ask him to call you.'

'Thanks again, Monty.'

'My pleasure.'

Ten minutes into my run across the nearby fellside, Bruno rang and I had to ask him to hold until I found shelter behind a rock. I said, 'Sorry, Bruno, I couldn't hear you for the wind noise. I didn't expect you to call so soon.'

'I can ring back if it's easier?'

'No, no, I'm fine now. Did Sir Monty tell you what it was about?'

'In brief.'

I told him about my confrontation with DJ and asked if he knew anyone higher up the Deadwood food chain.

'I don't, but I can find out.'

'Would that take long?'

'A couple of calls. If the people I need to speak to are available, I should have something for you in an hour.'

'Good. Thanks. I'll be home and showered by then.'

'Okay. I'll call you.'

'Thanks, Bruno.'

'Goodbye.'

I pushed the phone into the zipper armband and set off toward the ridge, wondering what Bruno Guta's life was like. He always seemed on auto. I'd never known him do small talk and couldn't imagine a social situation in which he'd fit comfortably.

Or maybe it was that I couldn't picture a social situation where others would feel comfortable around him. Bruno would just sit there smiling the smile that said, "I can see right inside your head, and you can see nothing of me."

58

I shaved in the shower, each razor stroke bringing to mind how close a man can be to bleeding. The next confrontation with DJ might be just hours away.

I was confident of beating him if he wasn't armed, but he probably would be. Maybe it was time to pull my ice-axe from behind the wardrobe and put it in the car.

For a few years now, I'd been wondering how I might replace the adrenaline rush of riding. Most jump jockeys had retired by their fortieth birthday, and I intended to do the same, to go while I still had the strength and energy to learn ice-climbing.

I'd bought all the gear, but I didn't want to do it part-time. The plan was to wait and then go at it all out. Until then, the boots, the crampons, the ropes, the technical clothing had been vacuum packed and stored.

The past scrapes I'd been in helped convince me that the ice-axe might one day save my life before it had bit into anything cold. I'd yet to use it but, from time to time, I'd haul it out and swing at imaginary Himalayan mountain faces...it was my version of air guitar.

When I went downstairs, still barefoot, I saw Mave in her customary tucked-leg position at her desk and I crept toward her. Without turning, she said, 'Nice shower?'

I stopped, 'You must have some hearing. I was in stealth mode.'

'Smelth mode more like. It was the smell of the gel that gave you away.'

'More like the antiperspirant. I had to layer it. I think the sweat might be on in Deadwood tonight.'

'You're definitely going?'

'Strike while the iron's hot, and all that. Speaking of which, remind me to put my ice-axe in the boot.'

She stopped typing and looked up, 'You think that's a good idea?'

'If DJ and his friends are armed, I'm going to need something to…subdue them with.'

'Eddie, you subdue people with pepper spray, or water cannon or maybe Tasers. With ice axes, you kill people.'

'Well, let's hope DJ knows that, too.'

'I thought Bruno Guta was going to help you?'

'He said he'd get me the name of Mister Big.'

'Well, wait for that and bypass DJ.'

'I'll be doing my best to bypass DJ, but we'll be in Deadwood, and that's where he hangs out.'

'So, ask Bruno to come along.'

I put a hand on her shoulder, 'Come and sit with me in the kitchen. I'll make you a coffee.'

She sighed and got up and followed me, saying, 'If Bruno can't come with you tonight, you should skip it until he can, or until Sir Monty can maybe give you someone else.'

I filled the kettle, 'As we speak, Alice is probably finishing packing.'

Mave folded her arms and stared at me. I opened my arms and said, 'What? Why are you looking at me like that?'

She pushed a chair out with her foot, 'Sit down,' she said. I sat, smiling. Mave said, 'Whatever zone you're in this time, check yourself out for a minute, so I can talk to you.'

Still smiling, I opened my hands on the tabletop, 'What's up?'

'Eddie, seriously, switch off for a minute, will you? You've been building up to this all day. I knew when you went out running, you'd come back like this.'

'Like what?'

'You ran the ridges, didn't you?'

'Yes. Why?'

'Because you hammer along there with nothing above you and picture yourself at the top of the world so that everyone else, every problem, every danger is below you.'

I laughed, 'Mave, you-'

'You work yourself up into one of these vision scenarios like you do before a big race. You ride it a hundred times in your mind until everything comes out perfect. You're doing it now. I can see it in your face, and you need to come back to earth for long enough to protect Alice.'

'What do you mean by that?'

'Oh, don't go all defensive on me now. I mean ask yourself what will happen if you're the one left bleeding in the gutter this time. What happens to Alice?'

'Well, you come with us, then.'

'And do what, fight off DJ and his team like Wonder Woman? Think about what you just said.'

I continued staring stupidly at her. She said, 'Wind your neck in…drop your shoulders. Sit back and just think about what you're planning.'

And I did…and the muscle tension steadily eased until I sat half slumped, forearms and hands loose on the table, the fire gone from my eyes, steadily clearing my vision until I could see how right Mave was. I glanced away from her…looked down and lowered my head.

I saw Mave's thin little fingers slip into my field of view as she reached to take my hand. Slowly she squeezed it and we were startled when the silence was broken by my ringing phone. I pulled it from my shirt pocket. Bruno Guta's name was on the screen, 'Bruno, hello…'

'Eddie, DJ works about four levels below the top man, a guy named Kelman Hines.'

59

In the dusk, Mave walked with me to the car as we discussed the best way to keep Alice cool. I said, 'Just tell her I was ready and packed for Deadwood when Bruno called. She's a big fan of Bruno, so if it looks like the cancelled trip is down to him, she won't be so upset.'

Mave said, 'I won't tell her about Hines or she'll be up and off after him.'

'If she gets too antsy, call me and I'll speak to her.'

'I will.'

I opened the car door then turned and hugged her, 'Thanks for talking me down earlier. I think Alice had become some kind of Superwoman in my head, rather than you.'

'Gee, thanks.' She put her arms around my waist.

I laughed, 'You know what I mean.'

She leant back and looked up at me, 'Mister Malloy, I always know what you mean, often before you do.'

'Just as well.' We kissed.

Mave stepped aside as I backed the car away from the sandstone wall of the barn, the flaring reversing lights spotlighting her so starkly in my rearview mirror that she seemed to live in just one dimension, like a photograph.

When I'd spoken to Dil earlier, I hadn't said why I was coming, but had warned him not to let Prim out of his sight. With her hold over Hines, I felt that Ben was almost within touching distance.

Dil was watching at the window and came to meet me as I wa
from the car. He began talking before he reached me, 'Eddie, do
say anything in the house, okay? I'm worried it might be bugged.'

I reached to shake his offered hand, 'Who would bug
house?'

'Take your pick. The more I find out about this Hines gu
more worried I get. And Vita has been real quiet since she's b
New York.'

'You think Vita might be bugging you?'

'I don't know. I just don't know. I don't feel like taking c
though.'

We walked across the yard. I saw Prim's outline as she stood w
her back to the window. I said, 'Dil, if your place is bugged, they'v
already got themselves all they need from our conversation last
night.'

He leant across, barging me slightly as he tried to look into m
face, 'How do you know that, though? How do you know they'
got exactly what they need?'

I stopped and turned, 'Dil, you started this. I don't know ar
You don't know anything. You're getting paranoid.' I pushed l
to start him moving again, 'Come on, let's get Prim.'

He caught my sleeve, 'Eddie, she won't talk in the h
'So where are we supposed to go?'
'The haybarn.'

We sat in a huge chair of haybales. The sweet smell and th
softness took me back to when I was twelve and had kissed
a haybarn, sitting on bales packed much more tightly tha
hiding us, hiding us from my father.

And it had not been night.

It was a July day in the holidays and she, Catherine, hac
bright with hope and dreams and I had been sweating with a m
of fear and excitement and I'd said sorry to her for my armpit
smelled so bad and she had said it didn't matter, said it in a
made me believe it.

'Eddie,' Dil said.

'Sorry, Dil. Long time since I settled in a haybarn for a secret talk.'

Prim looked haggard and hunted. Her dark eyes in the dim light had the look of a prisoner's in a condemned cell. I said, 'Tell me where you are now with your plans.'

Dil glanced at Prim. She turned her head away. He said, 'Kelman Hines says his guy will take the rap and do his time. Hines will pay him.'

'The guy who did it? Boffo?'

'Mike Boffo,' Dil said, 'He's only twenty-eight. Reckons he might get away with two years.'

'So, Prim, you're out of this, and now Hines is too. That leaves your father and Boffo to take the hit?'

Prim looked at me, then at Dil who said, 'Mike Boffo has made an offer to Señor Romanic…he wants another million to take the fall for him too.'

Prim would not look at me. I said, 'So Boffo soaks it all up, the mastermind, the tech guy, the betting man, the falsifier of bank accounts, the putter-in and taker-out of speakers, the sender of signals during the race…do you seriously believe Mac and his boss at the BHA will swallow that?'

'Gladly,' Dil said, 'I think they'll jump at it. One delivery, all nicely wrapped, no loose ends.

I nodded. He might be right. Mac would know it was bullshit, but his boss would tell him to live with it. I turned to Prim, 'Are you happy with that?'

She said, 'Eddie, I just wish I could rewind my life.' She looked away. Dil glanced at me as if to say "well, what did you expect?"

I said, 'Prim, how well do you know Kelman Hines?'

She shrugged, 'Haven't seen him for years.'

'That's not what I asked.'

Dil shuffled forward, the seat of his jeans rasping on the hay, 'This is hard for her, Eddie.'

I said, 'Dil, can you give me five minutes with Prim?'

'Why?'

'We're hardly strangers, are we? I'm not going to give her a tough time.'

He put an arm across Prim's shoulders and ducked to look up into her face, his heavy hair falling like a curtain to block my view. She mumbled something and Dil got up slowly, dusting off strands of hay, 'I'll go and fix some drinks,' he said.

As the sound of his footsteps faded in the night, Prim turned and held my gaze under the dim light. She said, 'I'm sorry for all this, Eddie, truly sorry. I feel like I dipped my toe in the water then fell right into a whirlpool. I wish I could go back to the start. I'd give anything to do that.'

'Wouldn't we all, Prim, wouldn't we all? I'll tell you straight off what will help, stop allowing Dil to treat you like some terrible sinner who must forever bow at the master's feet and do everything she's told. Dil is loving this, believe me. I always liked Dil, but since this kicked off, I'm not so sure I do any more.'

'He's just trying to protect me, Eddie, you saw that.'

'Prim, what he's doing is manipulating you, dragging you around on some kind of invisible lead, tied to him by obligation. He's making himself out your saviour here, but from what I can see it's your father who's saving you, and I might as well tell you now, I don't think you should be getting away with this. And I believe you don't think you should either…'

She dropped her head.

'…and that's what's bothering you most. You just don't realize it yet.'

She sighed and, with both hands, ran her long fingers through that black mass of hair, pulling it into a tight gathering. She looked at me, 'I think I do realize it.'

'Good. Now all you have to do is find a way to live with it. And what I have to do is find out all you know about Kelman Hines.'

'Why?'

'I want to know what else he might be into before I try to sell this bullshit story to the BHA.'

'I wouldn't know what else Kelman was into. He runs a big

company. He branched out into different parts, different services in racing, but as far as I know that's all he does. I haven't seen him for years.'

'But you had an affair with him?'

She glanced away, then straight back at me, some fire in her eyes now, 'It wasn't an affair. It was more a fling. Nothing serious.'

'It was serious enough to blackmail him with.'

She nodded slowly, 'Ouch,' she said quietly.

I said, 'Weren't you afraid of blackmailing him? Of him retaliating, threatening you?'

'He wouldn't do that, not in a million years. Not his style. He was a bit flashy, not unlike Dil in many ways, but Kelman was the type who'd moan about food if we were out somewhere and then, when the waiter comes along asking if everything's okay, Kelman would smile and say, "Perfect!"'

She went on, 'There was the business Kelman and the private Kelman, which was…well, he was timid. He was cautious, that was the main reason the fling never turned into…into anything more serious.'

'He backed out?'

'I backed out. Well, I finished it. He was making me feel I was the one sneaking around. I wasn't in a relationship at the time. Kelman was married. I got tired of it.'

'Did he talk to you about business?'

'No. We talked racing quite a lot. He loved racing.'

'But, other than the businesses you know about, the nutrition, the heart-rate monitors, all the vet-type stuff, there was nothing else?'

'Not as far as I know. As I said, he didn't talk business much, so there might have been.'

'Have you spoken to him since this all blew up in your face?'

'No. No, I haven't.'

'I might ask you to call him to arrange a meeting. How would you feel about that?'

'I'd do it if I need to, but…well, maybe talk to Dil about it first?'

'Prim-' I was about to set off again on another Dil lecture. In the end, I just waved my hand and turned away, then went out to find Dil. My intention had been to tell him that I believed Hines was holding Ben, but I couldn't risk someone warning Hines. Dil's focus was on juggling two women. His worries about the horses were over. All that my worries seemed to do was multiply.

60

I was home in time to hear the brass clock on the mantelpiece chime midnight. Mave and I settled by the fire with mugs of tea and a marked up map. I said, 'You've been busy.'

'Took ten minutes. Whatever Hines is doing crimewise, his lab business looks squeaky clean. All the properties belonging to Byerley Hines are listed on the website.'

'All the legal properties,' I said.

'Well, yes. I did some digging in the accounts, and I can't understand why people like Hines mess around with shit like trafficking and race fixing and whatever else he's into.'

'The race-fixing's a new one, though, isn't it? Prim's got him into that.'

'Maybe. But given his history, it's something he could have easily done years ago. He's got good relationships with racecourses, an army of vets, a lab full of bubbling chemicals...you'd have thought that offered more profit for less risk than trafficking teenagers, wouldn't you?'

'I suppose so, yes.'

She watched me, then said, 'It just doesn't compute, Eddie. Trafficking girls is organized crime. It's gang stuff, like drugs. It's competitive. It's dangerous. Hines owns seventy-two percent of the company he runs. Conservative estimate would make him worth ten million. Why would he piss around with idiots like DJ in places like

261

Deadwood? Is there a chance Hines could be working for somebody like this guy, Ember?'

'Monty ruled him out, didn't he?'

'I know, and he backed up your impression that Bradley's obsessed, and maybe even mad. But that doesn't compute either, does it? Jeez, he's a chief constable. They don't give that job to idiots.'

'Wannabet?'

'Eddie, I know you've bumped into some dunderheads in uniform, but not at that level.'

'Okay, okay. Maybe Bruno can go back and ask a few more questions…whoah, wait a minute! If Bruno warned DJ off and there was no comeback, then whoever runs DJ is afraid of Bruno. That computes, does it not?'

Mave looked away, her eyes in deep thinking mode.

I said, 'And Prim says Hines turned out to be a wimp in the end. Which would fit with him backing off on Bruno.'

Mave sighed, 'Which kind of stacks up on other things as well, I suppose. I mean, he's supposed to be this big villain running Deadwood, and suddenly Prim and her elderly father pitch up and say do this or else. Any self respecting crime lord would dip them in concrete and chuck them in the Mersey.'

'But maybe the beauty of it is that he's got Prim and the old man convinced he's just a vet who's built a decent business. If they had half a suspicion he was into all this, they'd have found somebody else to run the show.'

'But if he's so slick at hiding the criminal side, why didn't he get stuck into laying those horses once this Boffo guy had told him everything was lined up? We know that Prim's father was the only one who made any money on them.'

'Online, yes. But what about Hines's team of guys visiting the betting shops, all the offline stuff. Okay, you can't lay them, but he could have been betting two or three others in each race.'

'Except that Alice's diary showed that none of Ben's tracking of them fitted with the days the horses went wild…though I suppose there are plenty other betting shops.'

'Exactly.'

Mave sighed and picked up her pen and turned the map around, 'Okay, back to what we do know.' She pointed to an area on the coast between Southport and Blackpool, just where the estuary opens out. She had marked a number 4 beside it, as the fourth of the seven properties belonging to Kelman Hines. I said, 'It's not that far from Crosby where we found Ben's clothes on the beach. It's pretty remote, and it's close enough to Liverpool to be some kind of holding area for these girls they're trafficking.'

Mave said, 'And it's on the coast, which would make it easier to get the girls out of the country without worrying too much about the legalities.'

'Or to get Ben out of the country,' I said.

'No real reason to do that though, is there? It doesn't matter where they hold him, so long as it's secure and secret.' Mave turned her attention to a Google Earth print out, 'He's got three buildings on this property. I'm assuming the biggest one is the lab itself. This one here looks more like a house, with that path to the front door, and the lawn. Maybe a caretaker's place, or a manager. You wouldn't leave a lab unguarded, not one that's so remote.'

'Especially if you were holding somebody there,' I said.

Mave looked up, 'What next, then?'

'Well, it's not far, is it? I could be there in under an hour. Roads'll be dead at this time of night.'

'Why don't you call Mac? You're going to have to tell him about Hines anyway. Might as well have some support with you.'

'That would delay things at least twenty-four hours and Hines'll be nervous enough by now. He could be thinking of moving Ben, wherever he is.'

'Which means he could just as easy move him to there as from there.'

I stood up, 'Mave, we could spend a week on ifs and buts. That place is the most remote, the closest to Crosby and Liverpool, it's got to be favourite.'

'Maybe, but you don't know what you might be walking into. Why don't you call Bruno Guta?'

I smiled, 'You're getting as bad as Alice!'

Mave got up, 'Then, I'm coming with you!'

'Me too.'

I turned. Alice was in the doorway. Mave said, 'Oops! I forgot about you, Alice. Best if we both stay here.'

Alice just stared, her grey eyes dismissing Mave's suggestion much more convincingly than words could have. Mave sighed, 'I'll get our coats.'

I said, 'I'll get my ice-axe.'

Alice said, 'I'll get my gun.'

Mave and I turned and stared at her. Alice stared back, features hard and unmoving, then, slowly, a smile came up from her mouth like a cloud clearing the sun. She raised a hand and pointed at us, 'Had you then, didn't I?'

We laughed, as much, I believe, from relief as amusement. Alice said, 'Come on, let's find my Dad.'

61

To make the safest approach, we had to walk almost a mile from where we'd parked. Underfoot was scrubby duneland. The wind off the Irish Sea was gusty and unpredictable and when we heard it whip up, we shielded our eyes to keep out the sand.

I'd brought a flashlight, but only for emergency use. I assured Mave and Alice that the farther we walked from the streetlit suburbs, the more easily our eyes would adjust to the dark. One benefit of the wind was that it kept the clouds sailing along and the almost full moon was never hidden for long.

Mave's handheld GPS showed a big fat arrow and it counted down the paces to the target and we stuck to it until we saw the compound that housed the three buildings.

I'd expected a high fence topped with barbed wire but we found only a low wall surrounding the property. The driveway gates were low too, made of wood, and not only were they unlocked, they lay open.

Through the gates, closest to the sea, was a two-storey sandstone building, windowless, with large double doors. Beyond this was a building three times the size of the old sandstone one, and much more modern, though basic, with breeze blocks dominating above a brick—lined level about eight feet high.

This building too was windowless and seemed much more secure, with metal shutters at each end.

The last building, a bungalow, was the only one that showed signs of life in the light that came from two of its windows. We circled the bungalow, checking for an outhouse. Alice whispered, 'Do you think my Dad is in there?'

I said, 'If he is, I don't know what's keeping him there. No dogs, no fence, no security guard. I'm afraid we've backed a loser here.'

Mave said, 'It's almost half-past-two, why would they still have lights on?'

Alice looked at me. I said, 'I don't know. Maybe whoever lives there just forgot to switch them off. Or he could be an insomniac.'

'Or he could be guarding Dad.'

'Could be,' I said, 'time to find out.'

The wall around the bungalow was low, ornamental, enclosing flowerbeds already in bloom. I stepped over it onto a section of lawn and went to the window edge. No sound from inside.

I waited, counting out a minute, then eased across to look into the lighted room...empty.

I returned to Mave and Alice, 'This doesn't stack up', I said, 'It's as though there's nothing to protect, not even the lab.'

Mave said, 'Whoever lives there is probably in bed.'

Alice said, 'Did you try the door?'

'No.'

'Want me to try it?'

'Then what?' I said, 'Even if it's open, we can't just walk in. Might be some old guy lying in bed, he opens his eyes and sees us, he could have a heart attack.'

Alice said, 'I could take a look in the other rooms.'

Mave said, 'And what if DJ or one of the others is waiting?'

Alice shrugged, 'He doesn't scare me.'

I stifled a nervous laugh and looked at Mave. She said, 'Why not try and get whoever's living there to come out? There must be some kind of alarm around that we can set off.'

'Fire alarm?' Alice said.

We crept away to have a closer look at the other buildings.

The newer one had a red-boxed fire alarm at each end beside the roller shutters: "In case of fire, break glass." There was nothing obvious with which to break anything. Mave said, 'Use your axe.'

I held the shaft, just below the head. The first attempt was more a dig than a swing, and it caught the casing around the glass. I changed my grip and tried again. The glass broke. We all stepped back.

Silence.

We looked at each other. Alice hurried across to the sandstone building and beckoned us.

Beside the old wooden doors was a rusty fire alarm with just a few flakes of paint still visible. The glass on the front was filthy, but hanging from a short chain was a hammer with a round head, its handle crusted with bubbled rust.

I picked it up and rubbed the handle to make sure it wouldn't crumble completely. 'Might as well try this,' I said, and turned to look back at the bungalow. Still no sign of life. I swung at the glass.

It didn't break. Mave put a hand to her mouth, perhaps to stifle a laugh.

I swung again as Alice put her fingers in her ears. I missed the glass and hit the metal surround, sending a vibration along my arm, and a dull echo into the night.

Now Mave laughed nervously and almost started me off as I squatted to look closer and take more careful aim…

'Hello?'

A voice from inside the building.

'Hello out there! Is somebody there? Can you help me?' Much louder now, making Alice smile at the unmistakable voice of her father.

62

Alice punched the air and whooped and I reached to grab her arm and signal her to be quiet as we watched the bungalow.

Nobody came.

Ben called out again. I called back, 'Ben, we'll get you out in a minute. Just hold on.'

He didn't reply. We waited a long, long minute. Still no signs of life from the bungalow.

I went to the nearest boarded window and raised the broad edge of the ice-axe and with each crack of hardboard and each squealing nail, paused and watched the house. Nothing.

Two minutes later, we were inside and Mave's flashlight beam soon settled on the smiling Ben Searcey, though his smile faded when I told him to hold still while I aimed the axe at the handcuffs shackling him to a rusty radiator.

Mave held the beam steady on the lock. Ben leant forward. Alice held her breath, and I swung the axe, trying not to think of my failed whacks at the fire alarm.

The lock shattered in a zinging, echoing bang, and Ben smiled again as I hurried to the loose window board to check outside.

Nobody there…the only sound was from the wind and the sea.

In the car, Ben sat with Alice in the back. I said, 'How long were you there?'

'They moved me last night, so, through the night and all day today.'

'Where'd they move you from?'

'I don't know. That was the third move. They put a hood on me each time. The first two were houses, proper warm houses, though they had blackout blinds nailed onto the windows.'

'Have you been handcuffed all the time?' I asked.

'No, just with this move. Until then, they'd looked after me well, to be fair. Plenty grub and tea.'

'Who was it? Did you know them?'

'Three different guys. Never saw any of them in my life before.'

'Did they tell you anything? Why you'd been taken?'

'They weren't keen on questions from me, though they did want answers.'

'To what?' I said.

'Who my hacker was, as they put it.'

I glanced at him in the rearview mirror, 'The guy who helped you out with the stuff on Vogel?'

'That's him.'

'What did they want with him?'

'Somehow they'd found out I was waiting for an email. It was that same evening you and I spoke. I just needed confirmation about the bloke who had replaced the usual vets at the tracks where the horses were bolting, a guy called Mike Boffo.'

I nodded, smiling. Ben said, 'You knew?'

'I found out. But not as quickly as you did.'

Ben said, 'Well I'd asked for something else, too. Bookies are legally obliged to inform the Gambling Commission if they suspect money laundering is going on in their shops. After weeks of following DJ's guys into betting shops, I did some research and found that the shop staff should have been logging what was going on under The Proceeds of Crime Act.'

'But they weren't?' I said.

'Correct. I had called the Gambling Commission and asked if any POCA reports had been filed by the company Wannabet, which was the one that was always used by DJ and his gang. They wanted me to submit a formal freedom of information request, and I logged one, but they said it could be weeks or months. So I got my guy onto it. No reports filed by Wannabet.'

'Did your guy get into the Wannabet system or the Gambling Commission's?'

'I didn't ask. Made no difference to me.'

'Okay. Sorry. Go on.'

'Well, I started some checks on Wannabet and found it was owned by a shell company. I'd done some work on these shells before, and most people use them to hide something. Anyway, I asked my IT man if he could help find out who was behind the shell company.'

'Not easy,' I said.

'But doable,' Ben said, 'and he did it. Trouble was that by the time he sent me the email they had me, my PC and my phone.'

'How did they get your PC?'

'They took my keys and went into the house and lifted it.'

I shrugged, 'Straightforward. So you still don't know who owns the shell?'

'Nope.'

I turned to Mave. She said, 'Shouldn't be a problem. I'll have a look when we get home.'

Alice said, 'Was it the gypsies that got you?'

'What gypsies?' Ben said.

'We got a call from a guy saying you'd been seen leaving the Blue Anchor with two gypsies.'

'I wasn't in the Blue Anchor. I was out for a walk, waiting for some information coming in. It was near the Blue Anchor they grabbed me and shoved me into the van, the same one they brought me here in. But these guys aren't gypsies, well, not so far as I know.'

I said, 'How long did the journey take last night?'

'An hour...maybe a bit more.' A long sigh came out of him and his head went back on the seat. I said, 'We'll give it a rest until we get you home.'

'I'm starving,' Ben said.

Back at the farm, seated at the kitchen table, we watched Ben steadily make his way through half a loaf. He'd mastered his butter, marmalade and swallowing action to coordinate perfectly with the next two slices popping from the toaster into Alice's waiting hands. She was still smiling at the way her father was dressed.

He wore a black tracksuit and gold-coloured trainers. Alice said, 'I've never seen you so fashionable.'

'They don't fit,' Ben said.

Alice laughed, 'Dad, a Babygro would be too big for you.'

Ben smiled warmly at her and they held each other's gaze silently for a few private seconds. Alice said, 'They took your clothes the night they grabbed you.'

'How did you know that?'

Alice said, 'Because we found them that night on one of those metal statues on Crosby beach...soaked in whiskey.'

'Well, somebody thought my clothes were good enough for a work of art. Fame at last.' He raised his mug of tea in salute and picked up more toast.

Mave appeared in the doorway, 'What were they called, Wannabet? Double N?'

Mouth full, Ben nodded enthusiastically and I strung my next question out to give him time to swallow, 'So, if these guys get hold of the email that was meant for you, why did they have to hold you trying to find out who your IT guy was? They had his email address, and I'm assuming they have their own IT people?'

'My guy 's untraceable.'

'Did they even try to contact him to tell him they were holding you?'

Ben shrugged, as he reached for more toast, 'I don't know. Wouldn't have mattered. I knew the score if it all went tits up, I was on my own.'

'So, you didn't tell them who he was, obviously?'

Ben glanced at Alice, 'No.'

I said, 'Did you come across your old mate DJ while they were holding you?'

'Nope.'

I drank some tepid coffee, 'Mike Boffo, the vet, worked for a guy called Kelman Hines. Turns out DJ works for Kelman Hines, too.'

Ben stopped chewing and stared at me, then said, 'The Kelman Hines who used to work on track, years ago?'

'Same one,' I smiled, 'Not that there are many with that name.'

'I knew Hines,' Ben said, 'know him, I suppose I should say. He asked me to do an article on a lab he was setting up to research racehorse nutrition. Years ago, now.'

My turn to raise my mug in salute, 'Well, there's more on Hines, but I'm waiting to hear from Dil.'

Ben watched me. I could almost see his mind working. He said, 'I don't know why I didn't ask you this before, but how the hell did you find me? Did somebody tip you off?'

I looked at Alice, 'Want to tell him, and I'll see how Mave's getting along?' As I rose, I heard Mave get up too, her desk chair squeaking as she edged it aside.

I turned as she came into the kitchen, 'Any joy?'

Mave said, 'Wannabet chain of fourteen betting shops on Merseyside owned by a company with so many zs and qs in its name, it's unpronounceable. It was registered in Florida, USA seven years ago.'

'Any idea who owns the unpronounceable company?' I asked.

'Kelman Hines.'

63

We had gone to bed at 5 a.m. and were back around the kitchen table at 7.30. Not one of us had managed to sleep.

'Nessun Dorma,' Alice said.

We looked at her. Alice said, 'None shall sleep.'

Ben said, 'How did you know that?'

'Because I was sick of hearing it playing through the crap speakers at Royston House, so I asked.'

Mave said, 'Royston House?'

Ben said, 'The children's home in Leeds, the very last one.'

I raised my coffee cup, 'Well, Nessun Dorma to you too. We're all knackered. It's the first time for years I can say I'm glad I'm not riding today.'

Mave said, 'What next?'

I massaged my tired eyes, 'I don't know. Do we confront Hines, or wait until he realizes Ben is out?'

Ben said, 'Why not confront him before he knows? I get the feeling they were going to leave me in that bloody place for days.'

I said, 'That's one of the things that isn't sitting right with me. I mean, it sounds like they were looking after you pretty well before moving you there.'

Ben said, 'Three meals a day and about ten cups of tea.'

I said, 'Then, out of the blue, they dump you in an old, cold, unused building with no security...well, no obvious security. It's almost as though they expected us to find you.'

Alice said, 'If they expected it, why the move? Why hide him somewhere different?'

I said, 'But they moved him to where we found him at the first attempt, which suggests they know quite a bit about me, but, more importantly, about Mave and her skills. Now, I've never met Hines. Anything he knows about me,' I nodded toward Mave, 'about us, well, the easiest way to have got it would have been through Prim. He knows her well, but Prim says they haven't spoken for years.'

'Maybe she's lying,' Alice said.

'Maybe she is,' I said.

Mave said to Alice, 'You think Prim has stayed with you, promised to look after you, slept in your house, and all the time she's known where your Dad was?'

Alice shrugged, and glanced at her father. Mave said, 'If you had to bet whether Prim knew or not, what would you say?'

Alice considered, 'I'd say she didn't know.'

Mave said, 'You think she was genuinely worried about you and your Dad?'

Alice nodded, 'I don't think it could have been an act.'

Ben said, 'And Alice has seen plenty of acting in her life, haven't you?'

Alice said quietly, 'No more guilt trips, Dad, remember?'

Ben blushed, and he reached across the table to touch her hand briefly.

I sighed and rubbed my eyes, and said, 'Well, it's got me beat. My brain's too tired to sort through it.' I got up, 'I'd better let Monty know you're safe, Ben. It was him that put us onto the link with DJ and Hines.'

Ben said, 'I think I'd need ten lifetimes to pay Monty back for what he's done for me.'

I said, 'Do you want to give him the good news, then?'

'No...No, you do it, Eddie. Tell him I'll buy him lunch soon.'

Alice stood up, 'I'd better let Mum know you're okay.'

Ben turned quickly to her, 'You told your mother?'

A spark lit her grey eyes, 'She still worries about you, you know.'

'When did you speak to her?'

'I didn't. I sent her a message on Facebook.'

'How long has this been going on?'

'Dad! How long has what been going on?'

'Your contact with your mother.'

'Does it matter? Really?'

'Did it matter to her when you had nowhere to live? When you were in home after home? When you were risking your life in Deadwood?'

Alice went to him, her eyes wide, cheeks flushed, and she leant forward and she raised her voice, 'Did it matter to…' her top teeth were bared and she drew in her lower jaw and bit into her lip…she stared at him and tears filled her eyes and blood trickled out as her teeth went deeper, then she ran from the room.

Ben watched the empty doorway, and his eyes welled and tears spilled and as he bowed his head they fell straight like raindrops, and splashed on the old table.

I stood outside watching the sun come up through its cleft in the eastern fells. Below the farm, a sheet of mist almost hid Ullswater. The sun would soon burn it off and begin warming the lake. Another month and I might risk a swim, I thought.

I was reluctant to call Monty so early, so I sent a text message. Within a minute, he called me, 'You found him! Ben's safe?'

'He's fine, Monty, safe and well.'

'Thank god for that! Who had him? Where was he?'

'A guy called Kelman Hines had him locked up in one of his properties on the north west coast, not that far from where we found his clothes on the beach.'

'Who is Hines? The name rings a bell.'

'Started out as a vet, then went into different businesses and built up what's beginning to look like a small empire.'

'What's his beef with Ben?'

'We don't know, yet. And we don't know if Hines knows that Ben is out. We're just trying to plan the next move.'

'Anything I can do?'

I laughed, 'Probably! You've been an absolute star.'

'Not at all. A couple of phone calls, that was all. Delighted to help.'

'No doubt you'll let Bruno know that his good work paid off.'

'I will, of course. And don't hesitate to let me know if you need him again to help deal with this Hines character, though it sounds to me just a matter of a call to the police, if you don't mind me saying.'

'I think you're right. I just want to make sure all the theories actually produce some evidence.'

'Well, as I said, pick up the phone to me at any time.'

'I will, Monty, thanks. And Ben sends his thanks as well. Says he'll buy you lunch very soon.'

'I'll look forward to that. And tell Ben I'm so glad to hear he is all right.'

'I will. And I'll let you know how it goes.'

'Please do.'

I put my phone away and smiled at the sun as it cleared the felltops. Things were beginning to slot neatly into place. Unusual. And welcome.

As I turned to go back inside, the door opened. It was Mave. She said, 'Spoken to Sir Monty yet?'

'Just finished. Why?'

'Walk this way.'

64

I followed Mave to her desk. She said, 'Pull up a chair.' I got one from the kitchen. 'What's up?' I said, as she settled and touched a key to light her laptop screen. She said, 'I've just been looking again at those shell companies and one of my searches threw this up,' she clicked a link to open a page. I sidled closer and read the article.

It was about shell companies: what they were, how they were formed, which countries offered least resistance in setting them up. I said, 'I'd have bet that the Cayman Islands and places like that would have been favourite for hiding all this corporate ducking and diving. America's a big surprise to me.'

'Me too. Money talks, as ever.'

I turned to her…she wouldn't have had me read this just for the education, 'Good article. Your point is?'

Mave moved her mouse slowly and scrolled up to a tiny line of text below the article's headline: "By Ben Searcey"

I looked at her, 'When was that written?'

'Five years ago. And it's the first in a series by Ben, laying the foundations for the main subject, corruption in sport.' Mave clicked again and opened a PDF. Ben's name was more prominent on this. Mave said, 'It's three thousand words on match-fixing in various sports, Ben's sixth article in the series. I've learned a lot from it, main thing being that this is not the work of an alcoholic, or at least a practising alcoholic if you know what I mean.'

She watched me for a reaction. My sleep-starved brain could come up with nothing. I just sat there blinking, Mave turned again to the screen and clicked, 'The shell that owns the betting shops-'

'The shell that's owned by Kelman Hines?' I asked.

'Maybe. When I looked last night, or this morning, or whenever the hell it was, I checked the dates, which say Hines has owned that company for three years. But I've just been digging a few layers deeper in the server activity logs. The name of the owner and the date of origin were altered forty-eight hours ago.'

'Altered to Hines?'

'Yes.'

'From?'

'From a company called Valentine Elements Limited.'

'Who are?'

'Who are very, very protective of their privacy. I need to do more work on it.'

'Valentine, not Valentino?'

'Valentine.'

I rubbed my eyes, 'I knew this was too easy.'

'It was even easier for Bruno, or, more likely, whoever Sir Monty uses as his IT hit man, his tech equivalent of Bruno. You call asking for help. An hour later Bruno rings you with all you need to know about Wannabet. Or, at least enough to have us digging out our fine-toothed-comb for use on Kelman Hines.'

I looked at her, 'You think Bruno's involved in this?'

She stared at me...I knew that look and I tried again, 'Monty?'

'Since you asked for his help, we've been bumping into an awful lot of happy coincidences.'

The floorboards on the landing creaked, then the stairs...Ben came through the doorway, a hand raised, partly in greeting, partly in apology.

'All well?' I asked.

He nodded, 'The old wounds get opened from time to time...my fault.'

Mave said, 'Does Alice need some company?'

Ben smiled as he went toward Mave and put a hand on her shoulder, 'She needs some sleep, Mave, thanks.'

I said, 'Mave came across some of your old work when she was checking out those shell companies.'

'Must have been very old work,' Ben said.

Mave said, 'Five years ago.' Ben looked puzzled, then smiled again, 'My dry period. Alice, my wife, Alice, had finally seen sense and walked out. I begged for one more chance, which was actually my hundredth one more chance, and she came back.'

I said, 'I'll get you a chair.'

He raised a hand, 'I'm fine, Eddie, thanks.'

I said, 'It's too cramped here. Let's move to the kitchen. I'll make coffee.'

'I'm caffeined to the eyeballs, thanks,' Ben said, following me to the kitchen. I turned to Mave, 'I'm fine, Eddie.'

We settled at the table. Ben remained in confessional mood, the rawness from his row with Alice still obvious in his eyes.

He said, 'I got a great commission from The Times to do a series on corruption in sport, and I actually managed to stop drinking in July...' he pondered, 'yes, July of that year. Lasted all the way through, well past Christmas...got that behind us, and the New Year,' he smiled sadly, using his fingers to mark off in the air those two key dates, 'then, at nine months, as though I'd been pregnant with it, out it popped again at the National, in Monty's box...an old tale.'

'The wrong champagne day?' I asked.

Ben nodded, 'Monty was mortified. He was mortified, I was mortal.'

Mave said, 'Are you sure it was a mistake?'

Ben said, 'As in?'

'Could you have been given the alcoholic champagne deliberately?'

'Who'd have done that?' Ben said.

'Sir Monty?' Mave suggested.

Ben looked at her, 'Why would he do that? He was horrified when he realized what had happened, he even kicked off on the catering manager in front of all his guests, the only time I ever saw him lose his cool. It was the only thing that stuck in my mind from that day, how angry Monty was. Somebody got sacked for it.'

I said, 'It was Calum Crampsey. Remember him? Assuming you knew him. Big racing man. Loved a bet.'

Ben frowned and looked past me as though searching for the memory. I said, 'You'd definitely know his face, maybe not his name. He'd worked for Selby and Sampson for years. Covered the press room some days if he wasn't in the hospitality boxes. Used to pester the hell out of people for tips.'

It dawned on Ben and his look changed, 'Ah, I know the fella you mean! Nice guy, helpful, had been an assistant trainer when he was young?'

'That's him.'

'And they sacked him?'

'For bringing the wrong champagne. He was working as a wine waiter in that restaurant we went to for lunch the day of the panel hearing in Liverpool.'

'Was he? Jeez, I didn't even notice.'

'He stayed out of sight until Monty had gone and then when you and Alice left to catch the train he came and sat with Mave and me. Couldn't have been sorrier about what happened, but swore he'd brought the right bottle to Monty's box.'

Ben looked away, 'Poor bastard...what a day that turned out to be.'

'Calum said he wrote to Monty after it happened, apologizing. Then he told me he was sorry he did that, wrote that letter, because it was like admitting something he didn't do.'

Ben said, 'Did it sound like he was telling the truth?'

I shrugged, 'It did to me, but we all try and find ways out of the wrong things we've done I suppose. But if he was telling the truth then, well, what Mave said begins to make some sense.'

Ben reached and put a hand on my forearm, 'Eddie, listen, I don't know what I'd have done without you, but you're barking up the wrong tree here, I promise you. Monty's never been anything but helpful to me, well beyond the call of duty. I'll tell you just how straight he is. That day we're talking about in his box when I got so drunk I passed out. He found me a hotel, had his guy take me there and put me to bed, and next afternoon Monty comes to see me and hands me fourteen grand in cash.'

'Fourteen grand?'

Ben slid his chair closer to me, smiling, 'Listen to this,' he said, 'all of us at Monty's table had put money in a syndicate that day to try a perm on the Tote Jackpot. Monty brought me my share of the winnings. Fourteen grand, and, that Sunday, the state I was in, I had no recollection whatever of being in any syndicate. How straight was Monty doing that?'

I said, 'Well, he's not exactly wondering where his next meal's coming from.'

'Seriously, Eddie. Think about it. You know him almost as well as I do. There's no bad in the man. I forgot a lot of things, but I never forgot what he did with those winnings.'

'And what did you do with those winnings?' Mave asked.

The fire went from his eyes, and his head went down, 'I wrecked the rest of that year with it. I went on the biggest bender you've ever seen...'

'And what happened to your commission from The Times on corruption in sport?' Mave said.

Ben had that faraway look again, through the window at first and then his head steadily went down until he was staring at the floor. He said quietly, 'It was never finished.'

Mave said, 'Never finished, or you never finished it?'

'What do you mean?' Ben said.

'They didn't hire somebody else to complete it?'

'No, I don't believe they did.'

I said, 'Can you recall what your next piece was going to be about? I found six articles in the series.'

'I'd done some research on money laundering through betting, though it was very early days.'

Mave said, 'Like the money laundering DJ's guys were doing with the slot machines in the betting shops?'

'That was part of it. I'd been looking at on-track bookmakers mostly. Some had been paying astronomical prices for pitches, well above what appeared to be their value.'

I said, 'When you mentioned research, can you recall what sort of research? Had you spoken to anyone? Were you nosing around?'

'I had my routine. I wouldn't have questioned anybody I didn't know, or anybody I was suspicious of. Not at that stage, anyway.'

'Did you question Monty?' Mave asked.

Ben frowned and ran his fingers through his hair, 'I can't remember. I might have done...I probably did. He knew as much as anybody about racing gossip, and he liked a bet.'

Mave said, 'Can you recall the names of the people who'd bought those high priced pitches?'

'No, I can't. I might have some notes buried away on my...'

'On your PC,' Mave said, 'which you no longer have. Did you backup online?'

Ben shook his head, 'Just on a hard drive.'

'Still got it?' Mave asked.

'God knows,' Ben said, 'Haven't seen it for years.'

I said, 'How would you feel about talking to Calum Crampsey? I could book us a table for tonight.'

Ben shrugged, 'Fine. What are you thinking?'

'He'd have been working in Monty's box plenty of times. He could have picked up something that would help us here.'

Ben straightened in his chair, 'Eddie, you can't let him know, let anybody know you're suspicious of Monty. I'm not putting my name to that. You're on the wrong track here with Monty. I'd bet on it. You've been more than helpful to me, so I don't mind talking this through, but I'm going to have to pull out at some point. I might as well tell you that now. I owe Monty more than you could know. I probably owe him more than even I would know.'

'I won't say a word against him to Calum, I promise. I'll stick to what happened that day at the National if that makes you feel any better?'

He took a deep breath, 'Okay. Let's do that. It'll give me a chance to tell the fella to stop feeling bad about what happened. I'll settle for that.'

65

I checked that Calum Crampsey would be working that evening and booked a table for two. Ben was nervous about being seen in Liverpool. He was uneasy from the minute we set out to drive south, 'What if Hines's people spot us?' Ben asked.

'Hines never gave you any clue it was his people that were holding you, so why should he be worried? Besides, if Mave's right, he's not involved with DJ's lot anyway.'

'But if Mave's right, then Bruno lied to you and that puts us back on this same old roundabout with Monty. I know Mave's suspicious, and I know she's clever, but believe me, she's putting two and two together and making five.'

'Let's see what else she finds out.'

Calum was waiting just inside the door, smiling nervously. He shook Ben's hand and clasped his left shoulder with his free hand, 'It's been a long time, Ben. Good to see you again.'

'And you, Calum.'

He showed us to a table at the rear. The place was half-full. Calum brought us the soft drinks we'd asked for. I said, 'Have you time to sit for five minutes?'

'Sure. Of course!' He drew a chair out.

'How's your luck?' Ben asked him, 'Still punting?'

'Can't see me ever giving that up, Ben. I'm doing okay. Had a good Cheltenham. Aintree was so so. I'm probably in front for the season, though I suppose everybody says that.'

Ben said, 'You'll be doing better now you're away from all the duff information on the racecourse. Owners, trainers and jockeys are the worst tipsters known to man.'

Calum smiled, 'One or two of them are okay. You just need to be careful who you ask.'

The awkwardness that had been in the air stretched itself into a silence, and I resisted filling it, knowing it would have to come out at some point and the sooner the better.

Ben looked across at Calum and said, 'Listen, Eddie told me what happened between you and Monty and I wanted to say I'm sorry for my part. If I hadn't been there, it wouldn't have happened.'

'That's okay, Ben. It's a long time ago now. I just wanted you to know that Sir Monty made a mistake that day, and I think he knows it and I believe that's why he went mad when he saw you were halfway through that bottle.'

Ben reached to touch his arm, 'Listen, it's done now. Water under the bridge, as they say.'

'I know it's done, Ben, but it's important to me that you know I did my job properly that day. I knew that non-alcoholic bottle was for you. We had to order it in special. It's not the easiest thing to get. Still isn't. Worse thing they do is try and make the label and everything look as though it's no different from the normal bubbly.'

Ben said, 'It would have happened anyway. I'd been dry too long back then. I could have set it aside after the first glass. I just used it as an excuse.'

'But if Sir Monty had let me pour, it wouldn't have happened. He insisted on doing it himself. I've been over this a million times in my head. He must have picked up the wrong bottle. Must have.'

Ben said, 'I believe you. I'm just sorry for how it turned out for all three of us. You lost your job. Monty's been feeling guilty about me ever since. I wouldn't want you to think too badly of him. The guy's a gem, believe me.'

Ben didn't glance at me. He wasn't risking me pitching in to question him. But if he expected Calum to agree with him and reassure him, it didn't work out, because Calum just nodded slightly, folded his arms on the table and looked down.

Ben touched his arm again, 'Listen, I told Eddie this earlier. I was completely out of it that day, and Monty booked me a hotel room, got one of his guys to take me there, put me to bed, pay the bill, and then, listen to this, next day Monty turns up and hands me fourteen grand cash. Fourteen grand! I'd put money in the jackpot syndicate and forgot all about it and we won the jackpot.'

Calum's face changed. He went from humouring Ben with a pleasant look to a sudden quizzical frown and he glanced at me then back at Ben, who kept on, 'Must have been about twenty of us in it and Monty collected my share and brought it next day. I'd never have known. Never.'

Calum straightened, staring at Ben. Ben said, 'Believe me! Honestly, that's what happened!'

Calum said, 'I believe you, Ben. But the fourteen grand he brought you didn't come from a jackpot win, I can tell you that.'

It was Ben's turn to look quizzical, 'What do you mean?'

'The jackpot wasn't won that day. More than a hundred and fifty grand was carried forward to the Monday. I remember it well because I got sacked and then I had the first four winners in the Jackpot and I started dreaming about marching back into that box after racing and telling Sir Monty where to stick it. But I went down in the next leg, like everyone else when that fifty to one chance got up to beat the favourite.'

Ben just kept staring at him. Calum unfolded his arms and drummed lightly on the table with his fingers. He said, 'Whatever Sir Monty felt he owed you fourteen grand for, it wasn't for winning the Tote jackpot.'

66

Calum left us to talk things through. He sent a waiter to take our order, but Ben's appetite from this morning had been dampened considerably by Calum's news about the jackpot. He said to the waiter, 'I'll just have some soup, if that's okay?'

When the waiter left, Ben said to me, 'Should we ask Calum to keep this quiet for now?'

'I'll speak to him before I go. I'd been hoping we'd get him talking about Monty and what he'd seen and heard over the years, but we're going to have to be really careful now.'

Ben nodded, watching me vacantly, looking but not seeing. I said, 'Playing things back in your head?'

He blinked and focused again, 'I didn't imagine fourteen grand, Eddie. I know what I spent it on and I know what that did to me.'

'And maybe that was the plan.'

'For Monty to fund a long bender?'

I nodded. He opened his arms, 'Why? Where's the sense? What's the motive? He's done nothing but protect me since we met again.'

'A guilty conscience. Or maybe he wants to keep a very close eye on what you're doing now that you're sober again…Could be both, I suppose.'

Ben reached an open hand toward me, as though expecting me to place in it some proof. He said, 'Why, though? Why? That's the big missing piece in the jigsaw…the main piece.'

'Well, I know you can't remember if you asked Monty about the articles you were working on back then, but let's assume you did. It was about corruption in sport, right?'

'Right.'

'And the part you'd reached was investigating the purchase of bookmaker pitches on racecourses?'

'Correct.'

'Could Monty have been involved with those purchases?'

'It's not impossible. He's in the business of money lending, at the end of the day.'

'Money lending? I thought he was a trader in currency markets?'

'He tried some of that when he finished business school, but I don't think he was much good at it. He bought a few small independent companies who lend money to accountants and lawyers and professionals along those lines, dentists, doctors...reliable people.'

'Big money?'

'I think so. But very low risk. Monty was just a broker, essentially.'

'Why would they borrow from Monty? Why not go to a bank?'

'No hoops to jump through with Monty. A lot of these people borrow to pay their tax bills. Banks don't lend on that.'

I watched him, 'How do you know this? Have you questioned Monty about it?'

'Not in any detail. When we first met, he asked me if any of the top journalists might be ripe for approaching.'

'As customers?'

Ben half-smiled and nodded, 'He had the mistaken idea I was earning a lot of money back then...well, I suppose I was. I just didn't realize it.'

'If he lent to professionals, Kelman Hines must come into that picture, as a vet, I mean.'

'I suppose.'

'And Hines was pretty ambitious, obviously, if he was splashing out on labs and high-tech.'

Ben shrugged, 'I don't know, Eddie. I got the impression it was mostly short-term stuff Monty did.'

I groaned and massaged my face. Ben said, 'Maybe you're trying to fit too many things together here, Eddie. Prim started all this, remember? What is it you're thinking? Even if Monty did want to keep me quiet and stop me asking questions about those pitches, what's that got to do with Hines? They're separate issues, aren't they?'

'Except that Bruno pointed me right in Hines's direction when I asked him who the top man was in the trafficking racket. And that around the same time as Bruno was telling me that, someone was changing the owner's name on the shell company that owns Wannabet Bookmakers, changing it to Kelman Hines. And the combination of those two led us into finding you, who, by way of another ridiculous coincidence that lines up with the previous two, was being moved to the place we'd find you. Do you swallow all that, really?'

'Maybe Bruno was acting on his own?'

I opened my hands, 'Oh. Come on, Ben! You know Bruno does nothing without Monty telling him to.'

Ben looked over my shoulder and nodded in warning. I turned to see the waiter bringing the soup. 'Can I refresh your drinks?' the waiter said.

'No, thanks,' said Ben.

'I'm fine, thanks,' I said, 'But maybe you could ask Calum to come and see us if he's not busy?'

'Of course, sir.'

When he'd gone, Ben said, 'What are you going to say to Calum?'

'I'm going to ask him to keep all this to himself. If Monty finds out that somebody knows he lied to the tune of fourteen grand, the first guy he'll want to talk to is you.'

'Maybe that's no bad thing, Eddie. I can't see how we're going to get to the bottom of this without talking to Monty…I just can't.'

I looked at Ben, trying to come up with an argument against what he'd said. He spoke again, 'Put it this way, if you're right, and Monty's involved, he can't mean me any harm, nor you. He's had plenty chances to do all the damage he wanted.'

I nodded, 'Maybe you're right, Ben…maybe you're right.'

'Well, why don't we just go and see him?'

'And say what?' I asked.

'And say, Monty, where did that fourteen grand come from?'

67

Fifty miles into our journey home, Mac's name lit up on my phone. I hesitated…was there anything I didn't want Ben to hear on the speaker?

I answered. Mac said, 'You're on hands free by the sound of it. I take it you're driving?'

I resisted sarcasm, 'I am, Mac. All well?'

'You know we've got this new formal end to the season at Sandown week after next?'

'Uhuh.'

'I was thinking it would be good to tie all this wild horses stuff up so that everyone can relax on the last day.'

'That would be good, Mac. By the way, Ben's with me, Ben Searcey.'

They exchanged brief greetings then Mac said to me, 'I'd like to go and see Hines in the next forty-eight hours.'

'Officially? For questioning?'

'Yes.'

I glanced at Ben. He shrugged me a "why not?" and I said, 'Fair enough.'

'Good. What else do you know?' Mac asked.

'What I know and what I've been told are looking like two different things at the moment. We're going to make some calls in the morning to see if we can filter out the crap.'

'What crap?'

'The crap that we're trying to see through. Like the crap that's covering my windscreen just now…shit and squashed insects.'

'Very poetic. Should I be told about any of said crap before I speak to our man?'

'I can give you a better answer at this time tomorrow, I hope.'

'I'll look forward to it.'

'Okay. I'll call you.'

Mac said his goodbyes and the soft light of the phone screen faded to dark. I said to Ben, 'I mentioned to Monty that you wanted to buy him lunch…as a thank you. Why don't you invite him to lunch tomorrow?'

'Just me and Monty?'

'Me, too.'

'Okay. Where?'

'Let Monty choose.'

Ben shifted in his seat, 'Eddie, can you lend me enough to pay for the lunch?'

'I'll pay. Or should I say Vita will pay. You're still employed by her until we hear different, and this is part of your investigation.'

Ben folded his arms and slid lower in his seat, 'Well, I won't argue.'

Mave phoned, 'Will you be home soon?'

'Half an hour. You found something?'

'Managed to trace the previous owner of Wannabet, and probably still the owner, by the look of it.'

'Go on.'

'A company owned by Sir Montague Bearak.'

I looked at Ben. He looked to the heavens. I said, 'Nice one, Mave.'

'He has seventeen other shell companies, all of them own small groups of regional independent bookmakers across the UK.'

'It's beginning to make some sense, now, Mave, isn't it?'

'Money laundering. Big time,' she said.

'Looks like it. Ben told me Monty's upfront business is money lending. High level money lending. A broker dealing with respectable clients.'

'Nice front. I had a look at it. All squeaky clean, and very profitable.'

'Brilliant work, Mave.'

'Thanks. You can pour me a celebratory drink when you get home.'

'Gladly. See you soon.'

I turned to Ben. He said, 'I can't believe it...I mean, I believe it, but I'm, well, I don't know...'

'That first piece you did, the one Mave found online, was about money laundering, wasn't it? As part of your work on corruption in sport.'

'That's right.'

'Maybe that was what set Monty off. We were on the wrong track with the on-course betting pitches.'

'Not necessarily,' said Ben. 'The on-course pitches could have been used as a front for cleaning money, just as easily as the betting shops. In fact, they could shift a lot of the big sums through those pitches, the types of bets that are hard to get on with small independents.'

'But how could all the betting shops survive so long if they were taking losses through payouts to crooks? Whatever way they did it, the books still need to be balanced.'

Ben said, 'But if the crooks own the shops through a shell company then they can theoretically lose thousands as well. Supposing a guy has five losing bets at ten grand apiece, then the crook has a supposed winning bet for forty grand. He has a receipt for it to show the cops, but what they don't know is that he has also put the original fifty grand in to pay for it. No need for the bookie to identify the loser of the fifty grand. Not technically, anyway, for accounts purposes.'

'But you said there was some new Act where bookies had to declare any turnover they thought was suspicious, what was it?'

'The Proceeds of Crime Act. The one that Wannabet wasn't

following, and you can bet your life these other small companies were doing exactly the same.'

We travelled in silence for a minute, then Ben said, 'Eddie, I know I've worn you out by constantly defending Monty, but I just can't see any reasoning in this. I can't. Can you?'

'He's a rich man who wants to stay rich.'

'For what? He gives fortunes to charity. Why not keep it if he wants to stay rich?'

'Because it's a great front for a criminal. It bought the man a knighthood, didn't it?'

'But what else? He's got a couple of horses and a couple of cars. He didn't spend crazy money on either. He never married. Lives in a nice house, but hardly a mansion. He's never been a playboy. His biggest extravagance has been his private boxes on racecourses and entertaining his friends there.'

'Ben, the man could have hundreds of millions stashed in these shell companies. You probably don't know a fraction of what he's been up to.'

'I grew up with him. He was always one for helping people…always a peacemaker. He felt guilty about leaving our school to go to the private school when his old man won the pools. He was embarrassed when that happened…almost ashamed.'

'How long ago was that, though?'

Ben paused then said, 'How long since you were a kid, Eddie?'

'Long time. Feels like a long time, anyway.'

'And how much have you changed?'

'Completely.'

'Really? Everything you believed in? All the things you felt strongly about?'

'Well, they haven't changed, but they don't, do they? That's your character. You're born with it.'

'Just you? Not Monty?'

I looked at him, 'Ben, what do you want me to say here? Do I need to roll this out from the start? From Monty getting you drunk in his box, all the way through what's happened in Deadwood, then on to his ownership of a bunch of betting shops which you yourself discovered are laundering money? How much circumstantial evidence is going to be enough for you?'

Ben went quiet for a mile, then said, 'So, what's the plan?'

'I think it's time to give it to Mac, now, lock, stock and barrel.'

'Prim, too?'

I sighed long and low, 'Dil reckons he's found a way out for Prim.'

'Well, give me a chance to find a way out for Monty.'

I pulled onto the hard shoulder and pressed the hazard lights switch. Ben turned to face me. I said, 'Where am I supposed to stop here, Ben? When do I call it quits? Is anybody going to take the blame for this massive fucking mess?'

'Let me go and see Monty on my own and have this out with him.'

'You don't think Bruno will end up taking you for a car ride?'

'No. I don't.'

'Are you going to reel off all the evidence?'

'Yes.'

'Then he'll either tell you to phone the cops to come and get him or he'll have you killed.'

'At least I get to find out why he did it.'

'What about Alice?'

He smiled and raised a finger, 'That's a mean trick, Eddie. Emotional blackmail.'

I put my hand up. 'Guilty. Happy to plead that way to save you from yourself.'

He said, 'Alice would want me to do this.'

'I very much doubt it, Ben.'

'Okay. We'll ask her. If she says no, you can call the police.'

I watched him. He held my gaze, confident. Too confident. I said, 'No. You go and see Monty. But I come with you.' Ben smiled and offered his hand to close the deal.

68

Next morning, Ben was nervy about calling Monty. He pushed his breakfast around the plate. When he did take a mouthful, he chewed for a long time. I said, 'You'll be fine.'

He forced a smile and stared through the window at the bright morning. I said, 'I would call him, but it might just make him suspicious.'

Ben nodded. I said, 'You can't let him think you've got anything on your mind other than a thank-you lunch. He'll pick up on it. I'm picking up on it and you haven't even opened your mouth yet.'

Ben said, 'It's not just the confrontation, Eddie, since I was a kid I've felt ashamed of some of the things I've done. I hate the shame, but I can't get away from it. And every time I need to speak to Monty, what happened that day at Aintree makes me want to cry.'

'What happened that day at Aintree was Monty's fault, not yours. If anybody should feel ashamed about it, he should.'

Ben nodded slowly and looked away again with that thousand-yard stare and the sun through the window shone on his welling tears and his battered face. I remembered how shocked I'd been in the car park at Bangor hospital that morning when he had come toward me, almost unrecognizable. Then he'd smiled, and I had guessed at who he was. Now I had become used to his looks, his ruined teeth and the wrinkled and scarred paper skin of an ancient, made all the more curious by the man inside, the child, the born again…and watching him now, that same feeling of sadness that had overwhelmed me that morning came back and I understood finally why I had wept that day.

I said, 'I'll call him.'

'Would you?'

'Of course. Now, eat your breakfast. God knows, you need it!'

Ben smiled and dabbed his eyes pushing out the tears that had been waiting. I said, 'In fact, there's every chance Monty will be at Haydock today. Why don't we just casually drop by after racing and wait until his guests have gone?'

'You riding there?'

'I've got one in the last. I can hold off and travel late so you don't have to wander around the course on your own.'

'That would be good, Eddie. It would get this over with, too. It would kill me to wait a week to see him.'

'Literally, maybe,' I smiled.

Ben laughed. He laughed, and the sun shone, and for all that awaited us, the world seemed back in balance again.

69

My ride in the final race was for a woman who'd been training so long that, when she had started out, the training licence had been in the name of her head lad because the Jockey Club did not issue licenses to women. In the half century since then, she had never trained a big winner, but she had kept going and kept smiling and I'd never heard her complain about anything. Riding a winner f Constance McKenzie was on my bucket list.

But halfway down Haydock's back straight, I knew it wasn't go' to be today. Spring had brought the better ground, which helpec good horses gallop away from the plodders much more quickly t did the winter mud. Riccardjohnston, the bright chestnut I rode, w one of the plodders. He tried and he tried, eager to please his rid and unwilling to accept that the engine he'd been given at birth m not someday double in capacity.

We were last, a long way last...the others pulled so far clea couldn't hear the hoofbeats. Still he kept his head down. Sti' carried me. I patted his neck, 'I might borrow those speaker' stick them in those floppy lugs of yours and for one day you show them how it was done, wouldn't you?' And his ears flickec to listen for a moment, then his head went lower and on he tr

The clouds stayed away and as we entered Monty's glass-west-facing box, the sun was halfway set, holding Bruno G silhouette. He was at his usual place by the door leading onto the high terrace. Half a dozen guests remained, all at Monty's table, where the champagne bottles stood in Bruno's long shadow.

Monty saw us come in and he smiled and raised a hand and I saw the mouthed "excuse-me" as he rose to come and greet us. 'Eddie! Ben! How good to see you both!' He put a hand on my shoulder and one on Ben's and drew us toward him with what seemed genuine warmth. 'Come and join us. I'll order a fresh pot of coffee.'

They spread out, making room for two more chairs, and we sat and waited. We laughed with them, and joined in the banter and as I watched these men and women, each pleasantly drunk, I envied them their brief break from reality in this sheltered circle of sunlight, and I understood at last Monty's seemingly endless need for company without complications. Monty had never married. These regular gatherings of business associates, acquaintances, and minor celebrities provided him with a big happy family he could send home after racing, before the squabbles started.

Most importantly, they were people he'd never have to explain to.

It was close to sunset when the last couple left, accompanied by Bruno. Monty turned to us, smiling, 'Another day done, eh?' He put a hand across Ben's shoulder, walking him back to the table, 'Come and tell me now about all the excitement.'

We settled in our chairs. Ben said, 'Has Bruno gone? Is he done for the day?'

'Ah, if only, poor man. He'll see Colin and Angela into a taxi then take a break while I smoke my cigar on the terrace. He can't stand the smell, but it's the last true luxury in these days of health and safety and so-called political correctness. Either of you troubled by cigar smoke?'

We said no and he slid open the glass door, 'Bring your chairs. I'll stand. I'm sick of sitting down!'

We left the chairs and walked outside. All that was above us was the roof. Sixty-feet below, the enclosures were deserted: no punters, no bookies, no losing tickets. The cleaners had done a good job.

A third of the sun was below the horizon. Monty's cigar smoke rose in the still air. Ben swallowed hard, and Monty saw him do that and his eyes changed and he glanced sideways at me and immediately looked away again when our eyes met. Ben said, 'Monty, can I ask you a question?'

'Sure. Of course.'

'Remember that Sunday, the day after the National, when you came to the hotel and gave me fourteen grand?'

Monty nodded, trying to hold the smile together, but the panic in his eyes was desperately seeking a way out. Ben said, 'Where did the money come from?'

'The jackpot. We won the Tote Jackpot, don't you remember?'

Ben said, 'There was a carry-forward to Monday. I checked. The jackpot wasn't won on National day.'

Monty looked away slowly, toward the sinking sun, then he turned and dropped the cigar on the tarmac terrace and ground it out with his heel. 'I think we'd best go inside,' he said.

Monty slid the door closed and flipped the lever lock up. He went to the main entry door and turned the lock on that. We sat at the table. Monty looked at us, 'You both need to forget everything now, and get on with your lives.' There was no threat in his tone, just a tinge of resignation that seemed to stir the reporter in Ben, who straightened in his chair and said, 'What happened, Monty?'

Monty opened his mouth, but closed it again and his jaw muscles clenched. He composed himself, then said, 'Ben, I know this will seem a very odd question, given what you just asked me, but, do you trust me?'

Ben hesitated only for a moment, then nodded. Monty put his big hands on the table and leant forward, 'Go back to your family, to your daughter. Find yourself a home away from Deadwood, I can help you with that, and start the new life you always wanted. I'll help with that, too.'

'What happened?' Ben said.

Monty sighed and said, 'An awful lot happened an awful long time ago, and what I was left with became my life. It's a life I don't want you to have. It's a life I don't want anyone to have. The only good thing about it has been that I've been able to help and protect people I care about. I'm going to say-'

Ben said, 'You poured the alcoholic champagne deliberately.'

Monty held his gaze.

Ben said, 'The fourteen grand was to keep me topped up with booze until the project was dead, the writing gig for The Times.'

Monty massaged his gargoyle face with both hands, the damaged skin moving like cooling candle wax. He took a deep breath, 'Listen, Ben…' he turned to me, 'Eddie…both of you. I'm at the bottom of a pit that has taken thirty years to dig. What I've been doing, Ben, since we met again in Lime Street, is lying on my back in that pit and kicking furiously to try and keep you away from the edge of it. My kicking time is done. I can't buy anymore for you. All I can do now is fund you. I'll pay you to go away and be safe, you and Alice. If you want to go abroad, that's no problem. It might be the best option.'

I said, 'Who's threatening you?'

'Nobody's threatening me, Eddie. A man owns me. A man who can do anything to anybody and never pay for it.' He turned again to Ben, 'Ben, I want you to imagine yourself heading down the road toward hell. You don't know it's around the corner, but you meet me before you make the last turn and I tell you that you must go back, that you must not continue on any account because hell is around that corner. Would you listen? Of course you would.'

'I'd listen, but now I want you to imagine the same scenario…do you think I'd leave you there?'

'You could not get me out. Nobody could.'

I said, 'We can get you out.'

Monty said, 'I know your record, Eddie, and I admire you immensely. But ten Eddie Malloys, a hundred Eddie Malloys couldn't get me out of this. This man has never been beaten…will never be beaten.'

I smiled, 'There ain't a horse that can't be rode and there ain't a man that can't be throwed.'

Ben smiled. Monty shook his head and stared at his hands on the table top. Ben reached to touch his forearm, 'And you've got Bruno to add to the mix.'

Monty said, 'Bruno is my gaoler. He works for the man, not for me. You see my face? That's what I got when I cried enough. When, after more than twenty-five years I said I was done with it, finished, I was tied down below a drip, an acid drip, fixed to dispense once a minute. They set a clock for one hour. There was no car crash. No Bruno to pull me out. Sixty drops of acid melted my face and cost me half of my sight.' He pointed to his face...put a hand over his glass eye. 'I was left with this and a lifelong gaoler in Bruno Guta. And all I had said was that I'd had enough.'

I turned to check the door, then said, 'When will he be back?'

'Fifteen minutes.'

I said, 'That's time enough to tell us what we need to know to get you out.'

Monty shook his head slowly and said, 'How much more-'

I leant forward quickly and grasped his shoulder, 'Who is he? Name him. I'll get him.'

Monty stared at me. I said, 'You know, Monty, the last time I had this conversation, the last time I had to convince somebody? It was Alice, little Alice. I'm telling you what I told Alice. I fix things. I do this. It doesn't scare me. I've been offered jobs to do it professionally. I have people I can call on who can out-think Einstein. Sounds like this guy has brainwashed you into believing he's superman. I've done supermen. My CV is littered with supermen. Give me the guy's name.'

He looked at me, 'No.'

I said, 'Monty, your life is...you have no life. It's done with according to you. What have you got to lose?'

He said, 'Ben...Alice...You...Your family.'

Ben said, 'You want us to sign a disclaimer?'

Monty smiled, 'I want you to go home and look after your daughter.'

'My daughter would never rest if she knew about this. I promise you that. What made her risk her own life time and again was rage at injustice. Alice would have died for it. She told me that...emphasized it. What she actually said was, "Yes, Dad, I'd have died for it! Proper

302

died!" Proper died. Hear that?'

Monty nodded, smiling sadly. Ben said, 'You've protected me. It's time for me to protect you.'

Monty looked at Ben for what seemed a long time, then said, 'I'll tell you on one condition, both of you…' he glanced at me. I nodded. Ben said, 'Name it.'

'You send Alice somewhere safe for the duration. You too, Eddie. You send your family away. I'll pay.'

'My family's on the other side of the world. They'll be fine.'

'Your woman?'

'It's a package, Mave and me. Buy one get one free.'

He kept watching, waiting…I said, 'She won't walk away from this, Monty, I can tell you that now. She'll want to help, and there's nobody I'd rather have, whoever this guy is.'

He turned to Ben, 'Tell me you'll send Alice away somewhere safe.'

'I'll send her to America to visit her mother.'

Monty nodded, 'She will fly first class.'

Ben smiled, 'She'd flog the ticket and buy economy and give the rest away.'

I checked my watch. Monty drew a deep breath then said, 'I'm entertaining again at Beverley tomorrow. Can you come there, about the same time, to coincide with Bruno's break?'

I said, 'We'll come to work things out, Monty, but we're not leaving here without a name.'

Monty sighed and clamped a hand either side of his jaw, elbows resting on the table. His hands framed the scarred face as though he was holding an exhibit up in court, a final reminder. He said, 'No. Look, I'm sorry, but I finally, finally need to do the right thing. For my sake, as much as yours. Go home. I am not going to tell you.'

He stared at me. That eye had never seemed so dead. I said, 'Then I'll tell you…'

Monty's good eye twitched.

I said, 'Sydney Ember.'

Monty's head went slowly down until his forehead rested on the table edge, as though awaiting the fall of the axe.

70

We drove into the last of the setting sun along Haydock's tr
avenue to the big exit gates. The shock had kept us silent. I
to speak, 'You were right. Your instinct that Monty was so
right.'

'Yes, well, mixed feelings now, as they say.'

'We'll get it fixed. This Sydney Ember is the fella that Chief
Constable Bradley mentioned at that meeting. I think he believed I
was in tow with Ember. He wanted to bug my phone.'

'Who is he, Ember?'

'Bradley said he was a criminal they couldn't catch because he
always had a batch of receipts supposedly proving he had won all his
money from betting.'

'What kind of criminal? What was he into?'

'Bradley said his day to day stuff was organized crime. I got the
impression a few murders were thrown in.'

'Nice fella. Organized crime would certainly cover what's been
happening in Deadwood, but going by what Monty says, Ember
must be into a hell of a lot more than trafficking girls.'

'The thing is, he's probably doing it in every big city in
Britain…maybe Europe. Sounds like Monty's just been used as his
front man. Ember must own all those businesses that are in Monty's
name. Which, by the way, makes me wonder if that was the first time
Ember picked up on you. Mave showed me that article you wrote on

shell companies. Where did that fall in the series you were writing for
The Times?'

'Can't remember…second, maybe third…The one I was working
on when it all went tits-up was the business of buying bookmaking
pitches on course. Maybe we could…' He turned to me, 'Would
Mave take another look at the pitch side of things?'

'I'm sure she would. I'll get her onto it now.'

I pulled over and called home, feeling somehow that a hands-free
conversation might not be safe. I thanked Mave and told her we'd
be her in an hour. Ben interrupted, 'Ask her to check on Alice.'

I said, 'What's Alice up to?'

'She's on the spare laptop. Playing a game, I think.'

'Okay. Good.'

Mave said, 'That little half pitch that your tone moves up when
your vocal cords tighten?'

'Uhuh?'

'Anxiety or anticipation?'

'A bit of both.'

Ben said, 'Tell Mave to lock the door.'

I said, 'Mave, Ben's asking if you'll lock everything up until we get
home.' I knew she'd ask no questions.

'Tell Ben I'll do that now.'

'Good. See you soon.'

'Want me to call if I get a quick result on those pitches?'

'No, thanks. It can wait.'

'Drive safe, lover boy.'

'I'm smiling…You're picturing me smiling, right?'

'A rare projection in my mind's eye, but, yes, I am.'

I laughed, 'See you in an hour.'

When I put the phone down, I realized Ben was watching me. He
had a fixed half-smile. He said, 'You're a pretty cool fella, Mister
Malloy. How do you get to making off the cuff jokes when a man's
just told us we're probably going to die?'

I wagged a finger, 'The trick is in not believing him.'

His smile filled out and he nodded and settled back as we took the slip road on the M6.

At seventy on the speedo I hit cruise control. I said, 'How in hell are you going to get Alice to America?'

'Good question. I haven't spoken to her mother in years.'

'Even if you were on speaking terms, if Alice gets a sniff of the trouble that's brewing, she's just going to dig in here, isn't she?'

'Probably.'

'And?'

Ben said, 'I can only try, Eddie. If she won't go, she won't go. Monty can hardly backtrack now.'

'Don't be so sure. He seemed pretty serious to me. I think he's going to want proof she's safe, or, at least, your word on it that she's gone. I get the feeling that a lot of the protecting he's been doing has been of Alice. When you think of what she got away with in Deadwood, with DJ...if Ember's such a scary fucker, Monty must have had to pull some strings to keep Alice safe, and you, too. Now you know why you were getting so many cups of tea and biscuits when Monty's guys grabbed you.'

'They'd be Ember's people would they not, with Monty keeping them in check?'

'I doubt it, Ben. Ember's secret is to keep himself clear of any criminal association whatever.'

'So who did the acid drip on Monty's face?'

My stomach turned. 'You know, I wouldn't have guessed what happened, but it never sat right with me that Bruno just happened to be travelling the same road as Monty a minute after the supposed accident and then was able to somehow haul him out of a burning car.'

'Thus, happily landing himself the job of bodyguard for life,' Ben said.

'Indeed. And Bruno's going to be another problem. Ember must have some kind of right hand man, some, what's the word, consigliere? Ember might never get caught committing crime, but if Monty is that afraid of him, he won't be the only man running scared. So Ember must have some guy carrying out his orders. Somebody he trusts completely.'

'You think it could be Bruno?'

'I don't know. But he must trust Bruno enough to believe that Monty's not going to turn him. Monty would charm most people, and now we know it's all genuine. Ember would need to have been dead certain that practically living with Monty wouldn't see Bruno developing a soft spot for him.'

Ben said, 'Bruno does seem a bit robotic, doesn't he?'

'He doesn't do a great line in small talk, I'll give you that.'

'And DJ will have told Bruno what you did to him, so he's going to be extra wary of you.'

'Nah, Bruno would know that DJ's nothing but a fat kid wanting to impress his mates who don't have a brain among them.'

'I wouldn't underestimate Bruno, Eddie. Might be a big mistake.'

'I'm not. But I've dealt with harder men.'

'You don't know that yet.'

'Oh, I know it.'

Ben watched me, 'It's the same as riding, isn't it? You just won't allow yourself to believe anyone is better than you.'

'Correct.'

'A doubt-free life.'

I looked at him, 'Got to be, Ben. You can't win with a head full of doubts about yourself.'

'You never have any, ever?'

'Plenty. I just kill them off before I go out to ride. Euthanize them. Bang! Gone.'

'A handy skill.'

'A vital one. Listen, we've got off the track, here, what about Alice? What are you going to do?'

'I'll call her mother.'

'Do you think she'd go to Australia for a couple of weeks, with Mave?'

'I thought you said Mave was staying?'

'She'll want to stay, and I need her help. But I need her safe, too. Anything she can do for us here, she can do in Australia.'

'Would she go?'

'I think so. She trusts my judgement…well, most of the time. And she'll want to see Sonny. He's kind of like a dear old uncle. She'll be missing Kim, too. Marie, maybe not so much, but they get on well enough.'

'So, how do I talk Alice into flying halfway round the world? She'll already be getting antsy about the girls in Deadwood. Give her a choice between Sydney and Deadwood and she'd take Deadwood.'

'Oddly enough, her choice looks like Sydney the city, or Sydney Ember.'

Ben grunted in agreement and went quiet. After a while, I said, 'Maybe that's the answer in itself? We could tell Alice that we've got together enough evidence for the police to finally raid Deadwood and clean the whole place out, and it's them who want to keep potential witnesses safe so they can give evidence in court. Tell Alice you're both in the witness protection programme.'

'Except that I stay here and she has to go.'

'No need for you to stay, Ben, is there? You've done your bit. Maybe you and your IT guy could pitch in with Mave and work from down under?'

'That would leave you on your own.'

'Exactly, free from worry about the people I care for. I can euthanize doubt, but not worry. And I work much better alone.'

'You sound as though you mean it.'

'Never more so, Ben, believe me.'

He watched me for a minute then said, 'Danger means a lot to you.'

I hesitated, seeking an argument against that, then said, 'I suppose it does.'

'I hear it in your voice. You get excited talking about going this alone. It seems almost primal.'

I shrugged, 'I've never analyzed it.'

'That's why you ride.'

'Probably.'

He kept looking at me, then said quietly, 'Do you think you have a death wish?'

'I think I want to beat it. I think I want to say "give it your best shot". And I think that maybe I can get some kind of revenge on it for what it did to me, for what it did to my family.' I looked across. Ben watched, straight-faced and unblinking. I said, 'And I never even knew I thought that until I heard it come out of my mouth.'

'What happens when we're young stays with us, even if we don't want it to. You'll always be like this, Eddie, you know that? Excited about danger, about overcoming death.'

'I know it probably more than I know anything. Nobody and nothing ever beat that feeling for me…never will.'

'You lose in the end, though.'

'You never lose when you go down fighting, Ben. Never.'

71

Alice bought the witness protection programme pitch with considerable excitement at the prospect of finally nailing the traffickers. Mave proved me wrong about her respecting my judgement: 'No way, Mister Malloy. I'm bored enough here without being stuck among ten thousand sheep.'

'Ah, but with ten thousand sheep surrounding you, nobody can get close enough to do you any harm'

'Eddie, I'm not spending the next half hour going through a million sheep metaphors while you try to talk me into this. I am not going. End of.'

'Monty might not do the deal if he believes you're in danger.'

'Monty hardly knows me. This guy Ember doesn't know me at all. I'm way out on the periphery, so you just tell Monty you're not worried about me.'

'I am worried about you.'

'Then best have me where you can keep an eye on me. And where I can keep an eye on you.'

'Mave-'

'Shhh! Done. No more. Ben and Alice go. We stay. I'll buy their tickets, business class. Be nice to spend some of our money.'

'Your money.'

'Whatever. I'll speak to Ben and tie up the details.'

Next day, ten minutes into my trip to Beverley, I pulled over to a tree-covered viewing point on the edge of Lake Ullswater where the reflection of the afternoon sun lay smooth on the dark surface. I called Mac.

'Eddie? News?'

'Mac, you're becoming very, er, succinct, is that the right word?'

'Yes.'

I smiled, 'Oh, very droll.'

He said, 'Can we do the banter at some other time, when matters are less pressing? We need to move on this Hines case.'

'Okay, well, that's what I'm calling about. Remember when you put your job on the line for me to stop my phone being bugged by Chief Constable Bradley?'

'What's that got to do with Kelman Hines?'

'Bear with me, Mac, as you would say. It looks like Bradley was right about the guy he mentioned, Sydney Ember. I think he's tied up in the Hines case. Maybe not directly but the bucket load of brownie points that go with Hines will turn into a shitload for you if Ember is involved.'

'Eddie, why do I get the feeling you have your huckster's hat on here? Why am I getting the strong impression that you are calling to buy some more time, and buy it very cheaply?'

'It might seem cheap, Mac, but it'll be a good investment. For you, for your boss and for Bradley.'

He sighed heavily, 'Look, is there something in this Ember fellow, or is it just an excuse? And if it's an excuse, what is it for? Why are you trying to dissuade me from approaching Hines?'

'Which of those do you want answered first, Mac? You know that what I'm doing will be for the best. If it means a short delay on the Hines thing, it'll be worth it.'

'Your idea of what's for the best and mine are often entirely different. Now, you asked me to stay off the record with this, but I can't do that indefinitely. Sandown's coming up, remember that. I want Hines under arrest before the last day of the season.'

'You'll get it. I promise. I'm on my way to a meeting. Things should be a lot clearer after it. I might even call you again later. If not, then tomorrow.'

'Tonight, please.'

'Okay. Tonight.'

'Goodbye.'

'And to you, Mister McCarthy, and to you.'

I smiled as I pulled back out into the dappled shadows on clean, dry tarmac, and that primal feeling Ben had mentioned welled in me again and made me smile and drive too fast as I wrestled the car through the series of bends. Men could rip up the land and lay miles of straight motorway, but when it came to getting around all these ancient glacial lakes, quiet and still as they were, the water made the rules.

At Beverley, they race only on the flat, where the jockeys are smaller, the horses more expensive and the weather warmer. But, for me, it was lacking in danger, though my meeting with Monty might just make up for that.

I wanted to leave it longer this time before going up to his box. I had no appetite for socializing now and was afraid my impatience around Monty's guests would show. And there was something I should have considered before now: what would Bruno Guta think of me turning up at a flat meeting one day after spending so much time alone with Monty?

I waited until the car park emptied, then found a spot where I could see through the gates to the top of the grandstand. When Bruno came out, I would go in.

It proved a long wait, and it was close to seven o'clock when Bruno escorted a party of four down the stairs and toward the exit. I knew he'd wait outside with them until a taxi arrived, so I hurried across the enclosure and up the stairs.

I tried the handle on the heavy door of Monty's box. It moved smoothly down, and I went in, closing it behind me. Monty was on the balcony, smoke rising from his cigar as he watched me. I mimed a turn of the lock and he nodded and I spun the metal wing and heard the reassuring clunk. Monty waved me forward, and I went out onto the balcony.

He said, 'I was afraid you wouldn't make it.'

'Been here for hours. Thought it best to wait until Bruno took his break, this being a flat meeting.'

'I was a bit worried about that myself. Good thinking. Where's Ben?'

'Packing for a trip to Australia with Alice.'

He seemed to deflate, but it was the tension leaving him. He put a hand on my arm as he sighed, 'I am so relieved…so relieved!'

'Good. Ben wanted you to know how seriously he took things last night.'

'He's a good man. I feel so much better now. I don't really care what happens to me anymore. I'm rather tired of life, or, of my life, I suppose I ought to say. As long as your families are safe, I'm ready to take what comes. What about your woman, Mave?'

'Mave's staying.'

He looked at me, 'Is that what you want?'

'It's what she wants, Monty. I'll look after her.'

He sighed and looked at his feet for what seemed a long time, then slowly back to me, 'Eddie…I'm…I don't know how to find the words to explain to you, to try and make you see. You are dealing here with someone who is beyond psychopathic. He is a psychopath with full control over his decisions, a very, very smart man. The thing for you to take in is that Sydney Ember, when it suits him, places no value on human life. None. He is not some Mister Angry who lashes out or gets emotionally involved. He just puts out an order as though it's for groceries, to have people killed.'

I put a hand on his arm, 'Monty, I could sit Mave down beside you for an hour of this. It won't change her mind. I'm not being complacent about Ember. I trust your judgement. And Bradley left me with the same impression of the man. I'll get it done. I'll figure out a way to get it done. I promise you.'

'You talk with such confidence, Eddie. I'm torn between admiration and regret at your naivety. And I don't mean that unkindly, believe me.'

'Naivety can be good, sometimes. Want to go inside to make sure we're not overheard?'

He nodded and left the cigar burning on the edge of the brickwork.

We sat at a clean table. I looked around: all the tables had been cleared of bottles and glasses. I said, 'Quick work by the caterers.'

'They're a good bunch.' All his tension seemed to have returned. He said, 'You'll need to tell me where to start, Eddie. I can't function.'

'Want me to ask questions?'

He nodded and clasped his hands, 'Please.'

'How did you get in with Ember?'

'By accident. When I was starting out lending, I made the mistake of being sucked into providing capital for a very nice, very enthusiastic man named Michael Haberman who wanted to build up an estate of betting shops. He kept borrowing, kept expanding, kept showing me positive figures. So positive that I was persuaded to to turn the loans into investment and become a silent partner.'

'How long ago?'

'Thirty-one years ago,'

I nodded, He continued, 'All seemed well until Michael dropped dead from a massive coronary, and I discovered that all the good figures he had shown me were from laundered money. By this time, I had a healthy business of my own lending to established professionals. To continue providing finance, I needed a faultless reputation. Sydney Ember, who'd been launderer in chief, told me to carry on where Michael had left off or he would expose me as a partner in a money laundering business.'

'How many shops were there back then?'

'Fourteen, all on Merseyside.'

'How many now?'

'Three-hundred-and-seventy-six.'

'Nationwide?'

'Pretty much. Mostly around the big cities.'

I nodded, 'What else is he into, other than trafficking kids?'

'Big in drugs. Counterfeit brand names. Stolen bank cards. Online fraud, probably other things. I believe he's now into steal-to-order artefacts from the middle east.'

'How has he stayed clean?'

'He trusts nobody a hundred percent. He has two men working close enough to him whom he trusts maybe ninety percent. Bruno is one. I don't know the other, though I've heard Bruno call him Gerald. From what I can gather, Bruno and Gerald do what needs done and arrange everything on the criminal side. Ember owns nothing on paper. He's never been charged, let alone convicted.'

'Married? Girlfriends? Boyfriends? Anybody living with him?'

'Nobody lives with him. Nobody gets to see him at home without a full strip search.'

'A strip search? Even you?'

'Even me. Even Bruno, and, so, I'm assuming, Gerald.'

'What's he looking for, guns, wires?'

'Anything that could get him killed or arrested. Once you've gone through the search, and the house is locked down, he'll speak openly. The house is swept daily for bugging devices. He has an alarm system whose code changes every day. One button press on a handheld console or on his smartphone, locks the place down. Every door. Every window.'

'What's his IT setup, a big computer room?'

'Nothing. No PCs in the house. No internet connection.'

'None you know of, or none at all?'

'None at all, so he claims. He says no matter how good an IT team he could get, somebody else might get a better one, which would become a weak point in his defences, and he has no weak points, so he says.'

'Does he ever come to you?'

'Never. All business is done inside his house.'

My options, some of the ideas I'd come here with, were closing down and I was struggling to think on the fly. I said, 'The strip search, how literal? Who does it, Ember himself?'

'As literal as you can get. When you reach the locked gates to his

315

drive, you call him for a code. The gates lock behind you. When you get out of the car you call him again and he unlocks the house. Once through the door, you hear all the deadbolts slotting back into place. His set up means you are forced left into what he calls his 'Airlock', and you take off all your clothes, you turn around one full circle, arms fully extended, and you finish by spreading your legs and bending over…as best you can, in my case. Cameras capture everything and Ember is watching it live.'

'Fucking hell.'

'You go from there through a side door into the dressing room where you put on what's best described as a large judo outfit and a pair of slippers. You exit through another door into the hall and get your first live sight of Mister Sydney Ember.'

All the time he was talking, Monty was watching my face. He smiled sadly, 'Are you beginning to get the picture now?'

I nodded, 'What about female visitors?'

Monty considered…'You know, that question has never once occurred to me. I can only suppose that the kind of women who visit him at home have no problems with undressing in his company.'

'He must have had some…bona-fide women calling at the house, surely?'

Monty shrugged, 'I can only imagine that he must go out to them rather than have them come in. Or he lets them in but never discusses anything but the weather.'

I nodded, thinking.

Monty said, 'Now you know why the police have never been able to get anything on him, and never will.'

'Well, it helps me get a better picture of Bradley. I thought he was some manic-obsessive cop with a fixation. But years and years of trying to nail Ember must be like knitting fog.'

'Ember enjoys his relationship with the police. Bradley's not the only one he's pissed off.'

'What about when they come to check on him, to make him produce his betting slips and stuff. I'm sure they don't bend over in the air lock.'

Monty smiled, 'It's been years since they've called on him. The courts ran out of patience with search warrants when they were never finding anything.'

I shook my head, 'He must be sitting there like the grand old Duke of York.'

'A fair comparison. Lives on a hill, too. Fortress mentality.'

'What about your companies, so they wash all his income or just some of it?'

'All. That's why it was so hard for me to try and get out of it when he did this.' Monty raised his face to the lights. He said, 'Sydney Ember is the reason I never married. I would have so loved to have children. But I could never have coped with the worry and the guilt. He wanted to kill Alice and Ben. I told him I was done if that happened. No matter what he threatened me with, I told him, I'd be finished.'

'So he let you handle it your way?'

'Yes. And as you now see, I am hardly a criminal mastermind.'

I smiled, 'Was it your idea to put Ben's clothes on the statue and soak them in whiskey?'

He grimaced, 'I'm afraid so. A touch melodramatic, I fear.'

'It made me chuckle.'

He nodded and smiled sadly. I said, 'At least it told me Ben was alive.'

'Well, I'm glad about that.'

I said, 'Who changed the ownership name on the first shell company to try and steer us away from you?'

'Bruno arranged that, too. I didn't realize you knew about that.'

'Mave dug it out.'

He shook his head, 'That's bad news. Eddie. Ember did that as a precaution. If he knew you had got that far, he'd have taken control there and then. I don't know what you are planning, but this puts a tight deadline on things, believe me. There is nothing that happens that Sydney Ember doesn't get to know about.'

'We left no tracks, Monty. He won't find out about the shell company stuff through anything we've done. How the hell did he find out who was doing the wild horses scam?'

'Apparently the fellow who was actually doing it, the one who worked for Hines, was a bit loose-tongued.'

'Boffo?'

'That's it. Anyway, any crime happening in the north west, Ember knows about it. Even if Boffo hadn't talked, Sydney would have found out.'

'Did Ember lay any of those horses, or have a bet?'

'He's much too smart for that. The way he used that information was to avoid having those races on his records. Nothing criminal, then, you see?'

'So he does bet on horses and doesn't just clean the money through these fruit machines in shops?'

'FOBT, Fixed Odds Betting Terminals. I'd say only about thirty percent of the cleaning happens there. You see, there's no skill element attached to machines. It's impossible to argue that you can fund such a lifestyle just on machines. What he does is produce scans of his betting slips, suitably timed and dated. The police would then contact the relevant company to double check our records, and we confirmed the details.'

'So, you must be altering the times and dates on the tills so that he has slips which look as though they've been placed before the result was known?'

'Correct.'

'And how does he explain to the cops the fact that he's not been barred by the owner for damaging profits?'

'Well, as I said, it's quite a while since the police have bothered him at all, but he keeps everything going, continues betting just in case he needs all the records at some point.'

'So, when he was being regularly checked by the cops, what was the procedure?'

'He'd claim to travel the country, sometimes visiting shops just once a year so that staff had forgotten about him.'

'Did the cops ever ask to see the CCTV footage of the times he's been in?'

'Occasionally. Each shop has some footage of him, and the timecode was doctored accordingly.'

'So they, or you, I suppose, kept giving the cops exactly the same clip, just timed and dated differently?'

'Correct. Incredible, I know. But it's seldom the same officers checking footage, and they obviously didn't think to look back on previously requested clips.'

'So our Sydney is mostly sitting at home, while the cops believe he's roaming the country's betting shops every day? No wonder I've never seen him on the racecourse.'

'He seldom goes there. Though he, again through me, owns several pitches at the top tracks which are very useful for cleaning large amounts.'

'And it was those you had just bought when Ben was closing in with that series of articles?'

'Regrettably, yes. And painful as it was for Ben and Alice, what followed was way better than Ember's suggested alternative.'

I nodded, 'I'm sure.'

Monty sighed and massaged that rubbery skin, then checked his watch. I said, 'How are we for time?'

'Safe for another fifteen minutes, I'd say, but I'm not sure there's much more I can tell you. I hope what I have told you is sufficiently discouraging for you to have a rethink on this.'

'Why?'

'Because Sydney Ember is bulletproof. Nobody knows enough to convict him, except me, I suppose, and even then a skilful QC could probably make mincemeat of me. He won't convict himself, and nobody will ever record him surreptitiously.'

'What you've told me would easily be enough, I think. Would you give evidence against him in court?'

'Gladly, but I suspect Bruno would kill me at the first sign of any rebellion.'

'He trusts you enough to leave you alone, doesn't he? It can't just be at times like this that he gets a break, and you get a break, for that matter?'

'He has become complacent, I suppose. He believes I'm thoroughly cowed after all these years. But look, Eddie, I'm convinced Ember will have several get-out scenarios prepared to counter anything I'd say against him. I'm the one with my name on everything. On paper, I'm the criminal. Ember knows every single thing I could say against him. What we don't know is what he has on hand to discredit or disprove that.'

'We'll work something out, I promise.'

Monty smiled sadly and bowed his head. He said, 'The man's been under police surveillance for quarter of a century and has yet to spend one minute behind bars.'

I reached and grasped his forearm, 'We'll get him. Believe me.'

He nodded, but it was a resigned nod. I said, 'How do I communicate with you safely?'

'The racecourse is the only place I can be sure I'm not being monitored, Eddie.'

'Can you get away from your box if you need to, or would Bruno come with you?'

'No, I can get away. Probably couldn't stay away too long, but I come and go.'

'Check the papers for where I'm riding over the next few days and come racing at those tracks. You have a box at almost every racecourse, don't you?'

'All the northern and midlands ones, yes.'

'Stick to where I am. After each of my rides, and there'll probably only be two or three at most, come down to the paddock. I'll meet you there. We can make it look as casual as you like.'

'Couldn't keep that up too long, Eddie. Bruno would get suspicious.'

'We'll have a plan in place by the end of the week. Guaranteed.'

Monty said, 'You're a very reassuring man to have around. I wish it were under less trying circumstances.'

We stood. I shook his hand and clasped his shoulder, 'Remember what I said…I'll fix this.'

He smiled and bowed his head and seemed to take a long time to let go of my hand.

72

Before leaving Beverley, I took out my phone to call Mac, then put it away again and drove into town to buy some pay-as-you-go phones. I used one to call Mac. He said, 'Who's phone are you using?'

'Mine's broken. This is a throwaway.'

'What news, then?'

'Mac, will you stop saying "what news?" every time I call you? You sound like some ham actor on the battlements in a Shakespeare play.'

'My aim is brevity, Edward.'

'Since when? You're famous for dragging things out.'

'Which is exactly what you seem to be doing. Have you any news for me or not?'

'Yes. We need to meet.'

'When?'

'Tomorrow. In the morning.'

'Are you down this way?'

'I can get the early train to London…though, we'll need to speak to Bradley, too, so maybe you should come up here.'

'Why Bradley?'

'Mac, do you think I'm going to waste your time?'

He sighed, 'Okay. I could drive up tonight, though it would be well after midnight before I reached your place.'

'That's fine. I'll wait up. Pack a bag. You might need to stay a few days.'

'I'll need to clear that with Steel. I have meetings.'

'Are any of them more important than wrapping all this up before Sandown next weekend?'

'Probably not.'

'Then, get packing. And stop and call me when you're about a mile away. On this number.'

'Why must I stop and call you?'

'Precautionary.'

'Eddie…oh, never mind. I'll see you later.'

Next I used the new phone and called home, 'Mave?'

'Oh dear!'

'What's up?' I said.

'Things didn't quite go to plan at Beverley. You're using a throwaway phone.'

'I'll tell you about it when I get back. Mac's staying over tonight.'

'So, you have a plan, obviously?'

'Half a plan.'

'Half assed, did you say?'

I laughed. Listen, 'I'm calling on Dil on the way back. I'll be late.'

'Okay.'

'I'd ask you to wait up for me, but you won't go to bed anyway, will you?'

'I'll be here.'

'Lady with the lamp.'

'Until you get home. Then it's Lady and the Tramp.'

I laughed and I heard the smile in Mave's voice as she said goodbye.

I reached Dil's yard just after nine. He opened the door, unsmiling, 'I could have done with some notice, Eddie.'

'I was passing on the way back from the races. And I didn't want to worry you. Vita still in New York?'

'Yes.'

'Is Prim with you?'

'Yes.'

'Good. You want to talk in the barn or in the house?'

'About what?'

'Important developments.'

Dil sighed, 'The barn is probably still safest.'

'It probably is. I'll give you a minute to explain to Prim, and I'll see you in there.'

'What do I tell Prim?'

'Tell her we'll be back with her very soon.'

'Should I bring you a drink?'

'No, thanks.'

The barn proved too cold and depressing. We went to my car. Dil settled in the passenger seat with his chunky glass of whiskey. He said, 'You've been quiet.'

'I could say the same for you. How's Prim?'

'She's in denial. Keeps saying that maybe the whole thing will turn out to be a bad dream.'

'I think I've found a way to get her out of it.'

He lowered his chin and raised an eyebrow, 'I thought we'd agreed she's already out of it? Boffo's taking the hit.'

'I can get her out of it formally, with the police, I think.'

'How?'

'By trading her crime off for a much bigger fish.'

'At what price?'

'Hard to say. Are you willing to pay part of it?'

He stopped the whiskey glass halfway to his mouth, 'Pay as in?'

'I need Vita in on this working alongside Prim.'

He laughed, balancing the glass expertly so that the whiskey barely shimmered in the moonlight. I said, 'What's so funny?'

'Well, Eddie, things can't be so bleak if you're making jokes about them.'

'I'm serious. If Vita and Prim will team up on this, I can do deals for everyone, maybe even Hines and Boffo.'

'Who is this guy, the Godfather?'

'He thinks he is. That's why the edge is with us.'

'Oh, it's us all of a sudden!'

'Dil, don't push your luck. I could have taken the easy way out the night we walked in on Prim. Dumped everything in your lap. Do you want this all neatly tied up or don't you?'

'Tell me who this guy is.'

'No. You don't need to know and it would only put you in danger.'

'So, how am I supposed to persuade Vita and Prim if I don't know what the risks are?'

'You won't need to persuade Vita. She'll be up for it. I think Prim will be, too, but I might need your help there. We'll see.'

Dil was watching me with an odd, half-grin, his eyes fixed on me as though trying to work something out. I said, 'Why are you looking at me like that?'

'You sound like a man with a clipboard, just going through, ticking off things you need done, as though you were arranging a party or something. You seem, well, detached…from reality.'

I smiled, 'That's rich, Dil, that is really rich.'

'Honestly, if you could see yourself, Eddie. You turn up here close to bedtime, tell me we're going to bring down some guy who is so dangerous you won't even tell me his name, and it's like you're ticking off boxes. "You'll do this. Vita will do that. Prim will be helping with the other". You're like some factory charge hand giving out orders.'

'I'm in organizing mode, Dil, that's all. I'm sorry if it's not the dramatic performance you were hoping for. We've got things to do.'

'Then let's talk about them, figure out the best way.'

'No need. I've figured out the best way. You just need to do what I'm asking you to do.'

'End of? Just like that?'

'Just like that.'

He resumed the watching, but the half-grin had gone. He sat clutching the glass. I said, 'Dil?'

He hesitated, then said, 'What exactly do you need from me?'

'Get Vita back over here. Let me know when she's due, and we'll arrange a meeting.'

'What am I supposed to tell her?'

'Tell her what you've been putting off telling her since she went back to America. Hasn't she even called to ask about progress on the wild horses?'

'I've spoken to her once. She says she's busy with some deal and that we can catch up once it's done.'

'Tell her you've caught the culprit and the police want to interview her as soon as possible.'

'I'm not going to lie to her, Eddie.'

I smiled slowly, 'Jeez, Dil, listen to yourself? Will you listen to yourself?'

'What?'

'Look, call Vita when you go back in. I don't care how you get her back here. If she says she won't come, let me know and I'll call her.'

'And say what?'

'And say, Vita, whatever it is you're working on, there's something going on here that'll give you a much bigger buzz.'

He frowned, 'Eddie, what are you talking about?'

'Vita Brodie and what makes her tick.'

'Oh, so suddenly you know everything about women?'

'I know what floats Vita's boat.'

He shook his head, 'Are you on something? You been popping pills or smoking dope?'

'Listen, Dil, getting Vita here will be the easy bit. Your next job is persuading Prim to play her part in this, and that starts with a confession to Vita.'

Dil stared at me as though I'd gone mad. He said, 'How long have we spent finding a way to get Prim out of this? Boffo's lined up, isn't he?'

'Not any more. Not after I've spoken to Mac and to the police in the morning.'

'You're going to tell them about Prim?'

'I'm going to do a deal. No names mentioned until they agree to the deal. But once it's done, Vita and Prim need to work together and that means Prim telling Vita what she did…and, very probably, why she did it.'

Dil finished the whiskey, swallowed and said, 'You are mad. You are crazy mad.'

I turned the key to start the engine. I said, 'I have to go. I've got a meeting with Mac. If you don't want to speak to Prim about this, I'll do it tomorrow. In fact, don't tell her. She might do a runner. I'll tell her tomorrow. I'll do that, and you ring Vita. I need her back here in the next forty-eight hours. Call me when you've spoken to her. No time is too late.' I reached in the back and handed him two boxes, 'Throwaway phones. One for you and one for Prim. Just let me note the numbers, then I'll give you mine. All calls among the three of us should be made on these.'

'Until when?'

'We'll see.'

A minute later, I was holding his glass while Dil eased himself out of the car with the two boxes. He straightened and swept his fringe before taking the glass from me. I said, 'Prim will be just as important as Vita, maybe more so. Don't do anything to scare her off.'

Dil snapped to attention and saluted, 'Yes sir!' He slammed the door.

I opened the window and smiled, 'At ease, Grant. At ease.'

73

The lamp burned in the window, waiting for me and for midnight. Mave and Ben were at the kitchen table talking. I closed the door softly and said, 'I guess Princess Alice is asleep?'

Mave said, 'Had to recover the pea from under the twentieth mattress before she'd doze off.'

She watched my puzzled look, and Ben smiled. He said, 'You need to catch up on your fairytales.'

'I believe I do.'

Ben said, 'Alice, my wife, used to tell a joke about baby Alice saying to her at bedtime, "Mum tell me a fairy story.' And her mother would say, "Wait until your Dad finally gets home and he'll tell us both one.'

I laughed. Mave smiled. I said, 'Good to hear you're in fine spirits before your flight.'

Ben said, 'Can't say I don't feel guilty leaving you with all this.'

I put a hand on his shoulder as I sat beside him, 'It's all figured out, Ben. All slotting nicely into place. I've just come back from Dil's place. He's setting things up his end. Mac will be here in an hour or two and we'll get the formal stuff organized.'

He said, 'How was Monty?'

'Pessimistic. Better that way. He can celebrate all the more when this is done.'

'Want to tell me what it is you've got planned?'

'Not yet. Once you're safely hidden among ten thousand sheep in the outback, I'll let you know. Is Alice looking forward to it?'

'That's a change of subject, Eddie, and a very clunky one,' Ben said.

Mave said, 'He's crap at it, isn't he? In his mind he segues smoothly toward cunning distraction. In the minds of the would-be distracted, he crashes through gates and hedges and lands on his arse in the great wide open.'

I laughed, 'But the judges always give me a ten for effort.'

Ben said, 'Well, to answer your question, Alice is excited about her first trip abroad, and even more excited about coming back to stand in the dock and nail these bastards.' Ben flashed his eyes at me in warning, and I guessed that he feared Alice was listening.

I said, 'She's not the only one. From DJ upward, we should get the whole gang.'

Mave's glance moved between me and Ben, but she didn't turn around to see if Alice was in the doorway. I said, 'Just need to go to the loo. Been a long drive.'

I went past the foot of the stairs. No Alice. But that didn't mean she wasn't up there with her ear to a glass and the glass to the floor. My phone bleeped. I looked at the message from Dil: "Vita's not coming." At least he'd remembered to use the throwaway phone.

I pulled up her number and went outside. She answered at the second ring, 'My, oh my, everybody in England suddenly wants to talk to me. That cable on the floor of the Atlantic must be buzzing.'

'Vita, hang up and I'll ring you right back. You won't recognize the number, but answer it.'

'Okay.'

I got her back, 'How are you, Vita?'

'Intrigued is how I am. You are all using anonymous phones. Dil tells me you've caught the bad guys. Trouble is he couldn't tell me who they are.'

'I can.'

'Go on.'

'Not on the phone.'

'Why not?'

'Because Dil was wrong. We haven't caught them. We know who they are, but catching them is going to be very dangerous.'

'Call the cops.'

'We don't have the evidence. Yet.'

'How are you going to get it?'

'You're going to fly back here tomorrow and help us.'

'Is that right, now?' she laughed.

'Yes. It is.'

'You seem awful sure about that.'

'Because nobody but you can pull it off, Vita. You and Prim.'

'What, like some kind of Cagney and Lacey who can't stand each other?'

'You're only playing with her, anyway, as she is with you.'

She paused. I think she was holding her breath. She said, 'Nobody's playing with me, Eddie.'

'You believe that?'

'I think she'd want to, but she's not smart enough. Never will be.'

'Vita, she's a hell of a lot smarter than you think. Maybe even as smart as you.'

'Your compliments are cack-handed. Say what you've got to say, will you?'

'In an hour, I've got a meeting with Peter McCarthy. In the-'

'It's almost one in the morning over there!'

'That's right, which shows you how important this is and how quickly we're moving on it. In the morning we'll see Chief Constable Bradley of Merseyside police. Later tomorrow, Nigel Steel the CEO of the BHA will fly up to sit down with us.'

'All for somebody nobbling a few horses?'

'It's more than that, Vita, much more. At the very top is a man the police have been trying to nail for thirty years. He traffics young girls for prostitution and runs huge drugs rings along with a dozen other crimes. His solution to problems is killing and maiming. And we can't catch this guy without you. And that's not bullshit. Get a flight tomorrow. I'll meet you at Dil's place. If you think I've brought you here under false pretenses, I'll pay your return flight.'

'First class?'

'First class.'

'It's a deal.'

'Good. See you tomorrow.'

'You will…You will.'

That excitement was back in her voice, the tone I remembered from the day at Dil's when we were running through the Vogel tapes and Vita was buzzing. The buzz was back.

I tapped my phone to open Dil's' message and replied: "Yes she is"

Out of courtesy, Ben and Mave waited up to greet Mac before going to bed. He seemed touched by this as he settled across from me in the Snug with a glass of cognac. He said, 'How odd it seems to be in a house with other people…especially such warm-hearted people.'

'That offer to join our little commune is always open, Mac. You can get too used to living on your own down there in the Lambourn Valley. I speak from experience, as the saying goes.'

He smiled, 'Maybe once I've retired, Eddie. I can think of worse things. I like it here, oddly.'

'Oop north, you mean? It's not just flat caps and whippets after all, eh?'

'Surprisingly, no.' He raised his glass. I laughed.

He said, 'Tell me your plans.'

'You need to know first that the guy we're dealing with here, is a dangerous man. Once I tell you who he is, you need to accept that he might find out that you know his name.'

'Kelman Hines?'

'It's not Hines. This fella makes Hines look like a saint.'

'Who is he?'

'Sydney Ember.'

Mac frowned and I watched as his brain pushed his features around, working on the name. He said, 'Why does that ring a bell with me?'

'Remember when Bradley wanted to bug my phone? It's the fella your man Bradley thought I might be in with.'

'Ahh, indeed it was! Bradley was right, then?'

'Well, he was right about Ember!'

Mac laughed, then sipped his cognac and rolled it around in his mouth and swallowed it and smacked his lips and said, 'Tell me the plan.'

Mave was still awake when I slipped in beside her. She reached for my hand. I said, 'You know the cunning plan we came up with?'

'Uhuh?'

'It ain't going to work. Well, half of it might work.'

'Which half?'

'First half,' I told her everything about Ember's security system.

She said, 'Maybe we can work it so he'll let Bruno in with a laptop.'

'Ah, but he only trusts him ninety percent, which, by my reckoning, will leave us about ten percent short.'

Mave raised herself to lean on her elbow and look down at me, 'We'll just have to find another way.'

'We will. You're a genius, remember?'

'What doth it profit a man to possess a genius when the baddie has no PC?'

'And no trust.'

'And a penchant for surveillance even of the anus.'

I looked up at her, 'I think we need an anus mirabilis'

She smiled, 'I believe you're right.'

'Should we sleep on it?'

'I'll sleep on my front if you don't mind,' she lay down again.

'You do that. I'll lie awake and think.'

'Don't, the grinding of the gears will disturb me. Is Mac staying for the duration?'

'I think so.'

'And you reckon Bradley will provide protection?'

'Yep. After our meeting we become assets. It's often much better to be an asset than a person where the police are concerned.'

'Bradley's going to have to do some Herculean rule-bending here, isn't he?'

'He'll do it.'

'You're sure, aren't you?'

'Ember's his Ronnie Biggs. His lifetime project. He'll do whatever he needs to.'

'You've only met the man once.'

'That was all I needed. It took him less than a minute to get onto Ember once he started talking. He's obsessed, believe me.'

'But the plan you thought you'd be selling him is now just half a plan. Will he buy half a plan?'

'Probably not. I won't tell him about Ember's security arrangements.'

'I'd have thought he'll know them by heart.'

'Monty told me it's been a long time since the cops have visited him at home.'

She turned her head, 'Who are you trying to convince here, me or yourself?'

'Me.'

She squeezed my hand.

74

The sun was up as we waved Ben and Alice off in the taxi, its suspension bouncing on the pot-holed road. I watched until it turned left at the old beech tree, though I could still hear the engine. As the sound faded, I heard Mac say, 'And then there were three.'

Mave and I turned. He was standing halfway along the drive. I said, 'You must have fallen out of bed. It's only just gone six.'

'I rarely sleep past dawn these days, regrettably,' he said. He looked around, and up at the cloudless sky. He said, 'No flat caps, no whippets, no rain. I could get to like it here.'

We walked toward him, 'You'd miss the smell of horseshit coming up the Lambourn valley.'

'Not to mention the smell of bullshit from High Holborn.'

I laughed. High Holborn, in London, was where Mac's office was. 'Hungry?' I said.

Mac shrugged, 'You know better than to ask that, Eddie.'

I put one arm across his shoulder, and the other across Mave's, 'Let's go fry some eggs.'

After breakfast, I watched and listened as Mac tried to get in touch with Chief Constable Bradley using the cheap phone I'd given him.

'When do you expect him?...Can't you call him?...I know it isn't, but tell him it's about Sydney Ember. I'll give you my number.'

We counted it down on the big kitchen clock. Bradley called back in six minutes and agreed to change his schedule and meet us in Liverpool at ten. Mac said, 'We need ID.'

'Why?' I asked, 'Can't he meet us?'

'All formal meetings need to have attendees signed in. Just bring your driving license, passport.'

Mave said, 'I'd better get digging.'

Mave and I waited by the window in the reception area of Merseyside police HQ, while Mac went to the desk. Ten seconds later, Mac waved us toward him. 'ID time. Chief Constable Bradley's on the top floor. Access needs iris recognition.'

'Seriously?' I said.

'Seriously.'

I looked at him, 'This place is worse than Ember's house.'

'Very funny,' Mac said.

The young officer behind the desk said, 'If you'd just step up here and show me your ID, we log it to the iris image…just put your chin on that small ledge, please.'

We went in the lift unaccompanied. On the top floor, we had to go through the access door one at a time, after an iris scan. As we walked along the corridor I said to Mac, 'Seriously, how much does all this cost?'

Before he could respond, we saw Bradley in full uniform coming toward us, a sandy-haired man who was half a head taller than Bradley walked beside him. They stopped at a door and as we reached them, Bradley opened it and ushered us in, closing it behind him. 'This is Superintendent McConnachie,' he said. We introduced ourselves and shook hands. I said to Bradley, 'Before we start the meeting, can I have a quick word?'

Bradley looked at me for a few moments. I expected him to ask McConnachie to leave. Instead, he opened the door and motioned me out into the corridor, then closed the door behind him. 'What is it?' he said.

I walked five paces along the corridor and turned. He hesitated then came toward me, his hard heels clicking on the shiny tiles. I said,

'I think you might find this easier hearing the proposal on your own.'

'Easier?'

'Quicker. You'll get to Ember without having to jump through hoops.'

'I normally leave the hoop-jumping to others, Mister Malloy.'

'Call me Eddie. That'll be quicker, too.'

He shifted his weight and clasped his hands at his waist. I said, 'I can get you Ember, but I know how best to do it. And I need a deal for the people who'll be setting Ember up. You might want to hear everything on an informal basis first, that's all I'm saying. Once you know what's happening, if you want to bring the Superintendent in, I've got no problem with that.'

He said nothing, just turned and went back to the room. Within seconds, McConnachie came out and walked down the corridor without turning. Mac stepped halfway out of the doorway. I could see one, eye, one arm, and one leg and the finger he used to beckon me back in. Bradley was seated at a long, highly polished table. I said, 'Please forgive me, I need just two minutes outside with Mave. Just to reassure myself we can deliver every single part of this.'

Bradley said nothing, he just clenched his jaw and opened a notebook. I nodded to Mave. She followed me out and five paces down the corridor and she said, 'Why don't we just have the meeting here?'

I smiled, 'Listen, you know you said that the first plan was a doddle for you?'

'It was a doddle for anyone with coding experience. It wasn't false modesty.'

'I've got something a bit more challenging. I doubt it will be a doddle. I believe it will be a thing of beauty, if you can deliver, a thing of beauty.'

'You're talking art, here?'

'Art…and craft.'

'Shoot.'

Half an hour later, Bradley sat watching me, his fingers steepled below his chin. He said, 'You're going to need luck.'

'Just an absence of bad luck,' I said, 'there isn't a single reason this shouldn't work out.'

'Shouldn't and doesn't are two different things, Mister Malloy.'

'But you can't see any obvious holes in it?' Mac asked.

'Other than the rather large hole waiting to swallow me up if it goes wrong, no I can't.'

I tried not to smile as I watched him. I said, 'You'll do it?'

He looked at me for a few moments, then said, 'Yes. Assuming Miss Judge's tech work is approved by my team,' he turned to Mave, 'purely procedural. No offence.'

'None taken.'

Bradley said, 'And you're confident that Miss Romanic and Miss Brodie will sign the appropriate disclaimers, not to mention Mister Bearak?'

'We're meeting Prim and Vita next, but I'm confident.'

'Then all I should need is a day to pull together all the resources and agree coordination.'

I smiled, 'Good. That's good news.'

He lowered his hands and nodded. I said, 'Can I ask one final thing? Can we be there for the interview after the arrest? I want to see his face. We'll all want to see his face.'

'Well, since the protocol will be shredded by then anyway, I don't see why not. We have an observation room.'

'How many does it hold?'

Bradley smiled, 'Eddie, if you pull this off, we'll build an extension if we need to.'

75

From Liverpool, we drove straight to Dil's' place. On the final half mile, rounding a bend approaching the yard, I slowed as I saw two riders on Dil's horses. We passed them at walking pace and exchanged greetings. As the car window rolled back up I said to Mac and Mave, 'This is the first time today I've thought about racing.'

'As in?' Mac said.

'As in I'm a jockey and I should be driving to a racecourse somewhere to do my job.'

'A day off won't kill you.'

'That's not the point, Mac. This is the first day in my adult living memory that I haven't woken up frustrated because I have no rides booked.'

'Well, a change is as good as a rest, Eddie. And you can hardly fault yourself for being waylaid by something a tad more pressing than riding a novice hurdler at Sedgefield.'

'True…I suppose. But worrying.'

I glanced at Mac as we turned into the drive. He was smiling and nodding like a wise old man.

As we passed Arnie's cottage, I said, 'They might want to hold this meeting in the haybarn.'

'Why?' Mac asked.

'Prim got it into her head that the house might be bugged.'

'By whom?'

'She doesn't know. Just humour her, for now, will you?' I rang Dil's doorbell.

Fifteen minutes later, we were in the haybarn, on rearranged benches of bales. Their disturbance threw up a fine dust that floated in the sunlight coming through the big sliding doors. Mac had a sneezing fit that brought on a nosebleed and Dil returned to the house and came back with a roll of tissue.

Mac's blood stained the front of the haybale he sat on. Prim looked embarrassed, her blushing face still many shades paler than the scarlet two piece suit she wore. She said, 'I'm sorry. I'm up to high doh over all this.'

Mac raised a conciliatory hand and nodded as he held the reddening tissue to his nose. I said, 'Why don't we walk and talk? We could walk up the gallop.'

Mac waved and shook his head and said, 'I'll be fine. It'll stop in a minute.'

I said, 'You'd rather bleed to death than haul yourself a mile uphill.'

He smiled and raised a thumb and that seemed to break the tension as Prim smiled too. I said, 'That's the first in a long time I've seen you smiling, Prim.'

'Feels like years to me, Eddie. I just want this to be over now.'

'It will be. Soon. And I can arrange to have the house swept for bugs.'

'When?'

'As soon as you like. Tomorrow, probably. We had a meeting this morning with Chief Constable Bradley, the big boss on Merseyside.'

Prim's frown came back, 'Why?'

'To try and get this whole thing sorted out without you or your father, or Kelman Hines, or…' I glanced at Mac, 'maybe even Mister Boffo going to jail.'

Prim edged forward, her red skirt scratchy across the hay, 'You told the police?'

'No. I offered the police a deal where they get what they really want and we get what we really want.'

'We?' Prim said.

I swung my hand in a semi-circle, 'All of us. You, the BHA, Dil, and Vita. And Ben and Alice, Mave and me.'

She watched me.

Mac sneezed.

Nobody looked at him.

Prim said, 'That is some deal, Eddie. What's the price?'

'I don't know yet, but there'll be a risk for you, and for Vita.'

'What kind of risk?'

'We won't know until you take it. The police want to make sure the risk is as low as possible. That was part of the deal. But it could go wrong.'

'How wrong?'

'That'll depend on how quickly the police can react if things start looking bad.'

She turned to Dil, who swept his fringe and tried to look as though he had masterminded everything. Prim said to me, 'Will it put my father in danger?'

'No. It shouldn't. He can stay in Spain while you and Vita try to pull this off.'

'Shouldn't or won't?'

'Prim, I don't do bullshit. You know that. I suppose there's a hundred to one chance your father might be at risk, but I think he'll be okay.'

'Tell me what I need to do.'

'Vita's on her way here. Let's wait for her.'

Prim turned to Dil, 'You knew Vita was coming?'

He said, 'Eddie arranged it. He called her.'

Prim said, 'I'm not moving out of the house!'

Dil shrugged. Prim said, 'My stuff is staying in the bedroom!'

'Okay.' Dil said. 'I'll handle Vita.'

I smiled. Vita had handled him, and he knew it. Handled him, then dropped him. Dil was looking at Prim as though Mac and Mave and I weren't there. He said, 'I told you it would only be for a short time. She never meant anything to me.'

I stood up and dusted off my trousers, 'Should we leave you to it?'

Mac got unsteadily to his feet, still holding the tissue to his face. Mave rose on the other side of him. I said to Prim and Dil, 'We'll be back tonight, if Mac survives that long.' I nodded toward the blood stained haybale and said to Prim, 'DNA. Be careful. If Mac doesn't make it, they might decide Miss Scarlett did it. In the barn...' I glanced at Dil, '...with a very blunt object.'

76

That night, we met for dinner in a hotel five miles from Dil's place. I'd always known there'd be no haybarns for Vita Brodie, though it turned out that the possibility of the house being bugged appealed to her. She said, 'Dil tells me you can arrange to have the house swept for bugs tomorrow?'

'Bradley will take care of it,' I said.

Vita said, 'Since when did you become the boss of everything?' It was light-hearted and that familiar tone of anticipation was already in Vita's voice.

'Since Prim mentioned the house bugging, which gave me the idea for putting the deal together.'

'The deal with the cops?' Vita asked.

'The deal with everyone. I've one more man to see at Doncaster tomorrow, who's the kind of final link in the chain.'

'The Mister Big?'

'The good Mister Big. He'll get us to the bad Mister Big.'

'The one who nobbled the horses?'

'Nope. The one I told you about on the phone last night. The Godfather.'

I thought for a moment that Vita was going to rub her hands together. She said, 'Exciting. But I was told the man had been found who'd duped us with the horses.'

I said, 'He has been. A guy named Boffo who was sticking

speakers in their ears and blasting them with radio playback of howling wolves.'

Vita leant back in her chair and said, 'Ahh...so that's how it was done. That's pretty clever.' She looked around the table and said, 'Why didn't one of us think of that?'

I glanced at the reddening Prim then looked at Vita, 'One of us did.'

Vita, still smiling, looked around again. I said, 'Prim, over to you.

To her credit, Prim left nothing out. And Vita said not a word. She just watched Prim reveal everything as though it were some kind of private strip show. When Prim finished, she still had enough pride to hold Vita's gaze. They watched each other for what seemed a long time, then Vita smiled, wide and full, eyes and all, and said, 'You go, girl!'

Prim looked puzzled and on the verge of anger, when Vita got up and walked round the table to bend and hug her, 'I mean it' she said, and Prim slowly reached to put a hand on her shoulder. Vita straightened and said to Prim, 'You went to those lengths for Dil Grant? I envy you, Prim. I've never felt like that for anyone in my life.'

Prim aid, 'It was stupid. I was stupid. Look where-'

Vita clasped Prim's arm, 'We're all stupid. Every single one of us around this table, every person in this restaurant, and in this hotel and out on the sidewalk...we're all stupid in our own way.' She turned to us, 'Gentlemen, anybody want to argue with that?'

Dil looked a bit unsettled. Mac shook his head. Mave raised her hand and said, 'Guilty!' I said, 'Not me!'

Vita still had her hand on Prim's arm. Prim looked up at her and said, 'You were a bitch to me.'

Vita's smile did not dull, 'I'm a bitch to everyone when it suits me, Prim. A sad way to get your kicks, but there it is.'

Prim said, 'I'm not moving out of the house...or the bedroom.'

Vita sat down. She said, 'Don't rebitch me, darling. You've caught me on a good night. You're welcome to your...man.'

Vita's tone dropped just enough after the slight pause to rob that final word of its normal meaning. All Dil could do was revert to his lifelong comfort blanket in the fringe-sweep. Prim put her hands on the table and leant aggressively toward Vita, but before she could speak, Dil reached for her shoulder and eased her back into the chair, 'Enough, now. Enough.'

I said, 'Dil's right. From where I'm standing, Prim's been completely honest and Vita's been gracious. However it was that we got here, we're only at halfway. As Vita said, we've all made mistakes, but we've all got a chance to make up for them by nailing a man the police have been after for thirty years. They can't catch him. We can.'

Vita applauded, smiling, 'Inspirational, Edward, if a shade corny. And, speaking of we, where is Ben Searcey?'

'In Australia, with Alice.'

'Abandoning you in your time of need,' Vita said, 'what happened to the all in this together speech a minute ago?'

'The good Mister Big I mentioned to you, he wouldn't go ahead with this plan unless Ben and Alice were safe on the other side of the world.'

Dil, Prim and Vita stared blankly at me. Mac watched them. I said, 'Maybe I should have told you that first to try and get across how dangerous this guy is.'

Vita said, 'And how come we don't qualify for this assisted passage to Fort Sydney, or wherever it is they've gone?'

'First, because this very carefully prepared plan I've come up with can't work without you and Prim.'

'And second?' Vita asked.

'Second is I knew you wouldn't want to miss this, Vita. It'll make your juices flow.'

She smiled, 'Or my blood.'

'You can't have one without the other,' I said.

Vita turned to Prim, 'Are you up for this?'

Prim said, 'I'll hold until I hear Eddie's plan.'

Vita said, 'Scaredy cat!'

Prim did an eye-roll and a head lift. Vita said, 'What about Dil.

Any skin in this game for him?'

'Not really,' I said, 'but that's just the way the plan panned out. He'd have been all in with us if he needed to, wouldn't you, Dil?'

'Sure, I would. Of course.' But that damn fringe-sweep gave him away again, and Vita nodded and smiled once more. She turned to me, 'Okay, mastermind, let's hear the plan.'

I gave them enough to hook them, but not enough to sink us.

77

Next morning, the weather finally turned on us and I watched through the picture window the wind and rain ripping new buds from the trees and battering Ullswater into ragged whitecaps.

Mac came through from the kitchen and stood beside me. He said, 'Red in tooth and claw.'

'Me?'

'Mother Nature.'

I said, 'Look on the bright side. If it's like this at Doncaster this afternoon, the poor visibility will help no end in pulling off this stunt.'

'True.'

'What time are you meeting Steel?'

'I'm meeting him at Lime Street at noon.'

'Whatever he says to you, Mac, don't bring him to Doncaster. The last thing we need is him taking cold feet on this.'

'Don't worry. I'll drop him at Bradley's office. He can keep him occupied.'

'That's a bad pairing, Mac. If Steel does want to back out, he'll know Bradley is the only guy he needs to persuade.'

'Do you seriously think that after yesterday anybody could turn Bradley on this?'

'True.'

'You're just getting edgy.'

'Probably.' I slapped his shoulder, 'I'm going to pack my kitba'
Let's get this done.'

By the third race at Doncaster the sky had rained itself out and '
clouds looked drained and pale. The wind had got bored too,
headed north, firing just the occasional gust from its ex†
blowing the raindrops from the trees around the paddock.

On my third and final ride, I made sure the horse was given
chance, knowing he hadn't the ability to finish in the fi'
Galloping wearily toward the post with the few remaining st
I froze in my crouch above his withers, head locked, eyes d‹
though I had died in the saddle and somehow stayed uprigh‹.
strides past the post, I tumbled slowly off to lie still on my side in
mud.

I lay in the ambulance room, a drip in my arm, staring at the lights.
Mac was beside me, talking to the doctor, 'What do you think?'

The doctor said, 'Could have been wasting too much. I've s‹
that before where everything just seizes up after exertion. It's
body's way of asking for more liquid than it gets from you
sucking your toothbrush in the morning.'

Mac smiled. The doc said, 'We'll see how the saline go‹
no improvement in an hour, he'll probably need to spe
in hospital.'

Mac said, 'I'll hang around if you don't mind. Nigel Ste‹
to avoid any bad publicity about jockeys starving themsel‹
not up in an hour, I'll let our PR guys know.'

The doctor said, 'And here was me thinking you had
bastard's welfare in mind.'

Mac smiled again, 'He won't take it personally, will you,
I stared at him, stone-faced.

'See?' Mac said. The doctor walked away, shaking his
smiled at Mac, who raised his thumb. I heard Monty's voice fr‹
doorway, 'Is Eddie all right?'

Mac turned, 'Come in, Monty. Nice to see you.'

hands. Monty looked worried. Mac said, 'Doc reckons he needs a tad more sustenance before riding.'

'It takes its toll,' Monty said, then, to me, 'How are you?'

I nodded. Mac said, 'I'll leave you to it and make a few precautionary calls.'

I said to Monty, 'Shut the door.'

He did so and dragged a chair across to sit beside me. I told him the plan. He smiled warmly, 'Even if it doesn't work, it's brilliantly conceived. All your idea?'

'Teamwork. Mave and me.'

'How about the logistics? Won't everything need testing?'

'We'll do all the testing. Prim will deliver the kit.'

'How will I know it's working?'

'You won't. Not until afterwards.'

He looked away and his smile gradually faded. I said, 'All will be well. Believe me.'

He looked at me, 'It's a great plan on paper, Eddie, and you seem utterly confident it's going to work. But it will only take one wrong step and everybody's life changes forever. Your people need to know this.'

'They know it. And there'll be backup.'

'It's not me I'm worried about, Eddie, I want you to know that. It's everyone else.'

'They're covered, Monty. The biggest risk is yours. If Ember somehow susses it when you're in there, we'll have no way of knowing until he brings you out.'

'Ha! In a body bag, you mean!'

'Well, given how clean he likes to keep his nest, you'll be walking out. You just need to give the agreed signal, and Bradley's team will be on it in two minutes.'

He reached to shake my hand, 'I hope your girl can act.'

'Girls.'

'He won't swallow the takeover line, Eddie, too risky. I think Vita can rest easy. Miss Romanic is the one. If she can pull it off with Bruno, he might just do the rest.'

'All the better, then.'

He nodded. I said, 'Prim will kick it off tomorrow. Next move should be the day after, but we might need to delay until two days after. Depends on what progress Mave can make. You confident you can make the pass to Prim tomorrow?'

'So long as she's expecting it.'

'She will be. Good luck.'

'And to you, Eddie. See you on the other side.'

I lay for an hour as the doctor grew increasingly perplexed at my lack of progress. After another set of checks he said, 'Your obs are fine. How is the vision?'

'Blurred.'

'Better or worse than when you came in?'

'The same.'

'Headache?'

'Worse.'

He looked at me, 'Do you know that this is the first time in my career that a jockey has told me he's feeling worse?'

I tried to smile. The doctor said, 'You are definitely going to hospital.'

'I'll be all right soon.'

'Ah, normal service has been resumed! I'll be back in half an hour.'

Mac stayed with me throughout. As the doc came through the door, I struggled to sit up. Mac tried to help me. The doctor said, 'What are you doing?'

'Going home,' I said.

'Not on my watch.'

'I'm fine, Doc.'

'Half an hour ago you told me your headache was worse. Six weeks' ago you were in a coma. Two hours ago, your body stopped responding to signals from your brain. You need at least an overnight in hospital.'

Mac said, 'Doc, he doesn't want to be away from home, in case they keep him in and it makes things tough for his family.'

I weakly raised a hand to grasp Mac's arm, 'Mac!'

'It had to be said, Eddie. The doctor is right. You need at least twenty-four hours in a fully equipped ward.'

I said, 'There's a private hospital in Carlisle. I'll go there.'

The doctor said, 'The Regina? At five hundred a night? Fine, I'll just call your private helicopter to whisk you across, eh?'

Mac said, 'His partner can easily afford it. He's not kidding.'

The doctor looked tired. He sighed loud and long and said to Mac, 'There's no way I can authorize an ambulance to drive all that way.'

'I'll take him,' Mac said.

'You must be awful worried about PR right enough, Mister McCarthy.'

Mac smiled and said, 'I was kidding you earlier. We're old friends. We go back a long way.'

'No matter. I can't hand him into your care, even for an hour's drive.'

I said, 'I'll sign myself out of here. I'll go with Mac to hospital and spend the night there. I promise.'

'So long as there's no comeback on me, Eddie. But I'll tell you this, if a jockey is volunteering to spend a night in a hospital he is a worried man.'

'Just getting older and wiser,' I said.

He said, 'I'll get the papers.'

Mac reached for his arm, 'Will you do me a favour and call The Regina? That'll make things easier when we get there.'

The doctor checked his watch, and sighed once more, 'Okay.'

Once clear of the racecourse, Mac pulled over and phoned Nigel Steel. After a minute of trying to guess what Steel was saying, I gave up and laid my head back for the five minutes it took Mac to check everything.

He clipped his seatbelt in again and we headed west once more. I said, 'No problems?'

'Not yet. Early days.'

'Aha! Another vote of confidence!'

Mac smiled and said, 'Bradley's confirmed with the CEO at Regina that we're on our way and gone through his checklist with the guy again. Steel's organizing the press release for six-forty-seven in the morning and included Blake's direct number.'

'Blake?'

'Sorry, he's the CEO at Regina.'

'Blake's going to have to bring at least one of the doctors in on this, is he not?'

'Bradley talked him into handling it himself. Blake was in brain surgery in an earlier life.'

'In brain surgery? As a patient or a practitioner?'

Mac laughed, 'He was a brain surgeon. And Bradley knows him well, anyway.'

'Always makes things a bit easier.'

'It does. Blake says he'll keep it to himself as long as he can, but he might need to involve one or two staff members.'

'The more there are, the less I like it.'

'The less everybody likes it, Eddie, but we can't micro manage everything. Give the guy some credit. He's a highly accomplished doctor.'

'So was Harold Shipman.'

'Ouch! That was in very poor taste!'

'It was. I withdraw it.'

'Anyway, Blake's waiting for us. That'll get the first part out of the way.'

'And the fun starts tomorrow,' I said, looking across at Mac.

He said, 'Well, I'll say one thing, this is the first time you've tried to pull something off by informing all the authorities in advance.'

'Needs must when the devil drives, Mac. Needs must.'

78

Mave arrived later, carrying a small suitcase. She closed the door behind her, looked around and said, 'What a beautiful room.'

'I'm glad you like it. You're paying.'

'I am the year-round Santa Claus of the north country, air fares, hospital bills, maybe even funeral costs.'

'Cheer me up, why don't you?'

'Who needs cheering? For a man who is due to lapse into a coma at six-fourteen in the morning you look remarkably healthy, which leads me to ask, what the hell are you doing in bed?'

I smiled, 'I believe it's called method acting.'

'And I believe it's called being lazy.'

We laughed, more to ease the tension than anything else. Mave said, 'When's the sting?'

'First part today, I hope.'

'Prim and Vita both okay with it?'

'Yep. Prim maybe less so, but once she starts it'll be fireworks. She's all show business. Nervous waiting in the wings, but she'll blow them away when she steps out. She doesn't know that yet, but she will.'

Mave nodded and looked at me in a way I was familiar with. Today was the one day I didn't want to see that look, 'What's up?' I asked.

'My man in Newbury will need three days.'

I slumped slowly back to rest on the pillow. Mave said, 'Can you hold out for a three-day coma?'

'It's more about if everyone else can keep their nerve that long. Would it be any quicker if you travelled down there to help him?'

'There's nothing for me to do on it, Eddie. Remember last time he helped us on Jimmy's case? Same situation.'

'So there'll be nothing Bradley's team can do either?'

'Nothing except help get it here quickly once he's done.'

I stared at the ceiling. 'We need to cancel today. Cancel Prim. Put it off for forty-eight hours. Otherwise it's a three-day pressure cooker and somebody will blow.'

'That means rearranging a hell of a lot of other stuff, doesn't it?'

'Bradley and Mac would be the first to say better safe than sorry.'

I reached for my phone.

79

Next morning, the BHA put out the press release at six-forty-seven to say that Eddie Malloy had lapsed into a coma, which they suspected was linked to a previous head injury suffered at Bangor when Montego Moon had bolted, and that more would be known after a specialist's assessment.

It was one of the few times to be thankful that my champion jockey days were long gone. The news would stir a few racing reporters, but none would be rushing to Carlisle for comments from the medics. I asked Mac to include a paragraph asking jockeys not to visit until further notice.

At noon, I had my first formal visitors: Dil, Prim and Vita. Ten minutes later, a tech from Merseyside police arrived, introduced himself as Gary, and apologized for being late. I introduced the others and, as Gary grasped Dil's hand he said, 'You're the owner of the racehorse stables?'

'That's right.'

'My colleagues tell me the bug sweep was clean?'

Dil said, 'That's what they told me yesterday.'

'Good. Just double-checking that you knew.'

'Thanks,' Dil said.

Gary put a leather case on the table and opened it. He took out a gemstone brooch and held it up. It caught the sunlight through window. Prim said, 'Ruby?'

Gary said, 'Was that what you asked for?'

'I did. It's bigger than I thought it would be.'

'Probably to make sure we get plenty cover for the receiver. Is that the jacket you'll be wearing?

'Yes. Should I take it off?'

'Please.'

Prim gave him the blue, cropped jacket. Gary smiled and said, 'Talk among yourselves,' and he moved to the leather sofa by the wall.

Dil said, 'We could have done this at my place.'

I said, 'Except that you care so much for your dear comatose friend that you all felt inclined to rush to his bedside. Unlike last time.'

'I drove all the way to Bangor last time!'

'Indeed you did…three days after I was admitted,' I smiled, 'I'm only winding you up Dil. It's safer to do everything here. Not overlooked, as Mave and I were saying earlier. Not overlooked, and not bristling with bugs.'

Gary brought Prim's jacket, holding it by the shoulders, 'Want to try it on?'

Prim said, 'You serious?'

The fair-haired tech said, 'Trust me. It'll feel different. If it's too awkward, you'll fidget and mess with it and the broadcast could break up. Plus, if anyone sees you looking uncomfortable with it they could get suspicious.'

Prim stood up and pushed her arms through the sleeves, and frowned, and adjusted and fiddled with it, 'You're right,' she said.

'Want me to raise it an inch so it's not weighing on the lapel so much?'

Prim slipped the jacket off, 'Yes, please.'

Five minutes later, she was comfortable in it. The tech said, 'Try and keep it on in the car on the way to the racecourse. And, this will sound stupid, but be careful not to take it off once you're there. It can be an instinctive thing, especially if the room you're in is too warm. Once you start wriggling out of it, it's kind of difficult to change your mind.'

She nodded, 'And it won't suddenly whine, or bleep or something?'

'It's got no capability for audio out. Transmit only, so don't worry about that. Easiest thing is to try and forget it's there, otherwise, your fingers will go to it, believe me.'

Prim nodded again, then looked down at the brooch, 'Okay. Thanks.'

Gary said, 'We'll do a quick check, if that's okay?'

'Sure.' Prim said.

Gary made a phone call, 'Ready for on-site test?' He turned to Prim and said, 'What did you have for breakfast?'

'I was way too nervous to eat breakfast. Black coffee and three Hail Marys.'

Gary, phone to his ear, smiled and nodded, 'That was great. Thanks.'

Vita said, 'Who was listening to that?'

Gary said, 'Two guys in a white van parked a mile away. The same van will be parked in the centre of the racetrack once we're live. It has a logo on and the words, "Events Radio". There'll be backup officers with us in there.'

Dil said, 'Events Radio? Bit of a giveaway, is it not?'

Gary said, 'Just cover for us if anyone catches sight of the equipment. Any reasonably sized event will have a supplier of handheld radios on site.'

Dil nodded. Gary looked around at all of us, 'Any questions?'

Nobody spoke. Gary smiled as he picked up his bag and scooped his jacket from the back of the sofa, 'Good luck.'

At the sound of the door closing Dil said, 'Is all this really necessary? Monty knows exactly what's happening. It's not as though we're trying to catch him out.'

I said, 'Dil, Dil...' he turned to look at me, 'we've been through all this, and-'

'I know! But seeing Prim hooked up with it, well, she's nervous enough now, what's it going to be like in the box with Bruno hanging around? There's no percentage in it! We know what Monty's going to say.'

355

I said, 'Bradley wants it. He's out on a limb here. There might be a fair way to go before we get to Ember, and if Bradley hits resistance he's going to need something other than my word for it.'

Dil eased off a bit and leant back, his voice lower when he spoke, 'I'm just amazed Monty Bearak agreed to incriminate himself right off the bat.'

I said, 'Dil, if you wanted the perfect example of a man stuck between a rock and a hard place, this is it. Do I need to go through everything yet again, or is it enough just to remind you that this gets Prim and family off the hook?'

He swept his fringe and half-sneered, 'If it works…'

Prim said, 'Oh, fill me with confidence, why don't you?'

Dil went from loud to cowed and opened his hands, looking at her in what he hoped was a silent apology that Vita wouldn't see. But the sly smile on Vita's face had never changed since Dil opened his mouth and I had a sudden vision of Vita on a giant stage wielding a thin baton and a manic laugh as she conducted a theatre of chaos.

I said, 'One thing has changed…hopefully it will ease the pressure on Prim.'

Everyone turned. I said, 'We're delaying the first sting for forty-eight hours.' Prim's chin dropped and her shoulders relaxed as the tension was released. I explained what had happened. Prim said, 'I was relieved when you told me. Now I've got two days to worry myself to death.'

I said, 'Well, the good news, I hope, is that you can have a short practise run today, because Monty doesn't know yet about the delay, and it's not safe to call him.'

Prim rested a finger on her breastbone, 'You want me to go and tell him?'

I said, 'We'll arrange it so you just bump into him briefly and he invites you to his box on Tuesday. Two-minute conversation.'

'And what do I do for the next two days?'

'You do your gypsy princess vigil at my bedside, to build up some kind of alibi to convince the innocent that you're not part of the plot to kill me.'

80

Mave was the only one who kept vigil for the next two days. Dil, and Prim and Vita came and went, as did Mac, but these were precautionary on the very slim chance that Ember was watching us. There was no reason he should be, at least not until Prim had made her pitch, but I'd been unnerved by the fact that Ember had found out what Boffo was doing long before anyone else had.

Another who visited each day was a police firearms officer in the guise of a doctor. He was even supplied with specialist ID so that staff would believe he was an expert, working alongside Blake, on my case only. The name on his ID was MacCready. He did not tell us his real name. The purpose of his visit was to establish himself in case Ember had us under surveillance, and to set up the 'best scenario to give us the opportunity to apprehend an intruder': a euphemism for stopping Ember's guys killing me and Mave.

On Tuesday morning, Mac came in, wearing his 'bad news' look. 'How's the patient this morning?' he said.

'What's up, Mac?'

'What do you mean?'

'You've got something to tell me. You're crap at hiding it. We both know that.'

'Nothing major,' he said, undoing the buttons on his jacket and sitting down, 'Bradley's reluctant to release a recording to Prim, assuming all goes well this afternoon.'

'Why?'

'He's concerned it might go against us in court. It will be evidence.'

'It'll be evidence Prim already knows about, having been involved in the conversation.'

'But you want the others to hear it, don't you? That's where Bradley's problem lies.'

I swung my legs out of bed and faced him, 'Mac, I want the others to hear it so they can give Prim support and encouragement for the next one, which will probably be tomorrow, and then the big one, probably Thursday. Also, if Vita does need to play her part, she'll want to know what it's been like.'

Mac raised his hands, 'You're preaching to the converted. I'm only telling you what he said.'

'I'll speak to him.'

'Hmm, that's sure to go well.'

'Mac, come on, pitch in here! They've got to know the technology works, too! Prim's putting her life on the line here. Maybe Vita as well. They're entitled to proof that everything Bradley's team claim can be done can actually be done.'

Mac nodded. I said, 'You might also want to point out how ridiculous it is to be concerned about these tiny breaks with procedure given that he's driving a coach and horses through the rule book.'

'True.'

'Call him, will you?'

'I will when I get back to the car.'

'Do it now, Mac, please!'

He stood up and took out his phone and wandered slowly toward the window as he waited for an answer.

81

At seven that evening, the formal start of visiting time, Mac was back, along with Prim, Vita and Dil. I went to Prim and put my hands on her shoulders, 'You okay?'

She nodded, 'I think so.'

'It went well?'

'Eddie, all I can say is it passed quickly…very, very quickly.'

'Is that good or bad?' I asked. Mac held up a yellow memory stick, waving it, 'Let's find out,' he said, and handed the stick to Mave. She slotted it into the laptop. Mac said, 'The tech guys edited out all the early stuff. It starts with just the three of them in the box.'

Mave sat on the bed with me. Mac remained standing. The others sat on the sofa. Mave pressed play.

Monty's voice was first: 'Prim, it's been a delight to have you here as my guest. Is someone picking you up? I can arrange a car for you. Bruno will organize it.'

Prim: 'I'll get a taxi. Thank you…I mean, I don't want to sound ungrateful, but I'll get a taxi when…when I'm leaving.'

Monty: 'My dear, forgive me! I wasn't throwing you out! Please, I'll open another bottle.'

'No! It's not, well it's not social. I need to talk to you, to both of you.'

Three seconds of silence which seemed like ten.

Monty: 'Well, Bruno normally takes a break about this time, can't stand the smell of my cigars. If it's something you need Bruno's help with, I mean, is everything okay with Ben and Alice?'

Prim: 'Nothing's okay for anybody! Nothing! It's been bloody torture sitting through this whole afternoon waiting to tell you this. Both of you!'

'My dear, please! Sit down. Is the news about Eddie worse than we've been led to believe? I was planning to visit this evening.'

Prim: 'The news about Eddie is exactly why I'm here, but there's no point you visiting him. The longer he's in a coma the better.'

Monty: 'Is that what the specialists are saying. Isn't that rather unusual?'

Prim: 'It's what I'm saying. And it's what you'll be saying!'

Monty: 'I'm afraid you've lost me.'

Prim: 'Listen, just let me talk. All I need is for you to listen.' The volume faded as she turned her head, 'You too, Bruno! Please come and sit down. You're in this as well.'

Prim looked around at us and said, 'Bruno didn't wait for Monty to signal or anything, he just came over.'

The sound of chair legs dragging on carpet. Prim: 'Eddie Malloy knows what you've been doing. Everything. He knows you kidnapped Ben Searcey. He knows about all the betting shops you've got, about the bookies' pitches. He knows you're the hit man, Bruno. He knows about all the shell companies and that you're running those girls in Deadwood and that DJ and his gang work for you, and-
'

Monty: 'Prim! Prim…Prim…please! What on earth are you talking about? Betting shops? Girls? Eddie is a very good friend of mine. Someone is trying to make a fool of you, a very big fool.'

A loud bang on the table, then Prim: 'Stop it! We haven't got time for it! You haven't got time for it, and don't think you're out of it either, Bruno, and don't think you can get out of it. I've heard the tape!'

Monty: 'What tape? What the hell are you talking about? This is beyond a joke, Prim!'

Prim: 'Stop! You're wasting time. Eddie is this close to getting you! This close! Why do you think he's been coming to see you so often lately? Why was he staying behind until it was just you and him? He was wearing a wire! He's trying to get you to incriminate yourself so he can add it to all the evidence Mave found.'

Monty: 'What evidence?'

'The shell companies you own. The change you made to Valentine Elements to try and push the blame onto Kelman Hines. The call you made, Bruno, to tell Eddie that Hines was running the trafficking in Deadwood…Believe me now? Is it ringing bells, yet? Can we stop with all the fucking bullshit now? You're in charge in Deadwood, and you're the strongarm man! You tipped Eddie off on Hines, then you did all you could to push him toward me to get the blame for the horses…the phone call about the mystery gypsies at the Blue Anchor, remember? That tip off about Hines and then the highly convenient big pointy hand directing him to the Hines lab closest to the hub of everything that had been happening, which, surprise, surprise was where Ben was being held. Oh, how convenient all that must have seemed, landing it all on me!'

Long silence, then Bruno, quietly: 'It was you.'

We all looked at Prim. She smiled.

Prim: 'I didn't kidnap Ben Searcey! I came up with a plan, my own plan, to get Dil Grant away from Vita Brodie and it all just unravelled and now Eddie's going to hand me in, and you, and you! And I never meant to hurt anybody and now my father's in trouble, too. He's nearly eighty and he's looking at spending what's left of his life in jail.'

Silence…

Monty: 'You said evidence. What evidence. Where did you hear all this? Eddie Malloy is hardly going to sit you down and tell you everything.'

'Oh, Eddie sat me down all right, he sat me down and promised me and Dil he was going to find us a way out of this, all nice and neat and they'd get my father off, too and even Kelman Hines. And I believed him. I believed him, but my father knew better. He got the same guy who built the kit for the radio scam on the horses to go

361

and bug Eddie's house. So, what do we find? What do we find after all the promises? A recording of about a dozen conversations Malloy has had with his little genius girlfriend Mave, who, by the way, does all the work. She does all the work and Malloy takes the glory.'

I smiled at Prim, 'You got that one right!'

Monty: 'What's on the recording?'

'Everything. Everything I just told you, step by step through the stages. Through Mave finding the shell companies, the changes in ownership, the string of betting shops, the purchase of the bookies' pitches right around the time Ben was sober and writing that series of articles on corruption in sport. The articles you managed to stop by getting Ben drunk then giving him fourteen grand winnings from the jackpot that never was...everything. Oh, he did give you credit for not killing Ben Searcey, by the way.'

Bruno: 'What about the stuff in Deadwood?'

Prim: 'What about it? They put two and two together and made four. It wasn't exactly hard.'

Bruno: 'But what evidence have they got on Deadwood?'

Prim: 'Bruno, I can tell you, there's no point in you trying to get out of this. They know how loyal you've been to Monty. They know you pulled him from that car crash and saved his life and that you'd probably do anything for him. And, whatever your reasons, and I'm not saying you were doing anything other than obeying orders, but you're in this. No point trying to argue about evidence now, believe me.'

Bruno: 'There is a point. You said they've got evidence on the shell companies, the name changes, the betting shops the boss owns, have they got any evidence about what's happened in Deadwood?'

Prim: 'Nothing like what they have on the money laundering side through all the businesses, but it's completely logical that if girls are being trafficked too, as part of the business, that Monty is doing it and cleaning the cash through the businesses.'

Bruno: 'Completely logical is not evidence. Have they got any hard evidence on Deadwood or not?'

'Well, no, I suppose not. Not in the way you put it, though I wasn't concentrating that much on the Deadwood part. I'm only interested in getting my father out of this, and me. If you want to hear the recordings, I've got them on a memory stick.'

Monty: 'Do you have it with you?'

'No...didn't see the point. There's no computer here to play it on.'

Monty: 'Can you get me a copy?'

'No. No copies. You're in the same boat as me here. The last thing you need are copies of this floating around. I've got one. I'll let you hear it, but you can't keep it. You just need to hear everything I've heard. You know Eddie's voice well enough.'

Bruno: 'When? When can we hear it?'

'Tomorrow. Somewhere secure and private.'

Monty: 'Bring it to my house in the morning. Bruno will meet you and drive you there.'

Prim: 'Meet me where?'

Monty: 'Your choice.'

Prim: 'Where do you live?'

Monty: 'That doesn't matter. We will accommodate you.'

'Fine. There's a hotel about three miles from Dil's place, called The Century Oak. I'll have breakfast there and wait for you.'

Monty: 'Bruno will be there at nine.'

'Good.'

Silence...

Monty: 'I will see you tomorrow. In the meantime, assuming everything is as you say it is, have you considered what action might have to be taken?'

'From listening to those recordings, I'd say that's your department. And I'd also say, we have until Eddie wakes up, and that could be in five minutes, five hours or five days, but once he's awake, he could start talking. And, remember, she, his girlfriend, Mave, could talk anytime. It was her that dug out most of this stuff.'

Monty: 'Is she with Eddie?'

Prim: 'Been with him since he went in there. We visited this morning and we're supposed to be going back this evening. Mave is staying there. They have a bed for her. So, they are both going to be in the same place.'

Bruno: 'If Malloy has all this so-called evidence, why hasn't he already gone to the police?'

'Because he thinks he might have broken the law himself, well, him and Mave, in the way they've got all the evidence. She hacks company IT systems. She hacked your PC, Monty but found nothing. That's another reason I think Eddie wanted to wait and try and get you to incriminate yourself.'

Bruno: 'So what you're saying is that they don't have anything that will stand up in court, but you want us to handle your problem for you?'

Prim: 'Yes, I admit it, I do want you to handle my problem, but it's not for my sake, it's for my father's.'

Bruno: 'You tell yourself that to ease your conscience.'

Prim: 'Look, I'm not here for a morality lecture. I'll bring the recordings tomorrow. You listen to them. If you don't think you have a problem, fine. I'll walk away.'

Sounds of someone getting up, then the others. Monty: 'Let's talk some more tomorrow.'

Prim: 'Well. Let's hope Eddie Malloy doesn't wake up between now and then and decide he's too tired to carry on with this and that he might as well just give everything he has to the police and leave the legalities to them.'

Monty: 'Bruno and I will discuss everything this evening and we will see you tomorrow.'

Prim: 'Whatever you decide to do, it has to be watertight...times two. Malloy and Maven Judge. Watertight and permanent.'

Monty: 'We'll talk tomorrow. Bruno will see you out and arrange a car.'

Prim: 'If you decide to do anything overnight, will you call me first, on this number?'

Monty: 'I should think it's highly unlikely that we will need to call anyone, Prim.'

Prim: 'Just take my number, anyway...please? I have arrangements of my own to make if something happens to Eddie Malloy…and to Maven Judge.'

Bruno: 'You ask for a call. How do we know your place is not bugged?'

Prim: 'Because my father's man, the one who wired up Eddie's house, runs a sweep on Dil's place every day.'

Bruno: 'What's his name?'

Prim: 'There's no need for you to know that.'

Monty: 'Bruno, I think Miss Romanic has had enough questions for today. Perhaps you'd organize a car for her?'

Prim: 'I'm sorry to dump all this on you, Monty, but I need a way out, and so do you. It made sense to do this.'

Monty: 'Good night. We will see you in the morning.'

Prim looked up at us, 'That's it.'

All was silent for a few moments, then Vita began clapping, slowly and quietly and everyone joined in as Prim smiled and looked down the tabletop. Vita said, 'That was a bravura performance, Miss Romanic, bravura!'

Prim reddened as the rest of us added compliments. I said, 'That should give you confidence for tomorrow. You were superb.'

Prim said, 'This is going to sound really strange, but I enjoyed it. I was terrified, but I don't think I've ever felt more alive.'

'Ha ha!' Vita said, and clapped again, 'you've caught the bug! Let me tell you, it beats everything. Everything. Men become nothing. Money becomes nothing. You'll be hooked now.'

I looked at Dil. He was angry. Worse, he was trying to force a smile. Vita didn't even look his way. Nor did Prim, though that might have been to save him further embarrassment.

I stood up, 'Mac, anything else?'

'Bradley was delighted.'

I said, 'He doesn't look capable of delight, but we'll settle for pleased.'

Mac said to Prim, 'He thought you were superb. The whole team did. And everyone will be in position tomorrow and beyond. They can get you out at any time, on the signal.'

Prim nodded.

I said, 'Right. Ember probably won't do anything until he's heard the tapes. I can't see how he can track what we're saying, but there's a chance he'll track where you're going, so bear that in mind. And stick to the script when you're talking, just in case. Mac's found other accommodation to take him out of the picture for now. Prim might get tailed from Monty's, so we can't meet back here until the same time tomorrow evening. Normal visiting time.' I hugged Prim and kissed her cheek, 'You were brilliant. Good luck in the morning.'

She nodded, 'I think I'll be fine.'

'I do too, but you need to be prepared for Ember turning up. It's long odds against, but, as Mac says, you just need to say the get-out word if things go wrong. Bradley's promised that his guys can be in there in three minutes max.'

Prim nodded, 'Okay.'

'What's the word?' I asked.

Her eyes flared, 'Eddie! How many times?'

'Last time…what's the word?'

'Valentino.'

'Good.'

'I'm hardly going to forget my father's name!'

'Pressure's a strange thing,' I said, 'see you tomorrow night.'

82

The next day dragged us oh so slowly toward evening visiting. Blake dropped in three times, once to let us know that he'd had a call from the Racing Post to check on my progress. I said, 'And here's me thinking your car park is full of satellite news vans from across the world.'

'Been there and done that in a previous life,' Blake said, 'it can become quite addictive.'

'So they tell me.'

Mac arrived just after four o'clock. He was sweating. 'Warm out there,' he said, taking off his jacket. I smiled, 'See, the north continues to court you. Where's Steel?'

'Still lying low. Probably best he doesn't visit anyway. I'd guess we're being watched by now.'

'You'd guess? Didn't it work this morning?'

'Bradley wouldn't tell me anything other than that Prim walked out safe and sound.'

'He must have told you if the software worked.'

'Best I can say is that he didn't say it didn't.'

I got up from my seat on the bed, 'Mac, that was the deal! How else are we supposed to stay safe?'

'Bradley says that's his responsibility and that we can rest assured he will not be neglecting it.'

'So how are we supposed to know if this is running or not?'

'He said he hopes to be able to tell me more tonight.'

'Fuck!'

'Indeed.'

Mave said, 'Would he tell Steel?'

'I doubt it,' Mac said, 'and I'm not sure Steel would want to know.'

I said, 'He's a real leader of men this guy, Steel, isn't he?'

Mac opened his arms and shrugged, unpeeling the sweaty shirt from his sides for a second, showing the damp patches. I said, 'So we're no wiser than we were this time yesterday?'

'Well, Bradley did say that there had been some overnight activity at your place.'

'Overnight activity?'

'A two-man visit.'

'From Ember's boys?'

'Well, it wasn't from our side. I suppose it could have been Bruno and his guys, if they haven't told Ember yet.'

Mave said, 'They didn't make a mess, did they?'

'I doubt it. They'll be pros.'

Mave said, 'Pros can make the biggest mess depending on what they're looking for.'

Mac said, 'They were checking for the bugs that Señor Romanic was supposed to have arranged, and laying some of their own.'

I said, 'You were listening in to the listeners?'

'Bradley was. Fair play to him, he's thought of pretty much everything on his side.'

'Except telling us if Ember's in yet.'

'Bradley will have his reasons.'

'That wasn't the deal, Mac! And the plan was mine, remember?'

'And the plan was good, Eddie. Bradley paid you the compliment of taking it on lock, stock and barrel.'

'Then added a few rules of his own!'

'Calm down, will you,' Mac said, 'if Ember's boys are listening in here, they're going to be wondering how a comatose patient can make so much noise.'

'Bradley will hear me making some noise once I'm out.' I looked angrily at Mave. She frowned deep and dramatic and said, 'Go get 'em tiger!'

Mac laughed. I laughed. Mac said, 'They serving dinner soon?'

83

At seven, the others arrived. 'All well?' I asked as they trooped into the room. I was meaning to take in everyone, but my eyes fixed on Prim. She was poker-faced, but said, 'Okay.'

I went to stand in front of her, 'You're safe? No threats?' She shook her head slowly, as though exhausted. Dil said, 'It took an awful lot out of her. For nothing.'

'What do you mean, "for nothing"?'

Vita stepped forward, 'Your friend and supposed colleague in this, Chief Constable Bradley stopped his tech team from giving us the recording.'

I turned to Mac, who rolled his eyes and looked up and sighed, 'I'll call him.'

Mac went out. Vita and Dil bitched about Bradley. Prim sat into the corner of the sofa staring at the wall. Mac came back. He said, 'He just wants to make sure that what happens from here is decided by his team. He said that Prim knows what happened anyway, and she can brief us.'

'What about Mave's software?'

'He wouldn't say, Eddie. They're monitoring twenty-four-seven. He said he'll brief me along with Steel first thing in the morning, and that if you or anyone else here needs a briefing between now and then, his team will alert us.'

Dil said, 'They're watching all of us?'

Mac said, 'All of you, all of the time.'

'Like, now?' Dil asked.

'They know you're in here and when you leave they'll keep all of you in sight.'

'And what if they fuck up?' Dil said.

Mac said, 'They've been very efficient so far.'

Vita spoke, 'We're entitled to know what's going on. It wouldn't be the first time things didn't go to script with the cops. We ought to have an exit strategy.'

We all looked at Mac. He threw his "what can I do" pose and said, 'Bradley's not moving. I'll get Nigel Steel to press him. In the meantime, can I suggest that Prim briefs us on what happened this morning?'

Prim sat half crouched, elbows on knees, arms tight-folded. She looked down sharply, her black hair tumbling. Dil said, 'She's at the end of her rope.'

Mave said, 'Can we hold for a minute?'

I looked at her. She nodded for me to follow her and we went into the bathroom and closed the door.

We were back out within a minute. Prim was still seated. Mac, Dil and Vita stood and looked at us. I turned to Mave. She said, 'The memory stick we made up for Prim with the false recordings on it…I added a script that would switch on the webcam and microphone of any PC the stick went into.'

Dil said, 'Eddie told us that. But now we don't know if it worked, do we? Bradley won't give.'

Mave said, 'There's another script on there sending a backup into the cloud.'

Mac's eyes narrowed, 'Does Bradley know about the backup?'

'Not unless his guys were looking for something other than what I told them was on there. Even then, they'd need to be good…very good.'

Vita said, 'You could access this now?'

'Yes.'

Mac raised a hand, 'Look, I don't think this is a very good idea. If

Bradley changed his mind today about communications, it would be for a good reason.'

Vita said, 'How do you know?'

'I just can't think why he would want to withhold this unless he believed it to be in everyone's best interests.'

Vita said, 'But you don't know that, right?'

'Well, no. It's an educated guess.'

Vita said, 'Well this is educated company, so I say we take an educated vote on it. Those in favour of Mave running this movie raise your right hand.'

Only Mac kept his down, and shook his head. Mave lifted her laptop from the coffee table and placed it on the window ledge, then took to her keyboard. I turned to Mac, 'You staying to watch?'

'So long as it's noted I didn't vote for this.'

'It's noted,' I said.

Prim got up. We stood shoulder to shoulder. Mave adjusted the screen, 'Can you all see that?'

Vita said, 'Can we lose the big light?'

Dil switched it off at the wall. The weak glow from the lamp above my bed barely reached us, leaving us standing on the edge of darkness waiting for the film to start. Mave clicked the spacebar to run it.

84

We could see all of Monty's gargoyle face. Prim's loomed briefly into the picture as she said to Monty, 'You can't make a copy of this, you know that?'

Monty: 'Of course.'

Prim: 'You won't need it, anyway. Once you hear the voices you'll know.'

Monty: 'Indeed. Thank you.'

Monty's PC mics then picked up the sound from his speakers as the fake tape of the recordings Mave and I had made began playing. I said to Prim, 'Anything happen while they were listening to this?'

Prim shook her head, 'Nothing.'

'Was Bruno there?' I asked.

Prim pointed at the laptop as though to show us, moving her finger to the left, 'He was standing just off to the side.'

I said to Mave, 'Our chatter goes on for a fair bit, doesn't it?'

'Forty-seven minutes.'

'Can you fast-forward?'

Mave clicked and dragged the slider until we saw Monty turn and talk to Prim. Mave edged it back a bit and clicked play.

We heard Prim off camera: 'Believe me now?'

Monty: 'Leave it with us. I'll be in touch.'

Prim: 'Leave what with you? The problem's there…it's obvious! It's not going to get any smaller for you thinking about it! You haven't got time! He could be awake just now, for all you know.'

Monty: 'We will deal with it.'

Prim: 'How? I want to know how?'

Monty: 'As you said yesterday, that is our department.'

Prim: 'But I need to know what to expect, for God's sake! I need to know when!'

Monty: 'I'll call you.'

Prim: 'When?'

Monty: 'Soon.'

Silence…

Prim – her tone much more composed: 'Tell me that you understand what we're facing here?'

Monty: 'I understand.'

Prim: 'Bruno?'

Bruno (still out of shot): 'You should go home now.'

Prim: 'Are you going to do something or aren't you?'

Monty: 'Bruno is right. You should go home now. I will call you soon.'

Sounds of chair legs moving on a wooden floor, then a grunt, then a shot of Monty's left trouser pocket as he turned. Prim: 'Give me that!'

Monty: 'We need to keep it.' His left hand held the memory stick.

Prim: 'Why? You've just listened to every word of it. I have to take it back! My father said I must keep it! That was the deal when we spoke yesterday.'

Bruno: 'It was your deal, Miss Romanic. Go home.'

Prim: 'Monty, who's in charge here? I want that stick back! What if you decide not to do anything? You've got evidence that's damaging to me and my father!'

Monty: 'Things cannot run on your timeline, Prim. You tell us all this yesterday. Now you bring us evidence. We need some time to consider things now.'

Prim: 'You don't have time! It's the one single thing you do not have! Please tell me I'm not going crazy here in being the only person who can see this? I thought I was doing you a big favour. You are way, way much deeper in this thing than I am.'

Monty: 'I've been in business for more than thirty years. It would be remiss of me to make knee-jerk decisions. Now, please go home and wait. I promise I will be in touch soon.'

Silence. A heel scrape. A sigh. Prim's right hip moves into shot: Prim: 'What is it that's stopping you? If you're afraid of the consequences, I have a way out of this for you, Monty. Once you've done what you need to do, I have a way out of this. Guaranteed. You can disappear. Your business will be bought from you for full market price.'

Monty: 'That's good to know.'

Prim: 'Don't bloody patronize me! I hate being patronized by men.'

Bruno: 'But by women, you don't mind.'

Silence...Prim: 'Why are you both treating me as though I'm your enemy? I'm the one trying to keep you out of jail.'

Three steps. No heel-click. Bruno, louder now, closer to the mics but still out of shot: 'You are the one who wants us to murder a man and a woman who are your friends.'

Silence...Prim: 'Wouldn't you do anything to save your father?'

Bruno: 'Your father is an old man. He will die soon enough. What you want to save is yourself so that the American does not get Grant.'

'She's not American. She's a mongrel! A bitch. I am of the nobility, the Spanish nobility!'

Bruno: 'You are a gangster.'

Prim: 'I am a gangster? Me? Pot, kettle, black, Mister Guta. Pot. Kettle. Black.'

Monty, turning and walking away from the webcam: 'Go home, Prim. I will call you soon.'

Prim: 'I'm not leaving until you tell me what you're going to do.'

Monty: 'We will do what is best.'

Prim: 'Don't worry about afterwards, about being caught. Dil can get Vita Brodie to buy your business...at full price.'

Silence.

Prim: 'Vita Brodie has millions. She invests in lots of businesses.

Dil is certain he can persuade her to buy yours.'

Silence.

Prim: 'You and Bruno can just disappear.'

Silence.

Prim: 'Retire. Go to Argentina…'

Silence.

Prim: 'I will even teach you Spanish!'

Monty laughed softly. We all laughed and turned to Prim, who managed a strained smile.

Prim: 'Answer me!'

Monty: 'Go home.'

Prim: 'Fuck you! And you!'

Fast steps, heel clicks…Bruno: 'Spanish nobility, huh?'

Prim, from a distance: 'Up yours!'

Door slam.

We waited, as though it were some TV drama and Prim might storm back in. I turned to her, 'Was that exit stage left? For good?'

'For good,' Prim said, 'except that I forgot I had no transport and I had to walk until I was clear of the house before I could ring a taxi.'

We laughed.

I turned to Mave, 'Want to pause it?'

Mave clicked to pause then smiled at Prim and began applauding. We all joined in.

Prim said, 'They were genuinely pissing me off in the end. I had to bite my tongue.'

Mac said, 'That was you biting your tongue?' And we laughed, at the release of stress, at the safekeeping of Primarolo Romanic. Vita Brodie stood and drew herself up into a flamenco pose and cried, 'I am Spanish nobility!' even Prim clapped her hands together and laughed at that.

I said to Mac, 'So what was in there that Bradley thought was unfit for consumption?'

'Maybe it's what happened after?'

I looked at Mave, 'Picture and sound will have kept recording?'

'Should have. From ten-seventeen this morning.'

Mac checked his watch, 'That's close to ten hours. Are you planning to sit through all of that?'

I opened my arms and gestured around the room, 'Well, I ain't going anywhere.'

Vita said, 'The first few minutes after Prim leaves will be the most important, don't you think?'

I said to Mave, 'Should we see what happens next?'

We turned back toward the screen.

Monty and Bruno are in long shot, standing at the end of a table. Monty walks slowly back to the PC and sits down, side on, and puts his head in his hands. We hear the laboured sound of his breathing. From the table Bruno watches him.

Vita said, 'Is Monty in on this? Does he know he's being filmed?'

'Yes,' I said.

Bruno walks toward him until the webcam cuts him off at waist level. He says, 'Give me the stick.'

Monty grunts as he hauls himself to his feet. We see their hands as Monty gives him the stick.

Bruno's voice: 'The boss needs to hear this.'

Monty: 'We can handle this, Bruno, don't you think? There must be some other way. I can talk to Eddie. Things might not be as straightforward as they sounded on that tape.'

Bruno: 'Talk to him and say what? Please keep quiet or I might never invite you to my box again?'

Monty: 'All Eddie needs to do is sort out this thing with the horses. He's just stumbled on this. It's secondary. He has nothing against me. Or against you, I'm sure.'

Bruno: 'Then he should have settled for what he found when he discovered the woman was to blame.'

Monty: 'He still might. I think I can persuade him.'

Bruno: 'You overestimate your influence with people. If you could see yourself...performing, you would see how pathetic you are.'

Monty put his head in his hands again and said: 'Why should I want to go on with this bloody charade?'

Bruno: 'What else would you do with your sad life?'

Monty, looking up and across the room as though staring into the distance: 'Maybe I should take Miss Romanic up on her offer to sell out to the American.' He turned to look at Bruno and said, 'Maybe I should do that. Sydney can do his dirty work. At least my conscience will be clear.'

Bruno: 'Much too late for that. Come on. The woman is right about time. The boss needs to know about this now.'

Monty: 'You go. I've had enough.'

Bruno: 'You're coming with me.'

Monty, looking up: 'Sydney doesn't like to have me just turn up there. You know that.'

Bruno: 'He's expecting you.'

Monty stares at him as though he's been betrayed.

Bruno: 'Get up.'

Monty rises. Bruno: 'You walk in front.'

Footsteps...fading...the faint sound of a door closing.

The webcam films a silent, empty room. We watch the screen until Mave closes the lid. Even then we stand a while in silence until Vita says, 'So, they take that stick to Ember and he puts it in his PC and we get to hear his plans?'

I said, 'Ember has no PC.'

Vita said, 'You're kidding?'

I shook my head, 'He's nervous about technology. We were hoping Bruno would take Monty's laptop with him to Ember's place.'

Vita watched me, cold-eyed, 'He didn't.'

I said, 'No, he didn't.'

Dil got up and marched toward me, sweeping that bobbing fringe, 'Do you mean-'

The door opened. MacCready came in, carrying a leather case. He turned quickly and closed the door behind him. He said, 'Sorry, everyone must leave. Now. Except Mister Malloy and Miss Judge. Carry on as normal when you exit the building. Go home, or to your place of accommodation where you'll be met by the officers assigned to you and briefed. That's all. Please leave.'

Vita said, 'Hey, I need-'

MacCready turned on his heel. His look hardened, 'Leave. Now.'

Prim went out. Dil followed, then, slowly, Vita. MacCready said, 'You too, Mister McCarthy.'

Mac said, 'Chief Constable Bradley said-'

'Leave. Now, please. The chief constable's orders.'

Mac turned to me and offered his hand. I shook it. He hugged Mave, then left. MacCready locked the door and put the leather case on the sofa. He smiled, 'We understand that Ember's people might be here sometime after dark. We should have at least an hour for final rehearsals and preparation.' He opened the case. Fixed inside with broad elastic straps were three handguns.

85

MacCready said, 'Please sit down on the sofa.'

Mave and I sat. He said, 'As soon as visiting is finished, all admin staff will be replaced by police officers. This small wing, as you might already know, is dedicated to high dependency patients. Aside from officers, you two will be the only occupants of this wing. In the next fifteen minutes, you will be moved to another room in this wing where you will be under guard.'

I said, 'But you're staying here?'

'Correct.'

'You and one other?'

'Correct.'

'And you'll be pulling those sheets over yourselves and taking our places?'

'Your places will be taken, but not by us.'

'So who drew the short straws?'

'A couple of failed medical students, whose life is no longer worth living.' He said it with a perfectly straight, square-jawed face and, for a moment, it stilled my rising smile...then he smiled. He said, 'We have two excellent models provided by the hospital. They're made of very realistic synthetic materials, including, perfectly matched hair texture and colour.'

Mave fingered her fringe, 'You managed to get some old straw, then?'

WILD HORSES

MacCready laughed, and I was relieved to hear an edge of nervousness in it. No matter how professional or experienced, that edge of nervous anticipation is the final sharpener of the senses, especially when someone is coming to kill you. Mave sighed, 'I can't say I'll be disappointed to be in another room. I thought when you opened that case that I was going to have the ultimate crash course in weapons training.'

MacCready said, 'We couldn't afford to lose either of you, Miss Judge.'

'A PR nightmare,' I said.

He raised a finger and smiled, 'Got it in one.'

I said, 'How do you know they'll come to the right room?'

'Chief Constable Bradley assures us we are dealing with a highly professional criminal who's been getting everything right for almost thirty years. But…there will be armed officers in the other five rooms in this wing, that's including the one you'll be in. We also have body armour for you.'

Mave said, 'I'm guessing all these hotshots have not been performing drill in the car park before being marched inside in full uniform?'

MacCready said, 'Two arrived in a decorator's van this afternoon. Six more came in ambulances dressed as paramedics or patients. Others have been here since you two arrived.'

I said, 'I'm impressed. Either your boss is the most efficient cop in the country, or I've run into more than my fair share of organized constabulary chaos.'

MacCready said, 'As with most things, what you are seeing here is the effect of someone with a lot of clout…and, of course, if you are ever talking of me to the boss, a high level of genius.'

We smiled. MacCready checked his watch and said, 'Five minutes and we'll get you out and get the dummies in.'

Mave said, 'You could leave everything exactly as it is and achieve the same ends.'

MacCready laughed and began unpacking the guns.

Next morning, the high dependency wing was full of of very tired cops. A night of constantly bubbling adrenaline that had never found an outlet left everyone looking as though they'd been awake for a week. At nine o'clock, MacCready came to see us, his beard shadow and red eyes betraying how he really felt despite the positive tone when he said, 'Well, it looks like we can all safely have breakfast. I'm told there's a review meeting due to start at HQ right about now. More news later.'

The news came from Mac, in person, when he arrived just after eleven o'clock. He said, 'It looks like it's going to be tonight, during visiting. Monty called Prim and asked her to let the others know she would cover tonight and that they should all have a break. We expect that Bruno will be with her and he'll carry a syringe filled with a lethal chemical. He'll probably be armed, too.'

I said, 'I suppose the dummies are out, then, and we are back in?'

'If you're in agreement with that. Bradley wants to take it as far as he safely can. Ideally, to a point where Bruno makes it absolutely clear that his intention is to kill you both.'

'Lovely!' Mave said. I smiled at her. Mac swallowed. I said, 'I'm assuming MacCready will still be close by?'

'He'll be in the bathroom, armed, and there'll be two armed officers outside your door.'

I nodded. 'How sure is he this time? He obviously got last night wrong.'

'He didn't, actually. They knew yesterday that tonight was the plan but had to assume it was either a bluff or that it could have been moved forward.'

'Did MacCready and the others know that?'

Mac shook his head, 'Bradley didn't want any complacency creeping in.'

'Very shrewd of him, except that it's left him with a wing full of knackered cops.'

'They'll be replaced by this evening, except for MacCready who will be rested until eighteen hundred.'

I smiled, 'Eighteen hundred, eh? You love all this Top Gun stuff, Mac, don't you?'

He reddened, 'I can see the need for avoiding confusion.'

I said, 'How is Prim taking this?'

'She appears to be all right, but did say she'll be very glad when it's finally over.'

I said, 'Old Kelman Hines must be wondering what the hell's going on. First off, he's getting blackmailed, then he's trying to do deals between him, Boffo and Prim. Anybody handling that side? What if he pitches up at Dil's place today looking for Prim?'

'He's been spoken to…informally.'

'Informally? Must have been you who spoke to him, then?'

'I did. I'd have thought that the least of your worries right at this moment, Eddie.'

'Just trying to think what might go wrong before evening visiting by Doctor Death and nurse Prim.'

Mac looked at me and half smiled and slowly shook his head, 'You relish this, don't you?'

I turned to Mave then back to Mac, 'We relish being hellish. We're very, very glad to be bad.'

Mac looked puzzled. I said, 'From a kids' show on TV..a long time ago.'

Mac said, 'I spent my younger days in a rather boring environment, I'm afraid.'

I said, 'Your loss, Mac. Listen, one new detail on my tick list, how do I rehearse being in a coma?'

'Mister Blake will brief you on that and rig you up to the relevant equipment.'

'It's going to be kind of difficult getting my timing right,' I said, 'I'm guessing that MacCready will not be able to see what's happening. Nor will I. That leaves Mave and Prim to yell, "he's got the syringe at your neck!", which is cutting things a bit neat, don't you think?'

'It won't get that far, Eddie. MacCready will go through everything step by step.'

'Yes…first, raise the syringe, expel any air bubbles in case they damage the patient, locate the jugular…'

Mac smiled as he got up, 'Where would we be without graveyard humour?'

'The graveyard?' Mave said.

When Mac left, Mave said, 'It's going to be a long wait for visiting starting.'

'Well, at least we won't have to worry about how we are going to pass an hour with our dear loved ones. "Would you like some grapes? Chocolate? A glass of Lucozade? An injection of strychnine?"'

Mave watched me, 'Mac was right. You relish this. The more dangerous, the better.'

'You're not exactly shaking in your shoes yourself, Miss Judge.'

'Don't count on it continuing, Eddie. I'm shattered after last night. Come visiting time, I expect to be an utter wreck.'

There was a knock on the door, then it opened and Mister Blake came in, smiling, 'I hope I'm not interrupting anything?'

'Not at all, Mister Blake,' I said, 'just doing a final read-through of our wills. Do come in.'

86

At ten minutes to seven I closed my eyes and tried to still the nervous anticipation by listening to each tick of the clock and counting down the final six hundred seconds.

Our visitors were three minutes' late. The door opened. My hearing seemed ultra acute. Mave got up, 'Hello, Prim. Bruno. What a nice surprise!'

The 'mwah' of cheek kisses.

'No change?' Prim said.

'None. But we're trying to stay optimistic. Let me get you a chair.'

Bruno: 'I will get them.'

Prim: 'Bruno was saying that Monty sends his best regards. He has a nasty infection at the moment and thought it best to stay away until it clears.'

Mave: 'That's considerate of him. Please give him our love, Bruno.'

Chair legs scraping into position. I sense Bruno close by...smell his deodorant.

Mave: 'Will Dil and Vita be coming this evening?'

Prim: 'I'm afraid not. We'll be the only visitors.'

Mave laughed: 'Well, you never know that for sure! You don't know who'll drop by.'

Prim: 'I wish Eddie could hear me, Mave. I'd want him so much to know that this is nothing personal. I want you to know that, too.'

Mave: 'What? What's not personal?'

Prim: 'Bruno has brought something with him.'

A sharp intake of breath from Mave, then she said, 'Valentino.'

Bruno: 'What?'

Mave: 'There's a police officer standing right behind you with a gun aimed at your head. There are two more armed officers outside the door and two on either side of the outside wall by the window.'

MacCready: 'Mister Guta, stay seated. Raise your left hand, then bend forward very slowly holding the gun in front of you, and place it on the floor.'

I opened my eyes and looked at Bruno, 'Best do it, Bruno. Ember's finished. He's already in custody. You can have a few years in jail, or the sergeant can shoot you in the head. Second one is an awful price to pay for someone else's crimes.'

At noon next day, we settled in what felt like a TV studio at Merseyside Police HQ. Mave, Prim, Mac, Vita and Dil sat with me at a table. We watched a fifty-inch TV screen which showed the interview room, in which another large TV screen was fixed to the wall. At the centre of the room was a modern table with six chairs on either side. At the rear edge of the table, was a PC screen, keyboard and mouse.

We waited in silence. A technician came and went a couple of times. He said, 'It shouldn't be long. The chief constable has arranged lunch upstairs afterwards.'

At seven minutes past noon, we watched the screen as Bradley entered, followed by two men wearing suits: one dark haired, one almost bald. Two women came in and closed the door behind them. One of the women wore a grey skirt and jacket and a white blouse. The other wore a black trouser-suit and white blouse. Bradley gestured toward the table, 'Please sit down.'

The audio coming through to our room was as crisp and luxuriant as that in a cinema.

Mac said, 'Ember is the one with the dark hair.'

Vita said, 'Piggy-eyed, isn't he?'

Nobody responded. We watched them settle and adjust chairs. Bradley stood by the wall, behind the women and facing the two men. The woman in the skirt said, 'Ready?'

The bald man: 'When you are.'

She picked up the keyboard, typed something then clicked the mouse. The PC screen lit up. The woman set aside the mouse and said: 'Commencement of interview with Sydney Aloysius Ember. Also present: Detective Sergeants Collinson and Peters, Drummond Davis, solicitor for Mister Ember, and Chief Constable Eric Bradley. This interview is being simultaneously recorded on video.' She turned to the other woman, 'Detective Sergeant Collinson?'

Collinson edged her chair forward and put her elbows on the table, 'Mister Ember, yesterday you were arrested and charged with the attempted murder of Mister Edward Malloy and Miss Maven Judge, also known as Jolene Byrne.'

Everyone in our room turned to look at Mave. She smiled and kept watching the screen.

Collinson said, 'Mister Ember, where were you yesterday between eleven a.m. and one p.m.?'

Ember: 'I was at home.'

Collinson: 'Alone?'

Ember: 'Sir Monty Bearak and his assistant, Mister Guta called on me to discuss a project.'

Collinson: 'What kind of project?'

Ember: 'Sir Monty has a business which lends money to professionals. We know each other from occasional meetings on the racecourse. Sir Monty knows that my income as a professional gambler is such that I am cash rich. Sir Monty proposed that I might want to invest some of that cash in his business.'

Collinson: 'Sir Monty's account of your meeting differs substantially from your account.'

Ember: 'In what way?'

Collinson: 'Sir Monty says that he visited to discuss how best to deal with the problem that arose when Mister Malloy and Miss Judge discovered that for the past thirty-one years you have coerced and threatened Sir Monty into helping disguise the criminal source of your income.'

Ember smiled and turned to his solicitor. He smiled too. Ember looked at Collinson, then at Bradley and pointed to him, 'Chief Constable Bradley has been harassing me for what seems the major part of his so-called professional career about my income. The fact that he has plotted with Bearak to concoct such a preposterous lie, such an utterly ridiculous scenario, should be enough to see him relieved of his position. I intend to pursue that end through the courts. I've suffered many years under suspicion, which, by the way, is probably driven by jealousy at my success as a professional gambler.'

Collinson: 'Why would Sir Monty Bearak concoct such a "scenario", as you put it?'

Ember: 'I think my words were "ridiculous scenario".'

Collinson: 'At nineteen-oh-seven yesterday, Mister Bruno Guta was in room six of the high dependency unit at the Regina Hospital in Carlisle, when he produced a firearm which he intended to use in the murder of Edward Malloy and Maven Judge. Bruno Guta is associate of yours, and you ordered him to carry out those murder

Ember laughed, then he turned to his solicitor and said, 'I' laughing, but this is getting beyond laughable.'

The solicitor turned to Bradley, 'Other than these reported allegations outlined by your colleague, why are we here Ch Constable Bradley? We both know you have no evidence whatsoeve to support this outrageous charge.'

Bradley stood, hands behind his back, feet apart. His right h came into view and he raised it. He was holding something black a seemed to be pointing it at Ember, who ducked and raised an ar though to protect his face. Bradley said, 'What's wrong, N Ember?'

Ember slowly straightened and lowered his arm, 'What's th asked.

'A remote control for the television, Mister Ember. The up there, on the wall.' He clicked the remote and nodded to toward the camera. Everyone in the interview room turned to the TV. There was an edit countdown in large numbers, 4, 3, 2, 1…

Ember's face took up the whole screen, scowling, looking straight at the camera, 'What the fuck is going on?'

Monty's voice: 'Trouble. Big trouble.'

Ember, backing off a couple of steps and gesturing, 'Sit down.' Ember turned to his right, 'You too.'

The camera swings, showing Bruno Guta dressed in an oversized judo outfit. Camera turns again to Ember as he walks toward a high-backed chair, and turns, sits, then crosses his legs and his arms. He wears dark green chinos and a pale blue shirt, open-necked. His shoes are brown loafers.

The camera goes down and close, showing white judo pants as Monty crosses his legs. We see the slipper on his right foot. Camera comes up again and fixes on Ember. He says, 'Okay. From the start. Every detail.'

Monty's voice: 'It would have been so much easier if you had allowed Bruno to bring the laptop and play the recordings.'

Ember: 'Just tell me what she said.'

For the next ten minutes, Monty talks, occasionally confirming or checking facts with Bruno. It's a condensed version of Prim's proposal and the recordings made by me and Mave. Monty finishes by saying, 'What do we do?'

Camera shows Ember getting up, putting his hands in his pockets…

Then Ember stood up in the interview room and shouted at Bradley, 'Turn it off!'

Bradley said, 'Sit down.'

Ember's lawyer was pale faced, looking up at his client. Bradley said, 'Mister Davis requested evidence. Sit down. Watch the evidence.'

Slowly, Ember sat down, but he did not look at the screen. He stared at the table.

Back to the TV screen. Ember is in full shot, head to toe. He speaks: 'Well, it's all happening, eh? I thought we were doing the smart thing staying away from what Boffo was involved in. Maybe we should have taken a bit more of an interest…Frustrating when these amateurs become persistent. You understand now what I was talking about with Searcey? When these types start blundering around, it needs nipping in the bud. Properly, because they very seldom learn from warnings. They have a romantic view of life. Especially journalists. That's why they get into the trade. Woodward and Bernstein have a lot to answer for. They've probably caused more collective misery to generations of silly boys than they ever did to Richard fucking Nixon, whose middle name was Milhous, but I'm sure he will posthumously forgive me and understand my frustration with the press.'

He turns to look at Bruno: 'I owe you an apology. I should have left Searcey to you instead of indulging Monty in his movie script fantasy.'

Monty: 'It wasn't a fantasy. It was a decision to try and salvage some degree of humanity and decency from the disaster.'

Ember: 'What disaster?'

Monty: 'My life. My unfortunate association with you.'

Ember's head goes back. We see his dark nostrils as he looks to the ceiling. His face tilts toward us, looking straight to camera: 'Oh, here we go, another swim in the swamp of self pity. If anyone's entitled to feel sorry for himself here, it's me, don't you think? I indulged you. With Searcey five years' ago. Again this year. Then with his crazy daughter, who thought she was the queen of Deadwood when she would not have lasted two minutes without me agreeing to your increasingly bizarre requests.'

Monty: 'She's a child.'

Ember: 'She's deluded to the point of madness and everything I've let her off with has fed that delusion. And the least you can do now, Monty, the very least, is a simple acknowledgement that I was right and you were wrong.'

Monty: 'Things just didn't work out the way I'd hoped.'

Ember: 'As exclusively forecast by me, though even I didn't think the upshot would be the mother and father of a mess you've just told me about.' He turns to Bruno, 'Any word on Malloy?'

Bruno: 'Nothing new.'

Ember: 'His girlfriend still with him?'

Bruno: 'Hasn't left the building since she went in.'

Ember: 'Visitors?'

Bruno: 'Grant, McCarthy, Miss Brodie and Miss Romanic.'

Ember: 'None of his jockey mates?'

Bruno: 'A couple have called the switchboard and left goodwill messages.'

Ember: 'Not the most popular guy in the sport, then?'

Monty: 'Eddie's well liked. His friends from the weighing room wouldn't sit with a man in a coma. He'll get visitors when he wakes.'

Ember turned to him: 'The visitors he gets when he wakes will be cops unless we do a deal with this gypsy woman.'

Monty: 'If Eddie was bringing the police in, he'd have done it by now.'

Ember: 'It won't be Eddie who calls them, it'll be the Romanic woman.'

Monty: 'If you'd seen just how desperate she is to keep the cops out of it, I think-'

Ember: 'Bruno told me how desperate she is. That's why if we don't do what she wants, she'll go to the cops and try and trade it off the other way. No jail for daddyo, and she gives them the recordings.'

Monty: 'She says that's the only copy.'

Ember: 'And you believe her? She's the most sensible one among the lot. You included.'

Monty: 'So why didn't she take the recordings to the police first and try that deal?'

Ember: 'Probably because her old man would have had to give back the two million quid he took off the mugs on the exchanges.'

Monty: 'Not much of a price to pay given the alternative of trying to have two people she knows murdered.'

Ember, leaning forward: 'Monty, her marker's already down on what she thinks of Malloy. She nearly got him killed at Bangor. And it didn't stop her trying again. Or putting the other jocks at risk. She's fucking desperate!'

Camera looks to the floor then to Monty's clasped hands in his lap. Monty: 'Listen, I can do a deal with Eddie.'

Ember walks toward Monty, repeating the same word each time his heel hits the floor: 'No. No. No. No. No. No!' He stops in front of Monty, his face in full close up. He licks his lips: Ember: 'Do you understand?'

Monty: 'I want no part of it. I'm done. I'm gone. I'll go to Argentina, as Miss Romanic suggested.'

Ember: 'And take her with you as your Spanish teacher? You'll be staying here, Monty, doing what you've always done.'

Monty: 'I'm finished this time, Sydney. I'm taking no part in any killings, never mind those of my friends.'

Ember: 'Who's asking you to "take part"? Bruno will look after it. All you have to do is not bend my fucking ear about Malloy and just get back to the business.'

Monty: 'I'm out. Sell it to Vita Brodie.'

Ember: 'Not mine to sell, Monty. I'm sure Miss Brodie's legal team would find that something of a drawback come due diligence time.'

Monty: 'Then I'll sell it.'

Ember: 'And you think she'll accommodate me the way you have for the past thirty years?'

Monty: 'Con her, like you did me.'

Ember: 'Nobody conned you, except your ex-partner. Due diligence is what you were short of back then.'

Monty: 'Not heeding my instinct was what I was short of.'

Ember's face moves closer to the camera until his mouth is out of shot. His bloodshot eyes are large, out of scale. Ember: 'But what you had plenty of was greed…' His face pulls back and we see his mouth move, '…plenty of greed and a bleeding heart. Bad combination, Monty. Look where it's got you now. And your bleeding fucking heart means that I'm the one that needs to do the dirty work. Again!'

Monty: 'Hardly dirty for you. You've always enjoyed it. Well, you've always enjoyed getting other people to do it. Like me, and Bruno, and God knows who else.'

Ember laughs and turns briefly to Bruno: 'Hear that? He compares himself to you.' Ember turns back: 'Monty, you are an empty shell, my friend. No, not a shell. Shells are hard. You're soft, all the way through.' Ember keeps staring at the camera but points to Bruno: 'There's a hard man! You talk about doing dirty work? Don't make me laugh!'

Monty: 'So how many has he killed for you? How many more before he gets caught? And when he gets caught, what do you do, then?'

Ember: 'He won't get caught, because he's a professional. Professionals don't do bleeding hearts!'

Monty: 'No, they just murder people! For you! And they torture people with acid. For you! And they leave a man half blind. For you!'

Ember, shouts and points: 'Yes, for me! So people like you can leech off the back of people like us! Professionals! So you can go and sit in your fucking big box at the racecourse everyday, and give millions to charity and be Mister Nice Guy! Oh, sorry, Sir Nice Guy! So the murders brought you a fucking knighthood and the best that can be said for that is that you're probably not the only one.'

Ember turns slowly to Bruno: 'Get organized in the next twenty-four hours. I want Malloy and his clever little woman dead by midnight tomorrow. Use the gypsy woman. Visiting time will probably be easiest, but I'll leave it to you. Just get it done tomorrow.'

Bruno nods.

Ember: 'And make sure the gypsy doesn't make it home. She sounds like the biggest liability of the lot. Just make certain before you kill her she gives up all the copies of that memory stick. If you've got any doubts, get on the next plane to Spain and kill her father, too.' He turns back to the camera: 'You, go back to your bolt hole and our business. Don't call me. Don't come here with your special pleading for Malloy and his girlfriend. If you even think about doing that, just remember what they were about to do to you.'

The screen faded to black. Bradley was staring at Ember who had his head in his hands, elbows on the table. The TV screen flashed. Monty's voice came through: 'Sydney...'

Slowly, Ember looked up. The screen flickered, then 'eared' to show Monty looking at himself in an elaborately frame mirror: 'Sydney, such a clever man. So smart that once everyone d been processed through your incredible Airlock, your ego over. Nobody in a bloody judo suit could record you, could they nd so it would have remained, had you not chosen to do this my face…remember how funny you thought it was when I lost my sight? Remember your puerile joke? "Keep an eye out ne, Monty!" Well, I did.'

Monty raised his right hand to his face until the screen shwed the lines on his palm, until we saw from above his cheek his bottom lip, then the camera lurched in a deep swing and se and steadied showing a close-up of Monty's face…no mirror Monty smiled and it made that empty flaccid eye socket more grotes He said, 'Well, strictly speaking, Sydney, I kept an eye in for y The camera swung in a slow sideways arc, until we saw again the ror, and the eye between Monty's finger and thumb, filming everything Monty said, 'Goodbye, Sydney. I don't suppose we will meet again, though I would give a lot to see you on day one in prison. I understand their Airlock is not nearly as civilized as yours.'

A week later, Mave and I waited in the arrivals area of Manchester airport for Ben and Alice. The fallout from Ember's arrest had landed sweetly for Chief Constable Bradley and his team. Bradley had told me privately that on the day Ember was convicted and sentenced, he'd be retiring from the force.

Bradley had moved straight on to helping set up the complex negotiations for plea-bargains for Monty and Prim and the others involved. Nigel Steel, Mac's boss, was not nearly as accomplished as Bradley in the aftermath. Having hovered carefully on the sidelines throughout, he'd hurried to centre stage to big-up his part in the BHA's 'crucial role' in helping with the arrest of 'a master criminal with much blood on his hands.'

Mac had phoned me last night, 'Steel's getting press calls from all over the world and is making an utter balls of every interview. I'd told him to leave the police in the spotlight, but he wouldn't have it. Even if he wanted to take action internally now on Prim and the others involved, he's trampled in public all over any defence they might have had.'

I had said, 'I wouldn't lose sleep over it, Mac. So long as Prim and the rest get what was promised.'

Standing with Mave, waiting for Ben and Alice, one thing I did know was that Alice would still want her day in court. DJ would always loom large in her mind, no matter what Ember had done.

Mave said, 'Looks like they're beginning to clear from baggage.'

Tanned, tired passengers were filtering through from behind the partitions. I said, 'Alice will be breathing fire. She'd have been expecting to come back with a false identity to be spirited away by Special Branch.'

Mave said, 'I think that's your imagination at work rather then hers, Eddie.'

'Probably.'

We waited.

Mave pointed, 'There's Ben!'

All we could see was his neck and head behind the loaded trolley he was pushing. He smiled when he saw us and somehow those broken old teeth didn't look quite so bad against a deep tan. We waved, and laughed as he came toward the barrier, but we were already looking for Alice.

Then we saw her.

Walking beside Kim, holding hands.

Mave turned to look at me, but my eyes were locked to Kim's. He raised his left hand, pointing at me and mouthing 'Gotcha!'

Mave tugged my arm. I turned slowly toward her. She said, 'I think you just got your nephew back…for good.'

I nodded slowly, smiling, putting my arm across Mave's shoulder, 'Look at Alice,' I said, 'you'd think she'd never had a troubled moment in her life…look at her smile.'

Mave said, 'Young love, Eddie. Beats everything. Makes the whole world new.'

I squeezed her and she looked up at me. I said, 'You made my world new.'

She smiled slowly, and her eyes filled up, 'I did my best.'

'Hey, don't cry, you were working with crap material!'

She stepped away and punched my shoulder as Kim and Alice rushed us, all yells and flapping arms and through the melee I saw Ben standing with the trolley, watching us. And I realized that his battered smile and his optimism and his appetite for life had carried us all through this...yet he was always just out of reach, on the perimeter, urging everyone else toward their own second chance.

Ben Searcey. Reborn.

I hope you enjoyed Wild Horses.

All the Eddie Malloy books are available on Amazon as eBooks, paperbacks, and many as audiobooks through Audible.

I send out very few emails, but would be pleased to have you on my mailing list so that I can let you know about new titles in the series.

You can register on our website is pitmacbooks.com. There is also a Facebook page for Eddie Malloy

Best wishes and thanks,
Joe McNally

CPSIA information can be obtained
at www.ICGtesting.com
Printed in the USA
LVOW12s0528140616

492399LV00005B/224/P

9 781533 323910